INHERIT THE SUN

INHERIT

MAXWELL GRANT

THE SUN

COWARD, McCANN & GEOGHEGAN

NEW YORK

c. 1

The author gratefully acknowledges permission to reprint lyrics from
"Pack Up Your Troubles in Your Old Kitbag (and Smile, Smile, Smile),"
lyrics by George Asaf, music by Felix Powell, Copyright © 1915 Francis
Day & Hunter Ltd. Reproduced by permission of EMI Music Publishing
Ltd. 18-140 Charing Cross Road, London WC2H OLD, England;
Copyright Renewed. Published in the U.S.A. and Canada by Chappell &
Co., Inc. International Copyright Secured. All rights reserved. Used by
permission.

Library of Congress Cataloging in Publication Data

Grant, Maxwell.
    Inherit the sun.

    I. Title.
PR9619.3.G654I5   1981   823   80-25172
ISBN 0-698-11074-9

Printed in the United States of America

BL

JUL 8 '81

For Mary,
and the Clan Grant:
Colin, Helen,
Leigh, Jo, Lindy and
Cameron.

Foreword

This is a work of fiction and the characters and events are imaginary.

But the backgrounds are real, although I have taken some liberties.

Queensland and Northern Territory Aerial Services—QANTAS—is the Australian Government's national airline. But it was not always so. It started as a private airline and continued that way for many years. In my fictional references to it, from its start to the present, I have treated it as a private enterprise.

For the rest, one must look among the salmon earth and purple mists of the brown land to see what is real and what is not.

From the day I first visited the Territory, that great square in the north of Australia which may well be the last frontier left on earth, I realized it was the unseen things which moved there and gave the place its special meaning.

I would like to thank, once again, literary agent George Greenfield, of London and New York, for his continued help and advice.

Maxwell Grant
Melbourne, January 1980

Book I

THE
OVERLANDERS

The Carlyon family, founders of
Murranki Station in the Australian
Outback, realize both the benefits and
the harmful effects of the encroaching
civilization they helped to establish
in the wilderness.

1

If anyone had told Big Red's mother, on the day of departure, that before she was thirty she would look fifty, it is doubtful that she would have listened, and she certainly would not have believed it. Big Red—his name was Jim, but everyone called him Big Red—had not even been born then or even thought of, and Beth herself was no more than twenty-three, not a new bride, for she had been married for three years. But she and her husband Alan Brennan were still so young and inexperienced in so many ways.

Probably only someone as inexperienced as Alan Brennan would have attempted the Overland crossing he planned so close to the Simpson Desert. Perhaps if he had dropped his first name and settled for his second, that would have indicated that he had a rudimentary inkling of what the bush held for those who, in those early years, would take it on. It was certainly not a place for Alans, and certainly not Alans who were ex-Adelaide bank clerks at that. Yet in those times, particularly in Adelaide, the road north to the Territory was the road to Utopia: the great Australian dream of the great open spaces, for Aussie and Limey alike, and for not a few Yanks, although the latter slang term was about the only one that had been born then. But South Australia owned the Territory, really owned it, that great square up north, and few of the frustrated bank clerks and drapers' assistants who dreamed of the road there stopped to think that there was no road, and barely a track; that the water holes were few and unreliable, even if you knew them; that you must travel in the Dry, between May and October, if you would travel at all, else you would be washed away in the rivers past the desert; or that the desert was there, waiting on either side of you as you went north, ever north, over land which all but the most stupid would have described as desert enough itself, over this land traveled in bullock carts and donkey carts and horses by so many, so many with the stupid pioneer spirit, so many too stupid, proud or poor to acknowledge that on bad stretches the smart ones used camels. Later, when the water holes were better plotted, although it was Russian roulette for water in the Dry at any time, smart men would conquer and reconquer these most inhospitable of lands, but men alone, riding singly and with purpose, on a single horse, with water at saddle and the mail to go through.

But brave Alan Brennan, in his thirtieth year, in the year 1896, had decided, from his bleak bank window, to become a jackeroo, an Overlander, a man of the bush. He had a little money saved; he would go north and become a king of cattle. Why up north there were paddocks the size of England! Perhaps it was the completion of the Overland Telegraph in 1873, when he was a boy of seven, that had started this dream in his mind. But the dream of those ironbark poles and wires set starkly across the Continent, from south to north, set against the Outback sky, unsettled him daily. He read everything from boyhood on about those two-thousand-odd miles of line, from Port Augusta in the South to Port Darwin in the North, the building of which had some of the elements of drama and perseverance in adverse circumstances and climate such as were needed to build the Suez Canal. But this was no body of water; this was simply stout wood and wire in the desert. Yet Alan Brennan's clerk's mind, for it was that still in so many ways, saw only the upright poles and overhead wires, like columns of black ink figures. His mind did not turn to look down to the desert sands and spare mulga scrub or patches of spinifex grasses or the ever-absent water or the one hundred and one other difficulties that might beset the most experienced traveler in an unknown area where there was no concept or organization of wagon trains with leaders such as in the American West. The only organized parties were the Overlanders themselves, the drovers of cattle, and sheep in other parts, that group to whom Alan Brennan aspired to belong.

Of course the word Overlander, like so many, had variant meanings, and, technically, from his reading, he knew that the moment he left the environs of Adelaide with his wife and their few belongings (although more than any sensible man would have dared bring) he was an Overlander. He was overlanding from Adelaide way up to Darwin, or land south of there, cattle land where he would found a dynasty and with his accountant's mind and stout heart, make his fortune quickly, while enjoying the life of the great outdoors. If, as so many of his fellows in those days, he had not locked out the stories of those who died on the Track, as it was even then beginning to be called, if they had listened more carefully when the Overlanders came to town, instead of worshiping them as gods and hearing only the good parts of their stories, they might have stayed at home, where water was a few steps from the back porch, and temperatures did not rise as high as 127, and where those fully grown men, the Overlanders, did not cry for the loss of another poor beast in the heat.

Ah, but the telegraph line was there, something more tangible than the heat haze to hang onto in one's mind. Between '59 and '62 Explorer Stuart's push through what was then unknown Central Australia proved there was no inland sea, which some might have taken as a warning but did not, and indeed, it was hailed as showing that his route would be practicable for an overland telegraph, which would speed the opening up of the Continent. Burke and Wills and McKinley crossed after him, though farther east and dangerously close to that Simpson Desert Alan Brennan seemed to think did not exist and some do still, for it has never been tamed, conquered, really explored. So from 1870 to 1873, up went the line, from south to north, to join up with a cable from Java, which already connected to Europe, and link Australia to the world.

When built it was a triumph of physical endurance and, for Alan Brennan and his like, a disaster of psychological aspiration. For the bank-clerk dreamers of the world, here was something tangible to hold on to. In their mind's eye, they saw themselves traveling north as on a Sunday picnic, in easy stages, with the telegraph wire always nearby, the poles capable of being climbed and the wire cut, as the stories went, so that a line party would almost immediately appear, to save you from disaster. Well, although a punishable offense, sometimes they did, and sometimes they didn't. But there was more to survival in the bush, more to being an Overlander than being near the Overland Telegraph with a pair of shears in your kit, called in those days and sometimes still, your swag, which was about the only real thing Alan Brennan knew about the bush when he set out from Adelaide in April of 1896, with his young wife, Beth, who still had the look of a freshly washed baby about her, and could stand only a few minutes in the open sun away from the veranda even in the Adelaide summer and who, despite her bonnet, had, in the pit of her stomach, underneath her layered underthings and woven woolen dress, the most awful apprehension that this life was not for her, not even for her husband, to whom it had meant so much in the three years since their marriage that she had finally acquiesced.

She thought afterward that she was as much to blame as he was because there was a time she could have stopped it, thought she would, had decided she would, just one week before they were due to leave.

It would be a difficult enough subject to raise—the most difficult—for even then she was having inklings that she was stronger than he. She had waited her moment until after supper. They were on the back porch and because Alan had made the final payment that day—a thing she'd not known and which now made her task even worse—he had had a bottle of beer with the meal. This was a thing he rarely did.

He saw it as an extravagance, although sometimes he used it, too, to assert his manhood. If they had a tiff—and they had few enough—he would say, like a tough man of the town, "Right, I'm off to the pub, then, until you cool down."

She wondered if this might be such a night as she began to broach the subject. Would she hurt him so that he would have to take one of his twice-yearly refuges in the pub?

"Alan," she said gently, "Alan, I've been thinking about the trip."

"It'll be all right, really," he said, with a directness that took her aback. So he had been expecting her to raise it, and even as she began to register surprise about this, he started to take another tack and her heart sank further.

"I've wanted to tell you," he said, "I've tried so many times because I feel you don't really understand. I guess that's why I paid the full price for the tickets today. Buying the tickets made me feel I couldn't turn back, that we'd have to go."

He felt he was making a mess of it and she saw the pained look on his face and moved closer to him on the old couch on the back porch and took his hand.

"It's all right," she said gently, "tell it just the way it comes out."

"You know I'm not one of the boys," he said swallowing, almost in a whisper. "I mean I pretend to be but I'm not, you know."

She did know. She said nothing.

"I don't know, I guess I'm too serious or something. And then there's how I feel even in relation to you. It's like I get a funny feeling in my stomach and I sweat a lot, my palms sweat and my armpits and I get very nervous and haven't any confidence in myself."

She put her arm around him and said softly, with an upward intonation to make him feel he was being unfair to himself, "Alan—"

But he went on as if he had not heard her.

"I've got to go, you see. Out there I'll be free to prove myself. Other people won't be able to muck me up or get me confused. And it'll be a fresh start. They won't be the ones who laughed at me at school out there. They say in the bush everyone is equal and a man is accepted for what he is. That's all I want . . . a fair chance to show them what I can do."

After that Beth kept silent. Now she understood and knew there was no turning back for either of them.

Yet, even so, despite the apprehension, with the flashback innocence of childhood, she caught something of the lilt of excitement of any new thing, any new departure, any new adventure.

Part of the problem was that they left by train: train of all things to go overland. But the train Alan and Beth Brennan took their seats on was all part of the great illusion. The locomotive was modern and polished and shunting and steaming like any train about to depart from Istanbul or Trieste. There was a train and there were tracks. For nearly one thousand miles to Oodnadatta, just on the left, bleached rib of the Simpson Desert, there were railway lines. The infant railway had been fingering out from Adelaide for years, first to Gawler, Kapunda, Burra and Terowie, and then to Quorn and up past Lake Eyre's great salt plains so that now in 1896 it had finally reached Oodnadatta. It was the year and the time that Alan Brennan had been waiting for. Stock still mostly went on the hoof, up through the bush, and perhaps if the Brennans had started that way, started at Adelaide with all their false illusions, they might only have got a couple of hundred miles out and turned back. But to be able to go nearly a thousand miles by rail, and there purchase your equipment and dray and animals for the journey north made the journey sound easy. Somehow in those days, despite all the stories, Australians with the great bush dream were often as pathetically ignorant of the Outback as incoming Europeans and Chinese and Americans. In fact sometimes those from overseas fared much better, for they expected a country different from their homelands. To the would-be jackeroo living in Australian cities and dreaming out of office windows, there was the very real danger to think of the land out there as just an extension of the town's boundaries, or just a bit different from the city bush they picnicked in at weekends. None of them had seen a cow or bull so bloated with death from thirst that it had ballooned over on its side, stretched so tight and big that its legs, stiff with rigor mortis, seemed lost in its belly seared by the sun. Certainly none of them had seen a man or woman dead in this way.

Beth picked her way into the train beside her husband, past the conglomeration of men and sacks and boots and shovels and wooden chicken cages with live squawking birds, on the start of a two-thousand-mile journey like herself, the caged hens the only other female company on the train, which should have told her something. She was destined to be a "Missus" of the bush, a woman in the Outback, and she did not know how rare such an animal was.

But she sat happily enough, a big bushman with full black beard and head opposite her, raising his big hat politely in a welcoming smile while Alan tended to the luggage and then went to check the van which carried their few household goods.

"Good day, Missus," the giant bushman said cheerily from among the black hair and leather face as he doffed his hat, "off up the Track, then?"

"North," she said timidly, unused to such an easy, loquacious manner and not realizing that she was encountering in this dark, big, big man, with gray moleskin trousers and boots so big but so dry and scuffed they were the color of sand, her first experience of Outback hospitality. He was twice, if not three times her size, and his smile, although she did not notice it on that day, came from every inch of him. His mates up the Track, which was anyone from there to Darwin and back, called him Mac, or occasionally, the Bear, of which there are none in Australia save that small and infamous one, to which this giant bore no resemblance, except perhaps in cheery disposition and his ability to survive in the bush.

If Beth Brennan, who believed in God as much as her son was later to believe in the land, had known what lay ahead and in fright asked the Good Lord to book her seat, she would have been sitting where she sat at the very moment, as the big man, again with the overpoliteness of the early bushman to whom a woman was a rarity, leaned forward, this time only pushing his hat back a little and said, "Excuse me, Missus, but would you mind if I smoked?"

When she shook her head, again timidly, for part of her just did not know how to respond to such easy ways, he said simply, "Good-o," and smiling, leaned back and took out what she was later to learn were called the makings. She watched fascinated, pretending not to, from under her bonnet. It was not that she had not seen men roll cigarettes before, although her husband did not smoke, it was simply the incongruity of this huge man with huge hands making a perfectly shaped cigarette, rolling and licking and lighting, with such quick dexterity.

He gave her one quick smile as he lit up, and then settled back, after a deep and satisfying draw, pulling his large sweat-stained hat down now, almost over his eyes, so that he almost seemed to be smoking from under his hat while asleep. Beth sat there transfixed until Alan came back to break her reverie and she, in an uneasy way she couldn't quite articulate, almost resented his return.

Alan Brennan was, in fact, dark himself, though his hair was the traditional Australian brown, and he had a sort of reddish-brown suntan, for he had painstakingly exposed himself to the sun, during the Adelaide summer, in readiness for his great Outback adventure. Sometimes he overdid it, even in the Adelaide sun (which could be fierce although nothing in comparison with where they were going), and then he painfully rubbed himself with vinegar, or a cut tomato, or cold tea to draw out the heat. Once he'd got so sore he had to use butter. But he wanted to look Outback from the start, and indeed he wore moleskins like the man opposite him, and even the same boots and similar hat, for bush things could be bought in the city for a price. But somehow, sitting there, Alan felt that the bushman opposite him was watching him, sizing him up, from under the hat so worn and stained with so much sun and body salt. Alan had bought his bush clothes two years ago and worn them on weekends as much as he could, yet he knew, beside this man, they looked the newest of new and that everyone in the train, for none looked as green as he, would know he was a beginner.

But his thoughts were his own and on this day, as the train pulled out from the Adelaide station, for the 686-mile run to Oodnadatta, Alan Brennan sat himself squarely back in his seat, spreading his rather spare, tallish frame as much as he could, and looked out the window through his own reflected image and saw only an Overlander, even if his clothes were a little new.

He sat thus for an hour, staring away at the farms and the sheep and the still-green countryside, though with bleached grass showing here and there. In his mind he believed that his property would be like all this put together, only bigger.

From time to time he had spoken a word or two to Beth, and she to him, though she was reading Anthony Trollope's *Australia and New Zealand*. She was a schoolteacher from the area a little to the north of Adelaide, where her father had a few acres and ran sheep and some milkers. It was lush green pasture mostly, so she was a quiet, bookish person from a nice dairy farm and about as realistic and as equipped for the bush as her husband. In her mind, as it ran restlessly over Trollope's pages, in between stealing quick glances at her giant traveling companion opposite, the most precious things in her luggage were her books.

The sleeping giant opposite stirred, stretching first one side and then the other, before he took off his hat again, scratched his thick, thick black hair, and then replaced his hat properly this time and bent to rummage in a nondescript blanket roll which Alan eyed and believed to be the bushman's swag.

"A spot of tea then, mate, for you and the Missus?" the man said as his body unbent from the swag with his big, worn and sunburned hand holding the ubiquitous, cylindrical, quart-size container known as a billy. It took Alan some time to realize the man was addressing him and when he almost stammered in reply that his name was Alan Brennan, and this was his wife, Beth, the man stared at him as if he were speaking a foreign language to suggest that anything more than "mate" and "Missus," would be necessary. But the big man's stare was momentary and soon broke into a smile as he added, ignoring the introduction and going back to the importance of the question,

"So you'll have some tea, then?"

"We'd be delighted," Beth said, so hurriedly that her voice rose an octave and she blushed a little that she had sounded like a schoolgirl trying out for the church choir, and indeed that she had replied at all.

"If you've got enough, that is," she added, as if to make apology for the eagerness of her reply.

The big man tapped a bulging shirt pocket and nodded as he rose to walk down the passageway between the seats, producing a crumpled brown paper bag from the pocket. "You'll find some mugs and milk in me swag."

"Where will he get boiling water on this train?" Alan said disbelievingly, a little put out that his role of pioneer protector and Overlander had been usurped so quickly. He had obviously been unlucky enough to sit opposite the most experienced bushman on the train.

"Shouldn't we get the tea things out?" Beth asked, aware of her husband's distraction.

"You can if you like."

She bent, and soon found, among the blanket folds, a small hemp bag which rattled. Inside was a corked bottle of milk, another paper bag which contained sugar, and three chipped enamel drinking mugs, one unwashed with the tea stains dried but visible on it and a solitary teaspoon lying side-on in the mug. Just then the man came back and as he saw her bending and placing the mugs on the floor he said, "That's the ticket, Missus, floor or the ground—best table a man ever had." He sat down, placing the steaming billy beside the enamel mugs set among the space between their feet on the floor.

"I'll just let it draw a minute," he said, indicating the billy. "Now black or white and how many sugars?"

Alan made some effort at conversation now. "Both white

and two for me and one for my wife, thanks," and the big man gave him a huge smile, as if to indicate that that was the way, open and friendly, first lesson of the bush, and then added through his smile, "Right, mate," as he bent and poured, somehow managing not to spill a drop of water from the container which had no pourer.

"Might taste a little smoky," he said, handing the tea out, "got it from the engine."

Under her bonnet, as she took the mug offered to her, handle first, Beth compressed a slight smile. The bushman's right eye had seen it though, for he had a plainsman's peripheral vision, and for a moment she thought he was going to wink. Then she realized, as she sat and sipped the lovely, strong, hot tea, that he would never do that: he was too polite and, despite his cheery nature, too controlled. He would not embarrass her in that way.

Yet the sense of security which the presence of this big bush-man was already bringing to Beth was to be savagely challenged within a few more turns of the track. Scarcely had they finished their tea, so it seemed, but the train was stopping at a crossing. Beth looked out of the window—and had difficulty seeing, for although barely fifty miles from Adelaide, the greening of the countryside was already thin-ning. The dust had already pasted the windows with a thick mist, but as the train stopped at a crossing, she was just able to see a woman and a man beside a small cart being pulled by a donkey.

At first she thought the train was stopping to let them cross the tracks. Then, as she looked again and saw they were not moving, she realized how silly this was. The train would not stop for the people; the people would wait for the train. Well, what then? Why had the train stopped? She rubbed the window with her hands and a little dust gave way, though most of it was on the outside. She saw, or rather thought she saw, that the couple was really standing beside the donkey cart, with heads bowed, as if . . . yes, as if praying. Then she saw the bushman who sat opposite her. He must have slipped off the train quietly while she was looking out the window. He had been joined by the train inspector, and together they now spoke to the couple. There was much talking and shaking of heads. Something was dreadfully wrong. Alan had now joined Beth at the window. He was about to speak and then they both saw the woman beside the donkey cart burst into tears as the man with her and the bushman lifted a coffin down from the cart.

The man must have dug the hole before the train came along. Beth sat there transfixed. She saw the coffin go quickly and quietly into the hole. She noticed the stoicism of the two men handling the coffin. Their faces were etched into stone. She noticed the woman, crying still, now being comforted by the train inspector. She could hardly see the woman's face under her bonnet. But she knew she was crying well enough from the shaking of her frame. Beth saw all this, saw the Outback funeral in its stark reality trackside, saw how quickly the countryside had changed from green to brown, yet still did not fully comprehend, even when the bushman came back and the train moved on, leaving the hapless couple standing with their forlorn cart and donkey.

She looked at the bushman and he looked at her. He knew well enough what Beth was thinking. The man and the wife were there. Where were the children?

"It was their only child, right enough, Missus," he said at length, letting his words out slowly like exhaling a deep sigh. "It was very young, Missus, only a few months, really, and the heat got it. It's been so very dry."

"You don't mean they took it outside. . . ? My God, then they deserve—"

"They'd not done that, Missus, begging your pardon," he said, interrupting her before she could say more which she would regret, though, in time, when she understood better, she regretted even the thought. "They'd not done that, Missus. It was the dehydration. It can happen even inside. They'd had plenty of water. I checked on that. But it was just the heat, Missus, the overall heat. Some babies just can't take it, however much water they get and however much the mothers damp them down."

Beth could already have bitten her tongue for what she had said and meant to keep quiet, but now, because of what the big man had said, found herself going on.

"But that's dreadful. Isn't there anything that can be done?"

"They're doing it. They're returning to town. They're not suited to the bush, but they made it a long way this trip, I'll give them that."

"You know them, then?"

"Met once or twice, up and down the Track. They've come in from beyond the desert. It's a goodly trip. They'd have made it, too, if they'd had more than one plucky little donkey."

"Made what? Why did they stop here?"

He looked at her pained and realized how little she understood of distance and the country and miles not traveled by train and how many harsh lessons lay before her.

"The body was decomposing, Missus," he said finally, with the air of a man who believed the truth was always better in the long run. "They'd hoped to make Adelaide and bury the baby in their home churchyard but it was not to be."

"Of course," she said, "how silly of me," and bent to pick up her book once more, only to realize that her hands were shaking so much she could not hold it to read.

The bushman looked away. Alan had not seen and perhaps had not even heard. If he had, he had said nothing. He was still staring out the window at his new kingdom.

2

In all, the journey to Oodnadatta took two days, not because the distance was that great for a locomotive, but because in those days the gauges were not standardized, nor the timetables so strict. In addition, the train ran only once a fortnight and it brought the mail. There were frequent stops. There were frequent changes and delays. Toilet facilities for ladies, when the train did stop, were flyblown and over-poweringly nauseous, the smell, hanging, as it did, in the still and unmoving heat of the day. When the train had stopped at what could certainly not be called towns, at places which often had no platform, let alone a siding, there was, for Beth and even Alan, the first feelings of the aloneness of the bare bush. Even at noonday, one felt it. The dust was an inept and bilious yellow, stagnant as death and bleached bones. No wind moved across it; one felt that even if a breeze had stirred, the dust would have been too lazy to move. It just sat, not even thick enough to have character: sat dead on the hard earth beneath it, frightened to move in the harsh sun. If this was still civilization, in this pallid stillness, with some small railroad shacks and a narrow, sentry-box outhouse yards away at the back across even more dust, the smell and the amplified sound of the blowflies told Beth a sad story of the days that lay ahead.

When she returned from her first such expedition, the tall bearded man stood watching her and she bowed her head in embarrassment, although as she did so, she thought she saw a slightly pained look on his face, as if he wanted to say something, but couldn't.

She and Alan had known they would have to sleep on the train, but had not reckoned on the cold nights. Like so many others, they had expected the nights to be as warm as the days. Beth reluctantly, after tossing and turning half the night, accepted a spare blanket from her bushman friend's swag. But Alan refused to share it, and sat upright, trying to huddle to himself, so that the circulation from one part of his body would warm the other. He slept fitfully and awoke to the cheery first-light chatter of his never-talkative wife and the aroma of the bushman's fresh tea.

Of course food and drink were available at the stops, as the railway had promised it would be. But the stops never seemed to coincide with hunger and thirst, which was not surprising, for they had hardly been planned that way. The second night all the passengers—the whole train—ate handsomely at the stationmaster's house, if it could be called that, for it was more like a small, empty shearing shed. But by then they were within a stone's throw of Oodnadatta. So they bought odd things where they could, along the way, but somehow finished up sharing the bushman's "tucker," as he called it, from his tucker box, which was different, he explained, from what he would carry out on the Track, for his sister in Adelaide, whom he'd been down to see during the Wet, had packed it. She always gave him more than he needed, he said, so he was happy to share it, and in any case it was the bush way, as they would discover, and like or not they'd meet up on the Track someday when he was out of sugar or tea, and then they'd get their opportunity to repay him handsomely. Beth smiled and took his hospitality like a child taking lollies from her father, yet still a little reserved and in awe of this big man who should have frightened her but didn't. She was, in a way, more frightened of Alan's quietness, although he was warming to their friend a little.

Beth noticed the big man did not push things. He offered everything as part of the bush way, but never in a manner to indicate that Alan and she were ill-equipped for the bush. Yet in his almost every sentence and every move, displaying conserved energy, there was something to be learned if you had a mind to.

Alan did, however, question the big man about the Wet. It was the first time he had heard the word used that way, with such a finality of seasons about it, and the big man, who on Alan's insistence finally allowed that his name was James Carlyon, said that there were only two seasons in the Territory—the Dry and the Wet. The Wet was late November to March—or a month either side to be safe. The Dry was the rest of the year, when you worked flat-out against the onset of the Wet.

"Been a dry Wet, though, I hear," said the big man. "Driest Wet we've had for years. If I'd have known that I mightn't have come south to visit Sis for Christmas."

"We're glad you did," said Beth in genuine appreciation, again tripping over her words, for she had spoken with her mouth half full—a thing she would never do at home—of his sister's Christmas cake. This was too much even for Alan, whose own mouth was bulging with the rich rum-and-brandy mixture and, as he sputtered out, "Glad you did too," half the cake came too, spraying the bushman's face and front as he himself was about to take a huge bite. It was all too much and they all had to swallow the remainder of the cake in their mouths to prevent further spraying before their irretrievable laughter ran through the carriage. The bushman sounded like a bull in full charge, he laughed so long and loud. Alan was very apologetic, but the bushman kept saying what a good shot he was, in between bouts of laughter, how a man had to aim well to score such a direct hit with Christmas cake at two paces, and somewhere in that cake-and-laughter exchange, as the bushman finally stood and shook the cake from him as if it were a dozen insignificant flies, Alan came willingly into the ambit of his huge friendship, too. After that, for the rest of the trip, he began slowly to ask about things like the spinifex grass and the mulga scrub, the low bush tree that gave some of the country its gray, ground-mist look.

They had come up from Port Adelaide to Terowie, where the broad gauge finished. From Quorn, on the narrow gauge, they had left civilization, as they knew it, more and more behind, heading finally into the salt plains of Lake Eyre, one of the largest lakes in the world, yet a beautiful but desolate curtain raiser for the dreaded Birdsville Track to its north-east, Oodnadatta to its northwest, and the fearful Simpson Desert directly north and beyond.

"Know which side of the Overland Telegraph you're on," the bushman had said in response to Alan's remark about climbing a pole and damaging the wire if in trouble. "The Simpson Desert lies to the east."

As he said this, Beth realized that they would travel alone. Somehow, almost from the first offer of tea, she had automatically assumed this protector of hers would travel with them as guide. Now she knew how foolish that was to contemplate. He had generously given of his time, food and friendship in the open bush manner. But he would have his job to do, whatever that was, for he had not really said, and would travel over the country that lay ahead ten times as fast on his own. It was stupid to think she could thus easily adopt him. The next morning would see them at Oodnadatta and they would never see him again.

"I've got me plant at Oodnadatta," he said, as if reading Beth's thoughts again in a way which was most disconcerting, and she hadn't the faintest idea what his "plant" was and was too ashamed of her ignorance to ask. "I've got me plant of equipment and animals there," he went on, as if he knew she needed an explanation but addressing Alan first, in the way he had developed since their newfound friendship. "I'll be happy to see you set up first, though, if you wish it, mate," he added.

"We'd be very appreciative," Alan said.

"Right then, mate, we'll go straight to Afghan Town when we get in."

"Afghan Town?"

"Aw, yes, mate, although it's all part of the one flyblown place. But you'll need camels right enough. Wouldn't send you north to the Alice without 'em. Only thing out here, really. Some'll tell you different, but you'll need camels and the nearest we can get to a couple of honest Gyppos to take you through. Should take your camels as far as Newcastle Waters if I were you. Can't go any farther because camels can't eat ironbark—poisonous for them. From there on it will be horses or bullock drays."

Beth was looking at Alan distraught. The bushman knew why.

"We might get one or two pieces of small furniture on the camels, Missus, but you'll be best to get what you can for the rest at Oodnadatta. Didn't want to tell you earlier, but there's no point to it, really. Camels are best, believe me. You'll see some with their wagons and furniture, but camels are best— camels and just you and your swag for the Centre is what I always say."

She knew he would not have said it if it were not so, and if she had to sacrifice her furniture, so be it. But the books would stay. She would leave everything else if she had to, but the books would stay. Oodnadatta was the head of the line— the northernmost station—yet there was no station. The train stopped where the rails stopped and no one, perhaps because of this very fact itself, had as yet seen the necessity to build a station. After all, what need of a platform when there was no need to wait for another train and there was nowhere else to go by train?

The mail train had brought water in wooden-hooped barrels to Oodnadatta and it was this that was unloaded first with a complete disregard for passengers. The couple of cattle trucks which the engine had also hauled were unloaded next, giving those newcomers, who had an eye to observe, the order of bush preferences. So far as the townspeople of Oodnadatta were concerned, it was water, cattle and mail, in that order. Then the straggly, dusty town would turn itself to how it could make money out of those on the train stupid enough not to know how to spend it.

Money, as it is to so many bookkeepers, was a constant source of worry to Alan. Despite the fact that they had all but lived off the bearded bushman on the train, his hundred pounds had now dwindled to ninety-eight. The major part of the journey was still to come—and the most costly. He had not reckoned on what was already becoming a major factor in Australia's history: the cost of size, the cost of distance. The farther he went from Adelaide, the capital of the state of South Australia, which in those days owned the Northern Territory, the costlier things became.

South Australia, despite some metal discoveries and wheat and sheep, had been subject to administrative problems both locally and in London. The economy had suffered and the 1890s Depression had hit South Australia early. For the past three years Alan had struggled to keep his job and had had to accept a cut in salary. Perhaps it was to his credit, sometimes one of the few things Beth ever credited him with in the later years as she told and retold the stories to her sons—and especially to Big Red, her firstborn—that he stuck to his dream of the Outback and wealthy squattocracy, the term already in vogue for the aristocrats of the land. For the land *was* opening up. It was harsh and unforgiving, but it was also lush and plentiful in its vagarious season, and fortunes were being won: wheat and sheep in the South; copper, silver and gold up and down the country; and, in the North, beef.

Alan had always in a sense known that his hundred pounds would not do. But it had come to a point where he had had to try on that or not at all. He knew he would have to find work as a drover or suchlike first, work for which he was at the best ill-equipped, but he believed that somehow his head for figures and the opportunity of the Outback, plus his little capital, would give him his start. It never entered his head that he might lack those essential extra elements to make these things work: the judgment and the imagination to tie one thing to the other so that together they grew.

As he stood down from the train, and held his hand out for Beth, Alan hoped that this was his new beginning. It was a dusty, dirty place and no one had told him of the rainbowed soils and hills that lay way beyond the town and might have brightened his day. So he held his hope as bright as he could in his inside shirt pocket, where his main valve was pumping with the dreams of his youth.

South Australia, despite its many difficulties, had pioneered land legislation in Australia, fighting Britain for nearly a quarter of a century for laws that finally the Mother Country had passed. A man could now buy land in his own name and receive a certificate of title making it his. It had been this change of law that had finally brought Alan forth to start on his dream.

His thoughts were diverted by the detraining behind him of their traveling companion. There was no doubt that the welcoming committee was for him. It was true that there were only three, but the warm shouts and laughter suddenly brought the Oodnadatta railway station alive. There were two blacks and a white man. The Aboriginal men were tall with an uncannily graceful bearing which their youth and bright smiles did not diminish. Their bush shirts and hats and moleskins and boots far outdid Alan's and between them they held the most magnificent horse Alan had ever seen. It was a roan full of proud snorting fervor and making noises as welcoming as those any dog ever made to its master. The horse was beautifully brushed and groomed and its coat shone against the dust like the moon in a clear night sky. It was saddled with the particular early Australian stock saddle which was later to become famous the world over, bridled with green hide, which is the untanned variety, but worn shiny with wear, like the saddle, and a credit to the stockmen who stood beside it, almost as erect as sentries, yet shouting excitedly, "G'day, Boss, g'day, Boss."

"G'day, boys. You look after Firecracker plenty good?"

"Plenty good, Boss. Plenty good. But him glad see you back, Boss."

"Me, too," the big man said, walking over and hugging the animal's head as it nuzzled him.

The other man who had stood silent all this time, smiling approvingly, was dressed similarly to the bushman, although his shirt was pressed sharp with creases, as if it had come fresh from a Chinese laundry, Beth thought, as indeed it had.

"Charlie," the big man beamed, holding out his enormous hand as soon as he had finished hugging his horse, demonstrating again to Beth, who was now beginning with her teacher's mind to learn some basic bushcraft, that it was certainly water and animals in that order, and then human beings.

"You needn't have come this far south to meet me. You knew I'd be along presently. How is the mob?"

"In great condition. They're beautiful, I tell you. Truly beautiful, Bear, truly beautiful."

"I bet they are if they're yours. I bet they are. Well, I'll try not to lose more than ten percent for you, God knows I will, but I hear it's been an awfully dry Wet."

"God knows, that's true enough. But He also knows you've never lost more than five percent of a mob of cattle, even over two thousand head, on any overland drive you've ever bossed."

The huge man shook with laughter:

"You're right. By God, you're right, and I don't intend to start now. If the surface water is bad, then, by Jesus, we'll dig on our hands and knees for it, won't we, boys, to keep the cattle watered?"

At the use of the profanity the big man stood suddenly erect, turning with military precision even for his big frame, directly to Beth. "Sorry, Missus, got carried away." He doffed his hat again which, Beth was also realizing, was an Outback mannerism designed to expiate all sins.

"Alan and Beth Brennan, meet Charlie Swanson," he said with a flourish, surprising both Beth and Alan with the formal use of names. So there was a time and season for all things in this Outback land as elsewhere.

"Charlie's a big station owner a little to the north and he's come all the way down here to make sure I take his bloody cattle—begging your pardon again, Missus—to a buyer in the Barklys, despite the fact that he sent a telegram to me in Adelaide and I wrote him back that I would do it."

The big man was smiling good-naturedly.

"I had to come to town anyway," Charlie muttered, in between raising his hat to Beth and shaking hands with Alan.

Beth, still somewhat timid but certainly less so than she had been two days ago, noticed and later commented to Alan on the way that, although Mr. Swanson, as she called him, was the station owner, the bushman greeted him as an equal, and vice versa. In fact, the balance was almost in favor of the owner deferring to the drover. They were not to know at this stage, of course, although the conversation about stock losses overland might have told them something, that the man called the Bear was legendary among his kind—all of whom were men tall in experience and endurance. The wealth of the land was in cattle, and cattle were wealth only when marketed—either to other cattle stations for stock improvement and breeding or to meat markets in the cities. So the true king of this huge domain, the key to it all, was the drover king. The Bear, and the very few of his kind, who could cross thousands of miles of country with mobs of cattle thousands strong, with little feed, and even less water, and bring those stock in in good condition for market, these were the true aristocracy of the country. They were independent contractors, with their own plant of horses and camels and wagons and equipment, who hired their men for the drive.

Men such as Swanson knew the worth of drovers such as Bear. Swanson had ridden 250 miles from his station not only to make sure he had Bear, for the contract had really been set by telegraph and letter and the Bear had never been known to break his word—but as a mark of respect and for his company on the way back to pick up the herd—or mob—of cattle.

After a little more friendly talk the Bear announced that it was a dry day for a conversation, and even Beth and Alan knew what that meant, although the Bear did turn to Beth by way of explanation to say, "I have to admit I have been known to take a cool drink on a warm day, Missus, and it would be bloody inhospitable of me not to—begging your pardon, Missus—seeing we'll be spending Charlie Swanson's money, which I make for him, and if you'll excuse us, my boys—Smiling Sam and Lightning Ridge here—will take you for a nice cup of tea and perhaps a wash and a proper sit-down, if you know what I mean, at the stationmaster's cottage. You'll find his wife a charming lady like yourself."

Beth went red at the mention of a proper sit-down, although the thought of some sort of toilet comfort and washing the dust out of herself almost brought tears to her eyes at the consideration shown by this large, bulky man who was becoming more and more of an enigma and who, now back in his home environment, talked even more openly and honestly than on the train.

As she looked from him to his two black companions, she felt her first touch of love for the Outback *people*. She would always qualify it thus. Never, despite all the beauties it would reveal to her, would she ever allow herself to speak to her sons of love of the land, not even to Big Red, to whom it would mean so much.

3

Of all the times her husband might have chosen to assert himself, Beth was later to say, this was the worst of possible times.

She had noticed his bottom lip drop sullenly, of course, when he was not invited for a drink with the two men. She knew well enough that this mannerism, which she had started out being fond of when she had first met him on a weekend visit to Adelaide, was inherited from his mother. Alan's parents were poor, church mouse poor. They had migrated on the Assisted Passage Scheme from the Home Country, his father having been an Irish farm laborer. But what was a farm laborer's job in Ireland was very different from working in the wheat and sheep country north of Adelaide. Eventually, after several itinerant visits to the country, he settled down to odd jobs in the city, with his wife and one child, which was something he did thank God for, that his wife was unable to bear more children, because they were poor enough as it was. He drank much and worked little, and the woman learned, unconsciously, to drop her bottom lip at each new disappointment in her husband and her circumstances. The difference was, perhaps, that some inherent Gaelic strength caused her to have a second unconscious mannerism of turning that bottom lip in, turning it

34

into clenched teeth and an indomitable perseverance, for the sake of her son if nothing else.

In marrying Beth, Alan defied his mother, for Beth was Protestant. Perhaps, although she appeared timid, Alan was drawn to Beth's inner strength. Beth did not realize for some time after the marriage that her man would be alternately assertive and passive, the latter quality often being so much stronger than the former, and that his dreams of the Outback, of being a boss drover and then owning his own large cattle station, were the compensations which had begun in childhood for the true and enduring strength he believed he had but had never quite found.

So on this day, as they followed the happy black stockmen to the stationmaster's house, his independence chose to assert itself. It was true that he had come, despite himself, to admire the giant bushman and to regard him as friend. Yet there was in Alan that contrariness of friendship where like and dislike are close companions and, however friendly he and the big man were to become, Alan knew deep down that he would always feel inferior to this man, that he would always sense what his wife was trying not to show, that he would always be testing himself against the friendship. Perhaps, Beth thought, when she went over it and over it much later, Alan didn't know all this about himself. But he knew something. He sensed something, and now he was hurt: childishly hurt, but hurt nonetheless. She could see it as they walked and she kept saying things like, "I suppose they had private business things to talk over."

These sentences seemed to hurt him even more, for presently he began to reply to her, but never in the form of direct answers to her statements.

"Camels are best, are they? Well, look at that beautiful horse, that's what he's going to ride."

"But perhaps he's not going the same way as we are."

It was at this point that both learned another bushcraft lesson, although Alan missed much of it in his moodiness.

One of the two blacks, who had been walking quite a distance ahead, turned and with a broad smile, demonstrating incredible powers of hearing, not to mention a level of understanding which Beth was to admire more and more, said,

"That right, Missus. We go 'nother direction property belonga Boss Swanson. Only two hundred fifty mile maybe and good water end of Wet. But our Boss always take horse even if ride camel and walk horse easy case need him chase cattle."

Alan said nothing, but was furious at being shown up on such elementary things by a black boy. Both blacks had, in fact, stopped, waiting to talk more now that the conversation was to be opened, although they were often men of few words. Men! Beth guessed the elder to be twenty-one or twenty-two and the youngest barely sixteen, another fact which was no doubt not helping Alan's humor.

"Which are you?" Beth asked, addressing the younger man who had spoken to her, "Smiling Sam or Lightning Ridge?" She was proud of herself for remembering their names. But both young men began to laugh uncontrollably so that she blushed.

"They joke names," the garrulous younger one said. "Boss call us different name, makeup names, when he glad to see us."

"Oh, I see," Beth said, laughing herself a little now. "I should have known about Lightning Ridge, shouldn't I? Well, what are your real names?"

"Jacky, Missus," the talker replied.

"And your friend?"

"Jacky, too, Missus," he said smiling. "Jacky one and two."

"Please tell me what your real names mean," she said softly.

The talkative black never lost his grace of movement and stature, even when he was laughing about. He now said happily,

"Jacky Utmadatta . . . mean Oodnadatta. My people use it many years . . . mean 'blossom of Mulga.'"

"I see," said Beth slowly, putting her hand in Alan's, which was all she could do when he was like this, and beginning to walk once more. "And your friend?"

The other man now spoke for himself for the first time, although it was obvious that his range of vocabulary was much more limited than his friend's, whose English even Beth knew was unusually good for those times.

"My name is Jacky Emu, Missus," he said.

"Oh, that's a fine name," said Beth, making her own attempt at a joke about the speed of the ostrichlike emu. "I suppose you run fast."

"Fast when Boss after us, Missus," they both answered in unison.

They had reached the stationmaster's cottage, but instead of going in Alan said, very levelly now and with a quiet determination,

"Elizabeth, I'm going to Afghan Town to make arrangements for our trip if one of our friends will show me the way."

Beth was taken aback, but tried not to show it. She had expected something, but not this. She tried one near-neutral sentence, knowing it would be no use when he was like this. The mood might not last long, but it had to be acted out in almost reckless independence.

"You don't think you should wait for our friend?"

"You mean *your* friend?"

"Ours. We are strangers here."

"Better you wait, Boss. Camel traders very slippery, Boss," the talkative Jacky said.

"If you won't take me I can find my own way."

"I take you, Boss," Jacky said with a shrug of the shoulders, which was a habit they would learn most Aboriginals had, particularly those who had to deal with white men. Some found this easy agreement almost an indolence, or an inverted arrogance. It was neither. It was something more basic. Aboriginals really believed life should be easy, matter of fact, enjoyable and that individuals, if they didn't listen to good advice, should be able to make their own mistakes.

So, with a deep sense of foreboding, Beth went inside with Jacky Emu while Alan left for Afghan Town with the other, ever-happy Jacky.

When these hurt-schoolboy moods were on him, Alan certainly never appeared short of determination and willpower. At these times everything clarified in his mind with the tension born of anger. He strode off so fast, that the black, Utma, having tethered the roan, had to run to catch up with him and turn him in a slightly different direction, saying, "This way, Boss, this way."

Alan had it all worked out in his head, had for years. The others were fools. He had slaved for years in that damn bank near the edge of town where he could see the Adelaide hills. He had slaved and saved, as well as supported his drunken father and his mother who spoke very little to him after Beth moved in. Alan, despite his often simplistic way of thinking, knew this was not good for the marriage. But God knew it was the only way he could contribute something to his parents' upkeep and save as well. Either he would have had to take another house and have them live with himself and Beth, or move her in with them. The latter was the easier and cheaper course, for he would have been bound to take a slightly grander house for Beth. They managed. Beth kept teaching, so during the week there was truce between his mother and Beth, although the hidden resentment was so heavy in the air on Sunday mornings, on Mass mornings, that one could have cut it with a knife.

Yet through all this he had not lost his dream. As a grown man, he had, like a boy, done weekend errands for widows for extra money, done odd jobs such as cutting wood, or carting coal; and once or twice worked down at Port Adelaide when a ship was in. But now his dream was within his grasp. He was less than four hundred miles from Alice Springs, or the Alice, as it was called—and that was a good halfway. He'd worked it all out in his head over the years and his accountant's mind had to count for something. There couldn't be too many with his business sense up here. He knew the hundred pounds he'd saved was not quite enough to start as he would like, but he honestly believed if he could get north on the fifty pounds he had allowed, then he thought he knew from prices of recent properties in the Centre that he could buy for roughly one pound a square mile. And then he would buy cattle. Fats were around seven pounds. He hoped to find good quality scrubbers for five pounds or so up North, and build up from there. It would give him a very small mob indeed, but perhaps he could get the land a little cheaper so far north, although he was aware that some land, nearer good permanent waters, could be dearer. But if he could get a few square miles, and get started with a small mob, grazing freely, he could do some droving to build up his herd.

Oodnadatta had only become head of the line that year. So Afghan Town was then small, with Hergott Springs, which they had come through to the south, still a large camel train and droving center and southern terminus of the notorious Birdsville Track, one of the two perhaps most infamous stretches in the country: the Birdsville and the Murranji Track, up North in the Territory. They were the two. They were the true tests of drovers. Even then the Murranji Track was called the Death Track, and, although Alan did not know it, the big bushman held the record for the number of crossings and from that his new nickname of Murranji Mac derived. Now only the old-timers called him Bear. The Death Track of forty miles of cattle route from Newcastle Waters to Top Springs was worthy of a nickname on its own.

But Oodnadatta was building now as a center, with the train terminus this much farther north, and there were already the Bedouinlike tents and the mangy dog and manure smells of any desert camel camp anywhere in the world. In those days camels were the main transportation for more than half the continent. There were several mosques in the Centre, arising like mirages out of the desert, and the Oodnadatta one would be completed soon. The Afghans, as they were called, though they embraced several desert peoples, imported with their animals years earlier by the explorers, had two endearing characteristics: first, as worshipers of the Mohammedan faith, they did not drink alcohol; and second, their animals needed very little water. They could outlast a horse by days. The camels could pack about a quarter of a ton and eat anything, provided no one took them north of Newcastle Waters into the poisonous ironbark country. They were ideal. But their owners had all the cunning of desert peoples the world over.

Alan knew he would have to bargain, but having never

been to the pyramids, the thought of paying half now, and half when his guide had completed his journey, did not occur to him. His mind was fixed on not being taken down on the agreed price for the journey. No one had warned him that in the desert anything agreed on can be halved by a simple expedient, especially when one does not expect to see those particular clients again.

Of course, despite the dirty nature of the surroundings, all the color of any desert camp was there. To someone like Alan it was as if the train had been a steamer which had brought him into the foreign world of a Middle Eastern market, with all the chatter and smells of exotic foods and spices and campfires and camels and their tinkling bells and gaily colored harnesses and saddles and the few exotically veiled Muslim women.

Alan still had the idea of a comfortable home in his mind, and so when, after some fierce questioning and bargaining, he found that he could have two camels to himself and Beth, as against making up part of a train, for only two pounds extra, the bargain was struck. He had asked the man how he could do it for this price, but the driver, swathed in desert headdress with white beading and tassles and only his dark eyes showing, explained to sir—for here the clients were "sir" and not "Boss"—that he could do it for this money by his knowledge of the desert and the speed of his animals. This man was not a common camel herder, he explained to Alan. He was descended from the great peoples of the desert caravanserai, as indeed were his animals, the Prophet be praised. He would not travel with the common camel train. He, and a very few of his kind, could travel with two camels and two people and their luggage, like lightning across the desert. Did sir not wish to cross the desert in a hurry with animals as fine as his? See, here is Suleiman, here is Khalid. Are they not fine animals? The bargain was struck and the Aboriginal stockman stood in the background saying nothing.

They could take some of their furniture. Beth would be happy. They would have their own driver and train. Others were making such arrangements, though they looked to be either bushmen, or wealthier people, taking three or four animals and two drivers. But he had struck a good bargain and was happy. Even allowing for food he might still arrive with fifty pounds intact. For once at Newcastle Waters he was in the country he wanted to reach, and he was confident he would find a temporary job and lodgings for himself and Beth at a station there. He returned to the stationmaster's house in high spirits.

Beth's eyes flared with anger when she heard the news, though with great control she said nothing, for the stationmaster and his wife were there and the bushman who had just returned with Mr. Swanson.

"Which one?" the bushman asked of Alan, without a hint of annoyance that Alan had not taken up his offer of help.

"I didn't ask his name. He said he'd be over presently to load up. He *will* come—?"

"He'll come, all right."

"Abdul, Boss," Jacky said simply.

"Know him, Mac?" Swanson asked. He seemed variably to call the big bushman Mac or Bear, although Beth noticed the stationmaster and his wife called him Mac. To Beth's ear, Swanson's question had almost a statement in it, as if he himself knew only too well who Abdul was, and that was why he was being noncommittal, so as not to alarm her. She thought she might be imagining it, until Mac, for that was the name that seemed to fit him best, made an even more noncommittal answer than Swanson's question.

"Never heard of him. Surprised you have, Jacky."

"Not know him, Boss," the black youth beamed quickly, "just heard name as we left."

"I must have missed it," Alan said quite unconcernedly.

"Jacky'd give most men a good ten yards in hearing—in some country, ten miles," the big man said. "Sounds like a good deal, then, mate. We'll help you get loaded when he arrives. Setting off straightaway then, are you?"

Alan nodded.

It was nearly noon by this time. Alan now saw to the

unloading of their furniture from the train: two armchairs, an expanding rosewood table and four matching chairs, cast-iron mattress base, latticed with wire, and a feather mattress and pillows. There were a tea chest of books, a tea chest of cooking utensils, a tea chest of glassware packed in straw and wrapped in old newspaper, and four suitcases of clothes.

The big bushman strangely did not help with the unloading, but stood, after excusing himself to Beth, in low conversation with the others outside the station house.

Then he moved away for a moment on his own, watching the unloading, standing between the others and Beth. When he was sure all was unloaded, he moved toward her again.

"You'll pardon me interfering, Missus," he said, doffing his hat once more, "which is a thing it goes against me grain to do. But if you'll take my advice you'll take only your clothes, a plate, a cup and a knife and fork each, and a couple of blankets."

"You mean get rid of everything else, everything?"

The man nodded gravely.

"But that's why Alan got two camels."

"I know, Missus, and they can carry a lot apart from their passengers."

"Well, then?"

"The lighter you are the better. It's as I said on the train."

"Absolutely everything?"

"It's best. And don't sell it. You'd get next to nothing for it. We'll store it here and at Swanson's place so that one day, perhaps, if you have a mind to, you can get it again."

"But Mr. Swanson lives more than two hundred miles away."

"That's nothing up here, Missus, and I've spoken to him and he'll have his men lift the stuff up when they're next in town for stores. You'll not get the table on the camel in any case."

"But I must take my books. I *must*. We're going a thousand miles away."

"They mean a lot to you, then?" It was a question he might just as well have asked of a man about an old and worn-out bridle which had no value other than sentimental, his question indicating that the value folks put on things was their own business, but if something meant a lot to someone, that indeed was a value.

"Yes, yes, they do," Beth answered urgently.

The big man looked at her and smiled warmly. At the end of his huge smile he said,

"Tell me, Missus, can you cook?"

"Why, yes, of course, but what has that—?"

"Well, you trust your books to me and the next time I see you, you can cook me a roast dinner, trimmings and all, like my sister would, how is that?"

"But it's such a big country, how will you ever—?"

"I'll get your books to you. Trust me on that."

"Yes, yes, I surely will," said Beth, regaining her composure and becoming slightly more formal. "I surely will, and thank you."

"And you'll persuade your husband about the luggage and furniture? He wouldn't take it from me and in any case I'd not normally interfere in a man's business."

"I'll persuade him and I am indebted to you. We both owe you a great deal."

He turned to go, as if embarrassed, and then turned and roared, "Jacky," so that the Aboriginal lad immediately left off helping Alan and ran to the bushman's side.

"Water bags ready?"

"Sure, Boss, always ready, soak all night."

"Get me a good one."

"All good, Boss."

The big man laughed. "Can't beat them, you know," he said, turning to Beth as Jacky skipped off. "Have never got the last word with that one, particularly, ever. That's why they're so good in the bush, I always say—always got an extra answer in their heads. This one's a marvel."

Jacky arrived back with a canvas water bag, filled, and dripping from the outside, but bulging like a wineskin and stoppered with a cork at its china bottle neck on one of the square corners.

Suddenly the bushman was serious again, as he handed the bag to Beth.

"Your camel driver is responsible for your provisioning, Missus, but think of this as your handbag, as your purse, and carry it at all times. Fill it whenever you stop at a place where you know the water's good. Keep it damp and it won't leak."

"How will I know the water's good?"

"If the animals are drinking it, Missus," he said kindly.

"Are all bush people like you?" she said quietly, as she hugged the bag to her, feeling its refreshing dampness against her body.

"Don't know, Missus," he said, as he turned to go. "Never given it much thought."

4

Abdul arrived at one o'clock, with the two free camels already loaded with stores and strung out behind him. He had the determined, narrow-eyed look of a Riff rifle tribesman about him, champing at the bit as much as his animals to be off and moving. The beasts themselves were caparisoned in harness of red and tasseled mosaic cloth, slung with camel boxes aside each rump. Abdul soon had them kneeling; loaded Beth and Alan on separate beasts into the camel saddles; and then with a nod and a wave of his swish stick, like some Arabian potentate, shouted a command so that the animals were up and running, almost bolting, with Beth and Alan half catapulted with the force of the animal's movements, but somehow keeping their seats and waving backward, with one hand each, without daring to turn or let go with the other hand.

They had started late for the day, but Abdul made twenty miles before camping, finding a small creek with the remains of other campfires. His English was passable only, or certainly so he made it appear, and he spoke little as he swished the animals down for the night, unloaded, started a fire, made tea and unleavened bush bread with cold roast beef and then said,

"Sleep now, we start early."

He made no effort to help them with their beds and neither of them liked to ask. In any case, both were exhausted, having hardly slept since Adelaide, so they rolled out their two blankets, each on the softest-looking piece of earth near a rock under a tree, and as the night grew colder, perhaps because of that cold, or desperation at the already unbeliev-able harshness of the land they had come to, or because of the contract of love between them, they undressed under the blankets and clung to each other all night.

The next day was a day Beth would remember all her life. They were roused at dawn, with very little ceremony, and the Afghan pulling the top part of the blankets down so harshly with his, "Up, up, we leave now," that he exposed Beth's left breast so that she colored until she realized he had hardly looked and was already at the breakfast fire and readying the animals. He gave them cold beef and the now stale bush bread called damper for breakfast, like a sandwich but with no butter, to eat on the run. When Beth asked about tea, he begrudgingly gave her half-cold tea from a billy he was about to empty, telling her they must move far this day.

They did. They made fifty miles. The dust was like sand, and not far away there was real sand. The wind blew. They saw rocks, some gum trees, the common name for the famed and ever drought-resistant native, the eucalypt tree, and they saw one emu. My God, it really is a desert, Beth thought, as she felt her lips burning however hard she tried to keep her bonnet down and her head bent. And although, as they rode on through the noonday heat, she gritted her teeth and hoped for a stop soon, they had not seen the worst of it. Alan kept shouting at the camel driver to stop, but the man could not hear, or did not want to, and pushed on, hunched over as the wind came, which they thought must stop him but certainly did not. Beth had never been as glad of anything as the precious water bag which she sipped at from time to time, for their driver had made no provision for individual water bags for the trip. She worried about Alan but could do nothing and he had to wait until, a little after two o'clock, the camel driver called a brief stop at a clump of eucalypts around a water hole. He handed out water and some more cold beef and bush bread. Beth went to fill her now half-empty water bag and nearly vomited as, getting closer to the water hole, she saw a dead cow in it, bloated and ballooned on its side, its udders hideously and nauseously large as if they would burst any minute.

So this was Central Australia.

Alan was now arguing with the Afghan, but the man simply kept curling his gown and headdress tighter around him and shouting, "Cheap price . . . cheap price for speed. We go on . . . we go on . . . time is money . . . time is money."

It seemed incredible, as this man barely waited until she was sitting in her saddle once more before jolting the animal up with his order, it seemed incredible to Beth that a phrase like "time is money" could exist under these conditions. It seemed some sort of anachronism of the future, rather than the past, if there was such a thing. She ached from her bottom to her top. The backs of her hands were burned, as well as parts of her face, her lips were cracking in the wind, and her eyes were full of dust and of course she had rubbed them and made them worse. She was furious with the camel driver, furious with her husband, yet her temperament did not allow for open expression of resentment. So it tunneled down deep inside her, wrinkling her brow with a crease she was unaware of. Yet it had started. In that day, at that time, having to swallow her pride and her anger and ride on in that harsh heat of her husband's unthinking, selfish Outback dream, the premature aging process of the bush had begun. Of course the Outback could break a man's spirit. But there was, in the structure of things in that great outdoors for which Alan had longed for so long, a rule of inverse proportions. The life, after a time, seemed to leave a man fixed at young middle age, tanned and fit and more youthful looking than any of his city counterparts. For a woman, with the steam of stoves and washing and children and chores and dust, everywhere dust and a face cream of any description a long-forgotten dream, except perhaps for the Christmas mail from the South, the effect was just the reverse.

Some women, when they first set out, took dressing tables

and vanity mirrors. Yet they were never in evidence in visited homesteads.

This day they made their fifty miles but Beth and Alan had sunstroke, and could not eat, spending half the night vomiting, trying to keep even water down, and, in any case, so burned on the backs of their hands and parts of their face that they dare not touch each other.

The next day was more of the same; Beth trying to keep her mind occupied, like a prisoner counting the days, but calculating, from the relentless fifty miles a day the camel driver insisted on, the speed in the camels. The second day they had been in the saddle just short of seventeen hours. So that was three miles an hour. This third day turned out to be within minutes of the second. There was no wind this time, although the dust seemed as ubiquitous, and her strength was failing her.

It was 340 miles from Oodnadatta to the Alice. By the end of that third day they had done 120. They were not even halfway. Alan's sunburn conditioning in Adelaide had done him some good, and he was acting brave, but Beth knew that emotionally he was probably in a worse condition than she. That night, after another cold dinner but at least no longer vomiting with sunstroke, she broached the subject of turning back. He would not hear of it, but instead argued with the Afghan about the unbearable speed in the heat for his wife. The man's English immediately improved and he said that, if sir would pay him another ten pounds now, on top of the twenty pounds he had already paid him at Oodnadatta, of course he would slow down for the sake of madam. It was indeed a harsh trip for a lady. Reluctantly, Alan paid. He had now spent thirty-two pounds since they had left Adelaide, but the understanding was that this would take them as far as Newcastle Waters, at a more leisurely pace, although that had not been defined, and as this price included better provisions, which the camel driver promised to buy at the Alice, Alan still hoped to get North on his budget of fifty pounds.

The camel driver told sir and madam not to worry, to sleep

in and they would start later in the morning and go slower, for, as indeed sir now saw himself, one could travel too fast in the heat. Alan and Beth recognized it as desert blackmail, but they had no option. It was that or turn back. They went to sleep almost half contented.

When they awoke in the morning, the camels and the driver were gone. They awoke cold and the fire was well out. He was long since gone. They did not even have a billy or tea of their own. All they had, thankfully, was Beth's water bag, which was three-quarters full.

Beth held back a sob and began to apologize to Alan.

"I'm sorry. It's my fault. Perhaps if I hadn't mentioned turning back, you wouldn't have had to mention slowing down and he mightn't have taken off."

Alan was strangely subdued, almost as if the reality of the situation had not reached him.

"He didn't get my wallet, I was too smart for that," he said, patting his shirt pocket.

"Alan, we haven't any food . . . no food, no animals, no clothes other than what we stand up in."

"We'll live off the land. The Aboriginals do it. I've read a lot in books about how they dig for water and eat berries, and kill kangaroos."

"You've only your knife."

Just then Beth thought she heard a padding sound, the soft thump such as camel hoof pads make on the harder earth, so that for a moment she thought it was all a dreadful mistake—that their driver had gone off to hunt for food and was returning. Then she realized it was an audio mirage, often as common in that part of the country as a visual one. She was hearing what her mind was wanting to hear. She took a small sip of water and passed the bag to Alan. They had little shade where they were and the sun would soon be up. Alan was for walking on. Beth took no notice and slipped her petticoats from under her dress to tie to the solitary tree and rig into a shade. As she looked for broken branches to serve as two uprights for the outside edge of the shade, she thought she heard the pads again, this time a little louder, so that she wondered if she had imagined them or not. She walked a little farther, looking for branches, and then she was sure she heard something. She walked out from under the tree on such a track as there was and looked in the direction from which she might expect the camel driver to return. She could see nothing except the rising heat haze. Her heart sank. She was hungry and tired and, already again, thirsty. Then something, perhaps instinct, perhaps a rise in that same sound, caused her to look in the other direction. She looked, and, in the distance saw, she was sure, a camel, moving at incredible speed across a plain, swinging, now coming into direct line with her level of vision and coming out of the heat haze along the track like a dervish to battle. There was something black and upright on its back, graciously upright, and soon she saw it to be Jacky Utmadatta, his feet slung up casually to one side so she could not believe he still remained on, yet he seemed part of the beast, and she shouted to Alan to come and see as she saw this incredible smile come out of the haze.

Whether Alan had heard the padding sound Beth was never sure but he seemed almost disappointed to see the black man.

"I was just preparing to walk to the telegraph line and damage it so that someone would come for us," he said as his form of greeting, as Jacky seemed to swish the camel down and dismount all in one movement.

"You have breakfast now, man and lady, you have breakfast first and then I get help. I make fire. You not eat good."

"How could you know that and how could you possibly find us?"

"I track, Missus . . . what white man call *blacktrack*. Boss tell me follow you both, he plenty worried. I never more than two or three miles behind, maybe. Poor camps, Missus. No proper food or sleep or feed for animals. Those camels have plenty red noses, I bet."

"Yes, yes, they did," Beth said excitedly, as if she had noticed something and it was all part of the mysterious telepathy this man seemed to possess. "What causes that? I thought it might be normal."

"Blood, Missus, dried blood. Camels always have much maggots in nose. Good drivers clean out pretty good plenty often. Bad drivers let animals suffer. That Abdul plenty bad."

"So you knew him all the time . . . why didn't you tell me?" Alan said, his anger flaring against the black man and his boss for knowing so much.

"Boss never interfere another's business. That why he no tell and shut me up plenty quick when I say Abdul out loud. Boss no let people die, though—that why he send me to watch: maybe Abdul run off, maybe not."

"You mean he's done it before?"

"Hard to prove things in bush, Boss," Jacky said, busying himself at the tucker box now, which he had taken from his camel.

"You sit back relax, Boss. I cook steak and eggs, make tea. Pretty soon you feel better. Then I get help."

"All right," Alan said grumpily.

"You are a sight for sore eyes, Jacky Utmadatta, blossom of Mulga," Beth said, ignoring her husband, ignoring her usual reticence and kissing him on the forehead as he rose from the tucker box with a steak in each hand.

"Hung rump, Missus, plenty good. Look a bit dark but not blown in heat yet."

"I think if you gave me a witchetty grub or snake to eat I would trust you," she said.

"You want snake, Missus? Good snake near here I get and cook later."

"Goodness, no," said Beth, rather too quickly, and destroying what she meant to have shown as a willingness for Aboriginal bush ways. Then she looked and saw that Jacky was smiling. It had been a joke.

Alan sat all this time with his compass out, studying it and a map which Beth did not even know he had.

They ate the meal heartily, Alan appearing to have settled down and even entering into the spirit of the thing by helping Jacky to toast the bread over the fire at the end of a long sharp twig. For, unbelievably, in that tucker box of his, he had brought eggs, proper bread, steak, butter and milk, milk for the tea and it was heaven, the best of tea, slung in the billy with a eucalypt leaf, the best of tea Beth had ever tasted.

"Not always this good, Missus," Jacky said, as if reading her mind. "Tucker pretty good because only two days travel out of town."

Beth nodded and was about to say something else when Alan interrupted:

"How far would you say to the telegraph poles?" he asked, almost casually.

Jacky looked at him, his usual smile gone for a moment, his nostrils flaring as if he sensed danger.

"Thirty, maybe twenty miles, Boss. Not far, why?"

"I think I'll go and send a message so that they'll know where to find us. I think we should go there, break the cable and sit at the foot of the pole and wait. That's what we'll do. Beth can ride the camel and you and I will walk, Jacky."

"You stay, Boss. I send message and day or two my boss come, maybe less. No need walk one plurry yard further."

It was the first time Beth had heard Jacky use this word, which was a sort of Aboriginal corruption of the traditional "bloody," and it was the only hint in his sentence of slight annoyance.

"I'm telling you what's best," Alan said, that terrible boyish assertiveness of his, which Beth feared so, now rising.

"It best stay, Boss. I send smoke signal fire now and plenty soon my boss come. We stay here under shelter. You build plenty fine shelter, Missus."

Beth would have swelled with pride if she were not so distraught about Alan.

"Well, that's what I'm going to do. I'm going to walk to the telegraph line and send a signal I know will be received."

"You got to climb and cut wire, Boss—even that not easy. But poles long distance apart and easy walk under line and miss poles and then beyond that, Simpson, Boss. . . . Simpson Desert beyond that."

"How could I miss the poles? The line is that way—east, right?"

"That way, Boss, whatever you call it," said Jacky, nodding in the direction Alan had pointed, "line that way all right but easy to miss, Boss."

"How?" Alan said insistently.

"Willy-willy, Boss."

"Willy-willy?"

"Dust storm. Perhaps you no see wires."

"Nonsense. I'll stop if there's a storm."

"Twenty miles a long way on foot, Boss, if you don't know country. You stay, rest, you feel better soon. Here"—he produced from the tucker box a small wad of wax paper— "you rub this on sunburn and then give to Missus. You feel better plenty soon."

"Well, if you're going to stay here and wait, I'll take the camel to the telegraph line, then," Alan said.

"Alan, no, that's not our animal to take," Beth said urgently, but the black man was remarkably unconcerned.

"He better take camel and food and most of water if he going off on own, Missus," he said to her as if he were using the third person as a deliberate slight, rather than a mannerism of speech, yet doing it in a pleasant, relaxed way. This was about the closest Aboriginals got to wasteful, argumentative anger. Then he turned more directly to Alan and said, "But perhaps carry water bag, too, Boss, case camel bolts. Different riding alone from being part of a string, though this pretty fine camel and you welcome but Boss be plenty mad at me letting you go, I reckon. Not good idea, Boss."

The black man, or rather boy as he still appeared to Beth, now busied himself with the fire. Whereas Beth was expecting some sort of complicated blanket signal, the black Jacky simply built the fire up and said, "You move away, Missus, be plenty hot for few minutes."

"You mean that's all?" she said, as she took the wad of wax paper from Alan.

"That all, Missus. No one build campfire this big in daytime unless signal. Boss come soon. Come by nightfall, I reckon. If not by morning. He just across plain and over hills on way to Boss Swanson's place."

"What hills?" said Alan.

"They there, Boss. You want to walk to hills? I take you across plains to hills."

The black man had seen a chance to divert Alan's attention to a more practical route and had jumped at it with a keen cunning Beth admired, and her hope rose again. She was, despite their rescue, desperately close to tears. She feared for her husband. She did not believe he was in any real danger, for she believed her big bushman friend invincible and that, even if Alan did go off, when the bushman arrived he would find him. And yet, after the suffering of the last two days, why must he go? Why could he not stay? Her hope rose, and then he said,

"I'm going to the telegraph line. Are you coming, Elizabeth?"

"If you must go, you'll travel faster alone."

"That is the truth of it."

Jacky had wandered off to let them be alone for a minute.

"Alan, you mustn't go. You mustn't."

He looked silently at her and said only,

"Try to understand."

She had seen that look and heard that tone before. It was the day he had falteringly tried to explain to her why he had to come North. She knew what he was trying to tell her: this was the test he had been looking for. He was choosing this time and this Godforsaken place to prove himself. Yet still she tried.

"Alan, you mustn't go," she repeated. "For my sake, if for nothing else. It's too dangerous and I'll feel to blame because I made you ask the camel driver to slow down."

"I've got to go. You know that. Try to understand. I'll be all right. I've got my compass."

"But I'm sure Jacky knows what he's doing. I'm sure help will come."

"What if it doesn't come quickly enough? What then?"

"I don't know. All I know is that I don't want you to go."

His voice went strangely quiet then and he said, "But I must Elizabeth, you know that. This is the reason I came North—to show I can do these things. To be in the open spaces on my own, away from that terrible bank window. I love all this space. Despite the last couple of days, I've loved the space."

He kissed her, and then he and Jacky reloaded the camel and he kissed Beth again and left.

5

After Alan rode off, Beth was very silent for a long time and so was Jacky, although he took each of her hands and rubbed the now cold tea on their burned backs, and then gently on her face, taking her bonnet off and sitting her on a blanket under her own homemade shelter. He seemed not to mind that she was far away, and when he had finished with the tea and wiped her hands and face with a piece of flannelette, he took the wax paper she had absentmindedly put down on a log and rubbed it first on her lips, then on her face, and then on the backs of her hands. It smelled gamy and, still half away from her environment, she asked him what it was and he replied kangaroo fat. Then he put a blanket at her back against the tree, made some more tea and settled down hunched and cross-legged to wait.

Presently she dozed off and dreamed of her father's dairy farm and when she was a girl.

When she awoke it was dark and she was lying down with a blanket over her where Jacky must have put her. She heard voices by the fire and, as she raised herself on her elbow, saw that the bushman had arrived with the other Jacky.

She coughed and the bushman came over.

"This is a bad business, Missus," he said, making no attempt to hide his anger at Alan's action. "I've just been scolding Jacky for not keeping him here."

"It's not his fault. And besides, what could he have done?"

"Knocked him out and tied him up, that's what he could have done."

"Him plurry white man, Boss," said Jacky, coming over as if he felt it necessary to say something in his own defense.

"Well, that just means you tie him all the tighter to make sure he doesn't get away before your own boss arrives."

"I tell you Boss be plenty mad, Missus," said Jacky with his detached, matter-of-fact acceptance. He wasn't mad because his boss was, he was just stating that that was the way of things.

"I'll have to go straight on for him," the bushman said, his anger subsiding.

"You've only just got here, then?" Beth said.

"Just arrived, Missus," he said, unable to hold back a smile and Jacky looked as if he would burst.

"What is it, what have I said?" asked Beth, getting up now, with the blanket around her, and coming closer toward the two men near the fire.

"I think Boss just break all-time record any country anywhere in world, Missus, and you tell him just got here."

"Well, of course I didn't mean it that way," she said, suppressing a smile despite the desperate anxiety that was rising in her for Alan, now that she was awake. "I really am terribly in your debt. We'd be dead by now, both of us, if you hadn't had the foresight to send Jacky."

"Yes," the bushman said simply, "that's true."

His statement came at Beth like a knife in the stomach. She had perhaps thought she had been being a little lavish in her praise. But this man was in earnest, desert earnest, Outback earnest. It was nearly 1900 and in the cities or even in the country districts from which she had come, there were fine suits and carriages and houses and all the luxuries of European life. Yet the country's middle was the middle of nowhere and up here you could die in a day. She could not believe the assumptions of fantasy she and Alan had made for the bush, for the wondrous Centre and North. This night for her, despite her giant black and white companions and the friendly warmth of the campfire, was a night of despair. It was the despair of realization, which every bush traveler must face. But to come all at once in a rush at her, so that she began to tremble and feel faint, was a soul lesson she would never forget. The flames of the bush fire that night would have distorted the face of Christ Himself into an angel of evil. As the fire licked out into the night these were evil men and an evil place in an evil land. She would never forgive the earth on which she stood. Deep down, despite the loving changes of color and texture and the lush things it would give her to eat in season, she would never forgive the land.

James Carlyon shifted his big feet restlessly in the dust beside her, as if aware with a bushman's sixth sense of the unspoken hostility to his beloved land.

"I must be going," he said in a distant voice, a voice which Beth had not heard him use before. There was a tiredness in it, yet beyond that there was a tone almost of resignation. She wondered, momentarily, if even men like this giant James Carlyon sometimes tired of the bush, too, sometimes saw it as an unrelenting battle they might never win no matter how many times they conquered it daily. Perhaps this was the tone in his voice. She hoped it was this and nothing else.

"I'll take Jacky Emu with me, Missus," he went on, his tone unshifting, "and leave this hopeless smiling fellar with you."

"You're most kind," she found herself saying, although perhaps with as little heart in her voice as Carlyon's indicated he had for the task in front of him.

"Not at all," he said, in a formal manner, as if caught off guard, so that afterward she wondered, she wondered a great deal, just where this man had come from and when, since underneath his Australianisms and bush colloquialisms he had what she might have described as a cultured tongue.

"Will you be able to do anything in the dark?" she asked.

"The moon's not bad and I'm fairly confident your husband will have got only as far as the wire." He said this in a strange way, so that Beth was not sure what he meant; yet, in another way, part of her understood enough to ask her next question, however reluctant she was.

"Will you be gone long?"

The big man looked at her and she felt the warmth rising in him as his bush composure came back and he said,

"As long as it takes, Missus. We'll not come back without him. If he's gone beyond the wire, by accident, we'll keep going. We've got plenty of water and food for all of us, but don't you worry. You know either of these blacks of mine can dig in nine out of ten places and find water, or at least a frog under the mud deep down somewhere—and you can squeeze plenty of water out of a frog to drink and then cook the frog. They can find water in certain trees and when all else fails they collect the dew from the leaves overnight. So you are absolutely as safe as a house with my Jacky, here, Missus, and you just sit pat until you see us coming back—probably by tomorrow night, I'd say. But whatever happens, you understand what I'm saying, you stay with Jacky and he'll see you through. No wandering off, no arguing, just do exactly what he says."

Beth understood now, or thought she did. He was saying quite clearly, by implication, that if he and Jacky Emu did not come as soon as expected, or did not come at all, that she herself would be all right. But how could that be? Surely the bushman and the older Aboriginal could survive as well or better than Jacky and she. And then it hit her. Beyond the wire was the Simpson Desert. Against that, this camp and its closeness to civilization, she supposed, was like a city to the Outback.

She just nodded sadly and then forced a smile, which the big man and Jacky Emu returned as they rode off on their camels. But her thoughts were broken by a pulling at her sleeve.

"OK, Missus, OK. You worry not help men out there. We get you better now. You want wash while I cook supper?"

Beth was disbelieving: "Could I?"

"We spare billyful, maybe, Missus."

"You sure?"

"Plenty water all round this place, Missus. I dig for more if we run out. I see plenty water spots as ride in."

When she nodded he went to one of the camel boxes and

presently returned with a large cake of soap smelling strongly of carbolic, a small but clean towel, a billycan of water and a clean shirt and pair of moleskins, the ubiquitous cloth trouser of the Outback with the words, "You roll up legs they fit OK, Missus . . . you feel better clean bush clothes me think. You can wash under your plenty good shelter, Missus, and I be busy bending over fire. You plenty safe. . . . I no look."

At this show of consideration, at the deep thoughtfulness and sensitivity behind what she was beginning to see were the accepted norms of Outback hospitality, Beth Brennan finally cried.

She sobbed as she undressed and soaped herself, and felt secure in this black man's acceptance even of her sorrow.

Later they ate, and then he made her a bed of eucalypt leaves, with a blanket on top of the leaves and two other blankets to put over her. She rubbed some more kangaroo fat on her lips and then she fell asleep to the deep inhalation of the smell of oil of wintergreen.

6

It was four days before James Carlyon and Jacky Emu were back and Beth was not surprised to find them alone. In many ways she always thought the tears of the night they left were her tears for Alan.

"We found him on the edge of the Simpson, Missus, way beyond the wire. I hoped to bring him back to bury him here with a ceremony for you, but it wasn't practical, so we buried him right by pylon 13001 at the wire. We built a cairn of stones and that way you'll always be able to find the grave. We said a few words, Jacky some of his and I some of mine, so I hope that's all right and the line party which services the telegraph puts desert peas on the graves in spring. Sort of a tradition up here. They're beautiful flowers, Missus, really . . . big for wild flowers, big and pink and beautiful, and he'll rest easy out there. He had a thing about that telegraph line, didn't he? All those miles from south to north and connecting Australia with the rest of the world. Thousands of miles. It's a sad thing, Missus, but he got the space he wanted to breathe in for a while and now he'll rest in it forever and who's to say he's not better off there than if he'd spent his life in that bank he used to talk about, begging your pardon, Missus."

He doffed his hat then and asked Jacky to make some tea,

and he never spoke of Alan again. But Alan was with him, all right, Beth knew that—with him like every precious cow or bull lost on an overland drive, with him as another unnecessary death, of man or beast, as if he had to account for it personally and were some Outback Gabriel sent to warn unwary travelers and helpless beasts away from the devil's anvil.

They left the next day, walking the camels out across the plain toward the hills and Swanson's place. No one had asked Beth what she wanted to do and although the bushman seemed his normal self in conversation with the two Aboriginals, she felt a sense of strain between herself and him, so that after the words had been said they seemed to have come so much from a mind preoccupied elsewhere that it was as if they hadn't been said at all: like a dream one wonders if one has had.

"I'll try to be no trouble and get myself back to Adelaide as soon as possible," Beth said.

"We'll see, Missus. We'll see who's traveling where."

"I am dreadfully, dreadfully sorry for all the trouble."

She felt that somehow his nonresponse was a form of blaming her.

"I know, Missus, I know."

She couldn't understand how he could be so less kind to her than he had been at the start. She tried to be more formal again. She was riding on the second camel, behind him, with Jacky sitting close behind her.

"Where are you from, then, Mr. Carlyon; surely not these parts?"

He slowed his animal and looked around at her. "I'm from here, Missus, and nowhere else. Never been and never wanted to be."

He hunched over his camel more then, and they went a little faster, at the trot, Beth feeling dismally guilty and awed at the depth of the big man's feelings. She wished she might hold him and soothe him, and then, cut even more by the guilt of that thought and a feeling in her stomach she couldn't articulate, she put her head down and her thoughts away and concentrated on the ride.

The fact was, they had been drawn to each other, sexually and every other way, since the moment they had sat opposite each other in the train. But Alan had kept these feelings in check. Now with his presence removed in such a sudden way, neither Beth nor Mac could own up to their feelings.

Soon the lead camel, the unusual blue eyes in a face so dark kept sweeping the horizon. Mac was annoyed at himself for talking so abruptly to the woman and could not understand that, with the man now gone, as something that had stood between them, the dormant thing inside them both would lead to silly frictions. But he was not a man to dwell on his annoyance, particularly with himself. On that path lay death and danger. He had long since learned that lesson from the Aboriginals, though he would never be as good as they. But mostly he kept his energy only for the task at hand: it could not be spent unwisely on wasteful anger over nothing, particularly anger over anger; it must be kept for the far horizons and the noonday heat. Though the run into Charlie Swanson's, once over the hills, was picnic enough. God, he'd seen and done runs a thousand times worse. And he'd handled things worse, much worse than this thing with this woman and her husband. But the man should not have died. He should have tracked them himself but was fearful to do so because of his feelings for the woman; and that the man had a right to do what he wanted to do. He shouldn't have bothered about them other than to be neighborly and polite on the train. He should have given them tea and talked a bit and that would have been it. But they—she—had looked so defenseless. He shouldn't have gone off for a drink with Charlie Swanson. Then the young bloke wouldn't have gone off. He should have asked the young bloke for a drink, that's what he should have done. Would he be alive now if he had?

And he had known about Abdul, of course he had. They'd all known he was getting his fare together to ship out of Darwin back home. Never knew he'd be this stupid, though. God, if he ever caught up with him . . .

Well, he was certainly the greatest bushman of them all, this fellow leading one woman and two blacks over picnic country. He was such a good bushman that he'd lost a kid who should never have been let loose ten miles north of Adelaide, whatever one's belief about a man's right to choose. They should set up a dingoproof fence right around Adelaide: a fence to keep those purebred wild dingo dogs out and the people in. He was such a good bushman he'd lost a kid, almost shouted at the poor, bereft widow who was only trying to make polite conversation because he was being such a moody bastard, and now he was committing the compounding sin of worrying about it. He was great at Aboriginal logic, all right, at not wasting energy on things you could do nothing about.

But he did have to decide about the woman, that was true enough, for she was certainly in no fit state to decide for herself. Talk about a babe in arms, though she'd been pluckier than her poor husband—made of sterner stuff than he, he could see that from the start. She'd certainly have to rest up at the Swansons for a while. Then Charlie could get one of his boys to take her into Oodnadatta for the train. It would be no trouble to make a special trip. He'd just told her about him seeing what was doing to give him time to think.

Yet even as he allowed himself to think a little about what he really wanted to occupy his thoughts with, he realized it was unthinkable. It was madness. The best thing he could do for her was say nothing, do nothing and just point her little head in the direction, give her a friendly pat on the bottom and send her back home. This was no place for women, as evidenced by their scarcity. And he was an Overlander, the Overlander King, and, by God, he intended to stay it. What was he thinking about? He had Charlie Swanson's mob of cattle to get through and he'd lost four days already and it was going to be a very bad Dry, a very, very bad Dry.

But God, he loved it. He loved the dust and the mob and the crack of the stockwhip a mile long and the high hard sun and the search for the best pasture and the best water and how to recognize these and how to keep the pace up to the cattle and just right so that you kept them moving nicely and didn't let them spell too much so they got the idea they could die in the heat. That was the mistake so many made, resting them too much when they seemed too tired. Then was the crucial time to go on, however cruel it seemed, to keep them moving, moving to the next water and then to the market. But never straight to market. Move them fast through the heat and hard spots but never take them into market that way. He was too smart for that. Near every market he knew of fattening spots. He'd drive them till they nearly dropped to get them to those fattening spots, where there were good pasture and water, for the cities were all in the rainfall belts. Then he'd fatten and hand-feed if necessary and then drive them to market so that his clients got good prices.

You had to know your animals and your water spots and, even though the government was starting to put down artesian bores, you still had to know, that was the glorious part about it, you still had to know, it was your judgment against God's and the devil's, whichever came first, if either lived in this land, it was your judgment of the shrinking, death-filled day once you left one water spot and started out for another, only to find it dry and have to go on, reading the state of the land and the trees and the desert frogs to guess where the next best water might be and whether that might be another dead-dry claypan, too.

And that Murranji Track, the Death Track they called it up North, way up North where he one day hoped to settle, why that was the best of them all: the best and the worst, where minutes and sometimes seconds could mean death. He held the record there and it was there they had christened him Mac, Murranji Mac, for he'd drunk the Boss's whiskey and done a Highland dance round the campfire that night, and then an Irish one too, for he was half Scot and half Irish, though by that time he'd been christened with the new name.

He was doing a lot of damn thinking this day, that was for sure. Perhaps he was getting old. He was nearly forty and had been a bushy all his life. He'd wanted a place of his own once and he still did. That land out toward Arnhem Land was the place. He made good money as a drover but he sent a lot to his sister and his only chance was to find water. Five thousand gallons a day, regular supply, was what he needed—five thousand gallons a day that no one else knew about, that is, so he could claim the government water bounty of a hundred square miles of land and two hundred pounds for stocking. That'd be a good way to start. He reckoned that land near the Arnhem Land area would have plenty of unknown waterfalls and springs and even rivers. Still unsettled except by the blacks. But it was dry, too. Everywhere was dry and harsh except in the Wet, and then you couldn't move. It was a thought, though. But that really was another country, an unknown country, the last frontier in the last frontier land, and he doubted that she'd go, or put up with him going off droving because he'd been too long in one place, or mustering, because he'd be lucky to run cattle at the rate of one and a half to the square mile. And the two black blokes, would they go? And then he realized what he was thinking.

7

Charlie and Muriel Swanson were getting on in years now. Charlie was one of the few left who remembered Mac's father, who had been one of the first white men into the Territory. His father had died of natural causes, though when drunk one night Charlie Swanson had admitted that he believed hardened arteries might have hastened the end a little. "Your old man, the drover, you might almost say the Territory's first drover, was a fearsome man on a horse and a fearsome man with a bottle, Mac, I have to tell you," Charlie had once said.

Muriel Swanson had arrived on the scene just in time to prevent Charlie going the same way. "She was, she is," Charlie had been known to say to Mac and others on the odd occasions on which he might now get drunk, "a bloody Methodist missionary, so help me God. Sent to save the blacks, she saved me—well, bloody near. Perhaps she knew that was the only way she'd get a mission school built up here."

Muriel ran a mission school on Charlie's 640,000-acre property and saw Beth as a gift from the Lord. For Muriel was more missionary than teacher and her charges were long on the Psalms and Biblical names and very short on reading and writing and sums.

Beth sometimes thought that Muriel Swanson decided her future. The moment she arrived she put her to bed, to bed on a feather mattress with feather pillows and the most freshly laundered sheets she'd ever seen. She rubbed elder flower ointment, which was wondrously cooling, on her sunburn, and then sat on her bed and insisted on spooning the fresh beef tea into her herself.

The next morning Muriel told Beth that Mac had already left on his long overland drive with the mob, because the Dry was getting worse and time was running out. It was going to be a very bad Dry, she said, and wondered if Beth might mind helping out at the school, which might be better than traveling anyway, at least for the time, and who knows, she might come to like the place, but she was free to stay or go and Charlie would send her to the next train in a week if she wanted to leave. Mac had said to give her his regards and say he'd take her south to Adelaide at Christmas if she wanted to go.

"But you must see something of the countryside before you go, whatever you do," said Muriel. At these words, Beth, who was still in one of Muriel's borrowed nightgowns, and had not been outside, quaked. Charlie, sitting at the breakfast table puring huge cups of tea, laughed. "She thinks she's seen enough of the countryside for a lifetime, luv, I'll wager."

Muriel had curious quiet depths to her for a missionary. Beth expected her to answer but she said nothing, just brushed a couple of loose strands of hair back and straightened her silver-rimmed glasses and smiled quietly.

They chatted small talk for a time over breakfast and then Muriel said, "There'll have been a bath drawn for you when you're ready and I thought if you didn't mind keeping me company you might like to ride over to the school with me and have a look and then we can go and pick some flowers."

"Pick some flowers—?" Beth was incredulous.

"Yes. Would you like that?"

"Yes—yes, I would . . . but I thought—"

"I know. Everyone does. But here, you see, the desert does blossom like a rose. There's not a part of the desert there isn't some kind of wild flower. There are more than two thousand known varieties already, and I know you've had a hard time of it, but it is spring up here, and the flowers are out everywhere, even over by the telegraph line, and I thought it might help you to know that."

Beth choked up and nodded and hurried to have her bath. But Muriel Swanson had reached her, as she reached everyone, with her deep love of her adopted sunburned country. When Beth emerged in jodhpurs, boots, blouse and wide-brimmed hat with a chin strap, which Muriel had had the staff lay out for her, Beth had already decided to stay. Whether it was good for her to go from one extreme of the country to the other so quickly was a question she often later asked herself.

Yet if there had been any doubt still, it would have been dispelled in the soft, late-afternoon light, as Muriel, when she saw Beth could handle a horse well from her days on her father's farm, took her for a ride to a hill from which they could see Ayers Rock in the distance. Beth had never in her life seen so many purples and pinks and reds and browns in earth and rock and hill and mountain. They stayed until sunset and the memory stayed with her forever and it was the closest she ever got to loving the land.

Mac was not in fact heading for market this time. Charlie had seen that the north end of the North was starting to open up, particularly in the Barkly Tablelands area in the North-East, out toward the Queensland border. It was good cattle country and Charlie had just sold two thousand head to two stations up there, twelve hundred for one and eight hundred for another, and Mac was on his way with them. The station owners could have bought in Queensland, of course, and had them overlanded from there. But Charlie was known for his mobs, and his good breeders, and his cattle were used to the drier conditions of the Territory compared with the lusher pastures of much of Queensland, although they had their Dries too, by God they did.

So Mac was out and running with a big mob, pushing to the Barklys, out to break another record, out to play his death-duel poker with the land.

He would travel over a thousand miles and it should take six months—four months there and two months back, or less if he made good time.

Beth had been so happy those months that the news that Mac was late back made her weak inside, though she put on a brave front, for the months had not been without some infusion of the stoicism which the land taught.

But she had been so happy. For a month she had mooned about, feeling guilty over Alan and genuinely missing him, though less daily with a speed which worried her at first until, caught up in the capacious arms of the Rainbow Range station and all its staff (for with nearly a thousand square miles it was like a kingdom with the station house its capital), she came alive again, perhaps more alive than she had ever been. She learned to joke in a way she had not dared to before; she learned to let her feelings show more, as if prodded by some dormant pubescence that had not seen light before. She rode and she taught and she slept and she ate and her tiny frame put on weight but she did not worry, for something told her that Mac wouldn't like a scarecrow, and slowly she had begun to realize that what Mac would think mattered to her. She would never be fat, but her body had blossomed into a riper thing, like her spirit inside her, and somewhere in those months it had come accepted that she would stay.

But Charlie had been betting on Mac being back within five and a half months, and however much he told her that six months was a bare minimum for even the greatest, which indeed Mac was, she still worried. When the six months were up Charlie fell to other excuses and no one had kept from her the telegraph from the Barklys that Mac had cut a week off the four-month record and turned straight around to come home. So after the sixth month had passed, Charlie fell to excuses like, "Well, you know what he's like, Beth, he'd stop and help any lame dog, begging your pardon—stop and help any traveler."

"Yes, of course, Charlie," Beth said. Muriel said nothing but adjusted her glasses and stroked her two straying strands of gray hair back into place, repinning them at the back with her tortoiseshell comb.

After six and a half months Charlie was saying, "Well, he's run across someone ill, ill on the track, that's for sure. He'd never leave an ill person too weak to move. He'd stay with him until he got better or died. Could be months. It happens up here. No doctors for hundreds of miles. Bush tradition to stay with a sick man and look after him. Could even have run across a man with his Missus and kids."

Charlie did not mention that it was also a bush tradition to send one of your blacks on for help or to tell people so that they wouldn't organize unnecessary search parties. Mac would have sent Jacky, who could make fast time even on foot, just to let them know he was all right. It was a bad business and Charlie was worried and would have to organize a search party for the bodies if they didn't arrive in another week, although because Charlie knew Mac would have sent a message if he was still alive, Charlie held little hope. And this poor girl, on top of what she'd already been through. Would she stay on now? The black children loved her and so did Muriel but Charlie estimated it would only be about another week before she cracked. He could see what she could not. Her concern now went beyond that of gratitude for her rescue and normal friendship.

The extra week passed and Beth did not crack, although she had taken to sobbing quietly at night, filling the crow's-feet that were already beginning to appear on her young face, though her high color, almost a suntan, hid them except when they creased white in laughter or a change of light. But during the day she set her mouth hard and tried to be cheery, or at least act as cheery as Charlie and Muriel were, although after lunch one day she mindlessly dropped and broke a plate.

"Damn this bloody land," she said as the plate, crashing,

broke into everyone's thoughts, which were away in the North, or wherever Mac was or was not.

"Isn't that the truth, Missus," Charlie said, lapsing back into his Outback colloquialism. Muriel said nothing.

Beth stood in half shock. It was not just that she had sworn and spoken in a way she never expected she would in her life. It was Charlie's answer. So sometimes they all felt it. It was there, unspoken, at the bottom of the well in all of them.

It was this strange love-hate relationship they all had for the land—the bush, the land, the precious bloody thing the men loved like a mystic mistress, loved like Russian peasants, scratching at it, cursing it, yet blessing it for all its charismatic vagaries, loving it in the Dry and in the Wet, in the dust and in the mud, as it seduced them in its unreasonable beauty all the days of their lives.

And now, despite everything, despite this added hovering horror, she felt it herself, this need to fight back at this strange, animate, inanimate earth. She saw herself drawn to it and she trembled. But she must hold this fear into herself for the time being.

Another week passed and that was seven months and now Charlie cursed himself for not sending a party out earlier, for the Wet was nearly on them. Perhaps that was it. Perhaps that was why Mac had not come and not sent a messenger. Perhaps he knew that there was not time for one to reach them before the onset of the Wet. But Jacky? The Wet might slow him down, but he'd get through, sooner or later he'd get through.

But now there was nothing for it and Charlie set about organizing a major expedition.

As they gathered for a meeting with his head stockman to make their plans, Mac and his two blacks rode around the corner of the station house. They had made the forty miles from the front gate to the home paddock without being seen.

"Thanks for the thought but I wouldn't go to all that trouble if I were you, Charlie," the big man shouted in as much high humor as Beth had ever seen him.

"Oh, Mac," she shouted with all the unfulfilled longing

since his first tender word to her on the train, pushing up in happy intonation on his name, "Oh, *Mac*," she said, running as he got down, his indirect greeting to Muriel of, "My, she's grown, I don't think we'll have to throw her back for another fish after all," overlapping her own words as he stood down and she stopped short of him, slightly embarrassed at her unprecedented show of emotion.

"How do, Missus," he said with his cheekiest of grins, tucking her close to his side under one arm as he headed for the station house and then, to cover his forwardness, for she was still a recent widow, however much he'd thought about her in the time away, he shouted, "Come on, Charlie, you old bastard, begging your pardon, Missus, I need a drink. We all need a drink. Me and me black blokes have found water and been to the Back of Beyond and it really is there. That's the real reason we're late. I didn't want to tell you in case we didn't find it or to spoil the surprise." He did not add who the surprise was for—and didn't need to.

Beth's heart jumped. She had known of the Back of Beyond before she had ever come bush, although she had heard more of it in the past few months.

She had learned that the ubiquitous phrase meant a mythical place to every bushman, a place in the perhaps unattainable distances which held the relentless threat of the unknown, the unforgiving nature of the land and yet, too, the promise of pure pasture in the mists of watered land.

The Back of Beyond was as far as you could go—and then beyond that; it was beyond the black stump and beyond the green hill; it was beyond the blue lake and beyond the mulga scrub; it was beyond the Red Centre and beyond the blue horizon; it was the place way out there at the Back of Beyond—it was the fartherest, finest, unfulfilled longing of everyman; it was the infinite distance in a land of infinite space; it was all their lost tomorrows on all their dreamed horizons. But it was there. It was real. Anyone would tell you that. One could always just see it in the distance and know that tomorrow, perhaps, he'd be there.

And now Mac said he'd found it.

8

The wedding ceremony took place in the mission school chapel on Christmas Day, 1896, in 126 degrees. It was only 120 degrees outside the wood-and-galvanized-iron building, and under the shade of the lemon-scented citrus gums by the cool-verandaed station house, in the lush home paddock rich with grass from the Wet, it was like a fairyland of crinolined whites and smiling blacks, so that Beth saw in her mind's eye all the great balls and wedding ceremonies she had ever read about. Of course it was, in fact, an outdoor barbecue, with her iron bedstead, which had been brought from Oodnadatta with her other furniture, serving as the cooking grill. When Mac had said she could take everything else, but the iron was too heavy and unnecessary because he'd make a base himself and stuff calico with bush turkey feathers for the mattress, Charlie had commandeered the iron-and-wire bed base for barbecuing. These were highly popular for such purposes but very hard to come by. They just threw some big logs down, Aboriginal style, propped the iron frame on rocks at each corner and threw the meat on, although on this occasion, because of the wedding and Christmas, they had turkeys and suckling pigs going on spits as well.

And even if it was not white tie and tails quite as Beth saw it in her mind's eye, some had come over six hundred miles for the wedding and the station's Chinese laundry had been very busy and moleskins and shirts had been bleached and pressed and starched so that with the handful of women in cool catalog dresses and the men shining and polished like some bushmen's barbers' quartet, it was, as Charlie said, a great group of two hundred guests of distinction, however dubious some of those distinctions might be. To Beth it was wonderful and she did not stop to ponder if it was indeed part of the Outback Code that what the land gives with its lavish hand on one day, it takes back twofold on the next.

She was standing with Charlie and her husband, who had persuaded her to taste a little beer. Charlie, as host, master of ceremonies, giveaway of the bride and adopted father of the groom, had partaken freely of the amber beverage he had provided (with no objection from Muriel) and kept calling Mac by the name "Bear," which had really been Mac's father's nickname, although some still used it of him, too.

"Now, Bear, my son," Charlie was saying, "what do you really intend to do up there in that wilderness—shoot dingoes and possums, if indeed they are silly enough to go up there, begging your pardon, new Missus?"

They had discussed it many times and indeed Mac was stocking his property from Charlie's herd, taking a small mob with him when he and Beth headed north leisurely after the Wet. But Charlie kept at him as if, in a way, testing him that it was right to settle down; testing to see if he had indeed found every bushman's Shangri-La; testing him, despite Charlie's drunkenness, to make sure he didn't feel it better to stay on with Beth living in comfort at the station house and Mac going off droving when he had a mind. Charlie had even offered him a partnership and in some ways Beth hoped he might take it, for secretly she had the same fears as Charlie, who had known Mac's father so well. Could such a man settle down after all those years on the track? If the urge was going to keep taking him, then better for his wife to stay secure here, raising a family, teaching school, with Muriel for company. Women were so scarce even in the Centre, as evidenced by the handful at the wedding. But where they were going there was none. And Charlie and Muriel had only two daughters, who were home from school for Christmas, and they already got on well with Beth. In a few years Mac could have the place to himself if the girls were free to come and go and get half the income.

It hadn't been spelled out this clearly, so as not to make Beth too anxious, but she knew this was what the conversation was all about—it was Charlie's last best try to get Mac to change his mind.

"What I intend to do, Charlie," Mac was answering, as he had several times over the past several weeks, "is get that water bounty I've filed for and finish up with a larger and better property than yours—or if not me, my sons. The future of the beef industry is in the North, Charlie, closer to the ports for shipping overseas."

"Maybe . . . maybe . . . but this country's still got to be fed, too. It'll be a long time before Overlanders like yourself are not needed, if that's what you're hoping for to kill the thirst for dust on the road forever."

"I'm ready to settle down, Charlie."

"Of course you are, and no man has earned it more," Charlie said, realizing he had gone a little far and meaning it with all his heart. "You've made us all rich by risking your hide all your life and no one has a better right to it than you do. We've sat at home on our fat backsides while you reaped us huge profits for very little reward. Here's cheers."

As both men raised their big glasses of beer, Mac said, "And to you, Charlie. This has been a second home to me, if I ever had a first, and I'll miss you and Muriel like the dickens."

"Well, we'll be here. It's not so far for a man like you."

"It's over a thousand miles, Charlie," Mac said, emphasizing something more than the distance, emphasizing how hard it would be on Beth, so that suddenly Beth felt a sense of loss, and knew she was saying good-bye to the Swansons forever, and perhaps to her last link with civilization forever, for at least at the Swansons they were still this side of the Alice, only 250 miles to Oodnadatta and a train to Adelaide.

For whatever reasons, her journey north, a journey she had in some ways felt forced upon her, had been interrupted nearly a year ago. Would not any sane, normal woman have immediately picked up her tattered petticoats and run south again, back to the waiting arms of her father and mother, who had not come up for the wedding and thought some sun madness had taken her and perhaps they were right; would not any sane woman have gone back to civilization, where farms were farms and not dry stretches of nowhere with cattle wandering aimlessly on unfenced land? Oh, there were wild flowers, all right, and the red and brown hills of the Red Centre. But it was so dry and so sparse so often. Yet here she was, beside this man, at her own wedding, ready to head north again. But her journey was being made in a much different state of mind this time, or should have been. No one had forced her into this. She had not been married to this man before he decided to go bush. She had knowingly, willingly, decided, albeit for a deep as well as adolescent love she held for him, to go north of her own accord this time. The conclusion was inescapable. Somehow, despite everything, the land had seduced her. She had heard and answered its Cyclops-siren call. The love-hate conflict of the soil had cast its shadow of beauty on her and begun its erosion.

9

Mac had not received his water bounty bank draft by the
time they were due to leave, but government departments
were notoriously slow. Mac was anxious to get moving at the
first break of the Wet, so he could travel slowly, take wagons
and all Beth's things and show her some of the countryside on
the way. So it was left that, when the money came, Charlie
would keep it for a small mob Mac had bought from him and
against a few other breeding bulls Charlie would send up the
next time a drover was going near, anywhere near that
Godforsaken place, Charlie had said, until they studied a
map and found out that there was a telegraph station . . .
well, if not within "coo-ee" distance, if not within shouting
distance, at least within a bloody hundred miles, although
strangely neither man was much of a hand at maps. Bushmen, like the Aboriginals, read their way from landmarks
and signs.

When Mac returned, he had secretly told Charlie that the
word up the Track was that Abdul had been seen in Darwin,
having lost all his money gambling there. So he was
stranded, frightened to come back, for he'd heard that Mac
was after him. Having lost his fare, he was looking for a job
in the boiler room of a ship. Mac now told Charlie,

"Put the word out that he's not to get a job until I get there,

Charlie, however long it takes. Then we'll see how he gets on out in the desert alone, Afghan or no Afghan."

Charlie nodded silently. He was not sure he agreed with the vengeance part of the code. But then he didn't have to risk his life daily out on the treeless plain.

Emu Jacky elected not to go, so Jacky Utmadatta immediately put in a plea for his lubra, Nora, to accompany them. Beth had been hoping that Nora, who worked as a kitchen lubra at the Swansons', would want to go, for if she hadn't it might have affected Jacky's willingness, although it was hard to conceive of him being parted from his boss. But for Jacky and Nora it was a long walkabout, nonetheless, out of their tribal boundaries and away from their part of the important Aboriginal system of extended families. Now the new place would become home, with no relatives around. But both were young, Jacky not yet seventeen and Nora just sixteen, and Beth was so glad of another woman's company she could have cried.

They were barely out of the Alice when Beth's period was a day late. Nora had told her a few days earlier that she was pregnant. Beth could not believe that a sixteen-year-old child could tell by looking at her, but Jacky assured her, "She know, Missus; she plenty smart midwife deliver plenty babies and have one herself."

"She what?"

"Oh, yes, Missus, Nora and me have baby but baby die. Many Aboriginal babies die plenty quick, Missus; many more since white man come, maybe. But OK, Missus, OK, we have more, but Nora look after you plenty good. You just do what she say even if you think it dumb Abo bush medicine, you do. She say you eat plant, you eat, Missus, OK?"

Beth nodded, smiling, because her period wasn't even terribly late at this stage and she didn't believe Nora could know by looking at her, however much you were supposed to be able to tell by the bloom in the cheeks. But then she was several days late, and then it didn't come at all. Yet she did not give in to their superior knowledge until the morning sickness came, and then when Nora offered her some pods to chew to stop the vomiting she took them willingly and finally banished from her European mind all ideas about under-estimating Aboriginals of any age.

They traveled in easy stages, Mac being overprotective about the baby and Jacky berating him, Jacky christened Happy Jack Utmadatta now by Beth, and sometimes even called Blossom by her, though when Nora tried it once Jacky threatened to beat her, as Aboriginal men sometimes do beat their wives, and Mac cautioned that, if he did, Beth must not interfere. But Jacky had made the threat in his relaxed, matter-of-fact way, and Nora took less notice than anyone, although everyone seemed to decide perhaps they'd stick to Jacky or Happy after that. Jacky kept saying the Boss was being too easy on the Missus and baby don't slow woman on walkabout down, and in fact Nora soon insisted on Beth walking some of the distance each day with her, rather than riding the whole time as she had been doing.

Their camp was very different from the other Beth had known. Although when on his own Mac roughed it, this time he had brought tent and mosquito netting, for there was malaria and malarial dysentery from which one could die in those parts. He had brought groundsheets, good, warm blankets for the cold nights, plenty of good tucker, including prime rashers of bacon for when the eggs and steak ran out; and each day they made bush bread, or damper as it was called, cooked it fresh unleavened and she came to love it and was soon making it herself. Each night Mac and Jacky seemed to find little oases for their camps, so that it was like a holiday to Beth. In the late afternoon Jacky and Mac would ride together, talking softly, pointing, perhaps remembering a previous crossing, an earlier time along the track, identify-ing a sign. Then, by dusk, they would be holed up somewhere, usually near fresh water, with vegetation and shade, and another type of eucalypt for Beth to smell and marvel at and taste the leaf. Mac and Jacky could play pretty good tunes on the leaves. It was the best of possible times for Beth in the bush and as her stomach swelled so did her contentment and they were all very happy.

They had come up through the Macdonnell Ranges, traveling the Track, the Stuart Track, past the Murchison Range to Tennant Creek, which even in those days boasted the most famous drink in the world: Tennant Creek Double Scotch Light Brown Ale.

They had gone on, straight on up the Track, not stopping to reprovision until they came to Newcastle Waters, where the Murranji Track comes out, or goes in, whichever way you look at it. Beth looked at the track and shivered, particularly when Jacky took her down to show her a sign burned on weathered-wood, packing-case crosspieces, nailed into a cross at the head of the track. It read:

> MURRANJI MAC,
> KING OF DEATH TRACK,
> WHEN HE MAKES IT TO HERE,
> HE KNOWS HE'S COME BACK.

Beth felt she could well do without some of the bleaker aspects of Outback humor. But Mac roared his loudest bull laugh when Jacky showed her the sign and said,

"It's a pretty good arrangement, luv; practical as all things in the Outback. If I don't make it, I'm sure of a proper cross for me grave, 'cause no traveler's going to mind taking time to dig when the cross is already there and he knows he's burying a celebrity. He also gets done a favor, because if he digs right there, he'll find a little spring farther down: water, pure water, beautiful clear water. It was finding that water that saved me life and broke the record, and the cross was put there to remind us all where the submerged spring is."

"How did you know to dig there, right at the end of the Murran-ji—is that how you say it—Track?"

"Well, it ends just a few feet shorter than it used to, m'luv. I knew to dig there because I knew I could go no farther, and if the water hadn't been there I'd have kept going for a frog and if there weren't any of those there, I guess I'd be through to England about now."

He was quite incorrigible, yet in a way she enjoyed the

notoriety, for although other travelers were sparse, they all
seemed to know Mac, or know of him, and some passed on
messages from down the Track, such as, "Charlie says
nothing's arrived yet but he's checking where the papers are
and not to worry," and some asked him where he was heading
and left letters for the mailman to be dropped at the next
property or word-of-mouth messages to pass on to people.
Beth realized that this was a hangover from the pretelegraph
days; this was the real bush telegraph and still very necessary. It was one of the things that bound the people together
up here. For the biggest unattended, undoctored and un-
peopled parish in the world, it was the closest and most inter-
dependent community in the world.

Beth realized then that as things like the telegraph line
came, so the spirit of interdependence of these highly independent beings would diminish. She felt then, with the baby
kicking now within her and her time almost due, that this
was a good time for her baby to be born, a good place to be
born in, and that he, for both wanted a *he,* though for
different reasons, would be one of the last of the true
bushmen before the cities reached out with their influence
into this last frontier. Of course she hadn't seen it then, and
she mightn't always feel that way, but she felt it this day as
on past the Murranji they pushed, hurrying a little now,
without pressing, for Mac hoped to make his homestead site
before the birth.

Up past Daly Waters they went, through Birdum and
Maranboy, Katherine and Horseshoe Creek. At Pine Creek
they swung east for Arnhem Land, with Mac waving a good-
bye into thin air at the Track and turning to Beth and saying,
"Wait until you see it, luv, purple hills and waterfalls and the
best pocket of country you ever did see. And there's the
biggest, oldest—must be over two hundred already—crocodile
you've ever seen, right near the station."

Mac thought this would be a point of interest, like mentioning something one could see at a particular zoo, but when
Beth reacted with deep sighs as though she were about to
have a seizure and miscarriage all in one breath, yet

managing to splutter out, "The biggest! Damn you, Mac, I've never seen any bloody crocodile in my life," Mac realized he wasn't on the safest of ground, for she still rarely swore, so to placate her he added, "Oh, sorry, luv. Well, the kid'll like him, then," which of course made matters worse. So then he called out, "Nora, get up here quick." But it was a false alarm.

It was indeed beautiful country. There were the purple escarpments Mac had promised, and waterfalls and gorges which took your breath away. They made good time, considering that they were now traveling away from the Track, across unmapped country, using only their knowledge of landmarks from the previous trip—although it was easy going on the open plains, more wooded often than African plains, but still sparse, with plenty of room to travel over the leaf-strewn dust of changing salmons and grays and ocher, and between the paperbark and cabbage gum trees. Two new varieties, Beth noted; only about another five hundred to go. But she still hadn't seen a scribbly gum, where it looks just as if children have scribbled in beautiful, innocent and delicate patterns on the fragile gray bark, so Muriel had said.

10

The baby was born at 12:10 A.M., according to Mac's gold half-hunter watch, on January 1, 1898, in a place and area which really had no name.

It was born in the open on a bed of bark and leaves by the yellow light of a hurricane oil lantern in a spot among rocks near a spring which they had found at twilight when they saw Beth would have the baby that night and they would not reach the place where they planned to build the homestead.

She was disappointed but in no shape to argue, for it was a difficult birth, because the baby, though a few days early, was huge.

Nora was the midwife and gave her pods to chew on to kill the pain and seemed to regard the light of a lantern, in addition to a campfire, a luxury. She did it all matter-of-factly, Jacky and Mac boiling water in their billycans and Nora's infectious chuckle as she urged Beth to push, somehow—in Beth's pain-creased mind dulled with the pods like alcohol—making it appear almost a jolly affair, almost an orgy of creation, as she lay wet with sweat and her legs deliciously immodest.

When the baby came and the cord was cut with Mac's sterilized shears, Jacky said softly,

"Big fellar Big Red, Boss."

Mac shook his head but then smiled broadly and nodded.

"What's he say?" whispered Beth.

"He's naming him for the biggest of all kangaroos. The Big Red."

"Oh, he's not red, is he? He's not like me? He'll get sunburnt."

They had put the baby in paperbark and were now washing it and Beth had not yet seen him.

"He's dark," Mac said kindly. "He's not red. And in fact that giant species isn't even found up here. He'd be nearly a thousand miles out of this territory, any Big Red up here."

"Big Red, Boss," Jacky said gleefully.

"What's he say?" Beth said. They handed the baby to her.

"Whether we like it or not his Aboriginal name is going to be Big Red—I think that's what he's trying to tell us."

"Big Red belonga billabong early on, Boss."

"And he says," Mac went on, "that he saw a Big Red at the billabong beyond the springs at dusk tonight"—he paused, watching Jacky make signs with his hands, and then went on—"the biggest he's ever seen and farthest north one has ever been seen, so that's his name and euro as far as Jacky is concerned."

"What's a euro?"

"Sort of a lucky sign."

"Well, that's good, then—?"

"Yes."

"Do you believe him?"

"About the roo at the water at dusk—?"

"Of course."

"I don't know."

"But he wouldn't say he saw one if he didn't, would he?"

"He might. But it wouldn't be a lie."

"How can that be?"

"It's very complicated, luv. There are over seven hundred and fifty tribes and at last count two hundred and sixty languages, not counting dialects. The beliefs can get pretty complicated. Go to sleep now, we'll talk tomorrow."

"I want to know."

"Well, as much as there's a general thing they believe, it's part of what they call the Dreaming, or the Dreamtime—their mythology. Jacky wouldn't see it as making something up. It would be very real to him. Sort of like giving the boy something that keeps his spirit safe."

"I don't think that's very complicated at all. I think that's lovely. Perhaps there is a big red kangaroo that lives beyond the rocks."

"Yes, luv."

She seemed contented at that and lay back then and presently was asleep.

"You one smart white fellar know all about the Dreaming, Boss," Jacky said cheekily as he walked past.

"You and your bloody Abo magic," Mac scowled good-naturedly. "Now she'll tell the boy about it and he'll be looking all his life for a Big Red up here. Now I ask you?"

"I see him, Boss, I see." He was deadly earnest now, and indeed it was not completely impossible that one should be up here. They were enormously powerful beasts.

"Well, one thing's for sure. I don't want to look into the eyes of a big red buck this night," Mac said.

"Me neither, Boss. Him plenty big animal and this one biggest I ever see. We keep well away from rocks." He was smiling again. There was no way of telling. But he almost had Mac convinced.

It was three days before they moved on, and they were surprised to find how close they'd been to where Mac on his earlier trip had found the water for the water bounty and where they planned to build their homestead. Mac and Jacky both guessed the distance to be about five miles, so they called the place where they had camped by the spring, Five Mile Camp.

The Wet had started, of course, but had been mild. But now it set in and for the next two months Beth lived in tent and wurlies, which were Aboriginal bark shelters with an incredible resistance to the elements, although the main thing she had to cope with, after growing up in Adelaide, was the high humidity of the Wet. But the tent and wurlies were dry enough, and Mac and Jacky had found a good spot among rocks and trees near the river, which gave good natural shelter and a rock floor for the tent, upon which Mac spread his groundsheets. Mac and Jacky and Nora had already named the river Crocodile River, but they did not tell Beth this until much later, and kept her away from it and rigged a shower for her to wash in with a punctured, rusty kerosene tin and rope behind a lee of rock.

Most of the crocs were the small twelve-footers, and the big one Mac had seen was at the place upriver they had called Five Mile Camp, where the boy, James Junior, had been born. Mac knew it was too big to be a freshwater one. He knew enough to know that his river must go back close to the Arafura Sea and that sometime this big estuarine or salt-water croc—for they could live in salt water or fresh—sometime in the past hundred years or so, he had made his way inland to a quieter spot. It made Mac feel good to have him there, though he was in no doubt about the serpent-strike capacity of the jaws and tail. But it made him feel good to have this link with the past. The old bloke had certainly been around before the time of the first white settlers in that part of the world. He predated even the explorers. So to Mac he was something related to human, and tangible, and part of the land and, if left alone, seeing they said the big ones lived to three hundred years or more, something that would know all his descendants. He determined the big fellow must not be shot unless he attacked or killed. He got no argument from Jacky, who had already mentally declared him sacred.

The moment the Wet showed signs of abating, Mac determined to go to Darwin. He had bought one young milker cow from one of the northernmost stations on the Track, but it was hardly the country for milkers and the animal was showing signs of weakness already. Beth was distraught to hear Mac say he must leave but she knew he was right. He would take his roan, Firecracker, who all the time on the journey up had been tethered behind the second wagon, except when Mac rode him short distances for exercise. He would take Firecracker and buy a goat in Darwin. Firecracker was now in excellent shape, the goat would go easily across the saddle in front of Mac, and he'd be back within the week. Jacky and Nora would, of course, stay. Beth and the baby would be fine. In a week he'd be back, with a second supply of milk for the baby just in case, and having placed an order for some things he'd need for building. He'd need plenty of tin for post capping; the white ants up here were fierce. Mac said he knew a man once who'd taken his boots off at night and by the morning the ants had eaten through all but the soles.

Beth was getting used to bush humor, yet she had seen a lot of white ants herself and she wondered if there might not be an element of truth in it. Anyway, Mac must go, that was true enough, though she knew nothing of his real reason for going, for Mac was sure the cow would survive for some time now that it had water and grass. The river ran back of what would be home paddock, where there was plenty of grass, through to the back of Five Mile Camp and beyond.

So he left for Darwin, left for the goat which he did not need, although it certainly would come in handy, left to settle an old score, like a bushman is wont to, left to find a man who had broken the most basic bush code of them all, the code of survival.

The tracks were still muddy, when there were tracks, and the rivers full, but he rode on relentlessly, the thing now high in his mind from where it had lain lower since he'd found poor Beth's half-bleached husband, dead of thirst and his own foolishness and the Afghan's duplicity. It was as if Mac had to wash the blood of Alan off his hands by the Afghan's death, before he would feel really free to call Beth his wife. He had kept all this from her, with this bushman's code of silence, but it had weighed heavily upon him and now he would have his revenge.

With so few police troopers, it was an eye for an eye up here, and indeed some, some more educated, who did not believe in God as Mac probably did not (if the amount of thought one gave it counted), said that in some ways the

Northern Territory had an Old Testament Judaic sense of justice and familial ties about it, and no need of the New Testament. It was just one big extended family, with each related to the other through a common bond of space and distance, each an individual member, yet each dependent on the other, locked in together through admiration, love and helpfulness until someone offended against the family. Then he had to be cast out and stoned, so that he could not do it again and so that others would not get the idea of leaving people to die in the desert.

Mac did not articulate all this for himself, but it was what he intuitively felt. He saw the thing he had set out to do as a thing as natural as killing a deadly snake with a stick.

Mac knew that if he rode to Pine Creek he could take the newly completed railway from there to Darwin, the railway built from the growing wealth of the gold discoveries in the Pine Creek area. But he was short on cash, though he had not told Beth; some of the Track areas could still be flooded at the tail end of the Wet so that he would be lucky to save more than a day or two; and in any case he wanted to get to know his own area of country. Pine Creek was over a hundred miles away. No, he would take the way through by Jim Jim Falls, one Jim for him and one for his son, and that would cut time off the route to Darwin, he was sure. He would pioneer that track and get to know the quickest way into Darwin, though he did not see how he could ever get the distance down much under two hundred miles.

Darwin was officially called Palmerston, although the British discoverer of the actual port had called it Port Darwin first, after Charles Darwin, and for many like Mac, it was still bloody Darwin, and why all the fuss by the bloody South Australians who owned it and did very little except maltreat the Chinese coolies who had come or been imported for the gold rush and the discovery of that wonderful pearl shell in 1884? Sometimes, just sometimes, Mac had a yen to leave his beloved dry Outback and go to Darwin and dive for pearl shell.

Well, Darwin was like any Barbary Coast of a town,

growing and spilling and incubating insidious vice and virtue, perhaps more of the former than the latter, which always seemed to accompany a port administered by remote control and the first jumping-off place at the end of the world, or the last starting place for the beginning.

Mac knew well enough where to look for men such as Abdul, hiding from the prying eyes of the bullockers and the teamsters, the cattle buyers and owners, the friends of Mac who would be looking for him.

But first Mac had a beer, ordered his stores to pick up next time and then checked the main telegraph office. Charlie had known he would go to Darwin as soon as possible and Mac hoped there might have been a message there and the 20 pounds Charlie owed him after all accounts had been settled. Charlie had wanted to give it to him, but Mac had said no, for indeed he really owed Charlie 180 pounds for the cattle until Mac's 200-pound settlement grant arrived for stocking up the hundred square miles the government also gave for the water bounty. Oh, well, he'd check again on his way out of town.

He now went straight to that part of Chinatown nearest the waterfront, to a small hotel run by a former South Australian and meat-slaughterhouse laborer called Hatcher. He was big and thick-chested, with a bald, shiny head and practically no neck. He was hated by the drovers, bullockers, teamsters and all legitimate cattlemen, for he was the middleman for cattle duffing, for rustling; he was hated by the younger Chinese, for he was the head of the syndicate which ran the opium trade and, even more despicably as far as Mac and others were concerned, the coolie-slave and bride-selling market. For those older and poorer Chinese, indented as labor, ten pounds for a sixteen-year-old daughter, or younger, was sometimes irresistible. And of course often they were passed off as house girls, as domestics.

To Hatcher's Coast Traders' Inn, Mac proceeded directly, having no doubt that somewhere under this man's nefarious umbrella of activities such a man as Abdul the Afghan would have sought to lose himself from sight.

Sometimes Hatcher served at the bar himself, sometimes

not. Mac had camped out overnight and timed his arrival for the morning and it was not yet noon. Hatcher was not in sight. Mac ordered a tall beer and waited, without saying anything else, for Hatcher to appear. They had had dealings before when Mac was convinced Hatcher had some cattle (belonging to one of Mac's clients) at a holding paddock just outside town. Part of the brand looked newer than the other and very similar to that of Mac's client. There had been no fight, Mac had just knocked out the two guards at the paddock the next night and taken the cattle. But there was certainly no love lost between the two, quite apart from Mac detesting the man's profiteering from the weaknesses of others.

Presently Hatcher came, without Mac having to ask for him. He dismissed the other barman to the other end of the bar and stood looking at Mac. It was a long, polished wood bar, though knotted and stained with use, as scuffed as the floor was underneath the sawdust, which looked like patterns in the sand in the light filtering down in corridors through the open shutter windows without glass. There were roughly chiseled and worn chairs and tables, worn dark with sweat and dirt and smoke, and not dry and white and clean through overscrubbing like station house chairs. The smell of opium and joss came from the rear and out front were a few seamen drinking rum, some Chinese still with their pigtails, and some locals from the town, but none in moleskins or drovers' boots. There were, perhaps, only ten in all, although Mac had no idea what the back room, past the opium bunks, might have to offer.

"Well, then, Carlyon, another drink is it or something else?"

"You'll know well enough why I'm here, Hatcher, unless you've stopped knowing what goes on in town and up and down the Track."

"I'll know, will I? Well, maybe I will and maybe I won't, but either way I'll sure as hell not help you."

"Fair enough. Well, stay out of it, then."

"Don't know if I can do that."

"I want this one real bad. Very personal."

"So I hear. Must have been convenient, though. I thought you might have come here to thank—"

Hatcher had barely uttered the word "convenient" but Mac had started to move, springing with amazing agility for a man his size, yet perhaps not so surprising for one so fit, flinging himself along his side of the bar and throwing his long, strong arms out as he flung himself so that he had Hatcher under the arms and was hauling him over the bar, hauling him up bodily, despite the man's size and weight. As the man's feet came through the air, kicking at Mac who had him hard in a bear hold now, Mac suddenly let go and threw, sending the man skidding into a pile of chairs.

The men in the bar had never seen a fight quite like this one, for they knew of Mac by reputation but had not seen him fight. Knowing Hatcher's considerable ability with his fists, and having seen that exercised many times, they settled back for a fair dinkum pub stoush, a hard-fought fight that might last, with luck, perhaps hours.

It was over in minutes. Mac, like his bushmen counterparts and Aboriginal friends, had long learned the lesson that only one thing counts in a fight, and that is to win; there is no point in letting the other man land even one blow on you for no reason. Mac was not in the fight to fight Marquis of Queensberry rules, nor had he ever kept them in any other fight.

As Hatcher went to get to his feet, Mac was intent on positioning his body. Hatcher began to stand up and, when he was just at the right height, Mac let go the most vicious kick to the groin—a kick, the men in the bar said afterward, that was the worst they had ever seen; nearly made him throw his beer up, said one, the thud was so hard and the look on Hatcher's face so excruciating. Hatcher, nevertheless, was to make one more attempt to get up, although it took a few moments.

When he did at last almost stand, Mac was positioned again, knowing that position is everything in a fight, as important man to man as an army's deployment in battle. So

Hatcher got his body up and then made the mistake of lifting his head to look. He had no idea Mac was so close, yet at the same time was surprised that Mac did not have his fists up and was, in fact, rubbing his ear. Hatcher looked as if he might at last land a punch, but just as he went to lift his arm, Mac thrust out in a straight-arm jab—not yet with his fist, but with the heel of his hand, hitting Hatcher right on the bridge of the nose so that, from the sound alone if not the blood, as Hatcher went down again, there was no doubt in the bar that the nose had been broken.

Mac looked around to see if he might expect any opposition or if the other barman might be stupid enough to produce a gun. But there was no suggestion that, with Hatcher out for the count, the nose being one of the most vulnerable parts of the head as Mac knew only too well, anyone would give trouble.

He walked through to the back room and searched bunk by bunk, dismayed at the creased and dissipated age and helplessness of the opium addicts. But he knew that some of the Afghans had the opium habit, too, and he was hoping Abdul might be just such a one. On the last bunk, in the farthest corner of the room, he found him deep in a hashish sleep. He shook him awake and knocked him out with his fist, just to be sure, and then carried him, slung over his shoulder, out the bar and back to where his horse was tethered nearer the town. He threw the man across it, called at the telegraph office again to find that still nothing had come and then went off to buy a pack donkey and a she-goat. Then he loaded the Afghan, who would be out for hours, across the donkey, tied tightly, slung the goat across the saddle and headed off down the Track.

This time he made no effort to detour. He knew exactly where he was going.

It took a couple of days, and when the Afghan awoke he let him ride the donkey, hands tied. When he camped he hobbled him to a tree and fed and watered the man, the way he did the beasts, but after he fed the animals, he fed the man exactly the amounts and types of food and gave him the exact same water stops as he had put together from the story of the journey which Beth had related to Jacky, and which he had questioned Jacky about but never Beth.

When he reached the Murranji Track he turned in, and that took another day, until the Afghan had been out the same number of days from town the Brennans had. Then he stopped and cut the man loose, left him right in the middle of the Murranji Track with only the words:

"You're a man of the desert and used to it so that although this is a worse place it's a better chance than you gave them. If you live, that's an end to it, but I never want to see your face again, never, ever again, near me or mine forever."

He had the exact same kind of water bag Beth had had, three-quarters full as hers had been, and he tossed it now at the Afghan and then turned and rode quickly back the way he had come.

11

Mac arrived to find Beth covered in mosquito bites and despondent. She looked like someone with hives. He quickly put out some kerosene flares and berated Jacky for not putting some vinegar on the bites.

Jacky'd had Nora applying goanna oil and said simply, "Not know kero and vinegar work, Boss," which was fair enough, for they'd not done much traveling in mosquito country before, or camped out during the Wet except once, when they got caught, and that was farther south. The baby had been bitten, too, though not nearly as badly as Beth. Beth had used the mosquito net, but somehow they still seemed to get in, she said, and she'd been up half the night fending them off, keeping them away from the baby and getting bitten herself. Beth knew that their ability to control these insects and the malarial dysentery they brought would be limited, and this added to her depression.

Mac comforted her very gently for two days, keeping the flares out though wasting precious kerosene, and pegging the tent flaps tighter. They would need more netting, that was certain, and he cursed himself for not having had the foresight to buy some in Darwin. He did all this in his methodical bush way, and if Beth noticed he was a little quiet, she put it down to her bad mood. It did not even occur to her that it might be the letter she had handed him after his cursing the mosquitoes.

Three days after Mac left, a member of a telegraph line party and an old friend of Mac's had ridden in from the main Track to deliver a letter left with him by the mailman. Such a system of leaving letters with people in the approximate area was a common practice, and the linesman had seized on it, making an appropriate excuse and winking at his boss, as an opportunity to see Mac for a good talk around the campfire.

He was sorry to have missed Mac and said he could not stay the extra few days and rode off after spending one night.

Mac was sure the letter was the one he had been expecting—the official bounty for discovering a previously unknown permanent water supply, which included the river and its falls, and, indeed, by coming into this virgin country, virtually untouched at this time, he hoped to discover many more and quickly expand his station and property, perhaps later linking up all the finds into one big station, at government expense.

Whether because of a sixth sense or Beth's preoccupation with the mosquito problem, he had simply taken the letter and said, "Oh, thanks, luv, that'll be the water bounty," and tucked it into his shirt pocket while he battened down the hatches for the mosquitoes. It was nighttime, by the fire, as he rolled a smoke after he'd got Beth and baby safely to bed minus mosquitoes, having pointed out that being very careful not to open the net without thinking was certainly a help, and having been scolded in return for this, before he got to read the letter.

The letter was from Charlie. There was to be no water bounty. The government had finally written, after Charlie's inquiry regarding Mac's original application.

The Commonwealth was coming. Everyone knew that. The federation of the Australian states would be completed in 1901. It did not matter that the Northern Territory was not a state. The South Australian government, responsible for the territory, was nevertheless hoping that the Commonwealth would assume responsibility, Charlie said. Either way, they'd decided not to grant the land or pay the bounty.

It was a bitter disappointment and Mac sat long at the campfire thinking. He had bought a hundred pounds worth of

stock from Charlie on credit. When the two hundred pounds
came, Charlie was to have kept his hundred pounds, plus
another eighty, for breeding bulls he would send next season,
and to have sent the balance of twenty pounds on to Mac.
Charlie had now said forget the money—keep the small mob
and he'd send the extra breeding bulls on anyway. But he
really knew that Mac would never go for that. Mac had five
pounds between himself and his family and starvation. Well,
not starvation; they could always live off the land: he'd done
that before. And Jacky had gone without wages before when
things were tight; there was no problem there. But what of
Beth and the baby? It wasn't an Aboriginal baby, and even
Aboriginal babies had a high death rate. He'd have to go
straight back to droving—there was just no alternative. He'd
have to kill one of his precious mob of ten cattle for food and
go straight back to droving and telegraph money back. Jacky
and Nora would have to stay with Beth, if indeed Beth would
stay, for he'd not force her. Technically not one inch of the
land was his, but they'd squat on it, the way any affluent
grazier might do, and pay for it when he was good and ready.
If he got a couple of good cattle drives in he could buy ten
square miles anyway, and perhaps pay Charlie for the cattle.
He'd not accept them as a gift but he'd accept credit and pay
when he could. But he'd have to give Beth the choice, though
he knew if he turned back now, that would be it for his
lifetime.

But he would wait for his moment. He would let the mosquito
bites wane and the humor improve before he broke the bad
news and broached the most important question of his life.

When Mac told her she wanted to say no. If it had all
happened a year later, she was sure she would have. She
desperately wanted to say no as the vision of Charlie and
Muriel's station swept through her mind. She saw the quiet,
normal country upbringing her son would have there, the
children she could teach, the companionship of Charlie for
Mac and Muriel for herself, the train at Oodnadatta which
would mean she could take the children to see her parents
every two or three years. It would hardly be much different

from the farm she grew up on, except for the heat, but she could get used to that, and Charlie and Muriel's was a palace of a place with so many rooms and servants and the laundry.

She knew Mac planned such a place or better for up here, but could he now achieve it? It had taken Charlie a long time and this part of the country would take longer. Even with the grant of land and money it would have been hard enough. But now this. And of course there was the factor of Mac's absence, the thing she'd always dreaded, that he would never really settle down in one place. She wondered momentarily if he was even glad. But she looked at his face as he told her and she knew better than that. He felt he had let her down, and their son, too, so early in his life, and he was determined to make things right as soon as possible, no matter how many desert crossings it took.

Perhaps it was this bush-quarried pride of his that decided her; perhaps it was her unwillingness to make the decision rather than leave it to him to do what she thought would be best for the boy despite Mac's hurt pride; perhaps even the presence of the baby and the way he occupied her time so and tugged at her nipple and finger so freely so that she felt another part of her had been born inside, quite apart from the baby; perhaps this creature of the North she had given birth to gave Beth a false sense of omnipotence, causing her to believe she could be all things to all men and all conditions. But she did decide to stay. She owed this man so much and it would break his heart for them all to go back along the Track, like a ragged army in retreat. So she had used a bush phrase she had learned, a phrase necessary for such a country where nothing but the earth below the dust was permanent and even that eroded. So she said,

"Let's give it a try for a year, then, and see how it goes."

"Fair enough then, Missus," he said, beaming back with his old confidence, "a man can't ask for more than that."

Sometimes, when Beth thought about it a great deal, later, her whole life seemed patterned around annual repetitions of such phrases of hers and his, as if in the Outback this was what one had instead of marriage vows.

Book II

BIG RED

12

It seemed to Beth afterward that the next several years passed so quickly, in retrospect she could not even stop them mentally in slow motion long enough to see and feel and know what had really happened. She could not even work out why Mac had never got more than a handful of cattle and ten squares of property; never got more than the most basic of station houses, built up on stilts against the heat, rain, and white ants. The old shack Jacky had built that year when Mac had had to go straight back to droving was still there as a storehouse and an ever-present reminder that their property was a far cry from the Swansons, who were both dead now, with the daughters having to get a manager in. It had taken Mac two years to get the ten square miles and pay for the cattle. But by then, the second child, Billy, had been born. Beth determined to have no more children—to save money as much as anything—but they never seemed to get ahead. She never knew why, but there was always something. No matter how hard Mac tried to build up the mob, he never really got to commercial-herd size. Many of the calves they had to kill for themselves, and if it had not been for Beth's vegetable garden she wondered if they would have ever survived.

One of the great problems was, of course, the distance and the prices. Each time they went into Darwin—not often—

prices of even essentials, such as tea and flour, would be up. She had long since learned to do without butter. Part of the problem was that Mac could never fully concentrate on being a grazier of cattle because he had to keep going off droving. The money was so good even Beth could not deny that this was the best thing to do. And, of course, after Charlie and Muriel died, both within a year or two of each other, and the daughters got a manager in, she and Mac were virtually tied to the Far North anyway.

Life was not without its good times. Jacky, who had been only seventeen when Jim Junior was born, was now only thirty-five, and indeed looked no older than her son, who soon would turn eighteen. He and Jim Junior were inseparable companions, more like brothers than anything else. Jacky called him Big Jim, or sometimes Big Red, had since birth, through baby-playing times with him, through Aboriginal bush games and hunting times. Sometimes Beth resented the bond between them, which was stronger than any ties between herself and her firstborn and probably, although the boy adored his father, closer even than the relationship of father and son. Mac loved the boy dearly, closely and wisely. If Jacky were closer to him, it was only because he spent more time with him. Jacky and Nora, despite all their optimism, had never been able to have more children. They had accepted it stoically, in the manner of their race, and of course there were always other blacks from that part of the bush camping nearby, with their children, because Mac was so friendly to them and always giving them food.

Sometimes Beth thought Mac's generosity contributed to what she mentally called her family's lack of advancement. She had only used this phrase once to Mac and he had deeply resented it. Although the station was not as he had dreamed, not as either of them had dreamed, certainly, still he loved it and felt only partly *un*fulfilled. He had his own place—no mean feat in that country in those days; he made good money droving and was still King of the Track. But Beth had needed more, and she wondered what she would have done if the third son, unplanned, the third son, Douglas, and the apple of her eye, mind, heart, body and total devotion, had not come to her in her thirties.

But she was now forty-two and knew she looked a bad ten years older and had learned not to look in the men's shaving mirror—the only one in the house—as she went by. The years had not been kind to Nora, either, whose hair was as gray as Beth's. The two women had borne the brunt of the housework and so many other things like woodchopping and gardening which one expected to be the province of men. But in that country there was always other harder work to be done, like chopping down trees, or scouring out white ant nests, or mustering, or hunting.

So for Beth and Nora, the birth of the youngest, Douglas, was a boon. It was extra work, but extra women's work, and somehow this boy fulfilled the return-love quotient which the other two boys, Jim and Billy, never had. So after Douglas was born Beth didn't mind anymore not having had a daughter. There were even times when she didn't mind the land. When Mac saw this he let her have her own way with the boy, a thing he had not allowed with Jim and Billy, although Beth had made her mark on both boys, educating them so that both were in many ways bilingual, speaking the good English she had taught them and using the bush phrases of their father and Aboriginalims of Jacky. But Jim, Big Jim, was the reincarnation of his father, and then some: he was big and tall and dark and strong and smart as a desert lizard, a wild colonial boy who would be a match for the men his father had come up against, and then some. Billy was only two years behind him in age, and in most other ways, although he was a bridge to the third boy and the mother so that young Douglas idolized Billy and looked up to him as protector in a way he didn't quite do to Jim. But then Douglas was only eight—a full ten years younger than Big Jim, which he had learned to call him from Jacky.

Beth knew that her view was jaundiced. She knew, despite her resentment for the months totaled into years her husband spent away, for the days the boys went camping out with him and Jacky and some of the itinerant blacks, that Big Jim and

Billy had had a wonderful childhood. After a time she even stopped despairing of them playing with crocodiles. Jacky soon learned how to deal with crocs from the local blacks, who could easily handle the freshwater Johnstone ones, the twelve-footers, catch and tie their snouts or play chasy games with them. The boys learned it, too. The only thing that worried her about crocodiles in the end was the great giant one, the saltwater one which she unwittingly had one day nicknamed Kismet. It was when she had been in a foul mood once when Mac had come back from a long cattle drive and gone to play with the boys at Five Mile Camp, before paying much attention to her. He'd come back at last and said, in a rather philosophical mood as he was wont to be after he'd been out on the Track:

"I love that old croc, you know. He's like this country, old but new: part of the last frontier. He's the past, present and future—the destiny of the Outback. He's old and beautiful."

"Kismet," she had replied half under her breath and certainly with no attempt to hide the sarcasm as she added, "like this country, old and beautiful and deadly."

But he had not heard the rest. His mind had stopped on the first word. "What a lovely word," he had said. "What's it mean?"

It had long ceased to amaze Beth that many bushmen did not know things, some book things which city people took for granted. And in some ways Mac had a breadth of knowledge which astounded her. She knew this was a genuine question, but the moment of attempted insight through sarcasm had passed for her.

"Fate," she said, her voice flat. "Just fate."

But the name stuck, and her husband and children saw it as a wonderful play name from some Arabian Nights tale.

Beth saw it as a large amphibious reptile.

13

There were good times, many good and happy times, like Christmases, when everyone was always wetted in. Mac always came home for the Wet, came home with his kick full of money and his horse strapped with presents, once even with a proper baby pine tree which they afterward painted with silverfrost and kept for years.

Yet there was always something. First there was the bad administration of the South Australian government, that he never forgave; the ever-rising prices in Darwin; the change to federal administration in 1911 when the South Australian government relieved itself of the more than five-hundred thousand square miles it had run at a loss for so many years and the disappointment that the change did not mean a new deal. In many ways it was worse and still the prices kept rising, and taxes too, and absentee British owners seemed able to get land and help easier than proper settlers like Mac. There were bad Dries and some bush fires and bad meat prices and at times, despite even his sons and how he loved to be with them, Mac wished he had never left the Track where, however harsh things could be, he knew how to deal with them.

The story of Mac's disgrace, which occurred about this time, would be told in the bars and the bush for many years to come. Those who knew the real truth of things would not tell it. But whenever have stories been told by those who knew and understood? To the common folk who do not do deeds themselves but only talk about them, their hero had lost his star.

And perhaps there was something in that. Perhaps these men, small bushies themselves, some with small spreads and all with some sort of account or other with the Stock and Station agent, had looked to Mac for help; looked to him to set an example. After all, was he not the legendary Murranji Mac? The fearless man of the Death Track? The man who had never let man or beast or the elements cow him? Surely he would stand up to the new Stock and Station agent. Mac was in debit, well into the red, they said. After he'd had that third kid and not gone droving, not gone droving to bring in the money but stayed with his Missus, he'd never seemed to get ahead. And it had been a bad Dry again, for the fourth year in a row, and on top of that, Dan, the poor old Stock and Station agent, God bless him, had gone and died. Not before time, mind you. He was seventy, not out, but still lean and quick as a desert rat until he suddenly said one night in the pub he was very tired and went home to bed and turned his toes up and that was that. Bad day for the Territory, though, bad day for the Top End. The management was absentee; down South, down among all those rich, bloody milk-cow cockies. No way they ever understood about the Territory. If it had not been for old Dan carrying some of the blokes himself and arguing with them down South and losing letters and all that, there'd have been hell to pay.

And now with the arrival of the new Stock and Station agent there was. He'd given everyone bills—bills of bloody account. Could you beat that? they said in the bar, as they talked it over. Could you bloody beat that? This young prick had actually given them all handwritten bills on printed company notepaper. That was an insult, that was. Like telling a man he was welching on a bet. But no matter. The word was that he was going to ride down to collect from Mac tomorrow. Mac was into them for fifty pounds and anyone owing fifty pounds or over was in for a very personal visit. Some visit. He'd be lucky to make it. He was going to ride down all right but he was not going to do the riding. He was going to be driven in a horse and buggy. Well, that shouldn't take more than four days. If he made it, that was. A lot could happen to a man traveling in that open country.

They plotted and they schemed and some even rode out of town a little way shouting at the Stock and Station agent that he'd get his comeuppance soon enough from Mac. Murranji Mac was not a man to trifle with, no, sir. Best to leave well alone, if you get my meaning, mister.

But Mr. Harold Hughes had someone sitting beside him in the buggy who suddenly turned to the assembled street gang shouting their jocularities and silenced them with a look. Some still called the police *troopers*—a term going back to the founding of the colony when the convicts were guarded by troops. It was not a term of endearment, although Constable "Trooper" Murphy was a fair enough man, his ancestors having been chosen to migrate themselves by some of England's top judges.

Of course some said afterward that if Murphy had not been there, the story would not have got out. Or if he had not been there, Mac would at least have had a fighting chance. This way, he had none. There were others who said Mac should have gone to jail. Some others said he packed it in before it started, that he didn't even put up a fight.

They made it to Mac's place within two days.

There was no love lost between Mac and Murphy, but each had a healthy respect for the other. Murphy had no taste for this job. And part Scottish or not, they were Carlyons. But legally the mortgage guaranteeing the debt could not be foreclosed. He had a summons. He hoped Mac would not make him use it. It would be a fearful reaction from a man like Mac. And the towny who sat beside Murphy in suit trousers and white shirt and black bowler hat and smoking tailor-made cigarettes would never rate a welcome at Mac's place unless lost in the bush and dying of thirst. Somehow all debt collectors looked the same. It was to do with the eyes,

Murphy decided. Shifty eyes. Bullshit eyes. Summons-serving eyes. The man was short and thin. He had blond hair but it was almost albino. He didn't wear glasses but kept screwing his eyes up as if he should have. He'd taken his coat and tie off but looked even more out of place without them. He still looked like a thin-nosed, shifty, bloody undertaker and he talked in such a moaning drawl that Murphy hoped Mac wasn't home, but checked his pistol to see it was loaded just in case as they drove up toward home paddock.

His wish for an easy encounter had hardly passed across his mind when he saw Mac shoeing a horse at the primitive forge back of the station house.

Mac unbent from his work and looked up, steely and silent except for the minimum of greeting:

"Murphy," he said, in an acknowledgment of hullo.

"Carlyon," the policeman returned, and then started to add, "this here's"—

"I know who he is. There'll be no trouble."

Even Beth was surprised to hear this as she came out of the house and round to the forge.

"I've come to settle the company's debt, Carlyon," the man said in a peremptory, almost dismissive tone. "Give me the money now."

Phrased this way, of course, it had perhaps an unintended but built-in hint that Mac might have had the money and been holding back. Even Murphy knew this was unthinkable, and winced when the man said it, but was surprised again at Mac's reaction as the enormous, black-bearded giant, now with some gray in his hair and beard, shrugged in a way that seemed to Murphy afterward, and certainly to Beth, that seemed to take Mac back into his bent-over shoeing position at the forge, as if he were about to go on with his work. But the shrug stopped there, awkwardly, leaving Mac looking almost cowed and submissive to this haughty young man, who now took out one of his city tailor-mades and lit it without even asking Mrs. Carlyon's permission.

Murphy thought that would do it for sure. So did Beth, for that matter, who was feeling more and more awkward by the moment, and feeling she had made a mistake to come out and that Mac was not wearing her witnessing of this too kindly either. Though she knew, too, that to walk out now might appear as if she were upset by his behavior. She stayed, awkwardly.

"He's not got the money," Murphy said irritably to the agent. "Get it over with. Serve him the papers. Here, I'll serve them."

But the little black-trousered man, at the point of handing over the papers, suddenly withheld them.

"No," he exclaimed superciliously, as if he had made some great business discovery. "No, not with this one. I'll offer him a deal instead of foreclosure. We've a smithy's at the Stock and Station store in Darwin for our clients who are Overlanders. If this chap will shoe for them, working for me for three months, I'll regard the debt as paid in full."

Murphy, who still had some pretensions to keeping a tiny part of the faith and was not a blasphemous man by nature, let out a slow and audible, *"Jeez-us."*

Beth was taken aback and held her breath. Mac stood motionless.

"Well, fellow, what do you say?" the agent repeated in his lordly, employer's-representative manner.

Murphy never repeated what he now saw to anyone. Nor Beth. Never. But she was to lie awake remembering it plenty of times thereafter.

Mac did not say a word. His frame was already dropped low, but this time he let his head fall, too, nodding in assent, though so slightly it was almost imperceptible, nodding and shrugging, but more in resignation, not the careless shrug of the Mac of old, not a throwaway shrug, but a shrug into oneself this one, a shrug deep down hunching into oneself so that even Beth had to fight not to turn away.

The two men drove off then, in the undertaker's buggy in which they had come, the management agent leaving instructions for Mac to report next week and Mac not even looking up. Beth went to comfort him but he turned away and went deeper down now to his shoeing, leaving her to run back inside, hiding her tears from him, knowing that he had done it to save the property for her and the boys, but wishing he had let it go and finally overlanded them back out of this dreadful wilderness which did such dreadful things to such fine people.

They never spoke about it, but if there was a beginning, a beginning to the erosion, this was it. Beth had known for a long, long time that she was anything but the woman Mac had married. But now, in whatever almost imperceptible manner, and for whatever laudable reason, he was also no longer the man she had married.

14

After Mac returned from smithing he did not go into Darwin much anymore. He rode out on the Track less, too, spending more time with the boys on the property. Mac and Beth both worked at acceptance of the changed circumstances, but the submerged resentment was there, and sometimes Beth wondered if the youngest, who seemed to cling to his mother so—to her great delight—sensed anything.

There was never any conscious decision on Beth's part to *use* Douglas: no actual decision more than any mother's. Indeed, for a long time she was not conscious that she was; and when she realized, it was too late: not too late to change for the boy's sake, but too late for hers. She—and Nora, for Nora had been part of the silent unmentioned conspiracy, too—needed him. He had come at a time when Jim was ten and Billy eight, at a time when Beth felt finished with life and finished with the bush and neglected by it through the demands it made on her husband. As the two older boys grew, they grew away from her and closer to Mac; and however hard she tried not to be jealous, she was—just a little, or some days, just a lot—jealous like any mother of two young sons would be who sees them rudely weaned from that infancy presence and intimacy mothers enjoy so much, that brief span of so few years and months when a mother has a child to herself, weaned from this early by the natural wonderland of the outdoors, the damned outdoors in which they lived.

Perhaps it was because of this that she put her foot down so strongly when it came to Douglas's turn to do those things and be those people (if only in imagination) that boys are wont to do and be in the bush.

Yet there was a natural reluctance on Douglas's part, too, she was sure of that afterward; positive, she said to herself, as if to salve the guilt she often felt when she wondered had she kept him from the bush too much, had she unfairly made him so much less like his brothers in so many ways; had she committed him to a path which would lead him away from the bush and into strange and threatening byways which would create a quite different future for her son, and indeed, make a quite different person of him?

Douglas was nearly eight when the thing happened which even Beth (with all her perception of the damage her overprotective motherly instinct might be doing him, yet which she could not help) never saw in its entirety. Only Douglas saw—and felt—that; saw, but did not understand, felt, buried and kept like a small piece of twisted yeast inside him.

It had been the sunniest of days, one of those times when the Wet was over but the harsh part of the Dry had not yet started, one of those days when the soft warm light of the sun touches everything. Everyone felt good. It was certainly a day for a picnic. There was even a spark of the old spontaneous warmth there between Beth and Mac. If there had not been, she doubted she would have agreed to Douglas's going. But Mac had asked, with a hint of his old jocularity and shine, if the Missus fancied a picnic, a walkabout as it were, but on horseback, or, better still, he would hitch up the old buggy with the hessian canopy, so that she and Douggie could travel in real style. He always called his youngest that, as if it were his attempt to keep bringing the lad into the circle with Jim and Billy. And Douggie, for his part, though he clung to his mother still, worshiped his father and his two brothers, although, truth to tell, of all, even sometimes Beth thought, including herself, of all it was Billy—the shining, laughing, irrepressible Billy, Billy who talked and kidded and treated him like one of the gang whether he was or not—whom Douggie liked most.

And, indeed, for all Beth's influence, she had nearly lost Douglas to the bush several times because of his affinity for Billy. And there was a strong streak of the dogged and stubborn Carlyon nature in Douglas, Beth was well aware of that. She sometimes thought later, too, that if she'd let him spend more time with Billy, perhaps that irascible jocularity of the Carlyons might have emerged, too. It had to be there, somewhere, didn't it? It was as strong as the bush bastardry and determination in all of them. But sometimes, later, Beth thought that because Douglas seemed to have missed out on the jocularity, his personality had had to develop more of other Carlyon character traits, albeit in a slightly different and worrying manner.

But at this time, on this brightest of nice days, her thoughts were much less philosophical, much more practical. The fact was, the fact had always been, since his earliest days, that Douglas squinted in the sun. It may have been that Beth had never let him become properly accustomed to it from the start, as his brothers had. This may have been part of it. But there was another totally other reason, too, which none of them had even thought of. Not even considered. Not even Beth. It was not uncommon not to realize such things in those days in the bush. And it was compounded, of course, by the fact that they all really believed the squinting was the result of Beth not letting him out in the sun enough and that, even at age seven, nearly eight, things would right themselves if he gradually got a bit more accustomed to the glare. It never occurred to any of them, and the boy had not realized, was not really old enough to realize or living in an area used to such things, to know that he was nearsighted. Not terribly nearsighted. But nearsighted enough to need glasses. But although Beth's grandfather had worn glasses, she did not know because he had been in the Home Country and she had never seen him. Mac's side of the family had never been known to wear spectacles. So no one had ever thought about it.

And certainly, on this day, with Douglas so keen to go himself, even the squinting took second place. Before she could say anything, when Mac made the suggestion over breakfast, Douglas was the first to speak out:

"May I, Mummy, may I. . . ? Just this once?"

She had had this feeling of having deprived her son of something before, and she made as if to force it back inside her again, but could not this day, not when she saw Billy wink at her youngest, not when she saw his tiny green eyes light up, the eyes that were neither blue like Mac's nor brown like the other boys'; not when she saw this. She was not made of stone. Even the bush had not done that to her yet.

"Well, perhaps if you promise me you'll wear your hat and not take it off—not for a moment—"

"Oh, yes, Mummy, please, I promise, I promise."

"Then I think it will be all right, just this once."

"You'll not come then, luv?" said Mac, who had picked the drift of the conversation.

She shook her head. She knew she would be in the way. If Douggie went out away from the environs of the veranda and home paddock at all, she or Nora invariably went with him. In fact he hardly strayed toward home paddock without the ever-alert Nora following him. This was not an Aboriginal trait, this overprotectiveness. It was something Nora had learned from her European mistress. But this day Beth could not refuse her son.

It was a day and a decision she would have plenty of time to regret.

Beth asked Nora to bring Douglas's hat. Nora looked reprovingly and went to get it. The hat was a proper Chinese coolie's hat, which Mac, under some sufferance, had bought in Darwin on Beth's insistence when the baby was first born. Mac said then his son would never get used to the sun if he wore that from the start. But in the end he gave in, as he did on most things concerning his youngest. It was a terrible way to split up human nature, but he had felt he had to let her have one child to herself, and he had Big Jim and Billy.

When Douglas was finally dressed—in Billy's cut-down moleskins, with boots, checked, long-sleeved shirt and his coolie hat with a handkerchief tied around his neck as well to shade it at the back from the sun—it was questionable if one ray of the sun would be able to touch him, except perhaps on the backs of his hands. And it was such an inordinately pleasant day that even his hands were not going to get hurt.

Anyway, Douglas did not object and Mac and his other two sons certainly did not, for they knew that that could hurt Douglas and in a strange way they almost loved him the more, the three of them, but Billy most, because of his apparent frailty, loved him with their bush instincts like predator animal parents will protect the weakest of the litter.

So off they rode, Mac, Jim and Billy, with Douggie hitched up behind on Billy's horse, holding tightly onto his brother around the waist and Beth and Nora, having packed the picnic lunch, waving from the veranda and Jacky, having his first quiet smoke of the day, having elected not to go on the pretext that someone should stay with the women. This was, of course, nonsense. They were often left alone. It was his way of saying it was a family outing, and indeed giving his blessing to the idea of the three sons riding off together with their father.

They rode first to Five Mile Camp, skirting around but not going in, and then down toward the river where it cut in and then out again at the back of Five Mile Camp. The purpose of this was to introduce Douggie to their crocodile friend. This they did in great style, for the old croc knew a good day like everyone else, and was out sunning himself on his favorite rock, and although they kept their usual safe distance and explained all this to Douggie, the croc seemed in remarkably good humor. It was strange, really, to think that one could sit and eat one's picnic lunch and be as safe as a house within yards of a creature whose species had such a lethal reputation, but that only a few miles farther along, and out toward the plains through which they would make their swing back home, after showing Douggie the sleepy old buffalo he had longed to see, one could be faced with such instant and sudden death from such a normally docile source.

They funned and played and threw Kismet some of their lunch leftovers and then saddled up to swing out toward Buffalo Plains.

Douggie was so entering into the spirit of the day that he had long ago pushed his coolie hat down over his back. It was hanging from its black string around his throat, and the other three exchanged glances without him seeing. Then Mac, with great fervor, as he saw something of himself in his son at last, began to explain to Douggie that the buffalo was quite different from the bison of the Old West in America.

The water buffalo, and the sleepy old buffalo at that, for he was always referred to in the generic singular, this laziest and most prolific of beasts, imported from Java many years before and breeding like flies in a manure heap ever since— was being increasingly discovered as a possible commercial crop of sorts, and already the buffaloers were active, had been for years, shooting for the hides mostly, with some value in the horns, Mac told his son. However, the thing to realize was that they were not really dangerous. They were just sleepy old water buffalo, too slow to get out of their own way despite their big sharp horns. If one did start to snort a bit and look as if he was going to make a run at you, you had only to stare him down, although Mac did add that it was always a good idea to keep a tree in sight nearby that was thick enough to run behind and break the buffalo's charge. But there was really no danger, he said, no danger at all. The old buffalo was so tired and stupid he just let the professional hunters come up to him and shoot him without a fight.

Mac and the two older boys had brought their rifles, and when Douggie asked whether they ate buffalo meat or not, they replied they certainly did sometimes, although he had never been allowed, but if they shot one and brought part of it back, perhaps because it was his first day in the bush, they could have a barbecue in the home paddock and his mother would let him have a taste of it.

"You want to help us hunt one up, then, Douggie?" his father said suddenly and with a warm paternal smile.

"Oh, yes, Daddy, please, please."

Beth was to rant and rave later about how three so-called experienced bushmen could let such a thing happen. But at the time, in the spirit of things, and given the normal behavior of man and beast, it should have been quite safe.

Anyway, Mac designated that he and Jim would "scout" a buffalo—preferably a young tender one. Douggie could have Billy's old rifle, which it now emerged Mac had brought along "just in case the young nipper wanted to have a shoot at something on his first real day in the bush." The rifle was only a .22, and really little more than an air rifle. But they did not tell Douggie this. He and Billy were to lie side by side in the thick undergrowth by a billabong they had found and which Mac knew would be just right for this purpose. He and Jim would have little trouble driving a water buffalo toward what the animal would see as the safety of the water. But waiting at the edge, in the direct line of his charge, would be Billy and Douggie. All of them understood the plan by now, except Douggie, who was not meant to. The idea was that Billy and Douggie would shoot simultaneously and this way they would be able to tell him that he had helped shoot the buffalo. In this manner, his father hoped to instill some bush confidence in him, to give him that smell of the hunt in his tiny nostrils which, inwardly, Mac really believed once smelled, once tasted, was the most addictive of opiates and would last a lifetime and soon cause coolie hats and sun squinting and all that rubbish to fade into memory.

He chose a spot by the billabong edge where there was natural cover behind a fallen tree. It was very thick and very old, but not so old and rotten with the water that it would not break a buffalo's charge if anything went wrong. The fallen tree they now sheltered behind was perhaps thirty yards forward from the billabong edge.

Mac and Jim rode off to the other end of the plain to find a buffalo worthy of eating and worthy of Douggie's first "kill."

Billy and Douggie snuggled down behind the log. Billy

loaded in the tiny .22 bullet and showed Douggie how to hold the rifle and pull the trigger. There would be no recoil, he explained, when asked by Douggie what that meant. All Douggie had to do, he said, was watch what he himself did and aim for the buffalo's forehead—he showed him by touching with his own finger the exact spot on Douggie's forehead. Billy explained that the buffalo could rarely be stopped with a single shot anywhere else in the body. Even most of his head was armor-plated with good solid bone. But if you got him in the soft spot just above the bone you could get him with one shot, or maybe two, he added hurriedly, because he wanted Douggie to think he had a part in it and Douggie was already better at arithmetic than all of them put together had been at his age. Billy wondered a moment if his explanation might have been a bit grisly. But Douggie was in his element. He was here, beside his big brother Billy, and anything Billy said was all right with him. Beaming with delight, Douggie settled back to wait, trying to look as much like Billy as possible.

They had been there only a few minutes, so it seemed, when they heard Mac and Big Jim shouting.

At the far end of the plain, just off to the side by another bend of the billabong, Mac and Jim had found a perfect young specimen to suit their purpose, standing alone—or so it had appeared—grazing near the water. They swooped in together, one from the back and one from the side nearest the water to cut off retreat in that area and to force the young bull buffalo in the direction of the distant bank where Billy and Douggie lay in wait.

What neither of them had seen, nor could have been expected to see, really, as they rode in shouting and waving and stampeding the young male, was its mother, lazing in the shallows nearby, hidden by the paperbark gum trees and banyans and mangroves and overhang of the vines. But as she heard the shouts and the startled and muffled panic of her son taking off in a wild charge away from the danger, the hunting instincts of the mother sent her catapulting into action of a different sort. Instinctively she knew where her son was heading—for the safety of the water but the longest way around—the direction away from the men who had come upon him.

She heaved her bulky frame up out of the water and along the sandy and muddied shallows of the billabong, knowing that her charge, if she were quick enough, would bring her out at the spot where her offspring was heading.

But halfway along the bank her instinct and trained senses picked up a second smell of men and she changed course slightly again with a hunting skill equal if not better than any Mac could have mustered, even had he known the danger.

Mac and Jim were halfway across the plain, the young bull three-quarters, when terror hit them as they saw the mother come out of the billabong behind Billy and Douggie.

Billy heard, turned and saw almost in the same instant.

Mac had his rifle up to his shoulder, sighting along the barrel as he rode, safety catch off, leveling, taking two pressures of the trigger and firing the bullet off, knowing that the mother buffalo was a very hard target shooting on horseback from this distance. His bullet hit just at the base of the armor plating on the head, which was a magnificent shot, really, but it had not felled the enraged and still-charging mother.

Jim had got a shot off at the young buffalo, hitting at the base of the neck from the rear, and it had gone down in a heap, stumbling over its forelegs.

Billy had sighted as he had turned and, for whatever reasons, had shouted instinctively, "Run Douggie, run," not stopping to realize, perhaps, in the response of instinct, that it was an eight-year-old he was speaking to, not a fellow hunter—an eight-year-old, or seven and three-quarters, really, and a nearsighted one at that, though no one was to know. Either way, as Mac's shot went home but served to enrage the cow even further, as Billy sighted to get off the one, single shot he would now have time for, he saw, in stricken horror, Douglas run off, not in the direction he had assumed he would know to run, but right into the most dangerous area of all, right into the path of the charging buffalo, who was now not twenty yards distant.

"Oh, my God, Douggie, fall, fall, drop down dead like cowboys and Indians, drop for Chrissakes, drop," Billy shouted in ever more agonizing tones until, miraculously, just when he thought the beast was on Douggie, the little boy fell outward, thank God, so that Billy was able to get his shot off as the buffalo cow launched herself for what was to be her last full charge. His shot went straight through the soft part of the head and she fell down dead a few feet from him, as he went racing to Douglas, who was whimpering in the mud.

"Oh, Douggie, Douggie," his brother shouted longingly as he picked him up and held him lovingly, *"why* did you run that way?"

"I didn't know anything was there," the child cried. "I couldn't see it."

It was Mac who worked it out eventually. He didn't want to face it, but when all the recriminations and the deeper resentment which now arose in Beth had been talked out at least for the time being, bush reasoning told him what had happened so that he said to her one day, "I'd take the kid to Darwin and have his eyes tested if I were you. There's reason for him not hearing the charge, given his age and the shouting and the state of fright he was in, but I only knew one other occasion when man or child didn't react instinctively correctly to a wild animal charging and that was an old fellar who needed spectacles and knew it, but pretended he didn't."

And that was how Douglas came to wear glasses and came—however hard he later tried not to for Billy's sake—to hate the bush. But if Beth had reason to be concerned about her youngest, she also had great cause for concern about the other two boys. Jim would soon turn eighteen and no one seriously pretended anymore that the war was not coming.

15

Beth feared the war more than the land. But to her eldest
son it was a time of great adventure. There was an overdrive
in the boy which his parents were hardly aware of. Both saw
Big Jim as largely a replica of his father, the pioneer drover.
But they did not reckon on how this might orchestrate
internally with Beth's relentlessly taught school lessons and
whatever Freudian phylogenetic elements may sometimes
evidence themselves with more primeval intensity in one
man than another.

Every newspaper brought home—and they were few
enough—every magazine thumbed and worn, he read and
reread. He'd known for years about the man experimenting
down South with the kite machine which flew in 1910. His
mind was on machines and the air, as well as on the ground.
He knew more about what was going on in the world, and
how the Territory had stood still, than anyone else in his
family and probably than most administrators at the time.

He would have run away to join up when war was declared
if he'd thought he could get away with it and his mother
would not telegraph the authorities. But the day he turned
eighteen, on January 1, 1916, there was no question but that
Jim would leave for Darwin the next day. His father had
already tried but been rejected because of his age.

Enlistment for the Australian Imperial Force had, of course, begun on August 8, 1914, just four days after Britain declared war on Germany. Jim, then coming up to his seventeenth birthday and champing at the bit to be going, was tempted to write to the government and ask why it took four days, although in July the Labour leader, Andrew Fisher, so he'd read, had declared that Australia would be with Britain to "our last man and our last shilling."

Jim read about it all. By mid-August of that first year, temporary camps and staging areas were being set up all around the cities, even on racecourses and show grounds, and it would be a racecourse camp to which Jim would eventually go for his brief training. But in the South-East Australian spring of 1914 the factories had just started spooling out yards of khaki woolen cloth with big safari patch pockets and copper-oxidized metal buttons with maps of Australia on them. There were the slouch hats, the wide-brimmed felt ones with snap catches so the brim could be pinned up on the left-hand side, or left down to give protection all around from the sun. There was the Rising Sun badge, adopted from the original Commonwealth Horse badge of 1902, a half circle of swords and bayonets radiating from a crown, and looking like a sunrise.

Jim thought it all wonderful and could not wait. He knew it was not a *Boys' Own Annual* story. He had the harsh realism of the bushman from the start. But he had the bushman's sense of adventure, too. And he knew he could shoot and ride. God, could he shoot and ride. He had the bit in his teeth, all right, and he hated the waiting as much as his mother hated the coming of his eighteenth birthday and her knowing that she could not stop him going and his father would not try.

So on January 2, 1916, the day after his eighteenth birthday, despite his mother's pleading, he rode off to Darwin to enlist. He had the confidence of youth, battle ambition as bright as armor, and the determination to learn to fly before the war was over. It wasn't that he didn't believe he could be killed; it was just that he believed he knew a few things the blokes over there mightn't, and that one way or another he'd be equal to it.

His father's silent longing pride watched him go. He had a desert dry taste in his mouth that they would not see each other again.

Jim hoped to fly but this was not to be. The recruiting officers took one look at him, and his address, and said, "Just about born on a horse, were you, son?" to which he replied, "Just about," and after they'd shown him pictures of the Light Horse in action, and given him the famous khaki slouch hat, pinned cockily up on one side, so he could see that they were indeed real emu feathers as part of the badge, he said he'd settle for the Australian Light Horse, at least for the time being, until he got over to the other side and got the hang of things.

They sent him to a training school but shipped him out after a few days, the instructors noting on his report that he rode uncannily, sighted along the barrel like an Aboriginal but was the best shot they had ever seen and they couldn't see any point to keeping him there longer for they were sure no one would ever teach him to salute an officer but they were certainly glad he was on their side.

The sea voyage to Egypt did not prove novel for Jim. He had seen steamers in Darwin Harbor before this. In fact, he resented the inactivity. Still, he had his horse to look after, having been allowed to bring his own. It was a descendant of his father's spirited roan, Firecracker, and bore that name, the horse and name a present from his father on his fifteenth birthday. But of all things on the ship which interested Jim, the significant thing was the issue of his .303 rifle. At home he had had the long Lee-Enfield of 1892. The same rifle had been used during his brief training-camp sojourn. But now, on the ship, they were issued with that most wonderful of weapons, the short Enfield with the long bayonet. It came out of a new wood box with the others, wrapped in wax paper and grease, with the dark wood grain, which would become darker with the sweat of use, showing bright in the sun on the deck, and the dull metal even shining, the brass butt cap

which housed the brass pull-through and wire gauze for
barrel cleaning even shining also.

Jim held it and drew it hard into the muscle part of his
shoulder, away from the shoulder bone which the heavy
recoil could fracture, throwing it up and down, practicing
shooting imaginary things in the sky, practicing loading and
unloading the five-round magazine, each rim of the brass-
bottomed .303 shells lipped alternately down onto the spring-
loaded ridged platform of the magazine so that they would
not jam when firing. A jammed magazine was death where he
was going. He practiced all these things so much the others
laughed at him, laughed at his boyish enthusiasm, for few
were as young as he, but he laughed with them, in his
father's bush manner, agreeing and saying, "You're right, I'm
a stupid young fool, right enough, but perhaps I need to
practice more than the rest of you, for this is a new weapon to
me." ᐧ

He said it without sarcasm or malice, knowing he was right
and they were wrong, but it was not the bush way to be a
smart arse, and they would find out soon enough, for he knew
the difference between the two models of the rifle to be
minimal. It was his mind he was training, training to act as
instinctively as a crocodile will flick at the enemy with his
tail.

So he practiced the bolt action, too, making sure not to
palm the bolt, for that could mean a broken hand or thumb if
it kicked back the wrong way. So he practiced holding the
bolt properly between thumb and index finger, and when he
was not attending to his horse or doing drills, he practiced the
crucial speed of this bolt action which took another bullet off
the top of the magazine into the chamber, and he practiced
with the graduated sights, knowing he should learn to use
these, though his eye sighting was accurate. He practiced
this, and getting the safety catch off quickly, and the bolt
action and the two pressures on the trigger, the first soft
pressure and then the hard click so that the rifle did not jump
off-sight. He kept his rifle faultlessly clean, using the steel
gauze pull-through and the oiling rags, sharpening and

oiling his long bayonet and practicing getting that out of its hip scabbard on his khaki shorts, too, so that when they disembarked he felt his fighting instincts were as honed as they could be and his body and his weapons belonged together and his hat badge shone and the ostrichlike emu feathers told everyone he was cavalry, and Australian cavalry at that, volunteer cavalry, destined for the charge on the legendary wells of Beersheba.

When they got ashore and into their billets, he succumbed to the cries of "baksheesh" and let one of the Gyppos take a photograph of him horsed and uniformed, bandolier across his chest and all. He did not stop to think, as he mailed this off home, of the effect it would have on his younger brother Billy.

Billy had, of course, told his big brother Jim that he would, in the bush parlance, be over "presently," but Billy was two years younger—well, two years and nine months—and Jim believed they would have the war won by then. In any case, once ashore in Egypt he had little time to think of Billy.

Jim had teamed up on the ship with the only other Territorian aboard. He was the same age as Jim, or just a few months older, and together they were the youngest in the party. He was from Darwin, and the others, who'd been in the unit and under training longer than Jim, called him "Bluey," because of his red hair. His name was Byrne, and Bluey Byrne seemed to fit. He was short, stocky and a garrulous, happy fellow who was already one of the most popular in the 4th Light Horse Brigade. He was the son of a Darwin public servant, although Jim did not know this at the time. What Jim did know, from his father's bush training, was the need of a good partner, such as Jacky. This happy fellow, Bluey, Jim believed, would be very good in a fight, despite his size. Also, although he joked a lot, in quiet conversation over a fag at night, rolling a cigarette on the poop deck, he knew the bush, there was no two ways about that. Live in Darwin he might, but he was always going out from Darwin on hunting parties. He seemed not to mind the nickname of Bluey at all, and in fact almost everybody in their unit, if not the whole damn army, had a nickname, including some of the officers, including some unrepeatable ones for some of the British officers, although all that changed when a Pommy general they called the Bull arrived.

The Australians reckoned that was a good start that he had a decent nickname. Then the word got around that he'd told some of his staff officers not to make such a fuss if Australian ORs such as Jim, the Other Ranks as they were called, didn't always stop and salute an officer. The fellar, who was known as Allenby, apparently reckoned that they could turn a blind eye now and then as long as the Australians continued to kill the enemy as effectively as they'd been doing since the desert war first started, hand fighting with their bayonets at the hods. Those camp outposts of palm groves marked the all-important wells which had to be defended at all costs. There the Australians, New Zealanders and British held back brutal Turkish onslaughts such as in the August of that year, 1916, when the Turks, who had already taken most of the British outposts, threw eighteen thousand troops in against the Romani encampment. The Australian Light Horse held back that first savage onslaught in the morning, Jim and Bluey in the thick of it and loving it. In the evening they regrouped and three light-horse brigades, plus the New Zealand Mounted Rifles and a Yeomanry brigade shoved the battle right back at the Turks until, suffering loss after loss, they had to fall right back to El Arish.

The Australian commander Chauvel had been the architect of that little thrust, and when Allenby came on the scene shortly after, he kicked Chauvel up to command the whole Desert Mounted Corps and become the first Australian to be made lieutenant general. The Australians would have done anything for Allenby after that; and did. They also reckoned he was pretty smart when he took hold of a wiry little fellow who'd been a sort of archaeologist, which was almost as good as being a bushie, a little fellow called T. E. Lawrence, or "El Aurens" to his Gyppo bloody army. But Christ, were they some wild bloody troops, and Allenby gave them all the ammunition and supplies they needed and let them bush-

whack the Turks at every stage to weaken them while he
built up for the assault on Beersheba and the push through to
Jerusalem.

The Brits had built a railway and pushed a water pipeline
forward as Allenby built up his infantry and artillery and
Lawrence ran wild. But the Turkish enemy had built up a
thirty-mile front from Gaza and Beersheba, and on the eve of
the battle no one was under any illusions about how hard it
would be.

16

Jim and Bluey were having a quiet smoke at one of the hods they were guarding. They always volunteered for, and got, the jobs of guarding these palm tree outposts. First, despite the little extra danger, it was their bush instinct that to guard the water was a good and vital place to be: you and your animals would not go thirsty so long as you held one. Second, it got them away from the officers and details or fatigue duties such as latrines. Those bloody desert latrines, they were something else. Stupid bastards, with all that sand-fly fever and malaria. Some of them knew nothing about flies, that was for sure. Some of their other mates thought they were mad volunteering for outpost duty. But at the outpost, too, you could have a good quiet crap to yourself, dug and buried away from those bloody, disease-carrying bastards of flies. And so far, touch wood, neither Jim nor Bluey had looked like getting fever. Besides, it was pretty safe the way they played it.

They'd got hold of a young Gyppo kid, half starving, and paid him a few pennies to sit up in one of the palm trees and watch while they had smokos down the bottom. When they'd recruited him in the town, as a sort of unofficial batman, to steal and scout for them, he had said his name was Abdul, which didn't cheer Jim up, because Mac had told him the story of that other Abdul and of Hatcher, but after Jim had told Bluey the story, Bluey had looked at him with that one eyebrow-raised stare of his and said,

"You're not gonna tell me you think all Abduls are related, are you, Jim?"

"Well, sort of."

"Well, they're related to each other the same way we are as a race, see, and if you pass up this golden opportunity to get us our own unofficial batman, you can whistle until the cows come home for any more shifty deals with me, see?"

"You're right, Blue, we'll take him. But you've got to explain in that sign language of yours"—Bluey was very eloquent with threatening hand language—"that I'll bloody knock his block off if he tries anything, and he's got to bring along some of the local booze as evidence of good faith."

Well, they'd hired the kid, and it was the night before the big push for Beersheba, and they were guarding the farthest outpost, with the kid up the tree and the moon fairly high and bright.

"Think we could risk a smoke?" Blue said.

"Yeah, I reckon . . . if we keep low. The Turks aren't very good shots."

"Some of them are. We weren't shooting our own men back there at Romani, and who do you reckon killed those blokes at Gallipoli?"

"Well, that's what I mean. You'd have had to be the worst shot in the whole world to miss those poor bastards stuck out on those slopes like shags on a rock."

Bluey let it drop. Carlyon had a particular sort of logic which always seemed to win arguments on the basis that however right you might be about what you were saying, his rejoinder would always be of the nature that of course you were right in one sense, but what he was saying was that this or that or they or them was not as good as it could have been. And of course in any situation in life, most people being slightly imperfect, that was always an unanswerable answer. But he did it lightly, and Blue didn't mind, and he liked the idea of a man like that guarding his flank, so he slipped his head down farther into the small dugout, and rolled a cigarette, where Jim had already lighted up.

If Bluey was prepared to let it drop, Jim was not. That was another thing about him. Once on a line of thought he rarely let go until he'd thought it right through. Sometimes he'd let the *conversation* on it drop, but you could tell by his silence and the way he sat and frowned a bit that he was still thinking it through.

"What do you reckon about it, though, Blue, killing all these Turks? How many do you reckon you've killed?"

"Ten, twelve, maybe. I don't know."

"Tomorrow'll be worse."

"That's the truth of it."

"You'll top your quota tomorrow for sure."

"This is a great subject, Carlyon. You've got a great sense of humor. How many you killed?"

"Twenty. Exactly twenty."

"You kept count?"

Jim nodded.

"That's a good way to get yourself killed."

Jim half-nodded. "Not if you're careful."

"In any case how can you be sure? Sometimes you're firing off in all directions—we all are."

"I know what I've hit and when and whether the shot would have been deadly, I've always known that however hard the fighting was. Of course, with the hand fighting we did with the bayonets at some of those hods, I didn't count at the time, I counted later. In fact I think I counted them all up later."

"Well, if you did that you can't be sure. That's how I counted mine."

"I'm sure. I'm sure about the numbers."

"Well, if you're so sure, what's the point to it—why are you so bloody keen to keep count?"

"Don't know. That's the funny part about it. It's just something I do. Perhaps it's like hunting, like the way since I shot my first rabbit and my first dingo, I've always known what I've shot."

"Well, this is a bit bloody different from hunting wild dogs and rabbits, if you don't mind me saying so, old son."

"That's what I'm trying to work out."

"Promise me one thing?"

"What's that?"

"You won't try too hard until after tomorrow. My old man's a pacifist, CO, whatever, and I've got enough doubts of my own. We might both be dead tomorrow night, you know."

"Maybe sooner. Now who's being cheerful? Anyway, I wasn't talking about doubts, I was talking about not having them. Don't have any. Just kill what's necessary to stay alive as always: even the hand fighting with bayonets is that way."

Just then a shrill crack of a single rifle shot slammed over their heads, well above their heads, high into the trunk of one of the three palm trees above them.

Carlyon was up and in position and firing in the direction of the shot as he shouted,

"Jesus, Blue, they're after the kid . . . Abdul . . . bloody jump . . . jump . . . what's the word for jump? . . . Tell him for Chrissakes, Blue."

They both kept shouting then, and both firing, for there were at least six rifles firing at them from the nearest sand ridge. After a few minutes they heard a thud behind them and Jim felt an awful thrust of anger and pain in his stomach and he crawled over and looked at the kid's face and body and knew he was dead and he was about a year younger than Billy and Jim cursed himself for being so bloody stupid.

He crawled back and started firing again.

"They're mean bastards, these Turks. So they really do kill women and children. There was no need to do that. Must have been there all the time and seen him go up in the moonlight. No need to shoot him, though; only alerted us. We've got to kill them now, Blue, you realize that. Got to kill all of them."

"There's six of 'em. Maybe more. Where the hell are headquarters? Can't they hear the shooting?"

"Well, we can't wait for them. And we're sure as hell not going out there. We've got to fox them in here. You make an agonized scream, then crawl over behind the tree trunk, fix your bayonet, make sure you've got a full clip and wait."

"They'll never fall for that in a million years."

"They might. We won't know if we don't try."

"We won't be able to see if they're coming on or not."

"I'll hear 'em. I'll listen along the ground. I'll be able to give you a few seconds' warning with a nod before they come over the top. After you give your death scream I'll shoot off a few more rounds and then give mine. Then we'll lie doggo in wait for them. Make sure you make your scream at the same moment as a shot lands just near you."

"Hah bloody hah—I've got a comedian at my funeral."

"Ready?"

"Ready."

"Good luck, then, Blue."

"And you, Big Jim."

Presently Bluey let out what sounded almost more like a blood curdling yell to Jim, but perhaps, from a distance, it would convince the enemy that it was the sound of a man's death throes.

Once Blue was in position, Jim fired a few more rounds and then, when the appropriate shot puffed the sand just near him like a golf shot, he let out an audible groan, and rolled over, but kept rolling to the side of their sandpit, knowing it would be harder to hear them coming from there but hoping that if they fell for the plan they would come over the top at the point where they thought the bodies had been hit. Blue had a direct line of fire if they did this and Jim would be almost at right angles to Blue's line, which was not cross fire but the best they could do. He held up three fingers on his left hand to Blue and waved to the side, indicating that Blue should shoot for those on the far left and leave Carlyon the ones closest to him. Blue nodded back as if to say, "Do you think I didn't know that?"

Jim quickly reloaded to a full five-round magazine and clipped his bayonet on. Then he put his ear to the ground nearest him and the direction from which they would come. They seemed to wait several minutes. Well, did they want the outpost or not? Surely they had been sent to take it and to start getting in behind them for tomorrow's battle? Or perhaps they just wanted water? Well, the water is here, boys, he thought, and you've got to come and get it if you want it, it's not going to walk over to you. Just then he thought he heard a sound like the rustle of sand in the wind. Then another. And another. They were coming all right. He rolled quickly back into his upright position, crouching on his haunches so he could move quickly and nodding to Blue furiously, although Blue was already alerted by his movement. This would be rifle firing from the hip at the crouch, and no mistake about it, so he'd better be good, but he knew he had to be in that position in order to spring, for there were six of them at least and he had five bullets and then that was it. Even relying on Blue, who was a good shot, to get a couple, he'd have to be able to load almost three times as fast as the others to have a prayer and even then he'd probably have to finish at least one off with his bayonet. Oh, well, no guts, no glory, as his father used to say when teaching him to stand and sight easy so you got off your best shot at a charging buffalo.

Next moment the Turks came over the top.

He let Blue, who had cover, fire first. It was a calculated risk, but he hoped that would give him the advantage of a couple of seconds that he needed. The moment Blue fired, Jim dropped the Turk nearest him, reloaded in an instant as the second Turk nearest was turning and, fortunately, lifting his rifle to sight. No time for that, brother, flashed through Jim's mind as he fired almost simultaneously with Blue's second shot. Jim had seen his third man, who had got farther into the dugout by this time, start to turn as Jim let off his second shot. Jim knew there would be no time to reload and he sprang from his haunches as the second bullet left his gun. He also knew he must reach his third target in one leap.

Even as he launched himself, his bayoneted rifle held tight into his side with the butt, Jim knew he would not make the distance. In midair, as the Turk realized what was happening and started to drop his rifle lower so Jim would not pass under his line of fire, at this exact instant, in midair, Jim threw his rifle out as far as he could at arm's length, with both hands, making it parallel to the ground, and thrust through the air with it scythelike as he landed. He felt it hit something and heard an agonizing cry. Then he was on his feet and thrusting, having heard Bluey's third shot and hoping that it had killed the other Turk who had been left standing but having no time to look. When he was sure his man was dead, he turned, and saw the others were, too, and Bluey was walking toward him, wiping his brow. Jim hooked his head back in the opposite direction as he himself moved up the incline nearest him to remind Bluey to check for any other Turks in the patrol. But there was none, and he noticed, as they each rolled cigarettes, that his scythe cut with his bayonet had been higher than he'd intended, and he'd cut the Turk half through at the waist, so he need not have worried about the extra thrusts.

Then the others came up from headquarters.

"What took you jokers so bloody long?" Jim asked.

"From the shots we reckoned there were only half a dozen or so and that you'd be pretty upset if we thought you couldn't handle 'em," the corporal said.

"Hah bloody hah," said Bluey.

Jim said nothing. He got out his shovel and started digging near the palm trees. Bluey helped him and they buried the kid, only three years younger than they were, and then headed back to the main lines where their horses were, to have some tucker and get ready for the next day's battle.

"One bloody Afghan eye for another," Jim muttered as he walked back.

"The kid was Egyptian, it's not the same."

"I know, but the principle is. Then six Turks for one Afghan, or Egyptian, or whatever."

"There you go again—worrying about the rights and wrongs of it. I told you not to do it until after the battle."

"It won't affect my fighting, but you can't expect me not to think about it now, think about it some more, now that we got the kid killed."

"It wasn't our fault."

"Wasn't it? Whose was it, then?"

"Ours is not to reason why—?"

"That's like saying you believe in a Something behind it all that we shouldn't question."

"Well, maybe I do. I think I believe in God but I don't mean He's responsible for the killing."

"Well, who is?"

"Perhaps it's just fate."

"Oh, the immortal Kismet."

"Done some reading, have you, bushie?"

"A bit. I've done a bit, towny. That's the answer they'd give out here, right enough. They'd say it was written. I wonder if Kemal really believes it was written for his men to die? Perhaps it's all a case of who's the least stupid on a given day at a given time and place. The kid was stupid to listen to us and we were stupid to ask him in the first place and stupid to put him up the tree like some bloody stupid generals and the Turks were bloody stupid to fall for that three-card trick. Perhaps it's all just stupidity and nothing to do with fate. Perhaps you just get caught if you're too stupid not to think ahead."

"No one can do that all the time. I'm sorry about the kid, too."

"I know. Let's get the last of his booze we've got left and drink it and get some tucker and then try to get some sleep."

"Now you're talking."

17

When the photograph of Jim in uniform arrived at the Back of Beyond, Billy let out a war whoop and went dancing around the kitchen like a Red Indian, shouting, "Come and look at this, Douggie, come and look at this."

"Over my dead body," shouted Beth, grasping at the photograph and almost tearing it as Billy snatched it back and headed up the passageway to what passed as the living room and where he knew Douggie to be at work on his sums.

"Let him be," Mac said quietly.

"Let him be—?" Beth shouted in exasperation. "Let him be killed, let them all be killed, is that what you're saying?"

"Come and read the letter. You read and I'll listen."

She shook her head, so Mac passed over the letter which had accompanied the photograph, and she read it sullenly and silently, saying nothing, and then passed it over to him.

He took it and read a little slower than she. She tried to busy herself making a fresh pot of tea at the stove. She threw some more wood chips into the fire and then took the heavy metal poker and pushed the black, wrought-iron, manhole-like cover back over the hole of fire in the stove. She pushed the damper open to give the fire more draft and then stood pushing the kettle back and forth with the poker as if to hurry up its boiling, but in reality delaying it.

She looked down at her apron and nearly cried when she saw how dirty it was. She'd meant to wash it yesterday but had forgotten. This was the first news they'd had of Jim, first news that he was even still alive, and she'd been distraught with worry but trying not to show it.

Perhaps it was Jim she was angry with, for sending the photo, perhaps it was herself for not being more understanding, perhaps it was Mac for not being quite fully the man in control of everything that he once was, but when he uttered the words, the simple words in his casual bush manner, as he finished reading, "Well, it sounds as if he's enjoying himself," she flew at him.

"Enjoying himself!" she shrieked. "Is that all you can think of? Is that all that matters—play and laughter and getting killed with great Australian good humor? Next Billy will be off before we know it and then you'll have lost both your precious bloody sons and there'll only be Douglas left, poor little Douglas. But you'll not get him. He's too young. And even if the war lasts a thousand years you'll not get him because of his eyesight. You'll not get a second chance to try to kill *him*. But the damage is done now with the other two. You never made one single solitary attempt to stop Jim, did you . . . DID YOU—?"

She had been shouting ever louder and louder all this time and he had tried to interrupt her twice, but she had turned on him and silenced him with a look; he had tried to interrupt twice because it hurt him so to see her thus, because even to hear her swear seriously, in a way she never had, except in occasional jest or that once which the Swansons had told him about, hurt him deeply and made him feel to blame.

But now there was silence and she stood poised above where he sat at the scrubbed white wooden table, poised there as if demanding an answer. There was no answer he could give except to shake his head and then move over to take the steaming kettle off the range, bending down to do it and appearing stooped, stooped as he had the day the Stock and Station agent had come. He was getting old, of course, and everyone gets a little stooped as they get older.

"You could have done something . . ." she had started again . . . "you might have tried to stop him going. There was a time you had influence—a time when you could have ridden into Darwin and they would have done anything for Murranji Mac. Or you could have spoken to the boy himself. He's a volunteer. No one said he had to go. But he did have to go, didn't he? He had to be like his father—or what his father used to be. If Billy dies, you—you and your blessed Big Jim son—will be to blame and I'll never speak to you again."

She had said it all now and suddenly she stopped, or was about to when something, a mother's instinct perhaps, made her look toward the door.

"Oh, Douglas," she shrieked, and then burst into tears. The boy stood at the door which Billy, who was now long since down home paddock, had left slightly ajar, stood wanly, wide-eyed behind his glasses, fixed there, staring, unbelieving, seeing and hearing his parents thus and then suddenly, because his mother was crying and running to him, scooping him up, he was crying, too, crying loudly now, the boy and the woman together as they went off down the passage to the bedroom, leaving Mac a forlorn and bent figure really, shrugging more and more into himself, more and more those giant heaving shoulders inwardly contorting, muscle upon muscle, muscle into muscle, as if muscle spasm was what a bushman had instead of tears.

18

There has never been, nor ever will be, Jim thought, a battle camp different from any other on the morning of battle. He had read about a lot of the great battles and talked to his mates, some of whom had fought in Europe before coming here. But it wasn't for these reasons that he knew all camps would be the same. He just sensed that whether there was mud or snow or sand, or dirt or dust, whether there was sun or rain or mist or no mist or smoke from an early artillery barrage or no smoke, the men were there for the same reason, the same reason on each side, to kill each other to stay alive and that was what gave each first morning breath and each and every movement a sense of poised and ruthless expectancy, a snort of horses' breath, the steam of fresh manure, the saber rattle of weapons being made ready.

Sometimes he thought he'd read too much as a kid. Bluey joked about his thinking too much and Jim made light of it and sometimes pretended not to be thinking but Blue was right enough. Sometimes he found it hard to switch off and sometimes it was bloody impossible, though he'd never admit it, and would crack a bush joke to cover it. But it was there, sure enough, and he was worried one day it wouldn't stop as he went into battle and then that would be something, trying to do two things at once. A good bushman never did that, particularly when hunting.

They moved only a short distance that day, however, and without engaging, as they had expected. They rested and then that night swung out wide and just before dawn on October 31 of 1917, they were within striking distance of Beersheba. The taking of Beersheba was crucial. Although they'd found some old Roman cisterns with water in them in the desert, the town of the wells had to be taken for strategic as well as water reasons. Allenby was engaging Gaza with the 21st Infantry Corps; the 20th would hit Beersheba head-on; the Desert Mounted Corps, under Chauvel, was to come from the rear and right side. Two full Turkish armies were against them.

At dawn two infantry divisions went in and the Anzac Light Horse attacked the heavily defended hills east of Beersheba to try to open the route in. It was late in the afternoon before these positions were secured. Tired and dirty and bloody and unfed since before dawn and their water bottles half empty, Jim and Blue prepared to ride again for the ever-relentless Chauvel, worshiped like Allenby away on the other front.

The charge they now prepared to make had some elements of the legend of the Light Brigade in it, though certainly not the stupidity of the commanders. The men knew the charge had to be made if Beersheba was to be taken and all the plans of Allenby and Chauvel and Lawrence and the others over so many months were to be successful. But they also knew they would be charging guns, horses against artillery, and it was a two-mile ride and at the end of it, if they lived through the shrapnel, would be the trenches.

The commanders gave the men their choice: they could fix bayonets, or ride with their bayonets in their hands like sabers. Bluey and Jim decided on rifles slung and bayonets in hand. It was risky, for it gave them no firepower. But they were horsemen, and just a bayonet in hand gave them much greater maneuverability, which they'd need for most of the ride against the artillery. They could always quickly slip their rifles off and down, ready to use; the reverse would be harder in saddle and waste perhaps crucial maneuvering time. If they made the trenches, chopping and hacking was the go there, as you rode over. A stray shot was just as likely to hit your animal as you.

And this was how it happened. They charged the guns and used every precision trick of horsemanship each had ever learned to try to anticipate and swerve around the volleying shrapnel and when they hit the trenches there was a double line of them but they took them like a water jump, this 4th Light Horse Brigade, took the trenches and dismounted for hand-to-hand fighting which was so often the way it finished up for the cavalry. As the Turks began to run, part of the brigade was ordered right on and into Beersheba itself, and Jim and Blue were quickly mounted and charging again against the now broken and weakened Turkish line. The 4th Light Horse and the Anzac Mounted Division now broke through completely, cheering as they went.

The push continued with Allenby's troops eventually forcing the evacuation of Gaza and the thrust going right on north until on November 19 they were poised to take Jerusalem, with British infantry now in the front of the advance and the cavalry and air force snapping at the Turkish stragglers.

The Turks now evacuated Jerusalem and Christmas of that year saw Jim and Bluey camped near the Jordan Valley.

"This war's going to bog down now for a while, Blue," Jim said over a smoko on Christmas night, guarding their eternal hod again, away from the others.

"So—?"

"So I think I might be able to swing that move to the Flying Corps I've always been wanting. The prohibition on crossing over's lifted now and they're short of pilots."

"They'll never let you out of the Light Horse, you're too bloody good."

"Yes, they will, I spoke to the captain this morning. He said, because of our records, though he'd hate to lose us, we can go."

"Why didn't you tell me?"

"I'm telling you now. Besides, I wasn't sure you'd go for it. You're not as keen on the air as I am."

"You can say that again."

"Well, then?"

"I can't go, Jim, honest. Sometimes I think I want to live a bit more than you do. Other times I think I'm scared and you've never been."

"Don't you believe it. They're going to give us a decoration for that hod shoot-up, by the way . . . captain said."

"No one ever tells me anything round here."

"He just told me this morning. I thought you'd be pleased."

"I am . . . it's just that—"

"I know, with the kid involved you'd rather have it for Beersheba and that was more bloody and we were better heroes then. Perhaps we'll get a gong for Beersheba, too. Anyway, the commendation has opened the door to the Flying Corps and I've got to go, so help me, Blue, I've got to."

"I know, mate, but they'll ship you out to Europe any tick of the clock now and the death rate in that Flying Corps makes the Light Horse death rate look like Amateur Night. Besides, you don't know flying. We could both ride and shoot like the devil before we got here and that's what's kept us alive. I'm not changing horses in midstream now, so to speak."

"That's probably wise, but how else am I going to learn to fly and it's going to be important when I get back in our part of the world. Could save me years."

"If you get back. And what about Firecracker?"

"You're definitely not going, then?"

"No, mate, sorry to split us up, but this cobbler is going to stick to his last."

"Fair enough. I've spoken to the captain about Firecracker. They'll keep him at brigade HQ for despatch riders, which should keep him reasonably safe, and have him dropped off at Darwin after the war. I hate to leave him but it's the best I can do and they'll look after him and they need all the good mounts they can get."

"Isn't that the truth, though. . . . Had it all figured out, didn't you?"

"Yeah, been working on it for a few months. Figured you wouldn't come but wanted to ask. You wouldn't have to fly, you know; you could be my observer if you wanted."

"No thanks, mate, it's really not my caper. Tell you what, I'll see that old Firecracker gets on the same ship as me and I'll put him in our paddock in Darwin, just out of town, until you get back, how's that?"

"That's a deal, mate, it really is. That way, too, if I don't make it back, I know he'll be well looked after."

"Don't be bloody silly. I'd take him out for your kid brother and see your folks. Heard from home lately?"

"No, no I haven't. What about you?"

"Neither of us have."

"You're right. Well, you know these are not the easiest of delivery spots and we have been moving rather fast."

"When do you leave us?"

"Next few days. The papers came through this morning and they're flying a few of us to England in the next few days for training."

19

It was not until his flying training was almost finished in England that a letter finally reached Jim. It was from his mother to say that Billy had run away months earlier—she supposed to enlist. He was then still only seventeen and she'd telegraphed the authorities but she said they'd had no word of him so she supposed he'd used a false name. She pleaded in her letter with Jim to send him home if he came across him. It was typical of his mother, who was so realistic in some ways, to think that their paths might cross. Still, they might have if Billy had headed for the desert and the Light Horse. Jim thought Billy might try to reach him. You could make special application to claim your brother's battalion for yourself. But if Billy was using a false name that would be impossible, though he didn't put it past Billy to have got one of the recruiting officers to look in the wrong direction or lose the list the day his mother's telegraph wire came in. Billy loved the bush, but he was a town person, too, spending more time in Darwin than Jim ever had, and well known for his drinking and gambling. He'd have known the recruiting officers, or known someone who knew them, that was for sure.

Jim thought about it for a long time and decided that, whatever happened, Billy was a man by every bush law he knew and that his father would want Billy free to make up his mind, though there was curiously no mention of his father in the letter. If he came across Billy, or Billy found him, he'd be free to stay. But the chances of them meeting were nil.

There was now a complete Australian training wing in England supplying officers and mechanics to the four Australian wings at the Western Front. Jim was posted as a flight lieutenant to No. 4 in mid-March 1918. The squadron, under Major. W. A. McClaughry, was with the First Army in the Lens-Lille area. Jim arrived just after Captain A. H. Cobby and his patrol had encountered Richthofen and part of his wing in a brief dogfight. The encounter, in which Richthofen is said to have lost four of his planes to the Australians, was prophetic. A few months later Australian Lewis gunners shot him down with their ground fire and it was No. 3 Australian Squadron of the Royal Flying Corps which recovered and buried his body.

Jim was annoyed at missing the Richthofen encounter, an encounter he might not have survived because of his inexperience, although he was beginning to feel at home with his aircraft, a Sopwith Camel (couldn't get away from the bloody things). The hunting instinct and keeping your wits about you was the same and being able to sight along the barrel made him as accurate in dogfights as on the ground. But if he was annoyed at missing that encounter, he need not have worried, for on March 22, a few days after he arrived, arrived to a mud which reminded him of the Wet back home, No. 4 Squadron was moved up into the Somme battle.

Somehow, despite all the hard hand fighting and charging the artillery in the desert, it had still been what Jim felt war should be like, the sort of thing he'd read about. When he first saw the Somme, flying down as low as thirty feet sometimes to scout enemy positions, he could not believe it. He thought he was old and wise and smart at twenty. He now grew up in a week. In a week of flying in the Somme, of being in that stinking atmosphere, of mixing with the mud-stained troops who kept their spirits up with bleak, black Australian trench humor—"What does blood smell like? Like dried shit in your pants before you go over the top"—in that week he was a different person and hoped to hell Billy was nowhere around and if he came across him he swore he'd send him home that instant. He had no way of knowing that his brother was fighting below him now—or was about to—for the Australians were being ordered up, five Australian divisions tired and weary and needing their tot of overproof rum before each new command of "Over the top," tired, but now with the reputation of being shock troops, tired from the third battle of Ypres but needed because things were not going well in the Somme.

As Jim flew over he could even hear the troops coming up singing, "Pack up your troubles in your old kitbag and smile, smile, smile . . . What's the use of worrying, it never was worthwhile . . ."

Well, he was glad he was in the air, whatever the casualty rate, for it was going to be bloodier yet, bloodier than it had ever been, on the ground.

Up from Hell Fire Corner the Australians came, the Australians the Germans hated and feared, for they had a reputation for shooting their German prisoners.

Jim saw the mud below, the dead horses and mules in the mud and the live ones dragging gun carriages up to the front, appearing to gallop almost too fast, as if awkwardly speeded up by some unseen magic lantern. There were the square-boxed ambulances, square-fabric or wooden-ply bodywork and square engine housings, full of men so shot up and caked in mud they could not undo their uniforms and puttees to have their wounds dressed until they reached the hospital. And the hospitals . . . He'd been to one to see a mate who'd been shot down over their own lines but who had run into some mustard gas. The hospital was full of these poor gassed jokers, all lying the wrong way round in bed, with their heads on the aisle so that the nurses could get to them quickly and keep washing out their eyes and noses and throats, all of which were spewing mucus, and the rest of them burned and blotched so they couldn't move, their scrotums swollen and blistered in agony.

From the air again he looked down at the slouch hats and

the helmets, at the Australians and the Poms and the Highlanders, as they filed into the trenches, soon up to their puttees in mud, with nothing but bully beef and biscuits, but somehow cheerful, walking over the plank pathways stretched over the trenches like thin railway sleepers joined to railway lines, walking on and on and digging in to go over the top again and so many of them knowing they'd never come back, never in a million years.

There were tanks and bogs and fogs and still nothing worked and Germany's defenses could not be broken. Whatever the bloody history books would say later, the blokes in the Flying Corps agreed in their mess one night in June that year—for there were plenty of arguments because the Australians were always mentioned as British—the British in the mess who'd been flying over agreed it was five divisions of Australians up there and some Highlanders and very little else, whatever the books would say later. They knew who broke through in the end in the way Australian troops had been used from the day of the Gallipoli landing. They didn't like it, some of the English generals, for it wasn't bloody cricket, but they used these volunteers all right, used them when it suited them, used them because they fought so fiercely and the Germans feared them so because many Australians did not take prisoners and just kept trying to keep going and break through and win and hold extra ground.

That night in the mess a young Australian officer who was going up as an observer the next day to see for himself heard Jim pontificating about this and came over and introduced himself and said, "Excuse me, but did I just hear you say, 'Strike me pink the square heads are dead mongrels'?"

"Probably did, mate. Have a chair and a drink. Was just talking about them starting it with the gas. Terrible thing that gas. Probably called the bastards mongrels, why?"

The officer sat down and took a beer. "Oh, it wasn't just that word," he said in a fairly toffy voice which told Jim he was from the South, probably Melbourne. A lot of the officers in the infantry spoke that way. "No, it wasn't just the word, it was the whole sentnece, really. Got a young bloke in my outfit who uses it all the time. It's not that unusual, I know, but it's just that he looks a bit like you. It's not his face, so much as his build and the way he walks and . . . well, the way he talks. I wonder . . . I can't quite recall his name—"

"Carlyon," said Jim quickly, "Billy Carlyon."

"Yes, that's it. So he's a relative, then?"

"Kid brother. He's all right?"

"When last I saw him about three days ago, before they sent me on this useless exercise. Oh, I'm sorry, I meant no offense—"

"It's all right, mate, we understand; don't like to be separated from our outfits ourselves. But where is Billy exactly?"

"Yes, well, I was afraid you'd ask that if you were related, that's why I was a bit reluctant to raise it. He's right up there in the thick of it, I'm afraid. We all are. I'll be back there in a day or so and then we're going on, right on through whatever happens."

"He's underage," Jim said quickly, "doesn't turn eighteen until October. Would that make a difference at this stage?"

"Of course it would, if you're reporting it to me officially. Are you doing that, Lieutenant?"

Jim looked at the officer squarely. "How's he enjoying it up there?"

"Having a ball, I'd say, and making a lot of money from the poker school we don't know about."

"That'd be Billy. What are his chances, would you say?"

"About the same as all of us—fifty-fifty and getting less every day."

"That's what I figured. Would he have to know if I dobbed him in?"

"I'm afraid so. I rather think you'd have to sign a form. You know how regulations are. He's obviously managed to get a forged birth certificate or something and the way the war is you could be trying to get him out of the fighting. We get an awful lot of letters from mothers protesting. But of course as an officer if you signed a declaration, that would be acceptable."

"No, it wouldn't," Jim said, "not to Billy. He'd never forgive me. Never. And I think I'd rather risk losing him than having to live with him hating me for the rest of my born days. He's one hell of a hater, that Billy of ours, that's for sure."

"We need all the haters we can get up there at the moment," the officer said.

"Of course, it was just a passing thought. Forget I mentioned it. Here's to you and Billy. See you both in Paris by the end of the year. Cheers."

Whether it was the news about Billy, or the cumulative fighting since his war had begun, Jim that night got himself into one of the sourest moods he'd ever been in in his life. He drank late at the mess and was still in an angry mood when he woke, dying of thirst after the dehydration of the alcohol. He went to get some water. It was just before dawn. Dawn when the Hun bastards would be getting ready to take off to strafe the trenches again.

He needed only a moment to think about it—to think that he must not think about it and he could be court-martialed. But God Almighty what a way to say hullo for Billy; welcome to the bloody dirty war at the front.

He got quietly into his flying suit and out on the tarmac to his aircraft without being seen. Just as he was about to get into the cockpit, a voice said, from underneath the next aircraft so it seemed, "I say, Carlyon, you're not thinking of an unauthorized takeoff, are you?"

Jim swung around to see the figure of his commanding officer emerging. Commanding officer—he was just in his middle twenties! He was a fierce man in a dogfight. He was English—Royal Flying Corps.

"No, of course not, sir," Jim replied, and then added, thinking quickly, "but of course if you had a special patrol you wanted to send up in a particular sector up front . . ."

The flying officer, whose name was Ian Jarvis, realized there must be a story behind it and soon had Jim telling him about Billy.

"I'm supposed to fly up to HQ for a briefing. Was just checking my aircraft. . . . I suppose I could take an escort. I suppose I should, really. I suppose we might manage a slight detour if we hurried. We'll want the enemy planes still on the ground, that's the idea, isn't it—limit their strike capacity at the trenches, at least for a day or two?"

Jim nodded, almost stupefied. He had great respect for the man's fighting ability but had thought him a bit stuffy up until now.

"Better get started, then," Jarvis said, pulling on his leather flying helmet and starting to climb in. "Follow me. I think I know the spot we want."

They were off and running within minutes, the thrill of the wind in Jim's face and his sour mood turning to the joy of the hunt as the dawn showed its very first signs of breaking.

It all happened in an instant. There never was a warning when they come upon you from above. But in seconds he and Jarvis were in the midst of a bloody dogfight . . . six . . . seven . . . to two . . . and they dived from on top of them. It had been silly to think no one else might be up early.

Jim's hunting instincts took over. He never really remembered a great deal until afterward when this happened. But he remembered in that instant that all his sourness came back, all his hate of the enemy and all his desire to protect Billy. He remembered thinking this as he rolled out automatically, out and away, and started to climb himself, but not in a straight climb, though some said he was the most unorthodox pilot they had ever seen. The truth was that he was without fear to a point of stupidity. Sometimes in dogfights the Germans got out of his way because they thought he was going to fly right into them and explode.

This happened twice in the dogfight now as he came back to get in close, not bothering to climb to get too much height, but trying to get his bearings. There was one on Jarvis's tail and he couldn't shake him. Then Jim saw the fabric rip with a quick series of puffs as the shots hit. Jarvis was all right. But he wouldn't be with the next round of fire. Jim swung his aircraft sideways, blindly not caring what happened so long as he put the German off his aim. He was so close he did more than that. Even Jim had not judged the distance well. His propeller almost clipped the German's tail as that pilot swung his aircraft violently away, giving Jarvis his much-needed chance to break.

In the next few minutes, as often happens, he and Jim got on top of the opposition. Jarvis had been pinned down but once loose he took three Germans out of the skies in quick succession. Jim got two and the others headed off. It was a magnificent score, really, and although they never made it into the area Billy was in, for Jarvis shook his head when Jim nodded to go on and gave a very firm home signal, it put Jim up in the top pilot register. He and Jarvis became firm friends and Jarvis taught Jim the dirty little tricks pilots learn to survive.

They talked a great deal, too, for Jarvis was an avid listener. He wanted to know all about Jim's property, and said, in the end, that he might even try settling in Queensland himself after the war. Queensland appealed a little more than the Territory, he thought. He knew someone who had a good idea for after the war, he said. "You might be interested."

"I might at that. Always interested in a good idea," said Jim.

Jarvis obviously didn't want to say more, so Jim did not press him. Jarvis promised to get in touch after the war and took his address.

Then things got heavier in the fighting and Jarvis was moved up to HQ and Jim forgot all about it for a while.

There was no breakdown in any statistics or newspaper reports to separate Australians from British. The German general, Erich Ludendorff, knew differently. The day the five Australian divisions, so weakened it was questionable whether they were still divisions, the day they broke through in the Great Battle of the Somme, Ludendorff called, with great respect, "Germany's Black Day," and it was this prolonged and finally successful attack which led to the statement that "the war was won by five Australian divisions and the 51st Highlanders." There was a rumor, of course, that there were also fifty British divisions around somewhere.

But it was over, on November 11, 1918. Germany signed the Armistice and, miraculously, Billy and Jim met up in Paris, at the café where the officer, who knew Paris, had said he would bring Billy to meet his brother. But the officer was not there. He'd got it in the last push, Billy said, which had been truly terrible, and he himself had got so that he needed that firewater overproof rum they used to dole out.

"Still, the old bush instincts got us through, Billy," Jim said. "Perhaps we were mad to come and God knows I've done some things I'm ashamed of, but we're in one piece and that's the main thing, although you seem to have a bit of a cough."

"Guess I caught a chill in the trenches," Billy said. He was not as garrulous as Jim. He was a poker player in conversation as in everything.

"Sounds like a gas cough to me," Jim said finally.

"Right again, big brother. Got a dose of it early on, just after I arrived. Nothing to worry about. Nothing that beautiful, bloody dry heat we're going to won't cure."

"It's the Wet."

"You're right. But it'll be the Dry before we get home." It was. And when they arrived at the property, having stopped only half a day in Darwin, they arrived to the news that their father had died on the Track in one of the worst Dries on record.

20

Jim could not talk to his mother about it for a long time. They had never been close, and it was as if each blamed the other, Beth feeling it might not have happened if the eldest son had been there, and Jim feeling that if his mother had liked the land more, his father would not have felt forced to push himself so hard to try to get on, for as the years passed his father had never regained his happy shine, working harder and harder, taking every extra bit of work, mostly out on the Track where he was the expert, taking the impossible jobs to try to build up the property.

It was one such job, Jim learned from Jacky, that had cost him his life. The postman went through each year, from Darwin to the Alice and back in the Dry, a single man on horse. The mail was life to the Outback people. One day a line party had brought the mailman in, sick, to the property. He had a bad dose of malarial dysentery, anyone could see that. The line party said they'd tapped the wire and telegraphed Darwin and when the telegraph office heard they were taking the sick man to Mac's place, they said to ask if Mac would take the job. In the Dry, at certain times of the year, and in certain circumstances, a few days later in the year can make an enormous difference. Surface water you might otherwise have been able to rely on, say, in the third week of June, might be gone by the fourth. This was the driest of Dries, Jacky explained, although Jim said he'd seen enough for himself on the way in from Darwin. Mac had known how difficult it would be, and Jacky had wanted to come. Mac said Jacky must stay and look after the Missus, and that he'd travel better on his own, because some places he'd be lucky to find enough water for the horse, let alone himself. So off he went, knowing it was the most difficult ride of his life.

"He go happy, though, Big Jim," Jacky said. "He ride out smiling and very proud like in old days when you born. His hair very gray now, but he ride out like he glad the spirit of the Big Kangaroo give him final battle, and when I hear he die I go out Five Mile Camp at dusk and sure enough there the big fellar Big Red bounding down toward the water hole at sunset and him your euro."

Jim put his hand benignly around Jacky's shoulder. They were standing down at the end of the home paddock, the last bit of grass left, grazing Firecracker whom he'd picked up from Bluey on his brief stop at Darwin.

Jim smiled. "Perhaps you're right, Jacky. Let's hope so. What about the details?"

"I tell you story already, Boss."

"Not all of it. I want the lot."

Jacky looked resignedly and shrugged in the Aboriginal way.

"I train you too smart, I think. You know line party talk Jacky. He die slowly, Boss, plenty slowly. Your father big strong man know desert almost as well as me, I reckon. All surface water gone, Boss, all creeks, billabongs, water holes, everything. So we have to use government bores and you know still not many. He use bores and dig. Distances between bores too great, Boss. Finally he have to shoot horse, but not before gets to telegraph and cuts wire. But down to digging deep and even undergound streams dry, Boss. So lives on frogs but they pretty dry too and line party not close. Arrive a day late, maybe two."

"And the body?"

"They salt him, Boss, and take him across to Boss Swanson's place and bury him there with friends and telegraph company sending down nice tombstone. He still Murranji Mac, Boss. He still King of the Track. He roam out there from North to Centre, Boss, like your Big Red roam."

Jim turned and smiled at him gently. He knew Jacky was saying these things to make him feel better, although he knew Jacky believed them. Sometimes he wished he believed in something as Jacky did—these wonderful, rich, rainbow-colored myths of the unseen things which moved on the immovable landscape, all the lovely legends of the Dream-time and all the Dreaming down to the present. Parts of him half believed, of course. But it wasn't really any good to half believe in a thing: that was like not believing at all. Still it warmed him to know that the rich and ancient tapestry of Jacky's mind really believed that now his father's spirit was free and roamed up and down the Track.

"We must see to the cattle, Jacky," Jim said at last. "How many do we have left?"

"Maybe twenty, Boss."

"That all?"

The black man nodded. "Maybe a few more alive out there, Boss, but I think maybe those who going to make it in here by now."

"So do I," said Jim. In years of bad Dry he knew well enough that if the cattle had not worked their way in from the unfenced free ranges by a certain time, they would be lying bloated on their sides somewhere. The cattle's instincts knew that they could not travel more than a day without water, so as the surface water began to dry up each year, they started to work their way in to the more permanent water supplies of the river and billabongs near the station house. But in bad years—and this was already a very bad year— many did not make it.

"Well, I guess we'd better get them all together and hand-water and feed them."

"Already done, Boss. Got them down by river."

"Of course. Not too close to the crocs?"

"No, Boss, they OK, even if crocs crawl up at night."

"Well, we'll keep the home paddock for the horses and let the cattle feed by the river and hope the feed lasts but it doesn't look good to me. I'll have to think of something."

"Big Red always think of something, Boss," Jacky said, and when he referred to Jim in this third-person way, as if he were talking to someone else about someone other than Jim, Jim always found it a bit disconcerting, and was never quite sure if Jacky might not be making a friendly joke at his expense. Certainly the expression gave nothing away. It was a smile, but whether out of fun or the smile of confidence in a legend, Jim did not know.

"How's Nora?" he said as they walked back to the house.

"Not bad, Boss, not bad. She and Missus and Douglas one pretty strong group."

"Yes, I bet. Doug go out riding with you much?"

"He not ride, Boss. He not go out in sun hardly."

"Of course, I just hoped that with Billy and me away—"

"That Billy, Boss, him some boy, eh, the way he get away from under Missus's nose and call in his IOUs?"

"Is that how he did it?" Jim said. "You know he wouldn't tell me, just kept smiling that smile of his, like 'She'll be right, mate.'" The darker mood had passed and both were laughing now.

"That how he do it all right. He hold IOUs from poker games on half the recruitment bigwigs. He been planning this maybe a year, I reckon. He made sure all the IOUs big and overdue and then one day he ride into Darwin and say, 'OK, you jokers, I calling in IOUs.' They say, 'Hold on, Billy, they're pretty steep—we need some time to pay.'

"'They're all overdue and I'm callin' them,' says Billy, 'although if I was at the front I wouldn't be able to call 'em and you jokers would certainly have plenty of time to pay and maybe never.' They enlist him pretty quick then, Boss, 'cause he look pretty old enough and they get him on troop ship plenty damn smart."

"I bet they did," Jim was roaring, "I bet they did. And now he's home and he'll be going back into town any day now to present them with the notes again, I'll wager."

"That right, Boss. He got them both ways now—illegal

enlistment and the IOUs. You no tell I told you, though."

"No, Jacky. I know about you and Billy and your secrets. I won't tell. Just try to keep him here for a few more days. He's good for Mum. She talks to him more and young Doug loves him so—perhaps Billy'll even be able to get him out riding. He sure as hell won't do it for me." There was bitterness in his tone. Douglas had welcomed Billy home as the conquering hero, barely acknowledging Jim and now avoiding him as much as possible. Diplomatically Jacky did not take up the point but said simply,

"He plenty book smart already, Boss, but Doug not a rider."

"You're right."

"How you feel, Boss? You look plenty damn thin."

"Tired, Jacky, very tired. I think I could sleep for a week. We got any milk?"

Jacky shook his head.

"Silly question."

"Got good buffalo steak hanging in coolgardie safe, though, Boss. Buffalo get plenty good now. Him better eating than cattle this year maybe and him cost nothing. Got steak and eggs and beef dripping for bread. Nora bake proper bread for you, Boss, and there the last of the beer your father kept for your homecoming."

"When did you shoot the buffalo?"

"Three, four days maybe."

"Knew I was coming, did you?"

"Aw, yes, Boss, I knew for a while."

Jim said nothing. He was not going to invite an answer that might tell him that the nonexistent kangaroo had told Jacky, or, worse still, the existent crocodile. He was tired and had wanted to cry ever since he had heard the news of his father. He would cry when he was alone, in the way his father and Jacky had taught him. He would cry, then he would sleep until he woke, and then he must think and see what would be done with the property. But first he would eat.

Ever since Mac's death Beth had been putting off the decision she hated to face. She knew she must decide whether to leave the property or stay. It was, of course, her home. Yet it had always felt more like a temporary camp, and as she got older she longed for the comforts of an ordinary farm or a city house or the comforts such as Swanson's station might have given them. She wanted to leave, but she felt it would be a betrayal of Mac. She knew things had wound down between them as the years had gone on and she felt guilty about it. He had always been good and gentle with her and she felt her lack of enthusiasm had taken the glint off that happy surface of his she remembered so well from the time he first spoke to her on the train. And of course things had been worse between them since the Stock and Station agent's humiliation of Mac. She had never been able to give him the same support after that however hard she tried and however guilty she felt.

So she believed she should stay for him, yet she wanted to go. She was determined that Douglas, now eleven, must have a public school education, one of her boys must, whatever that entailed. She hoped in a way that Jim would make the decision for her. Since quite early she knew she had lost him, lost him to his father's ways. Yet she was just barely aware, and had noticed it more since his return, that there was perhaps another dimension to Jim. Something ran under the surface which was almost too well controlled, which the owner was very quietly aware of and holding to himself quite deliberately, just as a beast of the bush may appear to be purring or growling contentedly on a rock in the sun yet is alert to everything within its wide field of vision, alert and relaxed and almost overconfident with a quiet ruthlessness of intent which is scary. Jim had this animal motor thing and it frightened his mother. He had great warmth and kindness and consideration and an enormous sense of duty and respect and love, but sometimes she thought it might be a long time before he would discover whether or not he had the gentleness, almost the softness, of his father. It was as if Jim had different things on the top of his shopping list of priorities. But perhaps this wasn't bad. Mac had had the gentleness and she, or the land, or both combined, had taken it from him and left him almost as dry inside before he died as his beloved dust soil. And it wasn't that Jim wasn't happy; he was sometimes, she thought, too rollickingly carefree happy, and this in combination with his determination and what was described in that part of the world good-naturedly as cockiness—perhaps almost too much faith in his own abilities— might make him pursue his goals with perhaps too much selfish determination. And he had that.

She knew her son better than he thought she did, better than their relationship certainly allowed her to express openly. But she knew him, knew that even now, as she sat watching him so happy with Billy and Nora and Jacky and young Douglas, wolfing into the food with all of them sitting at the big, long, scrubbed wooden table, she knew from his eyes behind the happy jocularity that he was planning things all right and perhaps she was wrong to worry about him and perhaps she was superimposing her own prejudices on what she hoped for him. Of course he did not even know what she hoped for him, or that she hoped anything for him, and if he had, he would not have cared, except in a polite way out of respect for her, the same sort of respect Mac had always shown her. She worried at the early maturity of her son who had turned twenty-one in the New Year of 1919 and was not surprised when after the meal he said,

"I'll be off now for a week or two, Mum. Billy's agreed to wait and take the second shift in Darwin when I return and Jacky's well in control of everything on the property. Want to have a bit of a relax and work out what to do. Anything I can get you?"

He always asked and she always shook her head but he always brought her something, like Mac used to do, even if it was a tin of butter.

No other property owner—and Jim was now that—would have dared leave in such terribly dry conditions. It was typical of Jim that he knew to stay around worrying would achieve nothing, that Jacky had under control what could be got under control, and that his time could best be spent away in town, talking to people, asking questions, thinking things through, working on the next move. The Dry—the 1919 Dry which was even worse than the previous year's—was a fact to be accepted. But it was a part of the whole, one of the given factors of the environment one could do little about. What was important was the overall plan. Beth knew her son would be thinking about three, four, five years ahead already. He always had. And he had even more reason now. There were so many things to do that his mind had then one thousand mistresses of planning. It was the worst possible time to fall in love.

21

When Jim rode into Darwin he decided to visit Bluey first. After all, he was now his best mate, and almost the only mate he'd known apart from his father and brothers and Jacky and one or two of the other local blacks who were friends of Jacky's, such as the young, irrepressible Crocodile Tommy, who'd shown them how to crawl out on branches over the billabongs to watch the crocodiles mating.

So he went to see Bluey, and this time called at his home. A few days earlier, on his way home with Billy, he'd gone to the agistment paddock first, thinking that if Bluey was not there he'd just take his horse and keep going with Billy and see Blue later. But Bluey had been there with the roan, Firecracker, in tip-top condition, and some other nice horses of his own. Said he was spending a lot of time at the agistment and after all the time in the war was finding being back home bloody impossible. They'd had a few beers and then the Carlyon boys had ridden on, Jim promising to come back as soon as possible.

He rode past the paddock as he entered town and Bluey was not there so he rode on until, after a few inquiries, for he knew only the main streets, found the address. It was a bloody mansion. It was on top of a cliff overlooking the ocean. As he rode up the path he came upon the type of house which

Jim had always associated in his mind with colonial gover-
nors' residences, tall and white and colonnaded, with a
square graceful tower and flagpole and Union Jack. It seemed
half a mile across the sanded drive and gardens to the front
door. Bluey was there to meet him.

"Saw ya from the tower," Blue said.

"Yer didn't tell me you were royalty. Yer said yer old man
was just a bloody public servant."

Jim was convinced that Bluey had been making fun of him
and said so, but Blue replied that he had never said his father
was "just" a public servant, he had said, in fact, that he was a
public servant, which he was, but what Carlyon had missed
with that thick head of his, was not *asking* if he was "just" a
public servant. He'd been a weekday public servant and a
weekend bushie, Bluey said proudly, and had got in early on
the Pine Creek gold discoveries. The fact that he was a
geologist with the government had probably helped a bit,
Bluey said ruefully.

"Just a bit," Jim said.

"Anyway, the old man finished up making a mint. Real
good bloke at turning a quid, so help me."

"I'd like to meet him."

"Yeah, he'll be along presently or you can see him at
dinner. He says he wants to meet you, too. Reckons you sound
a goer. Got some idea I mightn't be here if you hadn't been in
the hod with me that night."

"That's bullshit."

"Of course." Bluey was smiling his fat, happy, wide and
shining face smile again, sitting like a Buddha in the sun on
the front steps, despite the elegant cane chaise lounges on the
tiled veranda under the white wrought-iron lacework, sitting
there on the steps in the sun, smiling, as good-natured as
ever, sitting in his khaki shorts and shirt and sandals and
Jim felt very good to see him again.

"We better think about having a drink," Blue said. "The
sun's nearly over the yardarm. Want to have it here or go to
the pub?"

Jim looked sideways and said nothing.

"Yeah, that's what I reckon, too," Blue said, "the pub. We can see the old man at dinner. I'd told him you'd probably be riding into town to stay a few days. All right with you?"

"Anything that saves room and board is all right with me, cobber."

"Good. Come and I'll show you where the stables are so you can put your horse away. I could call a groom, but I reckon you'd hit me."

"That'd be right."

"I'll tell you one thing, though, Jim," Bluey said, more seriously, as they walked around the back to the stables and a wonderful view of the Arafura Sea and knowing that beyond that, and the Timor Sea, out there at the end of the right and left apex on each side, were the Pacific and the Indian oceans.

"What's that, Blue?" Jim eventually replied.

"Well, me old man had the bottom out of his pants when he was a kid and he started off as a clerk on a pittance and studied nights and anyway, what I'm saying is I can remember as a kid being poor, bloody poor, and this being rich beats the hell out of it."

"I will give that due consideration during my week of planning. This place has got to be as big as the administrator's residence, Blue."

"Bigger," said Bluey with fierce and determined pride.

"Sorry."

"I didn't expect ignorant cow cockies to know such things."

"Of course not. There's just one thing, though, Blue . . ."

"What's that, mate?"

"That bloody Union Jack on the bloody flagpole up there."

"Aw, yeah. Sorry about that. Forgot to tell you. Me old man's a Pom—a Limey, so help me."

"With a name like Byrne?"

"Yeah. An Irish Pom, would you believe?"

"Blimey, you poor bastard."

"Yeah, a bit of a weight to live with, mate, but there you

are. Not a bad bloke for a Pom, though. You might just like him. Doesn't whinge about the place. Loves every square inch of it and reckons it's been good to him."

"I'd say that might be a fair statement, Blue, but then it sounds as if he worked the land pretty hard for it."

Jim's use of "land" in this way was his highest compliment, and Bluey knew it.

"That's the truth, mate, but he's still got his pride in the Mother Country too—that's why he keeps the flag up."

"Better let him keep it, then, mate, you think?"

"I honestly don't think it would be decent to climb up and take it down at night. Besides, he'd like as not get on to us and have us locked up in the slammer for a night. Got no sense of humor about that flag."

"You're right. We'll find another one sometime. Let's go and have a drink. We're carrying on like two-bob watches. In any case I want to ask your advice about something."

On the walk down into town Bluey suggested they go to Hatcher's bar, "Just to pass the time of day, you understand."

Jim told him where he could put that suggestion.

"Only an idea, mate, only an idea."

"You've been home longer than I have and you're spoiling for a fight, you fat little red-headed runt."

"I'll start with you if you keep that up and fight my way through to Hatcher."

"It's an old wound best left and forgotten, mate. That score is settled."

"That's not how I hear it."

"What do you mean?"

"Billy's holding IOUs on Hatcher, holding heavy, I hear."

"That's nonsense, Blue. Hatcher'd never let him in the game."

"That's why he's so mad. Didn't know, he claims. Says Billy gave a false name and you know the kid doesn't look much like you. From what you've said, anyone would pick you a mile off for your old man, but not Billy."

"That's true enough, all right. I look like Dad, Billy's in

between, sort of half-blond, half-mouse color, and young Doug is redder like Mum, bit more your color."

"Well, that's it, then. Hatcher says he didn't pick the kid for a cockie even, let alone a Carlyon, and he gave a false name. Says it's well known he doesn't allow cow cockies into his games, let alone Carlyons, let alone people giving false names. Says the kid got the money under false pretenses and so far as he's concerned, there's no debt. Leastways, that's the town gossip."

"When's all this supposed to have happened?"

"Night before Billy shipped out for overseas."

"How much are the IOUs for?"

"Two hundred and fifty."

"Two hundred and fifty quid! Jesus, it's a bloody fortune. We could sure use that right now if we could arrange to collect it."

They had reached the nearest hotel now and turned in.

"Short of robbery, I don't see how," Bluey said as they ordered two tall beers, saw them come toward them cold, the glasses beaded and cold from the icebox, and put the ten ounces of rich, cold amber fluid straight down with the word, "Skoal."

"Bit thirsty over there, was it, luv?" said the barmaid, who had the glasses refilled so quickly Jim suspected she was used to Blue's drinking habits.

"Got a bit dry—and wet in the wrong places," Jim answered.

Then he turned to Blue and said, "Let's forget about Hatcher for the present and I'll see if I can work out a scheme to get the money out of him. Billy's going to be rich with all those other IOUs too, though."

"I wouldn't bank on it, mate. Those blokes are off the enlistment board now, and whereas they won't welch on a bet like Hatcher, they're going to at least want a chance to get their money back and going to be trying real hard and Billy is a patchy player. Great when he's on a streak but you know—"

"You seem to know more about him than I do."

"Well, I'd heard of him and stories about him before I met you. The town's my main parish, mate, and the bush number two, the way it's the reverse for you."

"True enough. Anyway there's just one more thing while we're on it, and then we'll forget about it, get drunk, meet your old man and go and look for some crumpet."

"Thank Christ, I was beginning to think you only went for Gyppo sheilas. Ever had a lubra?"

"No, no, I haven't. Why do you ask?"

"Well, plenty of blokes do here in town and they say it's worse out in the bush."

"Sometimes that's true, I guess. Can't blame them . . . so few white women about. But no, I never have."

"Any particular reason?"

"I grew up with a lot of the kids of the local blacks, kids like Crocodile Tommy and his sister Lucy, and Lucy's a real dish, I can tell you. A whole lot of us used to swim and play with each other all the time. And if Tommy and Lucy and I go for a swim even these days no one bothers to wear clothes, for Chrissakes. So I guess I feel more brotherly towards her, guess I'd feel as if I was rooting my sister or something. Why, got something on the go?"

"No, not really. Always wanted to though, and thought you'd know. Not much of a bush expert, are you?"

"Not much."

"What's the thing you wanted to ask me about?" Bluey said, sipping his second beer and leaning on the bar.

"The doctor . . . whether you know the local doctor."

"Everyone knows the local doctor."

"We don't."

"No, I guess not. What's the problem?"

"Billy. He got a dose of mustard gas and he's still got a bloody cough. Makes light of it and of course Mum doesn't know about the gas but I'd like to speak to a doctor about it."

"Why don't you send Billy to see him?"

"Now that's a silly question, Blue, you knowing his reputation almost better than I do. He's the local tearaway. Besides

Billy, you and I are men of dignified common sense. He'd never go. He might say he'd go. But he'd have to be dying to get him near a doctor. Anyway, is the doctor an all-right bloke? Would he talk to me about it without seeing the patient?"

"I reckon. We'll have a couple more, go round to see him, to put your mind at rest, then have a bite to eat and settle down after a few more cool glasses to plan the festivities of the latter part of the day."

22

All his life Jim had known, in many ways, only the comfort of harsh extremes: the Track, the tented house, the shack, the station house of minimum comforts. Sleeping out nights, at Five Mile Camp, on the rock ledge near his cave which he had played in since a child and which held wonderful Dreamtime secrets for him was, in other ways, the most comfort he had known. But it was still comfort of the outdoors. The war, in that final officers' mess in the Flying Corps at the front, had in many ways given him more of what other people see as traditional comforts than any previous accommodation. Not that he would ever swap his beautiful Five Mile Camp for anything; no sir. That was his home and his secret place, with its rocks and waterfalls and wild flowers and purple hills and mists and plains off in the distance and the salmon-colored earth and the young roos and wallabies bounding softly down to drink at night, quiet yet furtive for the crocodile as they drank at the water. He would never swap that for anything, no sir, no matter what.

But on this day, when he saw the doctor's house, just on the edge of town, it looked like a haven to him and the nearest thing to his idea of home he had ever seen. Just looking at the place from the outside, he believed, told him a lot about the people who inhabited it. Despite the onset of the Dry, bougainvillaea was strewn all around the place, an aged but nicely painted white timber home on stilts. But the stilts were covered with white latticework, crisscrossed, with all the reds and whites and purples of the bougainvillaea popping through, and this, with the red poincianas, yellow allamanda bells, and fragile red frangipani, made it look as if the house were a house of flowers, with just little bits of neat timber and windows and gently pointed roof here and there. But even the roof appeared part of some wonderful, lazy, happy garden with banana palms greening its edges and lapping the veranda and, in the garden, tamarind trees, kingfisher ferns, oleander, orchids, and, on the ornamental ponds, lilies, everywhere that ubiquitous, most beautiful Northern Territory water lily, purple and mauve-pink and every other shade between blue mixed with red so that you thought there must be a thousand varieties of the color purple alone. But the highlight, near the house, was a stand of pink lotuses, so tall they would have reached Jim's shoulder, tall and clumped together, their leaves thick and green and rich and huge, like some dark green inverted cabbage leaf, and beside them, stemming up into the sunlight like upturned crinolined triangles of pink, were the flowers themselves.

Bluey saw Jim taking it all in and read his mind, which on many things in the Outback was simple for one bushman to do to another if one remembered that first, last and always, as Beth had discovered so long ago on the train, everything in this part of the world was related back to water. First and foremost on any bushman's mind would have been *Where does he get his water?* Blue would have been disappointed, in fact, if this had not been what Jim was thinking as they walked in silent admiration up the flight of wooden stairs. But it was, and when Bluey said, "Underground stream, permanent underground stream on the property," Jim just nodded and said, "Of course," and they rang the bell and presently the door opened.

No one could have anticipated that this haven, inhabited by the kindliest of men, could house such bad news for Jim.

Bluey could not even have anticipated it, though he was certainly part of it, for his reason for getting Jim around to the doctor's so promptly was indeed that he thought it might help solve their urgent problem for after-dinner company that night. Blue knew that the doctor, by reputation, had the prettiest daughter in town. Nothing much was known of her in Darwin, for she had spent most of her life away at boarding schools in the South. But she had just finished school, was eighteen and a half, and, so the sewing circle said, according to Bluey's mum, ripe for the picking. This phrase had slightly more weight to it in Darwin's tropical climate and Barbary Coast days than in certain other places at different times.

Now Bluey knew that the doctor's daughter, Lisa, was not for him. But Bluey was bush smart and city-street smart, too, and realistic about his own prospects and those of his friends. He knew that his tall mate, Carlyon, with his rich, smooth black hair, parted and straight, with just the hint of curling over the ears, with his suntan and his enormous bush vitality and unusual amount of book education when he let it show, would be just the ticket for the prettiest girl in town, if the deal was packaged in the right way: and Blue reckoned he was good at packaging things. Had not his father struck gold? Bluey had learned a lot from his old man. So he'd package Carlyon and himself in together and he'd settle for the girlfriend. She was bound to have a girlfriend. As Lisa opened the door to her father's surgery, Bluey believed he could hear Carlyon's engine murmuring and smiled at the prospects of his golden package for the night. It is doubtful whether on this day, in this flower-bower setting, with this blond angel standing in the sunlight, that Bluey would even have admitted ever hearing of the saying that all that glitters is not gold, or Jim, for his part, would have admitted knowing the bush saying that there is no such thing as a beautiful-looking crocodile.

Bluey stepped in right from the start, rubbing his chubby hands, as essential to his talking as his mouth, rubbing them round and round, rolling one around the other, somewhat in the manner of an early Territory undertaker, or the first used-car salesman caught without a handkerchief to polish his product.

"Ah, Miss Stewart, what a pleasant surprise. I'm Brian Byrne, Patrick Byrne's son, known to your father, I believe, and this is my friend, James Carlyon, from the famous pioneering family who founded the Back of Beyond station, known for its fine cattle."

The girl at the head of the stairs had remained quiet all this time, looking Bluey up and down. Jim stood staring. Her hair was very, very blond and long and she had a soft caramel skin and tan and big, oval brown eyes, which seemed moist to him in that light. She wore loose cotton slacks, beautifully made, like some Jim had seen in the windows in Paris; her blouse was soft pastel silk, with two top buttons undone, as if burst with the stress of her large, tight breasts, and giving her a carefree, reckless look. There was something of this careless toss of budding strength as, having eyed Bluey, until he introduced Jim into the conversation, she turned, or rather threw her gaze in Jim's direction, looking him up and down, but rather quicker than she had Bluey, and then said,

"So you've come to see my father, then?"

She said it so quickly, Bluey was almost lost for words. But Jim had been thinking as well as looking, and afterward he was not sure whether it was her particular phrasing or just an accident of desire which caused him to reply, in a manner perhaps too forward for those times:

"I think we've come to see you both, Miss Stewart." His voice was soft and low and polite and determined. She half turned, hesitating for a moment as if she might walk off apparently insulted, but at the same moment looking back at Jim again, as if admiring his coolness, seeing perhaps in him a sense of presence and self-possession such as her own. At any rate she chose to put on the most pleasant of smiles as she turned back to Bluey and said,

"Of course our families are old friends, Mr. Byrne, and it's a pleasure to meet you and your friend. I've been rather out of touch with things, spending so much time down South—"

Bluey might have been shot down in the middle of his first sentence but he was recovering fast now and certainly not going to miss a cue like that.

"Well, as a matter of fact, Jim and I have been off to the war and are a little out of touch ourselves. We were intending to dine with my father and then take a stroll around town. We have some excellent mud crabs and it just occurred to me that you—and a friend for company—might like to join us if you're a little out of touch, too."

It was a plausible, perfectly timed masterstroke. Bluey had recaptured the ground magnificently, thought Jim, until he saw the smile on the girl's face and wondered whose plan this really had been and who had captured what territory.

"Why, what a delightful idea, Mr. Byrne. They tell me you have one of the best views in Darwin. I'm sure that would be all right if a friend came, too. You're sure it wouldn't inconvenience your parents?"

"Not at all, Miss Stewart. Not at all. As a matter of fact, my mother's away in Sydney and my father likes a good table. I'm sure he'll be delighted. We'll call for you, of course."

She smiled in a way that, when Jim was to reflect on it later, on so many of these times, almost conveyed a sense of accomplishment. She smiled and nodded, without directly replying, as if just accepting that that was the way it would be, and then said,

"Well, now, I suppose I'd better get you into the waiting room."

They went inside to a relatively cool house, cool with the stream underneath it and the flowers, a house as comfortable on the inside as the out. It was richly decorated in what Jim recognized from books as antiques: rich grained woods, and old, old and elegant, quite different from the rawer timbers and furniture he was used to. There were wonderful oil paintings in gold frames on the walls and a thick Persian rug on the floor, like some he had seen overseas and knew to be expensive. The floor boards which bordered the rug were deeply and meticulously polished and beside the brown leather armchairs in the waiting room were Queen Anne tables, probably of rosewood, piled with British magazines.

Lisa had left them as soon as she had shown them in and presently the surgery door opened and a short, thin man with gray hair and spectacles and the wisp of a smile said in the quietest of voices, "Come in, won't you?" His body was small and compact but light-framed and bending as he patted rolled wooden armchairs for the two young men to sit in, moving around his surgery to his rolltop desk beside the window, scattered with medical books and magazines and slips of paper and a tobacco jar and pipes in a drinking glass. Because the desk was beside the wall and anyway too tall for him ever to see over, he skewed his chair around and looked at the two of them and said with a kindly smile, the smile and his quietness and gentleness which made all but just a few words unnecessary and which Jim would always remember him for,

"Now, boys, what can I do for you?"

Jim explained about Billy's cough and his concern and that he didn't think he could persuade him to come himself.

The doctor kept leaving silences, or nodding, so that Jim kept on explaining a little more, as much as he knew, when it had happened, how long Billy had been hospitalized, what the doctors at the front had said and so on. In the end, the little doctor had the lot, or as much as Jim knew, without having spoken a word. Jim intuitively realized this and noted it as the sort of expert silence which a bushman prizes so much. Now the doctor spoke, very low and slowly:

"Of course it would be better if I could see him. But it doesn't sound like a bad case and it may not affect him at all. Keep an eye on him and if it gets worse let me know. If he catches anything, are you far from a telegraph station?"

"Pretty close. About a hundred miles."

Jim saw the doctor smile.

"Just a before-breakfast canter, Mr. Carlyon, like your father?"

"Something like that. You knew him, then?"

"Only by reputation."

Jim nodded.

"Well," said the doctor, "let's say you'll telegraph me if you get concerned and then wait at the station until I telegraph an answer."

His friendly tone indicated that he had finished what it was necessary to say, and that he'd talked a little more than normal.

Jim felt relieved. At least the doctor had not ordered pills or a mixture or insisted on seeing Billy. It couldn't be too bad. And now he knew who to come to if Billy got worse.

"I'll pay you now, if that's convenient," he said, thanking the doctor as he stood up.

The doctor just smiled as he opened the door.

"I never charge ex-servicemen, Mr. Carlyon," he said. "Good day, gentlemen."

Jim paused, wanting to ask if there was more he knew about his father, yet sensing the doctor would not tell him: at least not yet. So he simply said, "Good day, Doctor, and thanks for everything," as the doctor, his smile almost a happy, elfish grin in the narrowing door opening, nodded and then shut the door.

"Some bloke," said Blue, as they showed themselves out.

"You can say that again."

"Not a bad day's work, so far, you might say, and the best is yet to come," Bluey answered.

They were back in the sun and walking again now and Jim looked back at the house and then at Bluey.

"And you can say that again, too, Blue. I think I'm about to take a ride on the rainbow."

"Which one's that, mate?"

"The magic rainbow, so the Aboriginals say."

"You're pretty big on all their Dreamtime stuff, aren't you?"

"When it suits me. And it sure explains how good I feel today. You know that saying, 'This is the first day of the rest of your life'?"

"Sure do."

"Well, that's how I feel. I just realized the war is over, Blue. Just realized it now. We're home and we're in one piece and this is the twentieth bloody century of cars and airplanes and machines and progress and I've been worrying about the property and not realizing that this isn't only the beautiful last frontier, this is the last frontier of opportunity. I'm going to take this bloody land of opportunity by the balls and stamp my mark on it from here to the Back of Beyond and back."

"I'll drink to that. Let's find a pub."

They found another of the few hotels in town and set themselves up at the bar for a counter lunch and some beers, and talked of the war, and the future, and dreamed the dreams and talked the talks that are reserved for special times and special places when the future is still tomorrow and not yet today.

23

They had a wonderful evening. Jim, sitting in borrowed suit, shirt and tie, realized how little he knew, despite all his reading, of the luxuries of life, or rather of the things money could buy, for he had certainly never missed them. Yet in the presence of Lisa, perhaps because she handled them with such effortless ease, he began to feel them important. With her hair swept up and her semiformal dress, she looked like his imagined pictures of Louis XIV courtesans, though he was not sure he fully understood what that word meant. She sat on Bluey's father's right, and Patrick Byrne, a self-educated, self-made man of wide experience, staggered Jim with his detailed knowledge of every subject imaginable. Jim thought he himself knew a great deal. He knew nothing. This man knew more about airplanes, more about cars, more about machinery and the goings on in the world than Jim began to know.

But it was a salutary lesson and not lost on Jim, for his bush mechanism of learning, of picking up here and there and from everybody, of watching and listening and learning, took it all in. Of course his sense of cunning was as acute as ever, and although his experience of women was fairly limited, he believed he understood why Miss Stewart spent her time being enthralled by the conversation of her host, and almost ignoring Jim, who was on her right, with Bluey and the girlfriend opposite. The other girl was a cousin, the daughter of the doctor's sister, and she was quite tiny, and quite quiet, but with very warm, lively blue eyes and a generous smile, as if she were very at peace with herself and at ease with others. She had a tiny round face, a few freckles and midbrown hair.

She and Bluey were getting on very well. She was not pretty, but she had something, almost a wide-eyed wonderment in her face that certainly gave her beauty. Jim talked across the table to her a lot, not only because he liked her, but because although he was outclassed in this company, he rarely lost his sense of self-assurance, or confidence, or whatever, and he may not have tasted wine before, or seen as much hardware either side of the different plates that kept coming, but he was a hunter, a consummate hunter, and that's all this conversation on his left was about, his quarry was telling him she would not be easy game, so he talked to the girlfriend opposite. Of course Bluey did a great deal of talking, too, a great deal, which kept making the quietish girl, Katrina, whom they called Kat, laugh a lot. Bluey also kept leaning across the table with the wine bottle in a most unmannerly way, and saying to Jim, "Have some more plonk me, China, it's not bad booze."

Jim knew he was doing it deliberately to bait his father, in a half-jocular fashion, and his father kept glaring at him each time he said it, and once, good-naturedly, stopped and said,

"My son is somewhat of an expert at the Australian idiom, ladies, or so he would have us believe. In case the subtlety of that last one escaped you, it translates thus: 'China is an abbreviation of China Plate, rhymes with . . .' he paused as if the use of the word were slightly distasteful to him . . . 'rhymes with—mate.' As a matter of fact the China Plate idiom is British in origin—not Australian, although I confess to understanding little of the rest."

Kat said she found it amusing.

Lisa touched the back of Mr. Byrne's right hand, on the table, saying, "I do sympathize, Mr. Byrne . . . sometimes it must be quite hard to understand," yet she spoke it with one of those quiet, accomplished smiles of hers, looking at Bluey and then Jim, in turn, with her wet, wistful, confident look, as if to portray that she understood their position, too.

"You're right, Lisa," said Bluey, who was liberally oiled by now and well past the "Miss Stewart" stage, "you're right," he said, breaking another mud crab out of its shell with his hands, scoffing it, dipping into the fingerbowl and drinking half a mouthful of wine from a rather overthumbed glass in between each snatch of conversation. "You're right, Lisa, it is quite hard to understand, but it has some fine lyrical nuances, even in some of its coarser aspects, quite apart from historical derivations. But I wouldn't have said that on the whole it was any harder to understand than the vocabulary you learn at ladies' boarding schools in the South."

His father glared at him, but in a way that also conveyed a sense of pride in his son. Lisa dabbed her lips with her starched table napkin, smiling assuredly back with, "Oh, indeed, that is interesting."

But Jim rather thought it was score one for Bluey and, more importantly, thought that he had discovered a chink in the lady's armor. She was very good, damn good at games. But she had just demonstrated a tendency toward slightly slow recovery from full frontal attack. Jim began to plan his campaign.

After the port and coffee, for which they stayed at table, Patrick Byrne excused himself, saying the car and driver were at their disposal and he hoped they'd enjoy their tour of the town.

Bluey took them everywhere: to the dance halls, the bars, the views from the cliff and finally, always the place of greatest interest, Little Canton, the Chinese Quarter: alive—or dead —with Chinese and Aboriginal prostitutes hardly turned thirteen, with cockfights and fan-tan games and thick, hooded smoke of a thousand dirty pipes clenched in a thousand decaying mouths of yellowed opium teeth, pigtails and joss and Chinee laughter and despair. There were cattlemen from the Track, con men in silk suits from the South, drovers and buffaloers and dingo shooters. There were the smart town set, such as they themselves would have qualified for that night; fishermen, camel drivers, South Seas sailors, miners in from Pine Creek, Malay and Japanese pearlers and a few nondescript locals.

When they had seen it all, Bluey suggested a drink back at his place. It was still not late so the girls agreed. The house was lit up but quiet downstairs and they sat on the back veranda drinking Bluey's father's champagne from fluted crystal glasses with long stems. The night air was soft and warm. The Arafura Sea sluiced in below with its mixed Indian and Pacific ocean waters. Kat had shown some interest earlier in Mr. Byrne's fine collection of paintings and after a time Bluey took her indoors to show her.

Thus left alone, it seemed the natural thing for Jim and Lisa to walk. Presently they were at the edge of the cliff where they saw a path that led down to the beach. Jim looked questioningly at Lisa. It was still part of the hunting game. Each had been playing it all night one way or another: Lisa with the most delicious, well-timed wisps of conversation, conveying all the emotional intonations of a subtle and hidden voluptuous savoir faire, Jim with all the quietness and stealth of the stalker.

Anyway, she nodded as if it were of no account, and they began their descent. The conversation fell to swimming, which seemed quite natural, there being so much water about, and neither could quite remember afterward who started it, though Jim suspected it was Lisa with one of her throwaway lines, such as, "Do you swim much out there in the bush, Mr. Carlyon?" He recalled she had used "Mr. Carlyon," so it must have been her, using it as if to dampen down any sexual suggestiveness that might accompany the mention of swimming. But it was there nonetheless—of course it was. They both knew it and played with it mentally, the way so much conversation is submerged libido dancing in words.

"A lot," he answered. "A lot in the billabongs and water

holes, and there is a beautiful spring at a place called Five
Mile Camp. But you know, I've never swum in salt water."

"Never? Not even in Egypt?"

"Never. We always seemed to be at the wrong place at the
wrong time."

"Of course. I'm afraid I've never swum in fresh water.
Strange, isn't it?"

"Not really," said Jim, as they reached the sand and he
automatically sat to take off his shoes. She stood staring for a
moment and then sat on a rock nearby.

"I'm sorry," he said, "I should have thought. Would you like
to go back?"

"No . . ." she said rather overslowly as if half-thinking
aloud. "No," she said, "I rather think you need the walk. If
you'll just move a little away, I'll take off my shoes and
stockings."

"Of course," he said, his shoes and socks off now so that he
walked a few yards along the sand and turned to look out to
sea. He was unused to all this and felt a little awkward,
awkward enough to say, as she came up to him holding her
shoes and handing him her stockings squeezed into a little
ball to put in his pocket, "I'm sorry," saying it for the second
time within a few seconds, the words he hardly ever said. Yet
her words had really brought out his. Somewhere in that
sentence of hers she had dropped the pretense and thought of
him. There was no maneuvering in her saying that she
thought he needed the walk; there was an understanding of
his need for the fresh air and the openness of the beach after
the stifling and oppressive nature of the town.

They walked for a long time until finally Lisa agreed she
needed to stop and rest. Jim had asked her several times,
with the great civility now of an Outback man to a woman in
the Outback, with the overconcern of the strong for the weak
as it were, or at least that was how Lisa saw it and smiled
because it was so nice that she had unwittingly let her guard
down and found that her openness and honesty had been the
way into this strange man's heart, rather than all her
coquettish games, which she so often despised in herself and
yet most of the time was so unable to avoid.

As they stopped by some rocks and Jim led her over into the shadows of the shore away from the beach moonlight, he stopped and held her in front of him for just a moment, so that as they stopped their damp bare feet touched and he kissed her lightly on the forehead and then put his arm around her almost in a brother-sister manner and walked her to a rock and sat her down.

None of this was going according to plan for Lisa. None of it at all. She regarded herself as experienced. She had been the most popular girl in her school and although she had never allowed a boy to enter her, because of the conventions of the time to which even she was prone, because of the abject fear of conception, she had had many stolen darknesses in the school garden, in the dusty, cedar-paneled attic rooms which every school has hidden away as if for young love to experiment in: she had tasted the harsh and soft salivaed kisses, had known the hurried rush and rub of part undressing, the throbbing touching and wet surprise of puberty passing like a shadow outside the window, and known each time when buttoned and hooked again that these things were ecstasy, however forbidden, and one day she would not be able to deny their proper fulfillment. She had set her eighteenth birthday for her coming out and had waited six months for the right person and had turned on the porch that morning and thought to herself, *Yes, yes, indeed,* but now she was not sure because earlier she had wanted to be roughly taken and possessed, and would have been, she was sure, if she had not let her guard down, which was most unlike her, and been kind and understanding, if only for a moment, so that he had responded. So that she now sat on the rock, silent, confused, so confused that despite all the dates set for her coming out she showed herself not only a child but also a prisoner of her generation as she reverted to type, as the restraint of society inbuilt in her tempestuous and erratic nature took hold of her again like a changeable wind. She shifted irritably on the rock where she sat. He came over and sat beside her, taking her hand rather tentatively, as though the physical contact were no more than a continuation of the comradeship they had experienced as they had walked. But even as he began to think this, he knew it was not so, felt his desire regenerating itself, felt the past of chasing his black female playmates around their nude rock pool coming back at him now, no longer called boyish fun, but called desire, articulating itself now, so that suddenly, without either of them realizing it fully, the tables were turned. Lisa had become the hunted, and as he kissed her first tenderly and then harshly, her confusion became fear and her fear, desire and confusion again. Then Jim's hand was at her top, one hand there and the other pushing down hard over the outside of her dress, so that she gave a little cry, a vulnerable cry, so that both drew back, the salt of anxiety and wanting alive in their drying mouths as they paused, both gasping.

There was no mistaking Jim's intent. And had she not earlier wanted to be roughly taken and possessed? But this was not how it was supposed to be. She was supposed to have been orchestrating the noble possession of her. Now he did really want to have her the way she had wanted, but he was doing the doing, even now as his hand went gently down and under her dress to the inside of her leg. His gentleness confused her even more. Her stomach was heaving with anxiety as the conflict between her inhibitions and her driving urges pulled her so much this and that way that she said with almost a challenging truculence,

"If you want to make love to me you'll have to marry me." She almost surprised herself to hear the words and was not sure she really meant them at the time and she was annoyed when *he* said, "I'm not sure that's a condition I can meet or agree with, but I'll not try to force you," so that she found herself saying again, almost as if she were a passenger in her own conversation at the time, "Oh, all right then, let's have a swim. I've got to do something or I'll go crazy."

She was sorry their moment of intimate honesty had passed, and felt that it might not have come had it not been for her, that he was all prepared to take her against her will if necessary, which was what she had really wanted, so she could pretend to herself and her upbringing that she had had no say in it, no say in it at all. Now although the easy closeness had gone, the hunting-of-quarry mood was gone, too. But they did swim, and they did come together in the water and touch in nice ways. Later on the beach they hunched together on the rocks, drying in the warm night air, with Lisa overly self-conscious of her nakedness at first, until he started to tell her stories of the spring and rocks around Five Mile Camp again, and how he and his black sister playmates all dried themselves on the rocks there, and the high rise of desire in both of them had slipped back once more into the sublimation of gentle friendship as they dressed and took hands and walked slowly back up the cliff.

As they walked, each wondered if they would live to regret the moment not taken.

24

Bluey found Jim early next morning sitting at the base of the cliff having a prebreakfast smoke.

"Christ, you get up early, or have you been here all night?"

"Just arrived. Hope you didn't mind me borrowing the car last night to take Lisa home?"

"Oh, did you? Not at all. Didn't know you could drive, though. Just left the keys in it after I'd taken Kat home in case one of you could."

"Learnt in France. Had to do everything over there. If someone was coming in for a crash landing—as most of us were half the time—his mates often had to drive the Model T ambulance or fire car."

"Huh-huh. How'd it go?"

"She's an unusual lady."

"You can say that again."

"What about you and Kat?"

"Good company. Warmhearted. You seem a bit far away, though. You're not in love, are you, mate?"

Bluey had intended it as a humorous aside but Jim then started quite seriously to recount the events of the previous night, including a conversation that had taken place in the garden of Lisa's place after Jim took her home. Jim said it had been good fun until then, and he'd enjoyed himself. But when they got to her place, she'd taken him down to a seat at the bottom of the garden and they'd sat there holding hands and kissing, and gently touching a long time, so that both started to know they felt something deep and real for each other.

"I hadn't really taken her mention of marriage very seriously earlier, Blue, and in a way I don't think she had either—it was almost more an excuse for saying that she wanted to make love but something wouldn't let her. Anyway, we're in the garden, and it's getting pretty late by this stage: we've been sitting and talking and kissing and caressing and being very natural with each other like we were earlier in the evening for a while, which she says she finds quite hard to do. So we're sitting there, and she's been asking me about the Back of Beyond, and I've told her that you were joking about our spread and really we were all very poor out there and we talk some more and feel pretty good and I'm sort of telling her, not in so many words, you understand, that I like her more than most and kind of hinting that we ought to see each other a lot. And she ups and blurts out—and she's not looking at me, but at the ground, and I get the feeling that she's blushing, though I can't see her face properly—she blurts out as if she really means it this time, could we get married and go and live on the cattle station, that she'd like that, that nothing would matter if we could get married straightaway and have lots of kids and live on the property and be happy. Of course I say that I'm not sure happiness is quite that simple and I've got things to do and a name to make for myself before marriage slows me down and couldn't we be friends first for at least long enough to work out how we really feel. By this time she's got over the shyness or whatever it is, and it's like she was talking about what she was going to have for breakfast or something, though very serious, and she says if we don't get married right away, something will happen and we'll lose each other. She says it's very important to her because she doesn't feel she has to act like some sort of phony with me, but if I go back to the station and leave her she'll be the other sort of person again. What do you make of all that, Blue?"

"Too deep for me. How did you leave it?"

"Well, I'll tell you, Blue. I've been taught never to look a gift horse in the mouth. But I have also been taught to look before you leap. I've got enough responsibilities as it is. But I guess now I'll have to think about it for sure. I'll stay in town for a while, if that's all right with you, and try to work something out . . . try to get her to see reason. I mean I do like her."

Bluey nodded to say it was all right to stay as long as he liked and then added, "You love her, Red?"

"You know, everyone always says do you love someone, as if that's automatically a feeling you should know about and be able to recognize and . . . like in some bloody stupid books where they say . . . well, if you don't know, then you can't love her, because if you did, you'd know . . . well, I think that's all bull. All I know is that it's fun to be with her and it's like galloping wild 'cause she's a bit wild and also I feel very tender and protective towards her. But I don't know if that's love."

"Sounds like a pretty good imitation to me and it's not exactly a bad offer. Ever wonder if you think about things too much?"

"Never. Was brought up to. Must be one jump ahead all the way—that's the Bush Code and that requires thinking all the time."

"Ever occur to you that nothing's ever perfect—perhaps not even your Bush Code?"

"It's stood me in good stead," he said. It was only the strength of their friendship that stopped Jim being openly angry. Bluey could see this, but went on:

"But perhaps there's a place where it leaves off? Perhaps sometimes things should just happen?"

"You're more easygoing than I am, Blue. You can afford to be."

Bluey did not take offense. "You're right. I've had it pretty easy from the time I was about ten. You're right. Want a piece of advice from a mate, though?"

"Why not?"

"Marry the girl. Marry her as soon as possible. Otherwise you might live to regret it."

"And of course it is equally as true that if I do marry her, particularly this quickly, I might live to regret it. It's like saying—"

"OK, I know, I'll say it for you. . . . I've heard it so many times I could recite it in my sleep. . . . It's like the famous bush saying which your old man always used to teach you. . . . 'How do you know a crocodile is really a pet or not? . . . You don't know until—'"

"Exactly right."

"But that doesn't make it right in every case. I'm trying to get through your thick head that a lot of your bloody bush sayings don't *automatically* just fit. We're talking about a beautiful young lady . . . the pick of the bunch . . . the belle of the fair . . . the doctor's pride and joy . . . the envy of the town—"

"Let's get some breakfast," Jim said moodily.

"You haven't lost your touch," Blue said, as they got up and started back.

"How's that, Blue?"

"At letting a man know when the conversation is over."

They had hardly finished breakfast but there was the sound of a very loud banging of the knocker on the front door.

"I'll go," Bluey said to the Chinese servant pouring the last of the second cups of tea.

The noise was so loud, urgent and prolonged that Jim rose, too, and followed Bluey.

At the front door, breathless, and with her father's car still idling at the bottom of the steps, stood Lisa.

"What on earth's wrong?" Jim shouted before Bluey had a chance to speak.

"My father sent me to fetch you and said will you please come quickly? There's been a telegraph from down the Track and someone is terribly ill."

Jim's mind recoiled, thinking immediately of Billy.

"It's my kid brother," he shouted, "I'll come immediately."

His senses were clouded and he started to run out the door and down the steps toward the stable but as he passed Lisa he saw, in a blur, that she was shaking her head and putting out her hand to stop him and he had automatically chopped down with his hand to push her away when he heard her cry of pain as he connected, and the message of her shaking head reached his brain and he stopped, turning back toward her. She was bent over holding her arm in agony but managed to say, "It's a baby, a one-year-old baby at Top Springs and he's got scrub typhus by the sound of the telegraph and Daddy says will you please ride like the devil with some pills"—she paused drawing breath heavily—"and so help me if you ever get back you'll never touch me again."

"I'll be back," he said.

"Oh, God, I do hope so," she said desperately, handing him the sulfur tablets. "I hope to God so, for my father was in two minds to ask you and I persuaded him and it was only then that he told me that the reason he was reluctant was because with last year and this being so dry, you'll have to break your father's record of hours without water to survive."

Jim smiled and kissed her on the temple. "I'll be back," he said.

"You know where Top Springs is?" she said disbelievingly.

"Oh, yes, I know all right. It's at the end of the Murranji Track."

25

Within the hour he had changed and provisioned and refused Bluey's offer of company because he could travel faster and one rider would use less water; within that hour he had done this and left a dejected Bluey and a pleading-not-to-go-now-please Lisa and saddled the snorting, champing Firecracker who could smell the challenge of dust and distance like any racetrack stayer, and ridden off at a cracking pace. And the taste of excitement and the threat of death the hourglass held was with him, and his beloved horse and countryside, and would stay at elbow and flank and side until the last water hole was passed and the job done or not done, and then would haunt him all over again as, or if, having crossed one way, he managed to make it back.

The trouble with this journey was that it was quite unlike any other: a mercy dash was a very different kettle of fish because you had to throw a lot of your Bush Code protection plans away. Things like planning your start at a certain time of day, resting cunningly, spelling your horse the way it should be spelled, so many of these things would have to be thrown away if he was to have any chance of getting the sulfur tablets there on time to be of any use at all in saving the baby's life. But he must use all the cunning he had, nevertheless. He must still be cautious in what he did throw away—what parts of caution he threw out on the windless plain—or he would not survive at all. He would have to break the Murranji record of his father all right, but he would have to break it cautiously to survive. He would need all the lessons his father had taught him, and Jacky, and then some of his own, and then all the luck in the world. He would have to keep his mind off Lisa and his mind on the job, though she kept haunting him, her body fragrances riding up at him from the warm country he rode on and his memories of the night.

But the Murranji. . . ! Nothing mattered but the Murranji and it could take him five days and short nights to get there, for he had brought a hurricane lantern with him and would ride the trail at night, five days and short nights, or perhaps four if he was lucky to get to Newcastle Waters where the Track took off from the main Track, Stuart's Track, the great North-South route of a thousand different shades and surfaces, from the hard desert gibbers, stones worn as smooth as ocean pebbles by the wind and sand, from these gibbers to the softest sand. He knew he would pray for these surfaces before he was through with the Murranji; he had never ridden it before but he knew he would pray for the worst surfaces he had ever encountered rather than the 140 miles of desert corridor they called the Murranji; he had never ridden it but he knew every inch of it in his mind's eye as his father had told him about it. He had never been along it because his father said a man only rode it if he had need, real need, and he kept his son from it. It could save a man 1000 miles as a shortcut, 140 miles instead of 1000, literally, but you never used it unless you had to, and every time you gambled with your life and the lives of your men and cattle.

Just then Red heard a train whistle and it startled him both in its sound and the registration of his stupidity it caused. He was not used to trains and had not thought to check the schedule. The Pine Creek Mines train, my God, that was a hundred miles saved, or near enough, a hundred miles of rest for him and his animal at a good steady speed.

He turned his horse, the red-mixed roan, frothing and

gurling and snorting effortlessly as if he knew this train was no challenge for his best speed, no challenge at all for Firecracker. So the rider Big Red turned his red roan off the track and over the salmon earth of the near country and soon met the line and the train a little ahead and easily brought it within reach. Red kept the animal at full bore until they reached the cabin and flagged down the driver, who did not hesitate to stop, for flagging down anyone or anything in the bush, any sort of unusual signal, is read as trouble and immediate action taken, for the bushies know a life may depend on it, and the community acts as one, for tomorrow it could be your life someone is riding to save. So the train stopped and Red explained his mission and the driver jumped down and opened the planked side of one van and helped Red jump the horse up, and then himself, and in a trice was back in the cabin and piling on steam in a way that made Red proud, for he had not asked for it, but the driver was an old, gray gnarlhead, a lifetime Territorian for sure, and he would make the train do its best, cracking on pace like a head ringer, a stockman, cracks his long whip over the heads of his mob of cattle.

They made Pine Creek by the night and Red, rested and having eaten and his horse refreshed, said his grateful thanks and took time only to water before he was off again, his horse watered and two of his four canvas water bags full, hoping that this would be enough, hoping for reasonable water at least until he got to Newcastle Waters where he must turn off for the Murranji. But it was dry, so dry already, the second of bad Dries and threatening to be worse than the previous year which had been so deadly costly. But he had only filled two bags so far, for every ounce of lighter load counted and made as much difference to speed as those extra little lead weights made to racing horses, such a small weight over such a short distance, yet so significant. But he had decided, as he changed quickly back at Bluey's, that he must take four water bags for the Murranji and God and the devil knew that four bags were not even one decent drink for his horse, not one decent drink.

He reached Newcastle Waters in three and a half days, or

three and three-quarters to be precise, as he had secretly hoped to do, and arriving at night.

He would rest his horse four hours, and sleep himself four hours, and be away before dawn, by the light of his lantern, traveling the easiest stretch of the first 20 miles by night and ready to take on the worst 120 miles in the world for man or beast at the break of day. By any standards at all 140 miles was considered a two-day ride in what was called straight bush. Over difficult country, or bloody impossible country such as the Murranji, no one in his right mind would try to do the 140 miles in two days. But Red had determined he must cover the last 120 miles from dawn of the one day to dawn of the next if he was to survive if, as he expected, he found no water at all along the Murranji. For this was the Murranji's dreaded secret: at the best of times it had but a little surface water; at the worst of times it had none, absolutely none— none to be dug for and hardly a water-filled frog besides, though the water hole, if it could be called that, from which the Track took its name, was the Aboriginal word for frog.

There were, technically, three watering spots along the Murranji. Twenty miles in was the first of the three supposed watering spots which the pioneer drovers called the Bucket, after a leather bucket than an early drover had left there, and because that was about as much water as you were likely to find at the best of times: it sounded a colorful name to some; it was deathly bleak Outback humor at its worst. Indeed the Murranji was full of such things, like a wheelbarrow in a tree, left as a reminder by those who found the body of a man from the Centre who had determined to walk it with a big barrel of water in a wheelbarrow. It had seemed simple; it was not. So there were such grisly reminders, and Red knew where and when to look for them and that when he saw them he must spur himself on. Of course he'd been told, too, that each year added additional memorabilia of death: it was nothing to see just a boot on the track, or a belt, or a bleached bone. There were fifteen known graves.

So Red had started out, by hurricane lamp light, taking it first at an easy trot, for he was allowing five hours for the twenty miles, five hours to dawn, and then nineteen hours from there, a total of twenty-four, and six hours under his father's record of thirty. But his father had found water at the actual Murranji water hole in the middle of the journey. If this was dry, as Red expected it might well be, then he believed he must get in within the twenty-four hours, or as close to as possible, to survive. There would be water at Top Springs; this was permanent water and never dry. But what he was facing at this time of year was the dreaded of dread prospects which made the Murranji so infamous and gave to it the name of Death Track: there might be no water at all, not one single drop of it, for the whole 140 miles.

Plenty, of course, who did not know the Track, might have argued for traveling more by night than he planned, out of the heat of day, but such statements were ignorant and made by people who had only seen the start of the Track, where he was traveling now, by moonlight and lamplight, the easy stage, with the gentle padding trotting of the horse on easy surface and the benign coolabah tree, important because of its shade spread and because its growth on inland plains usually meant water under the surface for at least part of the year.

But even as he thought this, the coolabahs were thinning now and the earth beneath was hardening and he knew soon he would be at the Bucket and then, as light lifted, into what lay beyond. Twenty hours for 120 miles was 6 miles per hour, and he hoped to pick up on this average to allow some spelling, which he surely must, though at the front of his brain, at the very front and coolest part, the part which must remain cool however hot the sun, he knew that when in doubt he must keep moving, moving, pushing on and moving man and beast, yes, even until his beloved Firecracker dropped, if necessary, if that would bring him and the tablets within safe walking distance of Top Springs. He dreaded it but it might come to that and he must face that mentally now, that if it came to that he must leave Firecracker at the escarpment descent to Top Springs and go on the last ten miles on foot. He had known this, too, and carried always, as part of his bushman's swag, a small corked bottle of arsenic to give the animal to drink, for the ride was such that the weight of a gun would be deadly.

So he had only this and his knife at his belt, and what coolness he could keep in his head, as he pulled his wide-brimmed slouch hat down now, his wide-brimmed felt hat, the Light Horse Regiment hat, still with the feathers of that fastest of all ostrichlike birds, the emu, in his hatband as he rode up to the Bucket and saw what lay beyond, saw that what they said was true, it was a corridor of spikes, as well as bleached out deathly desert.

He rested for a moment at the Bucket and saw that it was dry. He was not surprised. A bucket evaporated quickly. It did not mean that the second water hole, the Murranji itself, would necessarily be dry. His father had found a nose bag full there in his dry record year. And if the Murranji, fifty miles on from the Bucket, was dry, then like as not Yellow Holes would be dry, too. Yellow Holes, named for its dry, sulfurous claypans, was another fifty miles beyond Murranji. Then from the Yellow, it was ten miles more to the Jump Up, which was where the Track jumped up and then started down through the escarpment for ten miles. There was no water at the Jump Up, never.

And then there was the corridor of spikes. As Red looked down, out, through and along it now, as the sun rimmed up, he knew that this particular sort of bush, this bush of no name, unique in all the world, was the final dreaded coffin nail of the Murranji. On either side, for more than a hundred miles, on either side of the Track except for the brief outbreak of the three water holes, stood something like boxthorn, yet bigger and more twisted and more deadly and, eerily, in the middle of the desert, black—dead black. It wrapped itself in twisted, gnarling shrouds for a hundred miles along the Track and up to fifty miles deep on either side of the Murranji, the dread of man and beast. Cattle which took fright could become hopelessly impaled so they had to be destroyed. So could a horse. So, too, a man. For the Murranji was full of spook holes in the sand where the hard earth might give way suddenly to soft, and a hundred and one other specters of landscape and leftovers of man which could, as the dreaded heat delirium began to set in, give fright to the strongest.

Yet, with no water at the Bucket, with the corridor of harsh land between barbed-wire bushes, and with the cruel sun soon to be overhead, he felt that huge and terrible feeling that all real bushmen feel rise like the best of life and hope in his stomach and chest, that curious mixture of self-preservation and self-destruction which makes fear hope and hope fear, he felt all this now, knew it to be his moment of reckoning, but felt this thing bursting inside him, like the greatest joy he had ever felt, and started out, saying unconsciously half aloud to himself, as the sun came up, that it was a great day and great to be alive and you wouldn't be dead for quids, would you, as bushmen were always wont to say in the land only they loved.

There was one other very practical factor which hastened his speed as he gave the horse its head, knowing for the time at least it was safe to do so. Quite apart from all possible haste to try to save the baby's life, there was the fact that every hour of every day, every minute of every hour, dried out what water might be there. This, of course, was why records were set and broken. No one was stupid enough to try for the Murranji record. It was simply that, once committed, once past the Bucket, really, there was no turning back, and you raced to stay alive against every extra ray of the sun drying out every possible drop of water that might be left. His father had never ridden his record by choice either. His ride had been in the early days when there were still wild blacks in the largely unsettled area in the west of the Northern Territory where the Murranji led. The blacks had attacked his father's party while they were scouting for explorers. Only his father had got away, taking the little-known Murranji Track. Later he would occasionally use it at the better times of the year as a calculated risk. But no one took it in dry times by choice.

But now Red had taken it by choice, if that was the right

word, for the action had been reflex, automatic. He was a bushman first and last, and if you had a chance to save a life you took it, that was the code, for tomorrow it could be you.

He tried not to think of the heat; he tried no longer to think of the past deeds on the Track of his father and others. He concentrated on making his riding as easy on his horse as possible, as easy but as fast, and reading changes in terrain and on looking for anything, any sign at all that might help him.

They traveled fast and they traveled well and by 1:00 P.M. the horse and rider were approaching, or so it looked to him through the mirage heat, a break in the corridor, approaching Murranji itself. He was now thirteen hours out—five hours to the Bucket and a brief rest and eight hours to Murranji except for one brief stop by the Track to walk the horse down and chance one water bag with a mouthful for the rider and the rest in his pannikin for the horse. Thirteen hours into Murranji. Three and three-quarter days into Newcastle Waters, a record in itself, and now thirteen hours into Murranji, another record and no mistake, and soon he would be King of the Track. But as he caught himself saying it to himself, he had reined in and stopped and now he looked at the dead-gray-and-excrement-colored claypan known as Murranji, the frog hole, and knew that it was dry.

He untied another water bag and took two mouthfuls himself now and felt as if he had had none, his tongue already swollen, and he gave the rest of the water bag by pannikin to his horse and patted and walked him and rubbed him down with his khaki army handkerchief and said good things to him and fed him by hand half the oats he had brought in his saddlebag and then one of the two lumps of sugar, little enough, but strength and love for the horse who counted more than he did on any such ride. He looked at his watch. They had been stopped fifteen minutes and he knew now that they would find no water at Yellow Holes. He was dead tired already and he feared for his animal and dared not sit other than for a moment as he broke out some bully beef for himself, forcing it down dry as he walked and stretched and kept Firecracker at a slow walk, too. He found a pebble and put it in his mouth to roll around and make saliva as he swallowed a little salt to stop dehydration and put a lump on his hand for his horse to lick.

Then it was back into the saddle and off, off for the longest ride in his life. However much he hurried it would have that excruciating agony of hurried distance where everything seems elongated and slowed down in the heat, that slowing down of the mental processes also, so one must fight to stay alert and in the saddle, and not wander; that period during which one sees something on the landscape and thinks one has seen it before, and wonders if it is similar to something else or has one indeed seen it before, earlier that day, traveling in circles? He felt all this, though he knew there was little enough chance with the carcass-enclosing, death-watch bushes that guarded the no-man's Track.

But stiff and sore and noticing his horse slowing with every mile, he rode on, seeing the wheelbarrow in the straggly eucalypt tree, which might have been friendly among the spike scrub if it had not been for its grim reminder. Still, it was a landmark. He was nine miles from the Yellow. He looked at his watch and it told him what he feared: he'd averaged his six miles an hour to the halfway mark to Murranji, but now he had fallen behind. He and his sweat-flanked animal were down to five miles an hour. Still, he'd rested for half an hour at the frog hole with no water which named the Track. He'd walked Firecracker down in late afternoon and given him the third bag of water and abstained himself. One bag left. Thirty miles to go. It sounded so little distance. And there might yet be water at the Yellow. But he knew damn well that even water at the Yellow, however, good that might be, and however much it might increase their chances, did not guarantee success. Those last twenty miles would be killers. Both were dead tired, much more tired and dehydrated than even he realized. Whatever happened, they must do the last twenty miles on stamina. One mindless faltering and the desert deliriums, which he felt even now he was fighting, could take over, even at night, and send them off in a direction from which they would never return.

There was no water at the Yellow.

There would now be no more water once the last bag was gone. But he had decided in advance what he must do if this happened and he gave all the water to the horse, looking around quickly but seeing that the earth was so dry it would not be worth digging for a frog, even if he had time. Water, animals, men, in that order: that was the Outback priority. It was his best chance, he knew that. Even if he fainted forward in the saddle, his horse would keep on while he sensed his rider still alive.

The next ten miles into the setting sun were the worst of his life. He vomited down himself and then he dry-retched. But he kept awake, although at every step his pounding headache threatened to put him into that unconsciousness from which he might never awake.

But he kept asaddle, just; and he kept all the time talking to his horse and to himself and when they reached the Jump Up he could have cried.

There was no water but they were out of the scrub and had started their descent. He had to slow the horse for care, though it was not difficult country compared with where they had been, and as the coolness of the escarpment shadows and the onset of night came to him, his headache eased. But he was still sick to his stomach and he did not know how his horse had kept going and he knew that this time, when you think you have made it, is the most dangerous of all.

Gently, ever so gently, he eased Firecracker on as they came out into the valley, eased him back into a slight canter so the horse would not give up and die so close now, perhaps only a few more miles in easy country, to the water.

Near midnight, twenty-five and a half hours after setting out, and four and a half hours cut off his father's record, he heard the gushing sound of Top Springs and cried as he unmounted and unashamedly kissed and kissed again the neck of his horse as he gently hand-watered and walked him and sipped ever so slowly himself from the same handheld billycan and marveled at the breed of this stallion that had brought him through and yet had the control of his breed not to rush the water and risk death at the last yard.

Soon they heard sounds from a campfire beyond the Springs, where the station manager had sensibly sent ringers out, his best ringers, to wait and help, and relay the tablets on for the last eight miles.

"My God, you're Mac's son all right," said the head ringer as he passed the tablets on to a cheeky lad waiting at horse to take them, "you're Murranji Mac's boy and no mistake. We've been searching from here to the Jump Up and back for hours but must have missed you in the dark. But never thought you'd make it in this Dry and certainly not tonight, though we knew, too, that if you didn't come tonight the odds'd be bloody long, judging from the time we sent the telegraph and used up the last of the water at Murranji on the way back. We knew you'd have no water, son, and that's the truth. We didn't even know if you'd start out. But we've been betting on it—on if you'd come at all and in how many days—and I have to tell you, son, you've just won me a bloody fortune. Knew your old man and I'd heard of you, young Red, and when I heard you were in Darwin I reckoned that you'd come, right enough, and no mistake, and that you'd know there was only one way to do it and win—come straight on through in a day and never look back and, by Christ, you've done it and I've got a present for you but I 'spect you'd like some tucker first."

They were having to hold him up now and walk him around and he nodded toward his horse as he gave the reins over and the weathered old ringer smiled a smile for a man who acknowledged his horse and shouted to a ringer, "Take this beautiful, bighearted creature and walk him till he's cool and if he's not well in the morning I'll have yer guts for garters."

They walked the horse and walked Red over to the fire and sat him down gently, giving him more water slowly at first, and then a cup of strong tea with milk and sugar and rum. When he'd had one the old man gave him another and then threw a steak on the fire.

After Red had eaten, the head ringer took off his hat, and scratched his fuzzy, gray, balded head, picking up a piece of timber by the fire as he did so.

He came over and sat beside Red and put his arm around him. "It's me grandson, you see . . . the baby you've ridden in for is me grandson. Got the scrub typhus and they said he'd die for sure, but I said, 'No, I'll ride in and telegraph the doc and perhaps he can find someone in Darwin who's man enough to try,' and when the doc telegraphed back that he'd ask Carlyon if he'd come, I cried, so help me, son, and I sat down by the fire that night and made something appropriate. If you'll allow me the privilege I'll set it up beside the other after the next Wet." He passed the board over. It read:

THE KING OF THE TRACK IS MURRANJI RED
WHEN HE REACHES HERE HE KNOWS HE'S NOT DEAD.

26

It was not until after the ride back, more than a week later, that the lesson of the Murranji Track came to Red. He had been tired out, of course, and been taken up to the station house to rest. He had stayed a week, as much for his horse's sake as his own, and then freely accepted the offer of the station owner that he would set up a plant and send his best horse ringers to take him halfway with barrels of water by bullock wagon to the Jump Up, and then water bags from there to the Murranji hole itself. It would still be a difficult ride for everyone, but the barrels to the Jump Up and extra water bags would make it easier, and he was confident he and Firecracker could handle a straight-through ride for the second half from there. This turned out to be the case, and ten days later he was back in Darwin, somewhat of a hero, the news that the record had been broken and the baby recovered having been telegraphed ahead from Newcastle Waters after he had overnighted there.

But the ride had given him the time he had needed to think, and it had changed him. Bluey's father was the first to notice it and commented the first night Red was back in Darwin but out on his own with Lisa, having refused the option of a double outing with Bluey and Kat.

"Your friend's a bit different after his ride," the red-faced Byrne said, "quite a bit different, I'd say."

"Nah, he's just the same," Bluey said. "He's just tired, that's all, and he's got to work things out with Lisa."

"She's decided she's going to marry him, I believe, but he'll refuse her. He'll ask her to wait."

"You reckon, you really reckon?"

"He might have even before he went, but he will now for sure."

"Why should one ride make such a difference?"

"Sometimes it doesn't. It doesn't have to be a ride. It can be anything. Anything simple, even. But with people as talented as your friend Red, it usually has to be something big and challenging like the ride, breaking someone else's record, something like that."

"But he did some pretty big things in the war—we both did, if it comes to that."

The thinly haired and shining Byrne smiled benignly.

"Of course. Perhaps the ride was just the end of the chain. It doesn't happen with everyone. It happens very rarely."

He was losing his son, he knew that. He was losing him in his train of thought, yet he knew the path so well, his mind took it without question, as if reliving the time it had happened to him. "He's seen through it, Blue, that's how he's changed. He suddenly knows what it's all about. Oh, it won't change his warmth and friendship, you needn't worry about that: in some ways it may even enlarge it. And he won't lose his sympathy for other human beings because that's part of his nature. And he'll ride out again, if he ever has to, on the Murranji, but he'll ride for a different reason."

"I still don't understand," Bluey said.

"It doesn't matter. I think you'll see it in time and it's something you have to see for yourself. It's to do with the notice, really, to do with the notice the old ringer is going to put up."

"Well, what about the notice?"

"He doesn't need it. Now he knows inside."

When Bluey told Red about the conversation later, Red just smiled quietly and said, "So that's what your old man thinks, is it?" as if not giving away whether he agreed with his view

or not, although Bluey noted that his father had been right
about Lisa. Red said he had asked her to wait, that he loved
her, as much as he knew about love, but he had to put his
family things in order first and would she wait?

"She won't wait," Bluey said.

"Well, she did tell me to go to hell, but then that's her
nature, isn't it? Maybe she'll wait, Blue, maybe she won't.
But I've got to get started first, come what may."

Bluey was finding it a little hard to get the length of the
conversation with Red. The changes were small, yet he
seemed more in control, less concerned, determined in a
quieter way rather than full of boyish enthusiasm.

Even when Bluey told him that, while Red was away, Billy
had been into town gambling and lost all the money owed to
him, Red seemed not to mind and said only,

"It's all right, Blue. The old ringer offered me the hundred
pounds he won on my ride, but I turned him down. He can use
it as much as I can, and, in any case, I know where to start to
begin to get the Carlyon family things in order."

"Where?"

"First, I'm going to collect all moneys owed to us."

"What do you mean? No one owes you money."

"Oh, yes, they do. I can remember many people my father
let off a fiver here, a tenner there, because they were short at
the time, at the start or the end of a drive. Some of them are
big men now. What hasn't been collected, I'm going to collect.
If they're on hard times and can't afford it, that's different. If
they're flush, they're going to pay."

"There's one debt you won't collect," Bluey said, feeling
irked and left out of a warm ambit of friendship, "there's one
you won't collect," said Bluey, "and it's not money owed to
your father."

Red smiled quietly. "You mean Hatcher . . . the money
Hatcher welched on with Billy. . . ? That's the first debt I'm
going to collect. We'll need that two hundred and fifty quid
right away."

"How come you keep saying 'we'?" Bluey asked, getting a
vestige on his sense of humor back.

"Because I want you to help me, Blue."

Bluey looked at his friend and started unconsciously rubbing his hands, one over the other, as he did when anxious or excited. Bluey was no Big Red, but he was no man's fool either. He had bush cunning, Irish cunning, and his father's business sense, though not perhaps his ruthlessness or level of perception. But he looked at Red long and hard and then said,

"Why do you want me to help you?"

"Because I trust you above any person I know with the possible exception of Jacky, and you know about books and accounts from your father, which I don't. You're also a good bushie: as good or better than Billy. I want you to teach young Douglas about how to do the books, because we've never kept any and it's time we started and he'll never be any good in the bush—doesn't like it. Then I want you to keep an eye on Billy and help him run the station with Jacky while I collect the debts and get started in another business."

"I'll have to speak to my father. He's counting on me to help him."

"I'll fix it with your father if you really want to help me. Even if it's only for a year or two, Blue, I need your help." There was the old warmth back in his voice now which was really all Bluey had wanted to hear.

"As mates?" he said hurriedly.

"As China Plates, and just for a year or two to get me going," Red said warmly.

"It's a deal, then," Bluey said, holding out his hand to shake on it; "it's a deal if you can sell the old man."

"Oh, I'll sell your old man, all right, Blue, and no mistake," Red Carlyon said, shaking his friend by the hand to seal the deal.

"I'm not so sure about that," Bluey said in his good-naturedly cynical way, at the same time motioning with his right arm, bending it in a charade of drinking and pointing upward to the sun to indicate they should head for a drink because it was past noon. Red nodded and they began to walk.

"I have just one request, Boss," Bluey said.

"What's that, my son?"

"That I be allowed to watch Hatcher thumping the hide off you."

"Oh, you'll get to watch whatever happens all right, Blue. Where do you think we're heading for a drink right now?"

In fact they did not go straight to Hatcher's but stopped in at the nearest bar. Bluey assumed Red was just having a couple of warm-up drinks, getting in the mood for the fight. At the first bar, of course, everyone wanted to buy Red a drink, because it was a cattlemen's bar, a drovers' and teamsters' bar, a watering hole for bullockers and buffaloers and any thirsty soul in from the dust of the Outback. To such men, who knew the bush, his ride was already legendary and would be told up and down the Track, the main Track from North to South, in perpetuity. Of a man such as Red, such men, despite their toughness and their years, stood in awe. He represented the best that was in them: survival in harsh extremes and over and beyond that, helping a mate.

So all wanted to buy him a drink, but he thanked them kindly and said that he would have only one beer but there was a small service they could do him if they had a mind to. He knew they knew that the Coast Traders' Inn, owned by a certain Hatcher, did not welcome the men of the land. Red had always been a believer, he said, as he sipped his beer slowly, in the principle of live and let live. But the fact was, he said, that a debt was owed and must be paid and he was going to collect. Now the men knew, he said, that he was not a man to back away from a fight on his own, but seeing he was going to collect a bet, and say a few words, a very few words, he wondered if they might not care to accompany him, and whether it were not the time, the police being in such short supply in the Territory, with troopers always out here or there looking for someone they couldn't find in the bush, whether it were not the time to clean up the blasted Coast Traders' Inn once and for all: clean out the opium den and the Chinese and Aboriginal child prostitutes and Hatcher himself, who everyone knew was head of the cattle duffing ring even if no one could prove it.

Everyone thought this was a fine idea, and by the time he

and Blue had visited the other couple of bars in town, there seemed little doubt that Hatcher's real day of reckoning had come.

They were nearly fifty strong, fifty strong riding men and hunters in calf-high boots and beards and armor-plated hands, skinned and boned and reskinned into metal by a thousand silent chores on a thousand silent days out in the silent country.

There were perhaps twenty other men in the bar as Big Red and his fellow Outbackers entered, with Hatcher standing at the bar and paling as the truth came to him. He was not fool enough to try to shoot, but he cast a sidelong look at the back room and Red knew there would be a nit-keeper, a man keeping watch who could slip out for the police if there was trouble, so he shouted to Bluey, "Get him," and Bluey darted for the back room and came back holding an Afghan in a half nelson up the back. The look of fear on the man's face, as he looked at Red as if he had seen a ghost, was enough to tell Red that the man his father had told him about had survived in the desert.

He turned now to the man at the bar. He was older and balder but still much as he remembered his father's description of him.

"You know who I am?"

The big man behind the bar nodded.

"Then you'll know I've come for Billy's two hundred and fifty quid."

"He was a ring-in. He knew Carlyons were banned from my game."

"No Carlyon is ever banned from anything while I stand and live and breathe," said Red, "and there'll be no welching on gambling or any other debts with my family from now on, unless a man is down on his luck. So put your money up or I'll knock your bloody block off and no mistake."

Hatcher knew he had no choice. He could still fight well but he doubted that he would win and besides he could see the others were in a fighting mood, though he had no idea the full extent of what was on their minds and thought to pacify them by putting up the money, which he now did, reaching to a secret drawer under the bar and counting out twenty-five red ten-pound notes.

He handed them over.

"Now the rest of the money."

"You'll not steal that."

"No, I'll not steal that, but hand it over." Hatcher gave him the rest of the money in the drawer reluctantly.

"Is that all?"

"That's all."

"Blue?"

"Yes?"

"Empty out the back rooms and bring me his fan-tan dealer."

All this was accomplished quickly, and as the bar filled with the teenage girls out of the rooms, pretty but pallid young faces with bodies barely covered, Chinese and Aboriginal, it began to dawn on Hatcher how far Red intended to go. Some of the men in the bar were Hatcher's and they had guns. But so did many of the others, the buffaloers and the wild dog hunters.

The fan-tan dealer was brought. He was a smooth-faced, black-haired young man, in traditional Chinese dress with pigtail. Red was surprised by his youth. He doubted that he was more than twenty.

"Now listen here, Chinee friend," Red said with a warm but determined smile, "listen and don't pretend you don't understand English too well, for if you can deal like they say, you'll get the drift of my meaning well enough. I want your boss's money and I want it all. I can't believe that a sharp young man like you doesn't know where it's kept."

A look passed between Hatcher and the Chinese.

"I no know, Boss," he said quickly to Red.

"You just a gambler, Chinee, or you like young Chinee girl too maybe? That part of your wages, each new Chinee house girl you get to test?"

Red knew that any decent Chinese, while some might still support the tradition of child bride selling, detested the prostitution.

The Chinese man's eyes now showed a full understanding of the situation.

"You let girls go, Boss?"

"That's the idea—let them go with the money they've made."

"Money under floor of opium bunkhouse, Boss. I show," the young Chinese beamed, and then, seeing Hatcher's glowering look, "but you protect me, Boss."

"He's not going to be around to hurt anyone," Red said, turning to the two tallest buffaloers in the bunch. "You think you could arrange passage for our friend here?"

The men came forward, smiling out from their enormous beards.

"You're not going to shanghai me? Christ, help me, they're going to shanghai me and it's the twentieth century," Hatcher was saying in ever shriller and more disbelieving shouts until finally he was gagged and bound and Bluey had come back from the room with the money, the Afghan still in tow, and asked what he wanted done with him.

They were both thinking of the boy at the hod.

"That debt's been paid, Blue. Tell him he's free to go wherever he likes once we leave. If he goes to the police it will be his word against fifty others: it was just the warning we had to stop while we got this business started. Tell him if he wants to go home we'll fix passage with a friendly captain."

He had said it all in the third person but the Afghan had understood well enough and was nodding his head.

"I know a good captain who'll fix it and not maltreat him," Blue said.

"Good. Go with the buffaloers and make sure Hatcher understands he'll not be hurt but he's never to come back here again, never. Not to any part of the country."

Bluey nodded and went off with the buffaloers.

The next couple of hours Red was kept busy tidying things

up. He arranged jobs on stations as kitchen and station workers for as many of the girls as possible, and arranged for several to be taken back to their tribal territory, although this was not possible for all, and some feared punishment from husbands they had run away from. But in the end all were taken care of, and the money shared out by the Chinese dealer, who said he was known as Fan-tan, though his real name was Wang Lin, and whose spindle-fine and thin fingers flicked over the notes with great dexterity. He had a quick and easy laugh and Red found himself warming to him. But at the end of the doings, when all Chinese and Aboriginal girls were accounted for with jobs, or Overlanders agreeing to take them home or to mission schools, Red told the Chinese that that was an end to it and he could go. If he said anything to the police, it would likewise be his word against that of so many others.

"You find station job for me too, Boss?" the young Chinese said, "me sick dirty town."

"You sick of the town, my arse. You'd die in the bloody Outback, so help me. Those slick fingers of yours wouldn't find enough to do."

"Good cook, Boss. Plenty good cook before became dealer."

"I'll see what I can do, then," Red said absentmindedly, shouting across the room, "This fellar here reckons he can cook if anyone's getting a plant together for a drive."

"Oh, no, Boss," the Chinese interrupted, "not drive, proper home. I cook for you."

When Red thought about it afterward it seemed stupid, for he could not afford a cook and in any case there were his mother and Nora. But perhaps the dream was already forming, or had been formed for years and was coming to the surface, or if the young man had not offered perhaps he would have gone looking, for every decent station house had a decent, fair dinkum Chinese cook, capable of cooking meals for twenty or thirty workers, plus drop-in guests from the Track, plus the family; and so it was, seeing beyond his means of the moment, he somehow said yes to the idea of the

Chinese cook, rather than the person of Fan-tan, the gambler, though he was to learn that a gambler's heart is often a generous heart.

He and the other men then decided that, since everything had been cleared up, it was time for a celebration. So they broke out some of Hatcher's liquor and toasted themselves, toasted rather overvirtuously, their victory over vice and corruption, telling themselves what great heroes they were, and Red the greatest, the pick of the bunch, the greatest mate a man could ever have, they said, as they staggered out the door to spread the new legend of Big Red.

Red watched them go. He'd had a few drinks but not so many he couldn't think straight. He now had 250 pounds, a station manager in Bluey and a cook. Tomorrow he and the men would sift Hatcher's holding herd outside town for brands they could identify and send back to owners, and the rest they would divide up themselves. He'd get perhaps three or four Brahman crosses, but good enough to get going again until he collected other debts and got money enough to buy some more, for the 250 pounds he had already earmarked for a special gamble of his own.

Soon he would leave for home to see things set up there. But first he must arrange things with Bluey's father, and then he must see Lisa. She was anxious to ride down and back with him, but he'd explained he could be away weeks and in any case, though he had not told her, his mother's future on the land had still to be settled, and he was very worried about Nora, whose health had been failing for years. He was concerned about how the loss of Nora might affect his mother or, and sometimes he thought, more importantly, Jacky.

When he thought of his lifelong black companion, he thought again of the land, the land he had so recently been back into and fought again, the land he loved and missed, the land of Five Mile Camp, the Shangri-La with the ever-lurking Kismet, the land of pink mists and purple hills and red earth and gray rocks and salmon dust and gray-red wallabies and Dreamtime and the whole earth where past and present were one and where he was at home and truly at peace. He thought of these things as he walked on alone, walked back to town alone, he thought of these things and he thought of Lisa and he thought how similar the feelings were. Their bodies had been a vortex for each other since the first swim and he was always full of things to tell her, and she to tell him.

So after the visit to Hatcher's he went to Lisa again, down into the cool-fronded Alice garden around the house of flowers, down into the lush, dark green parts of the garden, beyond the stream which ran under the house, beyond and down to where they had so often nearly made their love, and they made it now this once, and sighed and clawed and deeply drove but never made talk again so that he went away manned and mellowed but not understanding, understanding nothing more than she, but both believing they understood fully and would be faithful to each other for all time and both having that depth of first intensity, that excruciating love so touchy and fragile and so open to pain.

27

He left her in the garden at dusk, left her roughly blond and tumbled, with the smells of her and the garden still with him as he walked back along the road feeling fulfilled yet not fulfilled and wished he understood himself better and wondered how long it really took to be wise. He had bush wisdom, but each day added another feeling or experience or thing or word he was not wise about, did not know at all about, so that the store of what he knew and what he did not know seemed continually being drawn upon in different ways, pulling ways, so that he was glad of his bush wisdom to fall back on, and glad of the lessons of the bush such as he had learned down the Track. For when he felt the way he did now, he pushed the feelings he didn't quite understand underground, buried them there with the stores to come back to, and threw himself into another activity until the wisdom thing leveled itself out again. So he headed back, forcing himself to think of other things, steadying himself for the conversation with Patrick Byrne, which he had intended to have before seeing Lisa, if he had not been unable to stop himself going to her first.

Patrick Byrne was a tough negotiator, as Red had expected he would be, and as he poured Red a beer and said bluntly, "What's in this for me?" Red hoped he could ride through the conversation without having to show his trump card. He knew his trump card was good enough to win Bluey's father's approval; at least Red believed it to be. It was one of those obvious business developments that *had* to take place. The trick was to have the inside running. And because of a friendship, Red had just that. To mention it would be for Patrick Byrne to insist on a half share of Red's investment opportunity in return for help with the pearling. So Red would sit tight and bluff it out and hope he could persuade Byrne Senior on other grounds. Of course Byrne Junior was of age and free to do his own choosing, but he had himself put on the stipulation of his father agreeing, so that there was no ill will in the family business which Bluey certainly intended to inherit in good time and fortune.

"What's in it for you, Mr. Byrne," Red found himself saying, as if his thoughts had led into words quite naturally as the other man spoke, "what's in it for you is that you get me for your pearler—a straight swap—me for Bluey for two years."

"With due respect, son, that doesn't sound like such a good bargain to me. You don't know anything about pearling and I'm doing pretty well out of it already."

"For *only* seven months of the year," Red made certain his emphasis fell heavily on the word *only.*

"That's true for me as it is for all pearlers. We're as subject to the times and tides of the Wet on the sea as you are on the land."

"But is it the crew or the divers who don't like the months of the Wet?"

"Both."

"But when it comes down to it, you could probably avoid the worst of the monsoons and get an extra two to three months out of the season from the crew, particularly if you gave them a Wet season bonus."

"Probably."

"Well, then, I'll dive for you for that period for the next two years in return for Bluey's work in helping on the station and teaching me kid brother how to do the books."

"It's bloody suicide."

"It's bloody profitable if it works."

"If."

"That's my chance. Your boat can turn back at the first sign and cut me loose if you like. That gives you the minimum risk."

Patrick Byrne poured them each another drink and eyed Red Carlyon more carefully than he ever had before. Then he said,

"Let me try another question. What's in it for you? I'm going to be making all the money if, and I do say *if,* it works. Seeing you grew up in the North your education would have included the fact that in Australia we dive for pearl shell, not pearls, wouldn't it. . . ? That wasn't neglected out on the land, was it?"

Red shook his head.

"I know about the pearl shell."

"So I guess you also know that although we pearl for the shell, a diver will occasionally find a true pearl, occasionally a very valuable pearl, and that this belongs to the owner and we watch our divers so closely we even make sure we know where they shit so they don't swallow any pearls on us . . . so you don't know of some offshore pearl bed somewhere you're thinking of plundering for your profit and my loss, now do you, son?"

Red smiled and shook his head. "Whatever I find is yours, Mr. Byrne, for the period stated. You have my word on that. What's in it for me is that I want to learn about pearling and you're the best pearler around as you are at most things. I want to learn about pearling in the same way I want my kid brother to learn about bookkeeping and in the same way you want Bluey to learn about cattle."

"I never said that."

"No, but you must have thought about it, a man always expanding like you are. He's a good bushman but he'll learn more in two years with Jacky than he could in ten years with me or twenty years with some. It'll be a good investment in experience for both of us. I'll be ready to go into pearling if I ever get the cash and you'll be ready to go into cattle the moment the two-year term is over. Is it a deal?"

"Your Jacky that good, eh—?" Byrne Senior said, cocking one eye up as a businessman will do who has already made up his mind but wants to register his double-checking principle.

"That good," Red said. "The absolute best there is."

"Like me at diving—or like I used to be. You ever dived?"

Red shook his head. "Only in the billabongs. . . . I can stay under a long time . . . used to search for baby crocs underwater but not proper deep diving."

Patrick Byrne nodded quietly. "It's not the same. It's no picnic, I can tell you that. You'll need your wits about you, particularly the time of year you intend to dive. You really sure you want to try to kill yourself this way?"

"I'm game if you are."

"That's the trouble," said the old man, smiling resignedly. "Two seasons and no more, then, is that a deal?"

"That's a deal."

They drank down their beers and shook hands and then Red went off to tell Bluey and make preparations for his return to the Back of Beyond the next day. As he left the room he was smiling to himself. He had not had to play his trump card. But he would fix that tomorrow so that while he was back at the station, then out overlanding collecting debts, and then diving for his very life during the Wet, he would have a separate bet running for him all the time, in some ways the biggest bet of all and one he had the inside track on to be sure, something he had planned ahead a long time. He would send off the money and fix that tomorrow and then ride happily home.

The next morning he was up early, grooming and saddling Firecracker and then making excuses that he had to go into the town to find a farrier he knew, because he wasn't happy with the roan's shoeing after the tortuous ride along the Murranji and back. Patrick Byrne mentioned casually that their own groom could do it, displaying only slight interest when Red thanked him, but said it was really a job for an expert and he knew a man with special talents in the town.

"Which one?" asked Bluey ruefully, giving nothing away to his father but knowing damn well that Red shoed his own horses, shoed them as well as any farrier or better, and preferred to see it done properly by himself, however good the man's reputation, so that Bluey repeated his question, predictably as Red had hoped, "Which one and is it male or female?"

"Oh, it's like that, is it?" Patrick Byrne smiled over his newspaper, assuming, as Red had intended them both to, that he wanted to slip away for a quiet farewell to Lisa. But he had said his farewells there for a time, and it was the telegraph office to which he headed, after he walked his horse out the drive as Bluey shouted, laughing, "Be gentle with the animal . . . make sure you get that special farrier."

At the telegraph office he wrote out a simple message to be sent to a mate in Queensland:

"Count me in. Here's the two-fifty."

He signed it and handed over the 250 pounds to be telegraphed with a message to his friend Jarvis from the dogfight, the ace with whom he had kept in touch.

But now Red was penniless again and he would be returning to the station without stores except for a few essentials which he was pretty sure he could get on credit so that Bluey and the others would not suspect he did not have the 250 pounds. He'd say, in any case, that he was taking the money with him on the trip, to buy cattle if he came across any good breeders. That way, by the time he returned from his debt-collecting ride, he hoped the 250 pounds would be lost in a round figure. He felt a little guilty about not telling the others. Patrick Byrne would not like it when he heard. He'd feel he should have been told out of friendship. But he was a realist and would accept it. Bluey might resent it for a time but he doubted it. Technically it was Billy's money, but he'd only have lost it elsewhere and Red's gamble was as good as any other.

One thing was for sure: if the gamble didn't pay off everyone would know about it. But he'd given his word that he would tell no one for the time; that was part of the deal, probably part of the reason Jarvis had asked him in, knowing he could be trusted in addition to his background. So say nothing he would. And as he rode back to the Byrne home, to pick up Bluey and the stores and divide up the unclaimed cattle and head down the Track once more, the smile of pride and cunning in what he had done far outweighed any sense of guilt in keeping it quiet. If it came off, it would be a giant leap forward in his dream, which was formulating more and more. He would own a million acres before he was through, with a house like Patrick Byrne's and an interest in every industry this new and lusting last frontierland had to offer.

28

On May 19, 1919, ten days after Red returned to the Back of Beyond, Nora died.

She had grown weaker over the past few months. Beth nursed her, of course, but none of Beth's ministrations, not her beef tea nor the medicines from her small store built up over the years, seemed to work. Nora had known she was dying and so had Jacky. They had waited quietly, stoically, smiling knowingly and lovingly at each other with the long, warm friendship of the years, sitting holding hands for hours on end, Jacky at her bedside. Beth had moved her inside, she'd insisted on that. When Nora passed away in her sleep, Beth thought she should give her what she considered a nice funeral. She wanted to get her Bible out. But even she had learned better by this time.

They carried her body, wrapped in bark, the long distance to Coffin Swamp, where they placed it above the ground on a platform of gum rods set between two trees.

Jacky dressed himself in tribal dress, which consisted of only a fur-string pubic cover, and sat beneath the body for ten days with his spear and spear thrower beside him. Then he lovingly took down the bark bag and placed it in a log coffin and buried it himself and then went walkabout and was not seen for nearly a year.

During these weeks Red delayed his ride and worked close to the station house, though avoiding his mother as much as possible. Nora's death had pushed her into her quiet and circuitous rethinking of the past, as he had feared it would. It was as if she only came out of her tiny graying frame to open her mouth to eat a little at mealtime or to pass the bare necessities of conversation. There were other homestead lubras, of course, who happily did the work for little more than their keep, and some of whom she got on well with, but it was not the same, Red knew.

In a real sense there was now only one person close to her left. Mac, her great protector, was gone. Although close to Jacky in the early years, and still loved in every way by him, a shift had taken place at Red's birth which Beth well knew. The first object of Jacky's love and protection was the boy, the youth, the man. But for Beth Nora had replaced Jacky and filled in her mistress the need to have someone close to her who understood and loved the hostile land she had to live in, understood it in a way she never could. While she had that love bridge to someone she trusted who trusted the land it was all right. It was not good, but it was bearable. But now Mac was gone and Nora was gone and Jacky belonged to Red and would not sit by her day in and day out like an alter ego as Nora had done. No, she had only Douglas, her youngest son, now; and, perhaps because of her, he was even less a part of the bush than she was. Yet there was Billy, and she could talk to him for all his garrulous tomfoolery, and Douglas loved him so, and in her quietude she knew that if it had not been for this fact she would now, finally, have left this land which had dried her up both in and out.

Red knew what she was thinking and let her be and she, for her part, held her peace again as she had so many times in the past.

They all carried on as if nothing had happened and the three men spent as much time away from the house as possible, often camped out at Five Mile Camp. Billy took an immediate shine to Bluey, their senses of humor being about the same, and Billy's wildness and smooth, swift-talking nature being in some ways more akin to the town or city life that Bluey had known than Bluey's himself. Anyway, they played poker for matchsticks around the campfire and most times Bluey won: another point in his favor so far as Billy was concerned. Red was moody with Jacky gone and wandered way inside Five Mile Camp—where the others were not allowed—to sit around the fire and talk with Crocodile Tommy.

When Jacky eventually returned, Red thought things might almost be as they once were, or close to how they were when he was a boy, and his father's star shining so brightly and his mother so happy. He thought they might be almost this way, but knew, too, that they would never be again, knew that life erodes one way or another like the sand and red earth and that a whole generation had passed.

But Jacky, with his intuitive good sense and ways of his people, brought with him someone who for a time seemed almost capable of restoring the happy early past. Her name was Lily, after the purple lilies of the lagoon, and she was sixteen and full-bodied with never a stitch on as they came in from their walkabout, full-bodied with that slight hint of purple to her deep black body, and her full brown eyes sat out wild and happy from a round face with a mop-top of curly hair, black curly hair that had laughter in every shake of the head. So Lily came in to the Back of Beyond, naked as many of the lubras had often been in the old days, naked to show her beauty and part of Jacky's pride, so Red thought, as he saw the pursed smile on his friend's lips, naked himself, two tribal Aboriginals in from their long desert walkabout, the older nearing forty and the younger sixteen.

In they both came, laughing and smiling and lighting up the property with their stately bush beauty and telling by their actions those others who had sense enough to see that life is an eternal, contiguous thing for us all and that, for them, Lily was part of Nora's family and Nora still part of theirs and there was no real sadness to be held to for long in this land of ever-changing patterns. And, as he looked a second time, Red was sure that Lily's belly was slightly

swollen and that that was why she walked ahead in full
nakedness so that all might see that in the Aboriginal
Dreamtime, where all things are possible past and present,
Nora had already been re-created.

Jacky and the three men camped out at Five Mile Camp
that night, which infuriated Beth, although she really had no
time to worry, for she was already discovering that Lily was a
very different kettle of fish from Nora. She had a sixteen-
year-old fireball on her hands, a tribal young lady who, it
turned out, had never worn clothes, and saw no reason to
now, and kept shedding them at the most unlikely moments
no matter how much or how often Beth tried to put something
over her.

When the men came back, Beth pleaded with Jacky, who
just kept shrugging his shoulders and saying, "You get her to
wear something it OK with me, Missus, I no care," which of
course did not help the situation one iota and Beth was near
despair, for she was losing face in the eyes of the other
kitchen girls by not winning, until one day, suddenly, of her
own accord, Lily took a liking to a particularly bright tea
towel with a tartan background and piper on it which Beth's
parents had forwarded on years ago from a relative in
Scotland. It had seen better days, but Lily had never seen a
tartan before, certainly never that pattern of the Royal
Stewart tartan before, and she seized it from the hand of
another kitchen lubra the moment she saw it, and as a fight
threatened to ensue, Fan-tan stepped in and said, "Plenty,
pletty Missy, you wear," to Lily and had whipped it around
her waist and fastened the corners with knots and a back
sash of string before Lily could complain and when it was on
she strutted proudly around the kitchen and thereafter took
it off only on Beth's strong insistence when it absolutely had
to have a wash.

Beth, who resented yet acceded to the subtle ways in which
Fan-tan was taking over the growing kitchen, nevertheless
continued to complain to him about the rest of Lily, but Fan-
tan just kept saying out loud and chuckling, "plenty bare
bum and breasts this kitchen, Missus. . . . You no change

overnight and me no mind and they no care," and Beth knew that to be the truth of it, that to them it was nothing, though she had never accommodated her Presbyterian upbringing to their unusual ways of nakedness and unnakedness. So, in the end, she acquiesced and, in so doing, the power and control of the house passed quietly into Fan-tan's hands. She knew what this meant but did not mind. She was feeling her age.

By this time they had a series of small mustering yards built; they had the backbone of a small mob, mostly scrub cattle, but with some Brahman crosses among them and the possibility of a stronger breed; the station house had been extended minimally (for Red knew he would soon tear it all down and start afresh); Billy's cough had gone, thanks largely to a mixture of goanna oil and eucalyptus which Lily had insisted on rubbing in nightly, thus certainly winning over Beth despite the continued bare bottom and top in the kitchen; and young Douglas was taking to figures and books, although just having passed his eleventh birthday, like a duck to water. There was, for the first time in a long time, a vestige of a family on the Back of Beyond.

So Red rode off on his debt-collecting tour reluctantly, out into the aloneness of the bush again, his enemy-friend which would keep him company while he missed his family and the home he was building, while he thought of Lisa and plans for the future. For once things seemed discernible and bright, though you knew something would always be there around the corner, something unexpected, some Abominable Snowman of the desert, some new Murranji Track. This was his life, first by upbringing and then by choice, and his mind was already on the increasing numbers of buffaloers and crocodile hunters who were getting on their property and what this would mean to the family's future. Some were good men and friends whom he minded not at all, particularly those down on their luck after the war. But others, such as the dingo hunters, those men who hunted for the pelts of the oldest pure breed of wild dog in the world, the dingo men who were paid a bounty of seven shillings and sixpence a pelt for the dog described as a pest and the cause of the longest fence in the world, the dingoproof fence being built along the continent to keep them from the burgeoning cities of the Eastern seaboard, such men bore watching: some were bad and cruel men and all were taking things of value off Carlyon land. It was obvious that buffalo were becoming a commercial crop, that crocodile skins, like pearl shells, were already immensely valuable, and that dingo pelts at 7s. 6d. a time were not to be sneezed at. Such things would have to be thought about when Red got back and a decision made. It was true the real dingo pest area was to the west, and somehow he didn't feel right about profiteering out of crocodiles or upsetting the balance of the land. But the buffalo was an introduced animal, and was becoming a pest by multiplying so quickly and eating cattle grass and there there might be a lucrative free crop each year.

One thing Red knew as he rode out, unconsciously pulling his slouch hat down on his brow to shade it from the heightening sun, one thing he knew as he mentally chewed these things over, and that was that there would be many obstacles, known and unknown, and long, long hours of just keeping going, like one always had to in the bush, if he was ever to build the space for himself he wanted.

He rode the horse beneath him gently, though. Firecracker II was getting old and soon would have to be put out to stud to breed another generation. The mammoth ride had taken it out of him, but the brave animal tried not to let it show, although the rider on his back knew that like an aging sportsman he was still playing on gamely but past his prime. Momentarily, and only momentarily, for the huge, tall, dark man in the saddle still shone with youth, the rider wondered what he would do when this time came also to him.

29

By November of that year the money was collected, nearly 500 pounds of it without duress, and negotiations completed for another ten square miles of property. Beth had complained only slightly that there would be no station house additions yet! She still had minimal enough comforts, but she knew the order of priorities her son would follow as the night followed the day: land, animals, people, in that order. Begrudgingly she admired him but not without an unexpressed quiet resentment. Although her son, she had a part of her that resented seeing that he intended to do what his father had not been able to do, resented father and son really, for the pocket of vulnerability one had and the other did not. She knew, too, that in a sense this feeling, which she could hardly articulate to herself, was watched and known and understood by her eldest son and that frightened her—it frightened her that the part of herself she had given to him had given him these intuitive human emotional strengths as well as his physical ones. She wondered where his Achilles' heel was, and thought she knew and that he didn't, and wondered if he, too, sooner or later, would suffer the hurt of nonfulfillment at the hands of his beloved land.

But yet she watched him ride off with a certain pride, ride off to another adventure, back into Darwin just before the onset of the Wet, and she watched as she had always watched his father, never letting herself doubt for a moment that he would return but not really knowing what was involved in pearling.

And indeed as he rode off, Red was only too aware how precious little he knew of pearling, of diving and the bends, for all his swimming and diving—and he could stay submerged a long time—had been in muddied fresh water, hunting the baby crocs as game. Some would think this dangerous enough, yet he knew the diving to which he was heading would tax him more.

Yet it was to Lisa that his mind kept turning as he rode on, camped and rode on through the second day until by dusk he was near the town and the longing to be with her in the garden was unbearable now.

He reached the doctor's house just before nightfall: a still, silver, yellow twilight such as only the Tropics have. It was very pretty and still and quiet as he stretched out of the saddle after his long ride and looked forward to a bath and his time with Lisa and the good long times with her father over the table in which the doctor said little and seemed content to ask questions about the bush.

Red walked the steps as he had the first day and knocked loudly with confidence this time and soon the doctor came to the door, short and quiet and kindly in his glasses and thin cardigan, for there was a slight edge to the night air. He beckoned Red in and pointed to a chair and poured him a beer without asking and when Red had drunk that down and began to frown as if to say "Where is Lisa?" the doctor poured another one for him and sat closer to him and said simply,

"She's gone, son. She'll be back but she's not here. They're on their honeymoon down South. I'd advertised for an assistant and he arrived soon after you left. I needed a younger doctor: the town is growing and I wanted someone young. This young British doctor applied and I think Lisa had fallen in love with the photograph he sent of himself before he arrived. I'm deeply sorry but you know how she is: it has to be done quickly or not at all. She's always been frightened of decisions, so she makes them quickly, forces herself into unretreatable positions so she can't feel she's made the wrong decision. And she has to have people totally, fully, right from the start, or not at all. I'd hoped she'd change and she may and if she does it will be terrible for her, but in any case it's too late now."

It was a long sentence for the old man who spoke so little, but he had said it in his usual way, kind and to the point, though little was registering with Red except the deep, burning anguish. If he had an Achilles' heel, it was, as his mother had suspected, his tendency to trust some people too much, to expect of them what he expected of himself, to expect that, despite the signs of bush rogues and dangerous animals which he recognized so well, other people would live up to his ideals. It was not an unerring fault: it was a vulnerability and it had hit him now.

After he had thanked the old man and seen his eyes moist for him as he refused his offer of lodging for the night, after he had thanked the doctor and left the fairy-tale house that had meant so much to him, he walked his horse to the cliff, and then down the narrow cliff path with him where he had first swum with Lisa and there he galloped and galloped along the sand, driving hard into the horse's flanks to get the still night air moving at his face, and he rode and rode until he had cried himself out, for despite his size and strength and emotional stability in so many ways beyond his years, he was not quite twenty-two, and he had lived his whole life in the bush, and then gone to war, so that all his romantic, adolescent dreams had been stored up waiting for Lisa and inside he hurt like any young person deeply in love and deeply rejected for the first time.

Eventually he broke the horse to a canter and then a walk and he sat down on a rock ledge by the beach and the horse stayed with him and would not move and the young man sat a long time with his thoughts and his hurt, a hurt quite unlike any other, a hurt he could not, by action or design, attack with a knife and suck out like snakebite, a feeling of inadequacy which would ride deeply with him for many, many years.

The diving, which he had so looked forward to, became a mundane routine. He had not realized that they used helmet and hookah gear all the time now, and even the weather, he having persuaded Patrick Byrne to pearl in the Wet for the first time since the cyclone of 1910, seemed determined to be dull and monotonous. The captain was a wise and stubborn Scot who had explicit instructions from his master not to let Carlyon take any unnecessary risks. He more than fulfilled the letter of the law on this. At the first sign of the slightest squall, Red was brought up. This never took very long because he was never allowed to go very deep. When he complained to the captain the man just smiled and said, "I've orders to bring you back in one piece, and in any case I don't think I'd treat you any different if I hadn't. This is a dangerous business and slow to learn. It's also uneconomic for me to use you except on short easy spells. Obviously I use my best divers on the best jobs and for those, with or without helmet, no man will ever come near the Thursday and Torres Strait Islanders. Watch them and learn; get your deep-sea legs slowly. One day you'll thank me."

Red didn't like it. His body and mind craved excitement to wash the other things out of his system. But he knew the captain was right and, more than that, was a man of unerring judgment in his own domain, which Red admired, and would not change his mind.

At that time Australia was supplying more than seventy percent of the world's needs of pearl shell, mother-of-pearl, for buttons, ornaments and compasses. There were big fleets operating out of Darwin and Broome and the islands. There were armies of men in full diving gear, brass helmets and suits and lead belts and boots; men with oyster knives and bags, brushing their way past rock outcrops, looking for the precious shell many fathoms down, fed by air hoses from the luggers above. The Star of the West, worth ten thousand pounds, had been found two and a half years earlier, but no one went down with any real dream of finding such a prize in the black-lip or more highly prized gold-lip pearl shell, or at least Red did not in that Wet of the Christmas of 1919–20. It was as if all his senses were dulled and he monotonously went through the motions, not even trying to find a way around the system which suppressed his usual need for stimulating action, perhaps suggesting that there was part of him which was prepared, just for once, to let things be, and rest. And indeed, when the period was over, and he visited Patrick Byrne briefly, to whom he replied when asked how it had gone, "OK," and said nothing else except, "Thanks, and see you next year," and did not see the man's warm paternal smile or hardly hear him shout as he farewelled him, "Give Blue my regards," it did not even occur to him that a year earlier he would have demanded better treatment, to learn more quickly and have said that he wanted to dive for bloody pearls, not paddle around in the shallows.

Back on the station he started to work his sorrow out, free now to drive himself relentlessly, working twenty hours a day, up at five or even four in the morning, out alone often, out without his beloved Jacky, as if the land itself held some mystic prescription, out planning and marking areas that would later become mustering camps, or sites for windmill water bores as the property developed. He even tried fencing, knowing that every rule was against it at that time except for close to the station house. So he did it there, going into Darwin with the wagon for supplies, for the wire, for white-ant capping, but still unable to cut the fencing costs of posts and four-strand wire below twenty-five pounds a mile if he was lucky. So in the end he had to leave off because he could not afford it, though he'd finished single-handedly the fencing around home paddock and a couple of other paddocks for holding nearby, refusing help except occasionally from Jacky, banging his anger away with every angry blow of the ironhead mallet, punishing himself with every sinew strained and his hands half raw as he stretched the wire to tension tightness, out day and night, out in the dark before dawn and the dark after dusk, out with or without lantern until everything that could be done was done, even timber races and wooden cattle yards built near the house, too, and Red started to feel better as it came up to June.

Jacky and Blue worked with him then, as they started their small mustering drives, calf marking, castrating and branding. It was still monotonous, it was still doing routinely work he normally loved, but as the Dry wore on and the months passed and it was November and time for drafting the young cattle off into the yards and then driving their mothers away so the weaning was accomplished, Red began to feel himself again and got back some of his former balance.

He realized that friendship was getting in the way of business. Patrick Byrne would never let him dive the way he wanted to, and he could not keep a pearl from a friend. There was no strict rule about the pearls, as Patrick Byrne had well known. There was a captain's inspection, of course, as the divers came up, but everyone knew that although good pearls were not frequent, they were not infrequent either. In the 1880s off the West Australian coast one skipper had logged over one hundred pearls to eight hundred shells. The unwritten law was that if the diver could get the pearl past inspection, it was his, an unofficial bonus for the risks taken diving and because these days they were scarcer and a man had to go deeper to find them. Patrick Byrne had known the unofficial law as well as Red now knew it, but he had been cunning enough to protect himself by extracting a friendship promise from Red which he knew the younger man would not break.

So without saying the real reason why, and saying only that his father would not let him dive deep enough, Red told Bluey that he would not be doing another hitch with his father and he was free to go. Bluey said he was enjoying the bush life, and would stay on for part of the time through to the end of his second Dry, if his father said OK, which he was sure he would. By then young Douglas would have the rudiments of bookkeeping, because after all Red didn't need much more than an in and out column at the moment, did he, and not much of the in? After that, if he needed any help, Red would be in Darwin from time to time and could ask Bluey anytime. But it quite suited Bluey to get off a bit early, he added, because he had decided to marry Kat.

So just before the onset of the next Wet, both men rode into Darwin together.

On the property it would throw an extra load on Jacky and Billy but they were making just enough now out of sales to itinerant cattle buyers to afford two extra Aboriginal ringers. Red would dearly have loved to stay. But he knew that for the time being his chances of making bigger money quicker were elsewhere. And he was enough himself again to have formed a plan for the pearling venture. Last season, while pearling, he had met a Thursday Islander. Thursday Island was the center of the Torres Strait island group strewn to the North between the Cape York Peninsula and New Guinea. The man, named Kiwai, was of the more classic South Sea Islands type of Melanesian origins. He was tall, muscled smoothly brown and a descendant of collectors of human heads, with an excellent education at the hands of the London Missionary Society which from 1871 on had had a quite remarkable conversion record on the islands. Some said this was at least partly due to the fact that the islanders were such an adaptable, happy lot, once the head-collecting business had been resolved, that they never took Christianity seriously enough to do them any harm. Certainly when Red approached Kiwai with his proposal, the tall man, almost as tall as Red himself, with the straightest, whitest, strongest teeth that Red had ever seen, showed no aversion to the scheme. The Thursday Islanders' diving was legendary, and of the Thursday Islanders, Kiwai was the greatest, and Red believed that this man, with his culture and experience, would be able to smell a rich pearl at fifty fathoms, would be able to read the signs of the seabed as Red could read the desert.

But more than this, the man was in every way a born leader. Red knew he would be more than capable of running a fleet of pearling schooners, let alone one, which was all he had in mind at the moment.

So he found Kiwai, and signed on with him on the sixty-foot, schooner-rigged, pearling lugger *Queen Victoria,* passing himself off, with the help of Kiwai's recommendation, as an experienced deep-sea diver. It was a beautiful boat, yachtlike, with low bulwark lines, strong enough to work to windward whatever the weather and beautifully built to drift sideways with ease, essential to the divers below so that there were no sudden jerkings which could threaten the lifelines.

Kiwai and Red would work as closely together as possible. The plan was fairly simple, although depending on a good deal of luck. The aim was to find a pearl, or pearls, large enough to buy them a pearler for themselves. It would be a straight fifty-fifty split, with proper legal documents; although once secured, Kiwai would run the boat, Red would return to the property and get fifty percent of the profits.

Now divers were searched, and a boat like the *Queen Victoria* had a skipper smart enough to have a guard on the toilet, twenty-four hours. The guard stood with the door open while you squatted, the theory being that since what you were eliminating went straight into the sea and you could not stop the process to search for a swallowed pearl with the guard there. It was a great deterrent, for a man was unlikely to take great risks to secrete a pearl he knew he was going to have to flush straight back into the water.

Red's plan was this: They would work together as much as possible and Kiwai would point out to him the places where the most likely black-lip and gold-shells might be found. But they would not make their move until the last week of the season. Then, finding the pearl together, for Red knew he would need Kiwai's help, Kiwai must surface first, alerting those above that his partner was in trouble. Red would come up with the shell, but, within a reasonable distance of the surface, purport to have air hose trouble. Kiwai would dive in to unfoul the hose but would, in reality, cut the hose and help Red, still with headpiece on, to swallow the pearl or pearls through the cut mouthpiece and then bring him quickly to the surface.

But this would be the easy part. Red must then go for up to

a week, depending on which day they found the pearl, if they found it at all, without a bowel movement. Yet he would have to appear to the toilet guard to have one movement daily. He was fairly sure he could fake this by sitting awhile and then flushing. But the real problem was the simple stopping of the motions of nature. To this end he had brought with him a mixture of Lily's, who was proving to be somewhat of an amateur or not so amateur Aboriginal chemist. When one of the kitchen lubras had got dysentery (which was not uncommon in the Wet, when malarial dysentery was feared above all else), Lily had wandered off to the escarpment country near Five Mile Camp and come back with a bowl of white clay material on her head. It was, as they all agreed later, basically clay chalk, such as Aboriginal painters had been using for centuries. It was perfectly soluble in water, tasted like clay chalk and set inside like concrete. It stopped the runs in an instant. In fact, once a few doses had been taken, the problem was how to start the sufferer again after the tummy and bowel had quietened down. Red was not looking forward to the experience, but he was sure his bottle of Lily's mixture would stop him dead in his toilet tracks for more than a week. It would be agony, but it would be worth it. Once ashore, with his pearl intact inside, it would be a case for castor oil. The plan seemed foolproof to him, and Kiwai thought it a huge joke. The problem was the luck needed to find the right pearl at the right time, and then to get past the inspections. He felt confident no one would question Kiwai's decision to cut the air hose and haul the fouled diver to the surface for safety.

So for nearly two months, out in the ever-roughening waters of the North West sea, they dived, dived deeply, reading the signs and waiting their time.

The last week of the season came and they had pearled their way out to the forty-five-fathom offshore beds, which made both men happy. They worked through the seven days of each week without rest, and on the Sunday night at the start of the last week, Kiwai said the signs were good but they must start drifting down to fifty fathoms from now on.

This was the only thing that worried them. The other divers would say the pearl shell was good at forty-five fathoms. Also, fifty fathoms was a recognized dangerous depth, as well as a recognized depth for more likely pearl finds as distinct from the highly vaulable shell itself. It could arouse suspicion. They had discussed this at the start of the voyage and decided that, although friends, there must appear to be rivalry between them, with Red striving to learn, and be better than Kiwai perhaps a little too quickly. Thus they had contrived, while working their way from the shallower to the deeper water, to accept dare bets from each other, and the crew had already grown used to it, Red challenging in a good-natured way, and invariably being beaten by the champion diver Kiwai always managing to go deeper. Thus they hoped they had accustomed the men above not to pay much heed when their lines ran a bit deeper than the others.

On the Monday morning they made an obvious thing of Red betting Kiwai that he'd be the first to go "more than forty-five fathoms."

They worked at about forty-seven fathoms both Monday and Tuesday, and although there were several heart-stopping moments while they prised promising-looking shells open, they had to be thrown into the crocheted-rope bag as shell only.

On the Wednesday, at nearly fifty fathoms, Kiwai spotted a rock-ledge outcrop well below. He signaled, and Red followed, knowing this would take them over fifty fathoms, more of a risk for him than the practiced Kiwai. But he followed, feeling the pressure and knowing this would be nothing to the pressure he would feel in another way if he misjudged his time of rising, for you had to surface slowly, carefully, at a regular rate, adjusting to the pressure so that you did not get the bends. Kiwai, who appeared to have a watch inside his head, had taught Red how to do this by counting, which was fine if you were still coherent enough to count.

Anyway, down they went to their rock ledge and after some digging away at the sea-crustated shells with their diving knives, eventually Kiwai prised one loose and gave Red the

thumbs-up sign before he opened it. But when he did,
working with his knife in his bare hands, with his fingernails
almost iridescent against his black fingers, both men laughed
for joy with their eyes through their helmet visors when they
saw what was in the shell. They had hit a doubleheader. The
pearls were not enormous, but they were not peashooter size
either. There was one each and between them they would
certainly buy a pearling lugger. Kiwai signaled thumbs up,
realizing quicker than Red that it was not safe for either of
them at this depth, let alone Red.

They slowly rose to what they considered about forty-five
fathoms. There was a third diver down but he was out of
sight. They were confident they had not been seen. Kiwai had
reclosed the shell with the pearls in it. He now handed this
shell to Red and waved as he started his ascent. This was the
signal for the start of their plan. Kiwai would rise as quickly
as he could, certainly much more quickly with his years of
training than Red's body could take. But Red must still rise
at a reasonable rate so that Kiwai did not have too far to dive
without helmet and compressed air hose when he gave the
alarm. But for the moment they would remain in sight of
each other, with Kiwai just a little above but gradually
increasing the distance as they rose.

Fifteen minutes passed and it seemed a lifetime. Another
ten minutes and now Red was worried they were getting
dangerously close to the surface and might be seen from the
boat, which was stupid, for it certainly did not have a glass
bottom and looking up toward the surface of the water always
looked clearer than looking down. Then he worried that
Kiwai was staying too long with him, making it appear they
were too high for any real hose problem, or that they would
be seen by the other diver who must surely be on his way up
or, worse still, be above them. But the next moment his
thoughts were broken as something dropped suddenly upon
him so that his air was cut off for a moment and then he saw
Kiwai going up from him fast and realized that the Islander
had left nothing to chance. If he were to report a kinked hose
above, kinked it would be near where he would eventually

cut it—and indeed frightened would be the diver whom he would eventually rescue. Red marveled at the strength in the man's fingers that could bend the strong hose so quickly and thoroughly so that the rubber would show a kink line when they surfaced.

Red waited, and it seemed ages again, although it was only a few minutes before he saw the dark shape of Kiwai diving down towards him with his knife in his teeth. Momentarily it occurred to Red that it would be an easy matter for Kiwai to take the precious shell back from him to hold while he cut the hose and then stab Red and let him drop to the ocean floor. But it was a fantasy only and soon the dark man had taken the pearls out of the shell, held them tightly in one hand and then, while Red stretched his air line out for him, had neatly cut it close to the mouth so that the next moment, with the inrush of water, Red felt something go down, and hoped that he had swallowed both the pearls. Then Kiwai was taking his arm and pulling him upward.

It was, of course, farther to the top than Red had imagined so that by the time they reached it he really did feel as if he were about to drown and actually blacked out for a moment just as they broke water, so that there was no need to fake a near disaster. As they got the helmet off him on the deck he was coughing water and gasping in deep heaves for air and he noticed with a slight annoyance that his Islander partner was standing above him on the deck smiling broadly with that immaculate set of teeth of his and not even winded. The whole thing was so realistic that no one even thought to give him a mouth inspection, and that night, when the others were asleep, he drank down the whole bottle of little Lily's bowel choker.

Each day he went to the toilet, sat and grunted and groaned appropriately and was convinced that the guard did not even stop to consider that this poor diver might have been faking his bodily functions. Indeed the only person who had shown the least suspicion was the mate, who had said, "Why didn't you stay with him, Kiwai, and cut the hose before you came up?"

Kiwai replied that he was not sure what state Red was in, whether he was fully conscious or not. Once the hose was cut, he would have to be brought up quickly and Kiwai could not bring him up quickly while still in his suit. That was true enough, and an answer to a question they had foreseen and rehearsed, though it troubled them that anyone actually asked it. The mate, however, seemed satisfied, as most anyone was who asked a question of Kiwai about diving.

When they reached port late Sunday, both men headed for the town. But of course there was not a shop open which sold castor oil. Red found one shop that sold prunes, and bought and ate two jars, but to no avail. It was late on Monday afternoon, having quaffed a bottle of the oil on Monday morning, before the pearls came forth, out in the bush, beside a riverbed, Kiwai insisting with his broad laugh that he'd take his pearl washed, not unwashed, thanks very much.

They waited a week, sold the two pearls on the Chinese black market for 3500 pounds and probably at least 1500 pounds less than they were worth, and then approached a local representative of a ship-broking firm. Within another week the papers had been drawn up and they had their pearling lugger—not the newest and biggest, but a good sixty-footer and strong and seaworthy.

Red hoped he was right to put the money into this, rather than straight into cattle or land. He hoped this in the same way he had with the 250 pounds he had invested, on the inside information of Jarvis, his wartime chum, in the newly formed company across the border called Queensland and Northern Territory Aerial Services Limited. They'd wanted him to fly one of their Avro biplanes at first. He'd said no, but that he would be interested in joining the group of graziers they said they were organizing as backers. This suited his mate just as well, though he would have liked him as a pilot and Red would have loved to fly, too, but that would have given him no time at the property at all. Besides, he couldn't make enough money sitting in an airplane eventually to buy himself one to fly on his imagined one million acres of land. But after nearly a year of operation QANTAS was already going well and he knew now that that investment would be solid in a country whose vast distances held the key to its understanding.

So once again he returned to the Back of Beyond, a penniless capitalist, and thanked the God he did not believe in that cattle mated and produced a crop without asking for money.

30

That summer, if that is ever the right word for the Dry, that summer was one of the best he could remember at the Back of Beyond. He thought himself finally over the thing with Lisa; his mother, despite herself, had taken to Lily as to a daughter and supervised personally the birth of Jacky and Lily's baby girl; Billy seemed as well and happy as he had ever been; and for the first time, from the first three months of operation, there was a regular source of income coming in from the pearling lugger. He went to Darwin whenever the boat was due in. Kiwai would show his big white teeth to indicate the size of the profit and hand over Red's share. Back home they'd all wanted to know where he got the money, of course, so he said that he had in fact kept some money out of the main kick, and lied that he had put it into a gold-mining venture near Pine Creek which had paid off quicker than he expected so he had decided to take the money out and get into something more reliable. They believed what they wanted to believe and drank huge pots of tea around the scrubbed kitchen table and planned for the new station house they would like to build at the end of the next Wet and start of the next Dry.

Yet, with the unpredictability Red was learning to expect more and more, something unexpected always around the corner, behind the next tree, beyond the Back of Beyond, the Wet came early, very early, and very strong and heavy so that the mosquitoes were heavy, thick as a gas lamp fog around the hurricane lamp on the veranda, with even the kerosene outfires not stopping them, mosquitoes everywhere, and worse still, when the Dry came early with a sudden heat, incubating everything, so that it was a terrible year for malarial dysentery, and people dropping everywhere, and Billy caught it, and Red, fearful for his younger brother's weakened chest, rode to the telegraph station at once and telegraphed his doctor friend and said could he not come personally himself but got a reply that half the countryside was down with it and there was no special medicine other than what they'd used but he'd send someone with some more quinine pills so they did not run out and in six days' time Lisa herself came with the pills, a good enough ride in itself, seeing the rivers were still so high with the floods from the Wet, but Billy was dead by the time she arrived although they had not run out of pills.

He took Billy's body out to Five Mile Camp with an old gray army blanket over it, Lisa sitting beside him at the front of the rough cart, holding his left hand tightly as he cracked at the reins with the other in great urgency. He wanted to get his brother's body up into the cave at Five Mile Camp where it was dry. Then they would give him a proper funeral in home paddock later when it dried out.

His feelings for Lisa had not changed. They had matured, and so had hers, and there were many unsaid things in the hand-holding.

She waited at the entrance while he took Billy's body inside Five Mile Camp, and laid it in the cave and set a fire and nodded to Crocodile Tommy, who would watch over his brother.

They drove back in silence, each grateful for the other's presence.

The whole land was dank and putrid and it was still not dry enough to burn off and there was not enough kerosene to do the job however much they laid it on the billabong waters and stinking puddles and Red cursed the bloody property and the bloody lousy land and loved Lisa for doing the thing that mattered most in the bush, despite all his other feelings, loved her for her mud-streaked face and tired eyes and determination that had brought her through despite the rivers. And he told her as he put the bath in his bedroom for her and began to bring the hot water in from the kitchen that he admired her above everyone and he owed her and there was a mortgage now right enough which she held on him and his family and could call in any time in the future she wished. And she smiled beyond his words so that he understood and she stayed on to be with him until after his mother had left, left for Sydney with Douglas, once the threat of the epidemic was over, left in a bullock wagon with the few possessions she had arrived with so many years ago, left driven by Jacky as far as Darwin, left as she had arrived but with fewer men, she says mumbling, has lost two men to the land and does not intend to lose another, lost two to the land, she says, despite the fact that two sons went away and came safely home from the war.

Lisa stayed until Jacky returned and Red was over the worst of it.

He did not ask about her husband and she did not mention him, except to say she must be getting back soon. After she had gone, refusing the offer even of a ringer to ride with her, Red wondered about her strong, erratic, loving personality and how it understood the land, and knew he had made a mistake about her he would have to live with for a very long time.

They went down to Five Mile Camp then, Jacky and Red, and held a wake for Billy, good old gambling Billy, the happiest pick of the bunch, the tearaway kid who had no bloody right to die. They drank rum for days and were very drunk and Red painted himself up like Jacky, in corroboree paint with daubed chalk marks on the body, whooping it up for Billy who was buried in the home paddock, whooping it up for them all, the sad sorry sack of bastards they were to live in such a land they loved so, and it was then that they declared the land to be sacred, Five Mile Camp and for a mile around, the only damn black and white sacred land in the whole damn country if not the whole damn world.

Then they returned to the house in the middle of the night some days later, and got Fan-tan and Lily and the child out of bed, and used the last of the kero on the building, letting them save only the old scrubbed kitchen table and chairs, although there wasn't much else there anyway, and burned the whole damned place down. Then they all went into Darwin with all the ringers and the three bullock wagons, and got lumber and tin capping for the foundation posts against the white ants, and all sorts of things, including plenty more kero to burn off the last of the mosquitoes and start again.

Book III

THE KNOWLEDGEABLE GOOD DOCTOR ANNE

31

The next several years passed. The money came in from the pearling, from the cattle, and dividends from the airline were growing. They built the new station house, timber on stilts and nowhere near as big and gracious as that of Patrick Byrne's, but the basic structure was a mansion of a size and style for the Outback and painted white with some improvement made every year. Fan-tan and Lily ran the kitchen, now equipped with a giant cast-iron stove, and Lily's daughter Cathy had her mother's cheeky temperament. The pearling flourished. They now owned two boats and twice a year Red went into Darwin to see Kiwai and Bluey, whose father had passed on so that Bluey now ran the business. Bluey and Kat lived in the Byrne house now, with their children.

In Sydney, Beth, in a nice house overlooking the harbor, with Douglas working, going to accountancy school at night and Red sending money regularly, had found the ordered, quiet life she had always craved. She was tiny, old, frail and contented.

Red knew nothing of accountancy and economics, other than what he had observed from Bluey's father and Bluey. But he knew how to read things which went in cycles, what to watch for and what to expect, and he had that canny intuition which bushmen have. He did not know when the world depression would come; he did not even know whether there would be a great depression. What he knew was that the prices of things rise and fall, the price of everything sooner or later rises and falls, that was why it had been necessary for man to invent a "futures market," where men actually gambled on the future of things, for he felt he could hardly call it investment. Now he was no buyer of futures in things such as sugar or other crops, but he was a saver against the future, or rather for the future, and as the world went into 1929 and that terrible economic downturn that was to lead to those frightening, mournful food queues in every country, Red slaughtered all the meat he could get to market quickly, selling it without a profit if necessary, and took the cash, that cash and all he had saved, and waited and waited, trying to judge the bottom on the market, yet watching the government for devaluation and, late in '31, with an instinct Billy would have been proud of, he allowed for wages for two years and keeping everyone on, just bare wages and nothing else, and then plunged everything on a land-buying spree so that before he was finished he had nearly half a million acres.

The year 1933 was desperate. Kiwai was just hanging on and they were barely covering costs. The government had devalued currency twenty-five percent to help men on the land, but because Red had virtually only kept breeders, it didn't help them much. Besides, the devaluation was more to help the wool graziers, who needed it less because the price of wool on the world market was just starting to rise. But he and Jacky went dingo scalping, a thing they said they'd never do, and did it to keep the men on and themselves together and not to have to sell off one precious damn acre. So they hunted for the 7s. 6d. bounty which had never gone up but which the government had kept on, to keep the pest dog down and to give men employment. They hunted dingo and they hunted buffalo for skins and pet meat and they lived off the land and fish from the billabongs, the beautiful, big, tender barramundi being a staple diet that year, barramundi, and buffalo meat, and wild geese stew and the cabbages and other few greens Fan-tan managed to grow in home paddock. They had one milker, and really, compared with the rest of the country and the rest of the world, they were enormously well off. In those thin and sinewed times the land fed its people well. There was no drought; there was no big Wet. Even the cattle had feed.

They got through it all right and it was 1934 and Red was thirty-six and although he saw Lisa each time he visited Darwin, they met only as friends now, for her children were growing up and she had quietened down, although the old flicker was still there in her eyes sometimes, and when they had a couple of whiskies together in the late afternoon in the old flowered house which her father had left her they joked about the mortgage, and how Red had got on, and what it must be worth now, and she said that one day she might still collect.

In the spring of that next year, 1935, when the desert pea was out in flower, Lily turned thirty-two and somehow, though she had had a son as well by now, she looked prettier and fuller of ripeness and more beautiful than she had at sixteen. She was an effervescent spirit still, who kept them all on their toes, and got them well from their little ailments with the things she gathered and mixed, always wandering down by the river, or out near Five Mile Camp, although respecting its boundaries, to pick the eucalypt leaves or spinifex that grew near there. She used the spinifex a great deal, as all Aboriginals did and had for hundreds of years. The beating of its leaves produced something like a resin, which was really a thermoplastic, soft when hot but rock solid when dry, a useful glue for household use or for binding hunting weapons. So she was always wandering around collecting this or one thing and another, and although crocodile hunters were becoming an increasing problem and Red and Jacky had warned all the lubras to steer a wide course around any signs of these most despicable of white men, the lubras, especially Lily, took it about as seriously as the men knew they would, for they were all women of the bush, who believed they could take care of themselves, and, in any case, they did not believe anyone would try anything silly on Big Red's property. It was unfenced, like most large properties, for the cattle followed the drying-up water in at muster time, with the help of the jackeroos and ringers. The station employed over thirty now, and whereas it was sometimes hard, on an unfenced property, to stop or catch all the crocodile hunters, everyone felt pretty safe and believed the situation to be reasonably under control.

But one evening Lily was missed at dinner. Jacky and Red made light of it during the meal but immediately afterward went quietly about organizing a search. Red wanted to rouse the whole staff, most of whom were around the men's quarters, but Jacky shook his head and said, "You me track, Boss," and Red accepted that, whichever way it turned out, Jacky, with his Aboriginal instinct, felt the fewer people who knew the better; and of course he was quite right that it only needed the two of them, for he could, by blacktracking, find the path someone had taken, even by hurricane lamp in the dark. Two men coming by stealth would also be better than a noisy group if they were to surprise the crocodile hunters they believed they would find. The hunters rarely came in groups of more than four, largely because they often drove now, and three, really, in the front of a utility, or pickup truck, three in the front cabin was normal. So Red and Jacky loaded and slung their .303s and left with a hurricane lantern apiece.

The moon was not bad and Jacky soon picked up a trail though Red had a terrible feeling in the pit of his stomach for the first time for a long time, as bad as when he'd first heard Lisa had married, as bad as when Billy died. But Lily might be all right. She was smart as a whip and could run like the very devil. And there might be no hunters at all. She could have fallen or taken ill or have snakebite or been knocked around by a buffalo or 101 other normal things. She'd not be silly enough to get caught in a buffalo charge full on and she'd certainly get any snake poison out quickly by biting her own skin and sucking and spitting, so she could be quite OK, just weak and waiting somewhere for help. But Red feared the worst, and he could tell by Jacky's speed of tracking that he did, too.

They found her near some rocks about two miles from the camp. She'd crawled some distance to find a sharp stone. She'd been raped terribly, and torn about, and was badly bruised around the eyes, and Red saw Jacky rivet himself rigid, holding in his emotion with thousands of years of tribal instinct. He would cry later, alone, privately. But now his emotion held him like a man stamped out of black iron as Red took off his safari top and went to lay it over her, but Jacky bent rigid and stopped him and said, "Not yet, Boss," and looked by the light of the lantern, taking up each of her hands gently in turn, the tiny, thin-fingered hands where she had taken her own life by severing the wrist arteries with the stone, taking each hand gently and looking under the fingernails, knowing that Lily would not have died without telling him whom to look for.

"White man, Boss. She scratch bad. Face most likely. Crocodile skinner. Strong smell crocodile meat." It was said businesslike and rigidly and Red replied simply, "Right. Which way?"

"We blacktrack where happen first," he said, nodding stiffly now to Red, who lowered his shirt top longways to cover her head and most of her body and then followed Jacky off in the direction toward which he had already started to move.

For a blacktracker of Jacky's skill, even without the extra dread incentive he now had, it was an easy matter to find these foreign tracks on his native soil, these simple, treaded, rubber-tire tracks. He could have found them without a lamp. What stupid man or men had been so cavalier, so uncaring, so unknowledgeable about the property they were on, or the attitudes of black people themselves, as to be so confident?

Red knew the speed with which Jacky was working, and the route his tracking was taking, swinging around now, back and down toward the river. They would come on them soon enough, drunkenly and obliviously camped by the river, with their rifles nearby, thinking they were the only experienced hunters, these men who shot defenseless crocodiles from metal boats paddled out on the lagoons. But Red knew the speed with which Jacky was working and knew he must act quickly and somehow cut through the area where the black man had temporarily rigor-mortised his pain so that he saw sense through his reflex and controlled anger. So he caught up to him and took him gently by the arm and said, "Jacky, just a minute." ·

The black man stopped suddenly and stood still, as if he had expected it, stood still waiting to listen.

"How many, Jacky?" Red said. "How many at the spot where it happened?"

"One, Boss. Only tracks one on ground but car there; heavy tracks. Two others in car, you bet, Boss."

"One only, then, Jacky, however unfair that seems. We'll never get away with three and you're to let me do it, not you. You know how other hunters will make the troopers come after you if a black man is suspected."

"Good reason finish all three. All three guilty, Boss. Finish all three so no one tell."

Red did not question whatever invisible weight ratio in Jacky's head knew it was three. And he knew the black man was right in one sense that it was safer to kill all three. But if they just got the one and did it in the way Red was thinking, then the others might shut up. But if three croc hunters disappeared off his place, and some of their mates probably knew where they had gone, he could have every kangaroo and croc hunter in the Territory on his neck, not to mention the police.

He explained all this to Jacky over and over and Jacky kept arguing and saying, "No, Boss, three fellar come, three fellar go. We find now, Boss, we no wait any longer."

"Use your bush logic, please. If we take all three, their friends and the police will come and dud us for sure and then where will everything we've worked for be and what will happen to Cathy and your son? If we knock off the whole three they'll get me, too, sooner or later, so don't follow your Aboriginal logic through that I'll be around to look after your kids. Trust me, please."

At the mention of Cathy, so like her mother, Red saw Jacky's eyes moisten so he thought he would break, but then the black man drew on his inner resources in the way only he could and pulled himself up again and said, "OK, Red, we do your way but I shoot bad white and if anything go wrong with your plan I shoot three on spot, OK?"

"OK. That's sensible. But you'll let me try to talk the one out first?"

"When sure got all safely my sights, Boss," said the black man.

"That's a deal," said Red, and they moved on.

About half an hour later the car tracks ran out into tall grass and then, from a clump of trees, they could see a campfire and the car, and three men as Jacky had predicted. Quietly they slipped the safeties forward on their rifles as they unslung them and moved forward so they could see the men clearly. They were sitting around the fire in a small clearing, two men together and the third, a little more morosely, using the rum bottle they passed between them more than the other two. This man had bad scratches down his face. He was a thin and long-nosed man with a ferret face and harsh mouth.

Red held Jacky's arm tightly as he felt the black man stiffen even more rigidly beside him. Then Jacky nodded and Red nodded in return and Jacky moved around silently to where he had a better line of fire to all three men.

The campfire was only a short distance from them. Both he and Jacky were well concealed and Red now took a line of fire on the man with the scratches, sighting easily along the barrel and holding his rifle up as he now began to speak in little above his normal speaking voice.

"You're dead if you so much as twitch, you blokes. Don't do it, for Chrissakes, I mean it, so help me."

But even despite this the man slumped near the fire sat suddenly bolt upright and out of the corner of his eye Red saw the other two starting to look nearby for their rifles and he pumped off one shot at the feet of the jerked-up man, hoping that Jacky would not let loose yet and the one shot would bring the others to their senses.

It did. One of the men stammered out, "What do you want, for Chrissakes?"

"You know what we want. We want that scum over there. I'm not alone. There's another rifle on you all and it's a trigger-happy and deadly one. You two could have stopped it and you didn't, and God knows you deserve to die and God knows I and my friend will never forget your faces till the day we die. But if you two get up now and leave, get in your truck without your rifles and leave and never mention this to a soul, you'll live. If you mention a word to anyone, so help me, whatever else happens, I'll find you and kill you. Anyone asks, a croc got your man. He got drunk and fell over the side of the boat in a billabong. . . ."

"Don't leave me, Jesus, don't leave me," the other man whined and went to get up again, aimlessly, forgetfully, hardly knowing what to do, Red thought, as he dropped another shot at his feet and the man slumped down again and then vomited all over himself with fear.

At the sight of this the man who had spoken first said,

"You've got a deal, mate. We're not part of this. He's on his own. Just tell us what to do and when."

"You *are* part of it, and you'll always be part of it until you die, and you remember that over every drunken drink you ever have when tempted to tell someone. Your dirty, fuckin' bastard of a mate fell in drunk and a croc got him. Got that?"

Red's anger was getting at him now and for a moment he wondered whether he might shoot the three himself.

"Got it," the two men said hurriedly together.

"Then get up right now and go. Leave everything and go—"

They rose slowly and began to turn—

"And you, you scratched-face bastard, don't move—"

But the man's body was in a bent-over hump, involuntarily jerking with his retching and because he was, by the look of it, shitting into his trousers.

Red hoped Jacky could control his anger just a little longer. He hoped he would be wise enough not to let them hear an Aboriginal voice. He shouted across the distance:

"Whistle when they're clear. I'll keep this one in sight."

And as he said this, and heard Jacky turn to follow the others silently the short distance to their truck, Red fired his third shot, the .303 at that distance blowing the man's guts open, as he jerked upward and screamed once and then dropped. The men would now know the other was dead; that the man whose voice they had heard had shot him, so that if anything ever came of it, it was they against a white man, or they and the police against a white man, not against a black man, which might be weighted odds. But he thought he could be reasonably sure they would tell the crocodile story.

He heard Jacky whistle and knew the others were off. Soon he would have to face Jacky's anger at not letting him do the killing. It could be a longtime sore for Jacky, although he would understand well enough why Red had done it.

"You trick me, Boss," Jacky said when he came back. The words carried their own anger and hurt, even without their intonation, hurt for both men. "You say trust me and then you trick me. You know I think you let me kill man who rape Lily."

"I know, I'm sorry. It was the safest way. I'm truly sorry."

"We no speak about anymore," Jacky said, and this was a bad sign because it could mean he would freeze Red out forever in his lackadaisical dismissal way of things. He would do the things necessary to clear away the body and then he would bury Lily and then Red would know the real state of things. But he felt Jacky would come around in time.

"We've got a few hours before light. We must take this bastard's carcass to Coffin Swamp, Jack."

"Drop in river for crocs, like you say. Let them eat his lousy hide."

Red walked over and put his arm around his friend. "You know better than that. We don't want the crocs tasting human flesh and we don't want the possibility of human bones left over if the police do come. We must take him to Coffin Swamp and hide him like an Aboriginal body, however hard that is to take. We could bury Lily in home paddock, near Billy. That would be nice. She'd like that. Then she wouldn't have to be in the same place as this maggot."

Lily was a different generation from Nora and so Jacky nodded.

"I'll go and get our truck," Red said.

When he came back he and Jacky stripped some bark and wrapped the white man's body up in it and dumped it on the back of the truck and drove to Coffin Swamp where they left it and Jacky sat on the back of the truck with a leafed branch on the way back, wiping out the truck's tracks, although if any police came it could be months and then it was unlikely they'd bring a blacktracker with them at first.

Just before dawn they buried Lily beside Billy and agreed that they'd say only that she'd tripped and been gored to death by a buffalo. Those who knew about such things would know how unlikely this was, and those who knew could draw what conclusions they wanted from the absolute ban Red would now place on any hunters of any sort coming on his land without permission.

32

In fact Lily's going seemed in some ways to affect Red more than Jacky. The black man quickly forgave his partner and tried—for some time in vain—to console him. It was at this time that Red began his lonely vigils at Five Mile Camp, talking to himself, yet talking, too, to the crocodile. It was at this time that he started going into Darwin more, and reading everything he could lay his hands on from the library. It was at this time that Lisa's husband finally persuaded her that they must go South for the children's sake; it was at this time that Red, for the first time, seriously considered leaving the Back of Beyond. He told no one. But Jacky knew and said nothing.

In a way Red knew Jacky's matter-of-fact, fatalistic, fate-will-rule-in-the-great-outdoors attitude was the only one possible for such a country; in another way he found it, as so many thinkers in every country before him, totally unacceptable. It was there as a fact, yet it was unacceptable. Perhaps it was just unpalatable. It was only luck. You had bad luck or you had good luck. By hard work and care you could increase the chances of one and decrease the chances of the other. But there you were again: you had to fall back on the use of the word chance. Life was a happy gambler like Billy; life was a dead gambler. How, how, in the possible scheme of things could they have stopped what had happened to Lily? By keeping her inside? Could everyone be kept inside all their lives? Sooner or later a wind would come by and rip the roof off. Could law systems be devised to prevent men, such as the three who had come onto the property, being allowed out on their own to rape land and people? Of course not. It was luck. Pure and simple, it was luck. Who you got and what you got was luck. Happiness was your share of good luck. The rest was your bad luck. Everyone got a lot of the latter and a little of the former. Correction. He bet there were people, plenty of people, who didn't think they'd got much of the former; none at all, some.

It was at this time, mechanically, on Jacky's insistence, they imported some Brahmans of their own, and crossed them with their best, and built up their breed into the best quality you could get in the North, built up the cattle mobs and improved the property and got, with Fan-tan's help and Cathy, Lily's daughter, choosing some decent furniture and curtains and things for the property. The airline was booming; Kiwai had suggested they buy a third pearler and Red had agreed. Everything was going well, except he was still going through the motions, moody and restless and inverted deeply, at the root of it all a deep conflict over whether to stay or go. In thoughts he hardly allowed himself to have, yet knew were there, he knew he could run things now from Sydney, or Brisbane, or Adelaide, where Lisa had gone.

But instead he took to prospecting, riding on the third-generation horse now, riding to the west along the old Canning Stock Route, a deadly enough route of its own, riding carelessly enough to kill himself, but needing the solitude and not caring about the Geiger counter Bluey had given him, trying to get him interested in something. In fact, Douglas had suggested the Geiger counter to Bluey when Bluey was on a business trip to Sydney. He had suggested a great deal more than that. Bluey would have liked to have thought that Douglas had suggested the Geiger counter to get Red's mind off his depression following Lily's death. But it was simply Douglas's obsession with business and Bluey wondered sometimes if the growing rift between the brothers—worse because it was a silent, unmentioned rift—would one day flare into open hostility. Bluey knew it would if he was ever stupid enough to mention to Red the other suggestion Douglas had made on that trip to Sydney. The property needed modernizing, he'd said, the staff could be pruned and better handled. The first step was to get rid of Jacky, Douglas had said. Even Bluey had hit the roof at that and finally, finally after many hours arguing, extracted a promise never to mention it to Red. But Red's absence worried Bluey. Douglas was taking too tight a hold of the business reins, although Bluey knew Red more than capable of fixing that when he chose to. If he chose to.

Red had been gone now nearly a year and found nothing and did not give a tinker's curse and on the way back decided to detour and ride the Murranji again for the hell of it, hoping it would be as dry as hell, drier than last time. But it was not. There was water all along it each way and as fate would have it, there being so much bloody water, he went looking for drier country, something that would be a challenge, and crossed the main Track to head across country for his own place after he had left the Murranji and the notices, the two of them, which were still there. And many miles into the drier country the bloody Geiger counter went off like a quiet alarm clock and there was the stupid luck of it all: wanting to die sooner or later and preferably sooner at the moment, cursing the bloody country that could not even give him the challenge of a decent Murranji Track anymore, it had given him a fortune from its dried and cracked womb as if to say however many lives it took it was not all that way and there were always lush virgin valleys or purple escarpment hills of one sort or another such as those he had been shown now and whether he would exchange the land for the other things it did which he did not like was not for him to say, it was only for him to say what use he made of such things. But this was not an issue at that time. There was some interest in such discoveries, but only for the radium. Red registered his find and gave Bluey back his Geiger counter but it would be some years before they knew what they had lucked upon.

But Red thanked Bluey for his interest, like his old man, in new things and said that if the find had some medical use that was good, and it had helped him to start to get the blues out of his system, if Bluey would forgive the use of the word, but he'd had the bloody blues for over a year but was getting OK again now thanks to his friends.

Again, he threw himself into work, riding and mustering, buying and selling and improving the property until he had three-quarters of a million acres, and a giant mob of good cattle, turning over the right numbers each year to keep the mob good. Now stories were written about him, about his property and his pearling and about his big airline holdings, and when the reporters came to his property, although he had an airstrip, they were disappointed he did not have a plane. He said so was he, but he could not afford one because he kept putting all his spare cash into land. They laughed when he said he couldn't afford one, but he knew they didn't know you were always borrowing from Peter to pay Paul and never had any real cash of your own while you were expanding and then once you were expanded you needed capital to service all your investments. Anyway, he said, the strip was for the flying doctor and people such as reporters to fly in on, or for emergencies, and that for him a plane would be a toy, not an investment, and as they had actually commented, he did have one or two airline shares, one or two hundred thousand, actually, so he guessed he had a few airplanes flying around for him as an investment anyway.

But what about the war? they said. Wouldn't he fly again in the next war?

Was there going to be a next war? He didn't know. No one had told him yet. He might be a bit old to fly and a bit out of date on the latest aircraft. Did they ride horses anymore to war? He supposed not. Was he joking? Indeed not. Who would joke about a thing like that? Whether you could ride to war on a horse or not made all the difference. Airplanes were very good for transport for countries like Australia, but they had made war very serious. He was not sure he believed in wars anymore if you couldn't ride to them on horses. But if there was going to be a war as the reporters suggested, he was certainly looking forward to the rise in the price of beef.

It was about this time that, on the basis of some of these remarks, a young reporter who thought he was smart wrote a story which suggested that the young cattle king might just be the slightest bit eccentric. He did it cunningly without using the word. But he used the quotes about war and horses cleverly out of context.

Cathy showed Red the story first. She was eighteen now and had finished her mission schooling and next year would start nursing in Darwin. Her brother, whom they called Black Roo, was still only three. Fan-tan, who got fatter and happier each year, looked after him with the help of the kitchen lubras. Under the highly civilized and sensible Aboriginal extended family system, which was really how the station house was run, Cathy and Black Roo had several black mothers and black fathers, a white father, and a Chinese male nurse and nanny. They looked at the story over breakfast, the paper a week old.

Cathy read it aloud to them all. When she had finished reading, Jacky leaned over toward Red,

"Him plurry give it to you, Boss," he said, in his most deliberate and worst Aboriginalese, often these days reserved for tourists.

"Just as well you didn't tell him you talked to crocodiles, Uncle Red," Cathy said.

"You're right there, sister, he'd have looped the loop on that one for sure. Well, at least he spelt my name right. They say that's all that matters with publicity, isn't it?"

"But you no want publicity, Mister Red," Fan-tan said.

Red looked at him and then around the table. "Do you think we could settle on a common language for this family sooner or later so I know where I am? Is it too much to ask you all to speak English now and then? I mean I know I have problems myself sometimes, finding bush English a damn sight better, but at least I'm making an effort—"

"For the children's sake," broke in Cathy cheekily.

"Exactly. For the children's sake. Where was I? Oh, yes, the publicity. No, I don't want it, Fan-tan. I don't give a stuff about it—"

"That's an interesting English word, Uncle Red. Would you mind translating—?"

He looked at her warmly.

"You're getting too smart for me. May I continue? Thank you. I think that Uncle Doug in Sydney has let our success go to his head a bit. I mean it's no different from all those other jokers who are half up themselves there. . . ." Cathy suppressed a smile, knowing that he had broken back into half bush English himself now as much to tease her as anything and to bewilder Fan-tan who still had trouble with some of the vernacular. . . . "But let's say they do it their way there, and we do it our way here, and who's to say who's right? Douglas is running much of the business end these days and he says a certain kind of publicity gives you a solid business image; makes us look more like business people and less like the cow cockies we are, although I rather think I'm going to get a scorcher of a letter about this story. But he arranged for the reporters to come and I said I'd cooperate because he is my brother and has got a damn good business head. At least I think so because Bluey says so."

He loved these early-morning breakfast conferences, as did they all, before they were out and about and doing their chores for the day. They were a bit sweet-sour afterward sometimes, for both him and Jacky. Each man missed not having a wife and knew it was the price you paid sometimes for being on the land and so far away from settlements. In the early days, when his father was alive, it had been nothing for men of the Outback to go two, three, sometimes five years without seeing a white woman. It was easier, really, for the blacks. But Jacky had not gone walkabout back to his own people after Lily's death. He could not at first because of Red's despondency. But he had also explained that he hadn't felt like it at the time, hadn't felt like getting another wife, although the locals had pretty well adopted him and he slept with some of their women whenever he wanted. In this respect it was harder on Red, particularly as he was one of those white men who did not sleep with lubras. It was not a racial thing. The blacks respected the white men who didn't. It was a mark of respect by the white men that they did not hold the black women lightly. So Red had survived on casual liaisons in the town on his sporadic visits and had had plenty of time to regret that he had not been impulsive enough to marry Lisa when she wanted to.

At forty, although as fit as a mallee scrub bull, he felt himself too old now to marry and raise a family. Cathy, with the quick flicker and cheek of her mother, kept raising the issue, and she was probably the only one who could have got away with it. She kept asking him when he was going to marry and told him how she would pick someone out for him when she went to Darwin next year because she sure to hell wasn't one of those stupid black women who wanted an old man on her hands all her life. Under the extended family system, she saw Uncle Red as her responsibility if he did not marry, so she kept telling him that she was going to find someone for him "plurry quick as possible" so he ceased to be a liability to the family. If the worse came to the worst, she said, she would ship him off to America where they had a surplus of women and a matriarchal society.

"What do you think we've got here, you bloody little anthropologist?" he said, rising and dodging out the door as she threw the tea cozy at him.

33

The next year war was declared. Red decided to watch and wait and see if he got called up. Meantime he and Jacky carried on as usual, holding the absolute maximum number of cattle until the war forced the price of beef up. Black Roo played around the home paddock or rode with them on his pony and Cathy was already in Darwin. Otherwise life in the Outback was very much as usual for a time.

Early in 1940 Red and Bluey both got their call-up notices to report for medicals. In fact, Red got two—one from the air force and one from the army—leading him to remark when he arrived in Darwin to see Bluey that the services hadn't changed much on the administration side seeing they still couldn't count up to one.

"What'll you do?" Blue said.

"We mightn't be passed as fit."

"We'll be passed, all right."

"I don't detect that note of enthusiasm you showed during the last great conflict, Mr. Byrne."

"Perhaps that's because I've been through one great conflict and know what it's like, Mr. Carlyon. You don't seem so interested yourself, come to mention it. You might even say you show a greater interest in the price of beef."

"Have you ever stopped to think that we might be going

over there to shoot at the sons of the same bastards we shot at last time or, worse still, to shoot at the very same bastards who shot at us? Now what sense does that make?"

"None at all, except—"

"Yeah, I know, it doesn't make any sense at all unless you think of that little prick Hitler, and of Poland, and that he's not stopping. Besides, Paris was good, you've got to admit that."

"Will take us as long to get there this time as it did last. Maybe longer."

"You're right there."

"Well, what are you going to go for—air force or army?"

"Army, if I can swing it. I look at it this way: in the air force I'd be too out of date. I don't reckon they'd let me fly, and even if they did, how would I be up against some hot young jockey straight out of flying school or a professional pilot from the German air force? And they'll have 'em. But I have been rifle shooting all this time, and I do know one or two things about hunting. No, I'll go for the bloody infantry, although I don't like the walking bit, but they reckon horses are out."

"Well, we might get in together again, then. You realize that if they pass us fit we'll probably both be officers."

"Come off it."

"I mean it. We're certainties. With our records of service it's as good as a fixed race. Just about everyone from the first war's getting pips of some sort."

They had their medicals and were told that they were fit but they were to wait because they weren't taking "the old jokers just yet." Bluey wanted to tie one on the sergeant who had said that, but Red said that was no way for a potential officer to behave, hitting an NCO.

A month later they were told by letter they would not be called up as both were in essential industries: Bluey's interests included mining and Red's cattle grazing was certainly an essential industry. Moreover, the demand for beef was not the only thing that had skyrocketed and was making Red his fortune. The demand for mother-of-pearl, for that precious shell, had gone through the roof. The shell was an important component of compasses. Business was so brisk Kiwai had to give up diving himself. They now had five luggers and employed dozens of divers under Kiwai's supervision.

"What do you say about being an officer now, Blue?" Red said when he came back into Darwin after getting his notice too.

"I say pig's bloody arse to the army, that's what I say; what about you?"

"The same."

"Thought we didn't want to fight?"

"Only when no bastard was telling us we couldn't."

"You're right. What are we going to do?"

"Do you reckon, seeing we are in essential industries like, and that between us we own almost half this damn bloody country, or the only part of it that counts, do you reckon we might have a bit of influence with the brass?"

"I reckon. What you got in mind?"

"I've just got a whacking big order for beef from the army. How are your orders for iron ore?"

"Big."

"Let's both tell 'em to go to hell until at least a general comes to talk to us."

"Have we got any generals?"

"Good question. Make it a brigadier, you reckon?"

"I reckon."

"Yeah, we're reasonable men. We'll hold out for a brigadier. But it's got to be a field rank. None of this quartermaster's crap."

"You're right. Have another drink and we'll phone 'em up. Who'll we call, you reckon?"

"South-Eastern Command. General Officer Commanding South-Eastern Command."

"He mightn't have heard of us."

"He can look us up in records while we're telling him about how short he's going to be of his bloody beef and iron."

They made their call, being deadly serious when they got on the telephone and refusing all attempts to put them through to the Quartermaster's Corps. In the end they got the

GOC's adjutant who sounded sympathetic and said if they put in their absolute objection to being classed as "essential and reserved" industry, in writing, and an undertaking that deputies could carry on effectively in their places, they had a fair chance.

They did this, and before long were back in khaki, Red as a captain and Bluey as a first lieutenant, and on their way once more to the Middle East. Someone had been smart enough to look beyond age and occupation in their records to marksmanship and performance in the last war.

But their stint overseas was to be short-lived. When German infantry and tanks breached the Australian position at Tobruk and ran on toward the cliffs of the port, they had to be driven back in a fierce battle by the Royal Horse Artillery. As the tanks finally pulled back, the Australian infantry, having stood its ground against the heavy onslaught, counted its casualties. Bluey was OK but Red, who had run to pull some of his men out of the way of a fast-advancing tank, had caught a heavy piece of exploding shrapnel in the leg just below his kneecap. He was in agony and the kneecap hanging like a jockey's cap dangling by the peak. When the main relief of the Australian garrison of Tobruk took place in September and October, Red was shipped home. Bluey stayed until April 1942 when, with MacArthur withdrawing to Australia, the 6th and 7th Australian divisions, which included Bluey's regiment, were ordered home to join the American forces there.

But Red had arrived home, and was in the Darwin hospital, before the Japanese attack on Pearl Harbor in December 1941. His World War II service had lasted only a few months and he had been awarded the Military Cross.

At the hosptial the army doctors held several conferences over his leg and he told them to hurry up because Darwin would be next. Yet even he only half believed this, despite Pearl Harbor. And suddenly his attention was diverted from the war by the request that he give the doctors who were to operate on him discretion as to whether his leg stayed or went. Reluctantly, he gave permission. It was a long operation and it was not until two days after it that he heard the full story, or probably as much as he would get of the full story, from Cathy via the hospital grapevine. The two army doctors had been for taking the leg off. But a young lady doctor from the South had argued against this and, in the end, pulled her rank. She pointed out that although the man was of army rank, the hospital was still civilian, as was she, and the army doctors were using the hospital facilities. But she, as the civilian doctor, was in charge of the theater, the man to be operated on lived on the land and his leg must be saved if at all possible. She believed, with modern techniques, it could be rebuilt around the kneecap. The leg might be permanently stiff, but better that than riding with an artificial leg or walking. The fact was, said Cathy, that the army doctors did not have the modern techniques and when the lady doctor said either they assisted her in trying or she would not proceed with the operation without the patient being fully informed of what she believed to be the alternatives, they reluctantly agreed. With their assistance, she rebuilt the leg. Red did not know if he'd ever get full use back, but at least it was still there and he gratefully asked to see the doctor, who had already been in several times since the operation to check, though he'd been dopey for hours afterward, and she had said nothing special and he had hardly noticed her, assuming her to be just another member of the staff, such as a physiotherapist, for all his dealings had been with the austere army doctors.

The night he asked to see her she came in with Cathy after the evening meal.

"Uncle Red," Cathy said quietly, "this is Doctor Brown." Then Cathy kissed him on the forehead and left.

"Anne," said the doctor, taking one of her hands out of her white coat, "Anne Brown—don't get up."

He had started to pull himself up in the bed to shake her hand. She knew how much cutting and bone bruising she had done in her rebuilding and how much it would still hurt and she had seen him wince as the stitches pulled as well. She came over and he lay back onto the three pillows and brought his hand out from under the covers.

"That's better," she said, as she shook it. "Pretty sore still, huh?"

"Uh-uh," he said, shaking his head. "Not bad."

"Huh-huh," she said, nodding hers. "I think we'll dispense with the mock heroics so you and I can get used to being honest with each other. The liquid APC every four hours— and I apologize for not having anything stronger but everyone's short—could only be taking the edge off. But as the pain does get a bit better I want you to get used to telling me what still hurts and what doesn't. That way we'll get to figure out how soon you start your exercises and in what way."

"It hurts," he said with a sigh and then, suddenly, his eyes welling at the human sympathy and the realization hitting him that this girl, for she looked little more, had cared, really cared, whether he lost his leg or didn't, when the others hadn't, or hadn't known enough to care, he added, his voice almost breaking for the first time in his life and with the sob barely held back. "I'm just so bloody, bloody grateful."

She looked at him then, as he sniffed and inhaled the near tears back in, and took his hand which had lain outside on the covers after she had shaken it, took it and put it back inside the bed with a soft, caring touch and said, "Of course you are and I'm grateful for your thanks, but that's my job and I'm glad to do it and now I think you'd better get some sleep. I'll send Sister along with something we've got plenty of and I'll send Cathy back for a while until you go to sleep. Would you like that?"

Red nodded, but his eyes were filling again.

"Good," she said smiling. Her hair was soft and tan and wispy, softly rounded down to her shoulders, and she had large blue eyes and a soft and sensitive voice that slipped inside a person unannounced, as if hardly conscious of the woman it had come from, a low and quiet and caring voice. "Good," she added again in that voice, "I'll see to it, then. See you later."

He forced himself to say thanks, without a quaver, but although she had heard it, she had already turned, and did not turn back as she went out the door and he realized that she was not tall at all as he had imagined her to be while she was standing by him.

34

In this quiet way thus began what was later to be called affectionately in Territory folklore the romance of the century. For from that first meeting on, Annie belonged to Big Red. There was no question about that. Ask the hospital orderlies. Ask the kitchen staff. Ask Red's batman. Ask Cathy and the other Aboriginal ladies of the town. Big Red was squattocracy, Outback royalty. He had sent for the doctor to whom he owed his leg and given her his hand. What else was there? What else could it mean? Anything that might or might not happen after that would be seen as an anticlimax. She was Red's and Red was hers. That was how it was in the word-of-mouth onpassing of message after message down the Track, by horseman, by telegraph line, and now by radio transmitter linking the stations with Darwin. Indeed, all on the Back of Beyond, so it later transpired, knew all this long before Annie herself, who was—and just as well, considering her fierce independence, Cathy was to remark—blissfully ignorant of how the rest of the local population now regarded her. She noticed, of course, on her few trips outside the hospital to the shops, an added warmth toward her and interest in her doings, but put none of this down to its real reason.

When Red's leg was finally well enough for them to go out to dinner together for the first time, the whole town might just as well have been invited to take up vantage points along the route the procession would take to the hotel dining room overlooking the Arafura Sea where the bridal breakfast would take place. This was not an uncommon slang term in those days to cover a variety of meetings in a town of mixed races, of forever shifting populations of drovers and Overlanders, of whom there were certainly still some, of hunters of all sorts, and now of service personnel. For those who looked on, as Red and Annie left the hospital for their first meal together, this was how they saw it. It had added point this Saturday evening because it was known Red was to depart on recuperative leave the next day.

It was doubtful if any officer ever looked better in a uniform. Red's hair was still black, straight for the most, but with a little curling here and there and a graying at the sideburns and temples. He had the ruddy, healthy glow that the countryside gives to its people. His summer uniform had been gone over and over in the town's Chinese laundry. It was pressed clean and fresh so that the creases stood out. His Sam Browne belt and his boots shone, and he carried his peaked cap in his hand as he limped his way to the car from the hospital, supported at each arm by Annie and his batman.

Red could tell from the stares and waves along the way what was going on but he only smiled quietly to himself and when Annie said how friendly the townspeople were Red just added, "Of course," and left it at that.

They reached the hotel and went in, Red helped by the hotel staff. They took a long time over drinks on the terrace before they went inside for a meal. Later, amid the silver and the starched tablecloths, as they dipped into their fingerbowls of rose petals and lemon water and received yet another table napkin from the waiter, it was hard to believe that a war was going on: that within weeks Darwin would have its Pearl Harbor. But there were no planes in sight this night and they looked out from the big square window of the hotel across the ocean and it was the still and silver-pink thing of any tropical dusk.

They had had the fresh mud crabs with the coldest of wine, and now they awaited their grilled barramundi while Red discussed with the headwaiter the state of the strawberries and the Bollinger to come.

"I'm impressed," said Anne.

"Don't be. It's just that from the earliest years on, having treats is part of coming to town. Every time a bushie comes to town he gives himself a treat: a woman, a drunken binge, a present for the Missus he hasn't seen for two years if he's lucky enough to have one who doesn't mind the land—rather like a sailor getting to the last port before home."

"And which category am I?" asked Anne, who loved to tease him.

"Don't you know?" he said, turning her question around on her in a way she found disconcerting.

"Take your time," he added, looking at his watch. She did not immediately answer and went a little red so that he turned to talk to the headwaiter again about the strawberries. He was positioned in such a way as to be able to look across at her as he talked.

He winked at her from time to time, although his whole conversation probably only took a minute or two. His kindly looking at her made her a little self-conscious so that she imagined wrongly that the whole of the dining room was looking at her. The others, who filled perhaps half of the room, had taken the couple in with warm smiles as they had entered. But they would not stare, though anyone would have been struck by the scene and the look of Anne that night. For despite her professionalism, the objectivity her job demanded of her, there was another side, different even from the caring and loving aspect of her which so many of her patients, including Red, experienced. To the people of Darwin, hard-baked by the high cruel sun, there was a freshness of youth about her. Some of it may have been in the peaches and cream complexion, the classic tender and sensitive skin that goes with the notion of an English rose, which she had inherited from her English mother. Something clean and beautiful and unburned was as precious to the people of the

North to look at as life itself; and they looked at her with her brown hair and her skin of unfired porcelain as if she were some fairy-tale Snow White or far-off princess come to visit them.

This freshness had always been hers. She had had a happy home life in Victoria's Western District and at boarding school, the daughter of farmers in a land where Rolls-Royces and Bentleys were the norm, in the years when every fleece of wool was truly golden. So she had a freshness and a style and the clothes to go with it that stood out on that night in the Far North dining room as if it had been her coming-out party. She looked twenty-one and, indeed, was only five years beyond that. She had that just-left-school vitality and freshness this night (although she'd been out of university over two years), and she wore it with a complete unconsciousness. With her natural fair complexion, her full, longish brown hair, which she had combed up a little at the front to tie in a tiny blue ribbon in a bow, and her simple, pastel-blue tailored dress with a string of pearls and black patent-leather handbag and shoes, the effect was almost of a young girl on her first serious outing.

There was a sparkle of salt-tipped water in her eyes which spilled over into her conversation, her laughter, into her little skip of a swinging walk as she had come to the table earlier in a way that had made everyone alive, from the very first, to the ring of her presence.

She left Red's remark still unanswered for the time and they ate and drank some more as they discussed again her reasons for coming to Darwin and whether she intended to stay. She smiled to herself, for she believed she was not supposed to notice the subtle strategy behind Red's questioning. She knew that he thought her very independent, and very career-committed, and as reluctant as most women to settle in the real wilderness of the Outback. They had discussed none of this, but she perceived it to be so and it was indeed true what he thought of her. But she knew something extra that he did not. That was her secret. And tonight she kept it, leaning back into the steady, soft intoxication of the champagne and the breeze that now came off the water through the open windows, enjoying this all, and the delicious dinner and company, and keeping her secret intact.

So they talked again about her farm and her parents, and her medicine course at Melbourne University and how she had done her internship and then her first year toward becoming a surgeon until the war interrupted. He asked again did she like the North and what it was that had attracted her to it. She said she thought she liked it and that she had always wanted something exciting to do and the Royal Flying Doctor Service sounded the most exciting. She hoped to learn to fly. But she was also very interested in the infant mortality rate among Aboriginal children in the North. She'd read a lot about it as a child after she'd visited the Lake Tyers Reserve in Victoria. She believed that was what really made her want to come North originally—the conditions at Lake Tyers and hearing it was worse in the North. But the war had brought it forward. At first she thought of enlisting. Then she heard they were short of doctors in the North and decided to see if she liked it.

They talked about many things. But always it came back to that: did she like it and would she stay? She had heard from Cathy the story about his mother leaving, and part of it from him, and knew it colored all his thinking and that of so many others. The droving and overlanding tradition—and he was certainly part of that—held women as part of the towns. Those who did marry left their wives at points of civilization—indeed, more often than not the wives insisted on it. Some of that had changed, but so much of the Territory, the last of the country to develop, was still seen as a hostile environment for females. This was what the men of Outback bronze feared most: more than any privation of animal or climate. This was the Australian loneliness. It had nothing to do with a man's capacity to win or hold a woman. Because of the loneliness, because of the rarity of the station Missus, women were treated with a deference and respect that would have won any Outback man a husband-of-the-year award in any city. They were gentle men of strength. Anne knew all this, for she was Australian, though her parents were not, and because she had listened and observed in her short time North to add to her already considerable book knowledge of Outback peoples. She let Red ask his questions, but she kept her secret.

When they decided it was time to go he explained matter-of-factly he had taken a room with a view upstairs. He would have dearly loved to have taken her for a walk on the beach, or a swim, down the path that led from Bluey's place, he said, but with his leg it was not to be. It would be nice to sit and relax over a drink and look out to sea. Whether she wished to utilize his room or go home was fine with him. His batman would be outside again by now and he'd been told to wait to take her back to the hospital.

"I'll tell him he's not wanted," she smiled, as he went to get up and she steadied him, at the same time beckoning to the waiter. She asked the waiter to help him to the elevator and wait there.

She went to speak quietly to Red's driver, and then walked to the elevator, where Red was already inside holding the door open for her.

They got to the room with some difficulty and Anne discovered another bottle of iced champagne waiting.

He had his arm around her shoulder. She let him slide down onto the bed and then sat down on it with a sigh and kicked her shoes off.

"Tired?" he said as he loosened his tie.

"Suddenly bloody exhausted," she said. "Are the showers here good?"

"They used to be good before the war," he said.

She went off to have a shower and soon returned with a towel around her and then motioned him to stand up—which he did precariously on one leg—while she skewed the bed around so it was slightly more forward and full-on to the ocean view and the big French windows. Then she opened all the windows, threw back the cover and top sheet on the double bed, and sat him down and helped him undress. His leg was still very stiff and he still needed help. She put the sheet over him when she'd finished, moved the table with the wine up beside him and then dropped her towel to the floor and slid in herself. She cuddled hard with her thighs into his good leg, and he tucked her under his shoulder so he could feel her breasts against his side. They lay still a long time and dozed and woke and kissed and cuddled very softly, both exhausted but not wanting to lose the time together. After a while the worst of the tiredness was gone and while he lay on his back in the position he could not move from because of his leg, he put out his hand to guide her over on top of him. She took his hand from her buttocks and kissed it, giving herself time to think again. It took only a moment and she did not believe he noticed the delay. Then she slipped quickly over onto him and wondered if he knew her secret. There was no way he could, really. But she still wondered.

She woke early and went for a walk along the beach. She had not been sleeping well and wondered if it was the war. Last night she had slept better than usual. She had fallen asleep as soon as they had made love, fallen asleep half on top of him and tucked under his arm. It had felt so good to be loved and wanted. She should have told him, really, how good it had felt. But she hadn't told him and she knew why. To tell him anything, anything intimate about herself, she would have to tell him the other thing, her secret, and she was not sure she was ready for that yet. Not sure he was. She'd like to know him just a little better to be sure. But now, after last night, after a commitment of sorts, she felt she probably had to. Yet as she walked and thought of the pleasure and security in the night that he had given her, her secret slipped inside the shell of childishness again. She kicked at the sand as she walked, barefooted, but in her dress of the night before. Oh hell, she'd tell him at breakfast. But she didn't. For she turned around then and when she got back to the hotel he was still asleep and it looked so good and secure in there beside him that she took off her clothes and got in again and after a little cuddle as he stretched, they both fell asleep once more. They slept late and made love again. Afterward she helped him to the bath and then got in with him to help him to bathe. They had breakfast. They were so happy then it seemed not to matter. At least not for today.

After lunch the beloved Jacky, whom she had heard so much about, arrived to drive Red home on his recuperative leave. They had a couple of long cold beers together, the three of them, and once, although she could never be sure, but once, when Red was looking the other way, Annie would have sworn that Jacky winked at her. But if he did, it was the quickest knowing wink she had ever seen. Of course she was new to the Territory and did not know all those things about euros and spirits and the unseen things that moved which the Aboriginals knew about, or she would not have questioned whether Jacky had winked or not. She was like Beth before she began to believe that Aboriginals could tell things, such as being pregnant, just by looking at you.

The two men drove off in an old Ford car that was just one step removed from a Model T and certainly older than her new pale-green Chevrolet ute, her utility or pickup truck which she had managed to buy when she arrived, just before vehicles became scarce because of the war. She had wanted a proper sedan at first, but the ute was all the dealer had in stock, so she took it and now she was glad. In those days it was the modern bushie's vehicle and it gave more credence to her Outback identity. Her Outback identity. There was something she had to think about now that Red was gone. She was glad of the time to think, really. She supposed, if she were honest, despite all her claims of independence, he had in some strange way swept her off her feet. She could so easily have gone with him if she'd been able.

He had ten days leave. Then he had to return to be readmitted for rest and therapy. He was really barely able to go and should not have been let out in one sense. But he had pleaded with Anne for several days before that evening out. He said he knew the Japs might come soon and he must have a few days at home to see to his family and property.

Because Anne believed in a patient's happiness, she finally acquiesced, secretly hoping that he might ask her, too, which he had, and that she might be able to get a couple of days off. But the medical superintendent said it was not possible. So although disappointed, she was also now glad. It gave her time to think. She must have that. God, she had nearly told him. Yet she did miss him terribly.

She could not at first believe her restlessness on that Sunday night, after just one night beside him. Perhaps it also had something to do with his not being in the hospital. For weeks she had been used to being able to see him whenever she wished. Even in the middle of the night, sometimes, if she were on duty, or had even gone to bed but could not immediately sleep, she would get up again and dress and go in to see if he were awake and to ask him how he was as if she were just finishing off her late-night rounds. On a couple of occasions he'd not been awake and she'd caught herself taking his pulse so that he stirred half awake and then she had touched him lightly on the brow or arm, comforting him as you would a child, telling him it was all right and to go back to sleep, and not realizing, not really realizing until she got back to her own room and undressed and started to drowse off to sleep, that she had actually got up, dressed, gone down to this man's room, and woken him up so she could tenderly tell him it was all right and to go back to sleep again.

But often he was awake, reading late into the night, and then she would go and make some cocoa for them both, and bring it and talk softly about all sorts of wonderful things, and it was this, really, that brought them together in the end, so that it became unusual if she did not call in, and then she had enough confidence in the relationship to wake him even in the middle of the night with a cocoa and say she couldn't sleep. He never seemed to mind and, for all her independence, she had her security needs, too, and on that first night of his absence from the hospital, and on the other nights, despite all the thinking she wanted to do, she missed him terribly. She did not think it showed and perhaps it didn't, but when at lunchtime on the following Friday the medical super said to her, "Can you get yourself out there and be back *fresh* for work early Monday?" she said, "Can I!" so quickly and earnestly that he said, "Oh, well, go now, then. We'll manage for the rest of the day somehow and it looks like being a quiet weekend."

She asked the kitchen to make her some sandwiches and a bottle of cordial and send them up and she hurried upstairs to change and throw some clothes in a bag. The food and drink arrived and she grabbed her purse and keys and then, on an impulse of instinct, took her medical bag also.

She had taken only one step outside the hospital building before she returned for her wide-brimmed straw hat with the dangling red ribbon.

Then she drove to Army HQ to see someone she knew to get a travel permit.

At the petrol station on the outskirts of town she stopped to ask directions while she filled up. The man at the garage wore grease-thick hobnail boots, and trousers from an old gray suit held up with firemen's braces over his check shirt. He kept taking off his gray hat. The silk band around the crown was very stained and the sweatband inside the hat showed shiny as he kept taking it off and wiping it with his khaki handkerchief and saying, "I'd not go today, Missus, not that far . . . it's hellishing hot."

"But you can direct me?"

"I can direct you right enough, Missus, but can you remember?"

"Of course. But should I take a map?"

"Well, you should right enough, Missus, but can you read it?"

She was getting annoyed but she refused to register it. "If you show me I'm sure I'll be able to read it," she said. She thought he was overdoing the bushman bit just a little. Red had told her that the trees were marked with big daubs of white paint on both routes and she had purposely elected to take the easier Stuart Highway through Adelaide River and Pine Creek before the turnoff. This was easier, so Red had said, than the overland route which he used. It was true she had learned this listening to Jacky and Red over their drinks that previous Sunday, and had not intimated that she might ever make the journey herself, and in fact did not believe it had crossed her mind until that day. But now she was certainly not going to be put off. After all, she was a country girl; she was intelligent; and as she bent over the map the man sold her, which indicated even made and unmade roads or tracks, she felt there was no cause to worry whatever. Of course it was hot. So she bought a canvas water bag to hang on the front bumper bar of the car and filled it. That impressed the old man, although he still eyed her cautiously as she paid over her money.

"Anything else, Missus?"

She felt it was a test question, although the price she had paid for the map made her wonder if this was not part of his routine, if he didn't have a check list of twenty things to sell to unsuspecting townies going bush.

She looked at him quizzically.

"Groundsheet and flashlight, Missus."

"I'm not camping out," she said angrily.

"Never know, Missus," he said, without a flicker of anger himself.

"Oh, all right then, how much?"

"Three pounds, Missus."

"That's highway bloody robbery."

"It's the war, Missus."

"Oh, yeah," she said as she passed the money over and then saw in the distance an army jerry can of petrol.

"Can I have that?" she said, pointing.

"You can have it for two quid and two more quid to have it filled if you've got some more coupons, Missus."

"God, I'm glad I'm rich."

"You can't put a price on safety, Missus," he said, as they made their final exchange and she saw the jerry can safely into the back of the truck.

"I just think the price of safety might be lower closer to town," she said, not willing to let him have the last word, "it's just that I thought you'd know the directions better out here."

"That's the truth of it, Missus, if you're determined to go, but it's goin' to be a scorcher. Over a hundred already, I reckon, and not yet three o'clock. They reckon we're in for a hot weekend."

"It's only two hundred miles. I'll be there with a cold beer in my hand within four hours."

At the mention of that magic Outback password by a woman, the old man's attitude changed.

"Of course you will, luv, and good luck to yer. Turn off after Pine Creek like you said, and follow the map like I've showed ya and watch the trees like the dickens for them marks and you'll be at old Red's before ya know it."

"You know him, then?"

"Know him, Missus? Everyone knows Murranji Red. Tell him Boomerang says hullo."

"You've got to be joking—?"

"Well, I ain't, Missus. You just tell 'im. He'll know."

"All right," she smiled, and then broke into a laugh as she drove off. "I'll tell him."

35

There are signs of sorts in the Outback. Signs for some roads, signs for some tracks, signs for some properties. Even in the year Annie traveled, there were some signs on some roads. There were even some speed limit signs, while the bitumen lasted. But there were not then and there are not still, there on the main Track she traveled, or on the infamous Murranji, or on the Birdsville Track where some still set out and disappear without trace, any signs at all that warned of the danger of high temperature. It was, after all, heat that had killed Alan Michael Brennan, Beth's first husband, so many years earlier. It was heat that had killed her second husband, Red's father, Mac, near the end of the First World War years. When all was said and done, the great Northern enemy was not flood or fire or tempest or wild animals, however much at times these might whisk lives away in an instant. The real killer, the thing the bushman feared most, was the sun.

Sitting in the truck, Annie knew it was hot. But she did not know how hot. And, like so many before and after her, the car provided an unconscious but erroneous sense of safety. People saw their cars as part of civilization—as a little portable house which would travel anywhere. If it was hot inside the car, it was not much hotter than it would be in a weatherboard house and not as hot as it would be in a galvanized iron shed. Besides, there was some movement of air through the car windows, however hot.

At Adelaide River, Annie stopped and topped up the tank, just to be sure, leaving her spare petrol untouched. She also emptied and filled her water bag, but she did not think to check the level before she emptied it, as a bushman might have, to note the speed of evaporation.

"It's a hot one, Missus," the garageman said as she gave him the coupons and money.

"It is that," she said, but it was not until he gave her her change and patted the door and said, "Ouch—you'd better watch the temperature gauge, Missus," that she had her first qualm. But it was minor. She regained the ground lost by slight panic within seconds. "Of course I will, thank you," she said and waved as she drove off. It was stupid to be alarmed. She was still on the bitumen, though it did look as if the black tar around the gravel was starting to melt just a little. But that happened on any country road in Australia on any hot day, she knew that. What she did not know, and even the garageman had not noticed, was that the beautiful, fresh, pale green duco of her new utility truck was splashed with black like ink just beside the line of the running board.

She looked at the gauge and drove on. The needle was midway between the blue shading and the red shading. That was fine. It was only a fraction over normal. It was stinkin' hot in the car to be sure. But at least it was shaded. Her most vulnerable thing was her skin. But her face was not exposed. Her arm was, though, on the window ledge where it lay, and even as she thought it, it felt a little sore and she pulled it inside. Her armpits were rivers and from her forehead to her crotch she was sticky with heat and perspiration. She'd had a quick drink of water while she refilled the bag at Adelaide River. But she had some salt and glucose tablets in her medical bag. She was glad she had brought it. At Pine Creek she would have a couple of tablets and twice as much to drink.

She drove on and it was well past three now and the heat

should have been easing but if it was she hadn't noticed it. She had not seen another car for miles and she was becoming just a little nervous in the pit of her stomach. God, she hoped that was all it was: just nervousness. She hoped it wasn't the start of a migraine. She hadn't had one for ages. That was another secret and it now occupied her next several minutes. She focused her eyes for a moment on the road again. No. It was just the heat haze. For a moment she thought the double vision was coming. That's how it had always been: slight upset stomach, slight blurring into double vision and then the pain, the piercing pain. She pulled her black bag over toward her and opened it with one hand as she drove to make sure the red and white tube of Veganin tablets was there. Thank goodness. But it was not a migraine. It would have started by now. God, what was that? Was that a twinge? No, just a stiff neck. Too much sitting and staring at the road and that bloody thermometer. It had risen a bit, though. Marginally closer to the red. Marginally? Well, a bit closer. Closer to red than to blue, certainly. But that was to be expected.

She settled back then to calm herself down. She was being a stupid female and she must not let that conditioning of dependence get on top of her. Her objectivity and independence would be lost if it did. She bet Red and Jacky had sailed through the other day with probably only one stop for petrol. And she had a better car.

Just then she thought she felt her car buck slightly and swerve just a little to the side. Then it righted itself again and she was relieved, for she thought she might have had a flat tire.

A couple of miles farther on it happened again so that she almost lost control. Again she thought it was the tire and now had no alternative but to stop and get out to look. The heat as she stepped out was almost unbearable and she immediately grabbed for her sun hat. When she took off her sunglasses momentarily to bend down and look at the tires, she thought her eyes would burst, they seemed to react so violently to the glare. She told herself not to panic. To get back inside quickly and not panic. The tires were fine. She was all right. As she turned to get back in, however, she glanced at the road along which she had come. She had replaced her sunglasses, but she now took them off again and faced the even more glaring heat of looking down the distance of the road to make sure she was right, dreading to look as she did so. But she *was* right. And now she ran back into the car, jumping in and slamming the door in fear as she felt her feet burning. The road had buckled. Unbelievably, the road had buckled. She had heard of that but never believed it. She'd heard of horrible bush-fire stories like, Don't shelter in the galvanized-iron water tank lest you be boiled alive, but that was a bush fire. She had never believed temperatures could buckle a road like a roller-coaster track, up and down over a series of bumps. It must have happened as she had driven over the melted-down bitumen: the softest parts had given way so that she was actually going up and down little rutted hills. She looked at her sandals then and barely suppressed a scream as she saw the white of her sandals completely gone and her feet splashed up to the ankles with the almost alive black snakes of bitumen.

She steadied herself. She was being female again. Not all the road would be soft. She could control the car enough to make it to Pine Creek. Soon the roads would be unmade, hard as concrete, baked even harder by this sun. She took a mouthful of cordial, which was hot but it was fluid, and swallowed a combined salt and glucose tablet with it.

She took only a moment to do this. It was imperative to keep moving, she knew that.

But, miraculously, so she thought at the time, she drove on and on and no more bucking occurred. It must have been just that one bad spot of bitumen. She even felt cooler. That could have been due to the fluid and the salt and glucose, but she rather felt the hottest time of the day was over. It was only a fraction of a degree *less hot,* for no one in his right mind would have said *cooler,* but this, combined with no more melting bitumen, made the run into Pine Creek bearable. She filled up again—her last chance for both water and petrol—and had a good long drink and wash until she was thoroughly cooled down. If she had entertained any thought of stopping overnight at Pine Creek—hardly much of a place to stop—this last stretch had confirmed her in her determination to make the Back of Beyond by nightfall, on her own, as a surprise, with no one knowing. When she heard that the bitumen soon ran out and her turnoff was not far away, she got in and drove on, staggered to hear it had been 110 degrees in the shade but confident that the worst heat of the day was gone.

She drove on, her arm a little sunburned, her head throbbing a little still, as she expected it would, but no headache. The last stretch of clear road over which she had come, the time when the heat of the day should have passed, the lack of a headache: all these combined, as so many things in the Outback so often do, to give her that false sense of security, as she sat back in her car, feeling safe once more and thinking of the wonderful swimming hole Red had told her about. Indeed, though she had noticed that a drop of water she spilled while refilling the bag had sizzled over the ground, though she certainly knew that touching her door handles was like touching a hot stove, she had that mid-twentieth century belief in the invulnerability of the motor-car. She had watched to see that her radiator was filled, filled while the motor was running, though there was no doubt of any mechanic making that mistake in this climate.

With everything filled and checked she felt safe again as she traveled on to the end of the bitumen, saw the sign marked Crocodile River and turned off, relieved to see as she did so the very first large tree on her left daubed with a large slash of white paint and that the track beneath the car was indeed like concrete.

It was at this point, when everything seemed under control again, that the Outback elements conspired to take over. The apparent combination of factors that had led her to think the worst was over could now be seen as a trick. There was no time when anything was over in this land, in this climate: there were only good and bad stretches, and there was, over and above everything else, one irreversible factor which hardly any but the most experienced bushmen thought of, though to a doctor with a scientifically trained mind it should have been self-evident. It was the cumulative factor. She would have plenty of time to regret ignoring it before the end drew near. That factor was the killer in this land: the cumulative exposure to the sun for man, beast and automobile.

Not two miles out of Pine Creek—it could hardly have been more, she believed—the radiator boiled. Although refilled at the last stop, the metal of the radiator, exposed to that fierce heat all day, had not cooled. Yet it was not the radiator itself that was taking the main strain—it was finally the hose that could not, hour after hour, take any more heat. It was this that eventually gave up the ghost, although it took nearly half an hour for the hood of the pickup truck to cool sufficiently for her to lift it, so she could see. At first she thought it was the radiator itself. And certainly when, nearly in tears, she approached it with her flimsy embroidered handkerchief to try to take the top off, for she had no oil rag, it gave a hiss like a geyser about to blow. Standing back tentatively she leaned outward to touch the radiator cap. She turned her head even farther away. Then, still fearing that she would scald her arm, she distantly inched the cap off as steam kept searing out in bursts. But it was less than she had expected and it was not water. The radiator was empty.

So next, still very gingerly, with her whole body pulled in as with a deep breath so that it would not touch any hot metal, she leaned over to look down beside the radiator. She did not really know about radiator hoses but she forced herself to concentrate for something missing and soon saw that the thick, black rubber hose had been blown off at the end which attached to the radiator. But the other end that led to the engine housing was intact and she thought at first to try to get the hose back onto the radiator when it cooled, although the clip which should have held it was missing, obviously blown off along the road somewhere, and she did not know what she would tie it on with. She was just about to look in her black bag to see what she could find when she looked again and realized it would be useless. The rubber hose which still hung there was pitted with holes like a sieve. The boiling water had eaten it half away like moth holes of decay in a wardrobe sweater. She was stuck. She looked forlornly in every possible place a spare radiator hose might have been placed in the vehicle. But she had never even considered buying one and there was not one to be seen.

It was still searingly hot outside and in her panic she had been without her hat all this time while examining the damage. Now she noticed the first twinge of a light burning on her face and her eyes were sore with the radiating heat from the near-white track which she now realized had a reflective capacity which at least gave the bitumen one advantage. The bitumen! The time was coming when she would pray to be back on that bucking bitumen. But it was not yet. All she knew was that her radiator hose had rotted with the heat in the same way the bitumen had melted. But although panicked, and tearful, she was not yet fully distraught. The fact that saved her from this was her strong rationality. Even in this crisis, and she knew it to be serious enough, the rationality at the back of her mind told her that she was really not far from civilization. She sat back in the truck for a moment now and thought about that. It could not be more than two miles, she was confident of that, though to be truthful she had no experience of guessing distances in the bush, which was about as difficult as guessing distances over the ocean. But she thought it to be two miles. She was not to know, any more than any other inexperienced Outback traveler, that the miscalculation of distance was one of the very real tricks the devil played on his anvil of heated stone and track and sameness of scenery. It was over five miles but she thought it to be two, and after she had sat awhile and sensibly calmed herself down with a sandwich and a large swig of cordial, the hot and sickly lemon cordial, she knew she was right to leave.

It was against every rule of survival taught in school to any country children. You were not to leave your car except in the most unusual of circumstances. Stay with your car. Stay with shelter against the elements. Even in a bush fire stay and let the fire pass through, lie down on the back seat under a wet blanket, or just lie there without covering if you have none, and cover your head with your hands and let the fire pass. You have to be very unlucky for the petrol tank to explode. Stay with your car. If lost, stay with your car. The search party will know where to find you.

But two things made her decide to leave. First, so far as she knew, no one knew where she was. Nor would they, unless someone was lucky enough to be speaking to both Red and the hospital and realized she was not at either place. How she longed for Red and his experience now. How she hoped he might call the hospital. But she knew he would not, for it was not on the radio transmitter system—only the Flying Doctor base was. Second, she genuinely believed that she could, despite the heat, make the two miles back to Pine Creek before nightfall. She had, to the best of her knowledge, only taken one turn. So she ate another sandwich slowly, drank some more cordial and prepared to go. She emptied her black doctor's bag of everything except the Veganin tablets and the salt tablets. Then she placed the remaining two sandwiches and half bottle of cordial inside the bag with the flashlight. She put her hat and sunglasses on, took the map and water bag from the front of the car and started off along the track in the direction from which she had come.

At the Back of Beyond, two hours later, as dusk began to descend, Red sat with Jacky drinking beer on the back veranda. It was the one time in their life they could remember having plenty of beer. Although wartime, Red had managed to get some hops and they had brewed their own.

Jacky and Fan-tan had gone to great pains with the kerosene refrigerator to make sure the beer was thoroughly chilled, and after this hottest of days, with a record scorcher forecast for the next day, so the radio said, they were enjoying that best of all possible drinks at the best of all possible times of the day in the Outback, a beer so cold the glasses were running beaded rivulets as you drank and sat on the back porch.

Just then the radio transmitter started to crackle.

"I go, Boss," Jacky said, getting up lazily and wandering in. He came back after a couple of minutes.

"You better come, Boss. It Boomerang and he sound plenty full and keep asking to speak to the Missus."

"The hell he does. He must be full. Tell him to call back when he's sober if he wants something. Haven't heard from old Boomerang in years. My father gave him his first job as a ringer, remember?"

Jacky did not move.

"Aw, come on, Jack, I know he's a good old-timer but he'll call back if it's urgent. Probably just wants to put the bite on me. You know what he's like."

As he said this Red looked back over his shoulder to where the black man was standing. One look and he was swinging his body on his buttocks to get his good leg around to stand on. He knew that look of Jacky's. That was his sense-of-danger look. And whatever any other white man said, it had never let Red down, and as suddenly as he had seen the look, his mind had made the connection with the garbled message about the Missus.

"Christ, she wouldn't be so stupid . . . would she. . . ?" Red said as Jacky helped him up and they hobbled quickly inside and along the passage to the radio room.

Jacky said nothing.

Red spoke to Boomerang for nearly five minutes. The old man was drunk all right but eventually, piecing together words like *petrol* and *map,* Red got the gist of it. Then he had to question and requestion the man several times to make sure he knew the route she was taking and the approximate time she had left. Red thanked Boomerang profusely for calling, although the drunken man kept almost crying and saying he wished he'd called earlier and not got drunk. He was calling, he said, from the pub right now. Red thanked him and rang off. Then he called the Flying Doctor base to get them to get a message to the hospital to check on Anne, for there was always the chance that she had turned back. He hoped to Christ she had. When the message came through that she had not returned, his heart sank. He then radioed the police station and told the police he was preparing a search party but would they organize one from there, too? They agreed, and by the time he and Jacky were ready to go, the police had radioed back to say they'd spoken to the River and the Creek and she'd passed through the Creek between four and five. Could still be on the way, they pointed out. She could barely have made it by that time of night even if she had come straight through. Red paused for a minute and looked at Jacky. Jacky shrugged as if to say, "well, what do you expect in this heat?" Red nodded and asked the inspector to start the search whether or no, as a favor to him. "Oh, well, we've got nothing else on. I'll send the boys out from Pine Creek and get the trackers and reinforcements in at first light, how's that?"

"And a plane—?" pleaded Red.

"Jesus, there's a war on."

"There must be one light aircraft not being used. See if the Flying Doctor will lend us one. After all we may—" He checked himself as he realized what he was saying.

The policeman had now realized Red's level of concern and his bush instinct took over at the other end of the line.

"Don't worry, digger, I'll get one somewhere. Keep in touch."

"Thanks."

They signed off and then Red argued once more with Jacky about going. Jacky was all for leaving Red behind and he and Young Roo riding on horses. Red was for taking the car—"to use as an ambulance if necessary"—with him and Jacky in the car with supplies and Young Roo riding behind tethering a spare horse so that, if necessary, Roo and Jacky could search where the car could not go. It was also part of a larger argument of Red trying to get Jacky to believe more in the role vehicles would eventually play in the Outback. But although Jacky could drive and was indeed a good mechanic, he was certainly no convert. He was a horseman—probably the Territory's finest—and he made very clear his preference for things animal over things mineral. But in the end Red had his way and by seven thirty, loaded with petrol and supplies, they headed for the route they believed would bring them up on the other side of Anne's approximate position, given the direction she would have taken after leaving Pine Creek.

By this time of night Anne was getting really concerned. She was still not sure she was lost, because she did not believe she would have had time to reach Pine Creek by now and she might have underestimated the two-mile distance just a little. After all, it was only an approximation, she knew that. But earlier, while still light, she had been forced to take a turn on the way back. Well, no, not really a turn. After what she estimated to have been half a mile from the car she had come upon a fork with two tracks looking so identical she understood why she might not have noticed the other one on the way through. Indeed, anyone traveling at a reasonable speed along one of them, and looking straight ahead, could hardly be expected to have seen the other the way it would have merged so exactly from the side, traveling in the same direction as it were.

But now she was coming back—and of course that way the merging tracks presented a right- or left-fork alternative. She looked for a marked tree. There was one a few yards distant from the fork in the direction of her car, so that was no help at all. She looked at the surface of the tracks. It was so hard, any sign of a tire mark was impossible. No, it was up to her to guess: she wasn't going to be able to reason it out. She wanted to take the right-hand one. But she was a right-hander and she suspected that was the reason. Rationally, the left one appeared just marginally to look as if it belonged to the single track which led on from them both, although there was really no telling, for both tracks looked exactly the same as they came into a slender vee. Her one hope was that since they were identical, and therefore the same width, this really made them both the size of roads—unmade roads, but roads nevertheless. This gave her a slightly more comfortable feeling that both would lead somewhere. Perhaps one led to the bitumen and another to a property. That would be just as good, perhaps even better, given the time of night. Or, hopefully, both led to the bitumen—one coming out a little farther along than the other. To be closer to town would be the best, but either would do: she would feel safe at the bitumen.

She had paused a moment longer—and then picked up her two bags, whistled up her confidence and stepped down the left track.

That had been two hours ago. Now it was seven thirty, dark, and she was very worried.

She walked on for what seemed like the whole night but was in fact only three hours. The track still kept going, but she knew she was well and truly lost. She decided to stop and sleep. The noises of the bush at night were starting to frighten her. She would have been better to keep going in the cool of the night, trying to find a hill where she could light a fire. But she had no matches, she now realized, and in any case she still believed the track would lead her out somewhere in the morning. She, like others, believed she must get back to civilization sooner or later. She did not stop to think of trying to find a river or landmark to follow in the night and then a cool holing-up place for the heat of the day. Her mind naturally thought things would be easier in the morning. Her country upbringing had given her no experience of terrains like this. So when she found an outcrop of large basalt rocks near the side of the track she stopped and climbed up, finding a ledge she believed she could sleep on, half curled up and half upright, but at least off the ground away fron snakes and spiders, unaware that the latter was a fear that belonged more to other areas of the country than here. In the North nature has a much simpler, more direct way of exercising its hostility to mankind.

She had used her flashlight sparingly, tripping and cutting and bruising herself on branches and rocks as she sometimes stumbled in the dark. She now used its light to eat one more sandwich only, though she could have wolfed two. Then she drank a little water from the water bag, which she now realized had evaporated considerably and was only about half full after her drink. She took two salt and glucose tablets with the water. There was a slight uneasiness in her stomach and the edges of a headache in her head and neck. She hesitated for a moment, then carefully opened the Veganin tube and counted out the tablets. It was not full. There were just six tablets. She would need all of those and then some if she got a full-blown migraine. But having survived the heat that day, and having no way of knowing the forecast for the next, she swallowed two thankfully to ease her head and settled back to sleep.

She knew before she fell asleep that she was going to be cold. The temperature was dropping quite markedly now and soon the cold started to keep her awake. She got despondent then and started to hug herself for body warmth. Then she sniffled and knew what a fool she'd been. She'd wanted to surprise Red and it was a childishly innocent enough thing to want to do but how she wished now she had radioed to say she was coming. Would anyone realize she was lost? Was she really lost? Perhaps tomorrow morning the track would come out at the bitumen or at a property or even a mining camp. She knew there still to be some in the vicinity of Pine Creek. It couldn't be that deserted, the whole area, just because of the war. She fell asleep slightly comforted, not knowing that war or no war there were no people: this was it, this was the bush, this was the emptiness of the great bush continent.

The cold and squawks and squeaks of the strange night kept her fitfully stirring and restless. She awoke to the dawn, tired and anxious and stiff in every bone. She ate half a sandwich, stale and dry now, and drank some cordial which, with the stupid inversion of this willful land, so she told herself, was now quite cold after the night.

She relieved herself behind the rocks, thinking how stupid, too, was her ritual of hiding her private parts from prying eyes. There were no other eyes here and her water was gone within moments, the earth was so dry. It suddenly occurred to her how desolate the spot she was in really was and what a terrible day might lie ahead of her when the sun came up. There was nothing, just nothing for miles. She was at the end of the earth. This was no track. It had just looked like a track because it led off at the same width from the other track— doubtless the real track which she should have taken.

She thought for a moment about going back but knew instantly that it was hopeless. For she saw that what she had thought was a track had just got wider and wider and for at least a couple of hours last night in the dark she must have been walking across this broad plain which the so-called track had obviously led into. She could not work out the direction from which she had come in a million years; she could probably find any number of exit-looking paths if she walked in any number of directions. But most, if not all of these, would lead nowhere, too.

She prayed for an Aboriginal, but knew the days of their frequency in the bush were long since gone. She prayed for matches and wished to God she could find something in her black bag she could use as a magnifying glass to start a fire. She didn't even care if she started a bush fire although some fat, bloody chance: it would burn out in this plain—it wouldn't move from one pile of undergrowth rubble to the other. The few bushes and straggly trees were far apart and bone-dry as driftwood.

She collapsed sobbing on her rock and wondered about staying put. But the terrible other fact of bush aloneness now began to dawn on her. Even if she could stay alive a couple of days and even if a search party came, which it almost certainly would when she didn't report for work, there was no guarantee of being found in this country, not even by a plane. Certainly the chances of being found were very slim indeed without some means to signal.

She inhaled her sobs in big gulps, trying desperately to gain control again. She knew she had to be logical. She had to find something to signal with: that was the priority and as she thought that, her mind jumped. Her makeup purse. She must surely have put it in her doctor's bag with the other things. She must have. But she couldn't remember, and makeup was not one of her strong points. She wore it sparingly and then as much for the patients as herself. She looked hurriedly through her black bag. She must have missed it. Look again. Jesus, she was stupid. It was not there. No mirror.

She thought again about returning to the car. But it was impossible, she knew. And there was slight heat in that sun already. She must move. She had no shade at all. However difficult it might be she must walk until she found shade and water. Shade and water and preferably some high ground where she could take off her shorts and shirt and at least wave if she heard a plane. But she didn't like her chances. There was no sign of shade, water or elevated ground. There were not enough leaves on the trees or the bushes to give even a modicum of shade. She emptied the last of the cordial into the water bag, stuffed the Veganin and salt tablets into her shorts pocket and began to walk. Twice she turned forlornly to look back at her black bag staring at her from the rock ledge where she had left it. She was very attached to it and hated to leave it. She resisted the temptation to look a third time lest she be tempted to go back and get it.

As she walked, not so very far from her as the crow flies but in another country in terms of effectiveness of reaching her, Red, Jacky and Roo blacktracked. The boy had stayed beside his father and they had not stopped all night. They had brought a spare battery and Red sat in the car with lights on and the choke out so that he could move the car forward slowly on the idling motor just by disengaging the clutch slightly with his good left leg. Roo and Jacky blacktracked over every inch of the dusty track.

They had assumed, from the information from the garage, that Annie must almost certainly have got as far as the Crocodile River turnoff from the bitumen along the Pine Creek Road. This being so, they had decided to track every inch of the track, coming in at it from the other side, for any sign at all. They had discussed hurrying forward to look for her car but in so doing they would almost certainly wipe out any signs at all if she had turned off in her car or even walked forward for a time and then wandered off lost. No, it was longer, painfully longer, but they must cover the area to be absolutely certain where she had left the main track. If she hadn't left it, then she would be found in time. If she had left it, it was crucial to know where to be able to reach her in the shortest possible time once it got light. The three of them knew the increasing urgency as every hour passed in the night. She would not last past noon and be lucky to do that, water or no water. Red hoped the others coming in from the other direction might have more men and be working quicker. And he hoped they had experienced men who would not wipe out blacktracking signs, for it was damnably difficult enough as it was with the earth baked this hard.

Drinking water as they walked along beside the car, and then in front of it again, the aging Jacky and the young Black Roo did not pause. It was nearly 9:00 A.M. before they sighted her car in the distance and then with the great Aboriginal instinct and caution they looked doubly carefully for foot signs. They knew in an instant by looking at the car what had happened, and indeed Annie in her anxiety had left the hood up, the green metal hot already to the touch of Jacky's hand.

They drove around it and immediately picked up her signs where she had obviously walked over to the marked trees to check them where the paint was thinning. This encouraged Red. Perhaps she had walked out by now. But another quarter of a mile farther on told the story when Jacky and Roo quickly identified that she had taken the wrong fork. They stopped momentarily for a conference with Red.

"Bad spot, Jacky."

"The worst, Boss. Wild Boar Plains."

"I know. But she'll be all right until she reaches the other side. This side is all right, isn't it?"

"No side all right but this side better, Boss. Roo ride on you think?"

"I've been wondering. One horse, you reckon?"

"Got to take chance, Boss. We no reach her before noon this rate. One horse Roo read signs as much as can from horseback and not ride over too many. We keep going as we are. Car not such bad tracker, Boss," he added rather condescendingly.

"The lights were helpful last night, Jack, weren't they?"

"We track just as well horseback and lantern, Boss, but car OK while you ill."

Despite everything they both managed a wry smile and then the look of desperation returned. Roo knew what he must do. He took a spare water bag, some salt in a brown paper bag in his shirt pocket and a packet of jelly crystals in his saddlebag and rode off slung low in the saddle to read Anne's tracks as he went. The earth was so hard he was grateful when he saw she had started to stumble in the dark. But even with these scuff marks to guide him, it was still painfully slow going and he certainly could not gallop and he was barely moving his horse at a trot.

By ten o'clock that morning Anne could tell by the extreme heat that she had picked the worst of all possible days to be out in the sun. She realized that yesterday's heat had been but a curtain raiser, a warm-up to the deadlier main event. Now, right from dawn, the sun had been shining cruelly and relentlessly down on her as she walked, intent to hit her from every angle however hard she tried to avoid it and of course there was just no way her hat could shade the whole of her. Her arms and legs and the vee of her neck down to her breasts were continually smarting and she believed before very long she would have second-degree burns. The sun had even managed to get at patches of her face just up from her chin. And the hat did not fully protect her neck. She had had a full migraine since eight thirty and taken two tablets then with the last half sandwich. Now at ten thirty she took the last two and a little more water.

She knew that in another hour she would be unable to go on and that once she stopped, without shade, she would be dead in a couple of hours. She was being a doctor again now, even about herself. She could almost laugh at her own stupidity and her predicament. She didn't feel all that sorry for this particular patient now. She knew she was going to die and she would observe it with her morbid scientific interest. This attitude was part of the heat delirium which had overtaken her. She was seeing mirages now, hazes full of shade trees which disappeared when she reached them. And she had been wandering for the last half hour, away with the fairies on the hill, the fairies in the meadow, away back in childhood where the present was not happening, where the excruciating pain pounding that searing blood through her inflamed and burned and swollen little body—for she was not much above tiny of frame and should never have been on this plain alone—did not exist. The delirium had taken over completely now. When she lay down, taking off her shirt and placing it over a bush, she was a little girl again playing Red Indians with the boys in their tents. She had made a good tent to hide in now. And she had her hat to put her head on. Her legs were hot but no matter. She was hot all over. But soon she would be cool. Soon the pain would stop. She was going to go to sleep. That's what she was going to do.

In the car Red looked at his watch and saw it was noon. He could be out in his estimate by an hour or two but he knew now he and Jacky would never reach her in time. It was Roo or no one unless she'd had exceptional luck.

Roo, for his part, was just as anxious. Tracking had continued painfully slowly because of the difficulty of identifying the signs on this hardest of all terrains. Her black bag had been a bonus, though, for it had enabled him quickly to identify where she had spent the night. It told him he must throw caution to the winds and hurry if he was to reach her in time. Yet he could not become too anxious, for it was a big plain, miles wide and long, and she could have wandered anywhere. He stopped from time to time to look through his binoculars but there was still no sign of her. It was like looking for a single grain on an ocean of sand. He rode on and on, once missing her track so that he had to backtrack and

waste precious time. He picked it up again and realized what
the problem was. She had started to wander. How long ago it
was almost impossible to tell. He followed the meandering
marks on the ground, the brushed-against dry bushes, the
disturbed or squashed dry leaves, he followed them all and
read them all and hoped by his euro that he was not too late.
He expected to find her dropped somewhere now. He had
stopped looking on the horizon. He would find her soon
enough now. But would he find her alive? It was nearly one
o'clock.

Then ahead he saw her shirt. Then her. He spurred his
horse the last few yards. She looked so still. He could tell by
the way her knees were bent up toward her stomach in
involuntary spasm that she had got the cramps. But she was
so still.

He came jumping out of his stirrup as the horse stopped,
jumping down and running, uncorking his water bag as he
did so and splashing it over her face as he slapped her face
hard twice and grabbed, pulling her to her feet and hoping to
God that she responded. She had made no sound but he knew
this might mean nothing until he got the water and salt into
her. Still holding her upright with one arm and attempting to
walk her, he forced the nozzle of the water bag hard into her
mouth past her teeth, so hard it cut her lip and he heard her
groan. He jerked her head back with a downward pull on her
hair and forced some more water down. Once her body started
to respond so that she instinctively started to suck hard for it,
he eased the nozzle back so she would not take too much. He
slung the water bag on his arm momentarily as he reached
for the salt, pouring some on his hand and holding it up
saying, "Lick, Missus, lick good." The words came to her
distantly but she licked like a child and then vomited all over
him and he said only, "Good, Missus, more salt, you lick good
and we sip a bit more now and presently you start to keep
down. You no lie down on me, though, Missus, because you
not want to sleep 'cause Big Red coming and him be plenty
mad me let you die, Missus."

She began to sob uncontrollably then and the black youth

put her hat back on and led her to his horse and made her hold on there as he took a handkerchief and began to wet it and then wipe her forehead and pat her arms gently with it, for he could see how sore they must be. Then he led her gently over with his horse to the bush and made a tent of his blanket by tying it to his horse and the bush and using his horse as shade on the side. Then Roo took his shirt off and placed it on the ground and put Annie on it, admonishing her kindly that she must not lie down and there must be no more sleeping. He kept giving her little sips of water and little bits of salt to lick and then some jelly crystals to suck.

Presently he gave her her shirt to put on and she said childishly, "Oh, what about you . . . do you want yours back?"

He just smiled and shook his head. "You not worry nothing, Missus. Hour, maybe two, Red come."

She was trying to talk. She was trying to keep herself awake. She was just beginning to realize how close she must have come. It was a miracle, really. Surely a few minutes more. But she was too tired to think. Her headache was still splitting. She must lie down. But even as she leaned ever so slightly forward, the black youth's arm had come down as strong as steel to bar the way.

"You talk, Missus. However plurry hard, you talk me all the time. I listen, honest."

She could not help a smile.

"That better, Missus. It all over now. You be OK now, you know."

She hadn't of course realized. And now that she did, she cried again, quite hysterically, and the black youth bent down and put his arm around her and let her cry herself out. Then she felt a little better and took more salt and sugar and water and Roo trusted her to sit alone long enough for him to build up a few twigs for a signal fire. He lit them and sat with her, letting her lean against him until the others arrived.

The feeling was the same. It always was in the bush. Relief mixed with anger. Anger like he had felt so long ago toward the tiny Douglas in the buffalo charge. But he was wiser now, wise enough not to let it show—to control it. It had done no good then and it would do no good now.

An hour later she was sitting back against Red in the back seat, eating slowly but gratefully some of Fan-tan's legendary chicken sandwiches and listening to Red and Jacky and Young Roo argue about whether the car was a good tracker or not.

"Man on horse find Missus, Boss," Jacky said finally and that was the end of that conversation as the men all laughed.

She still felt abominable but it was not this that prevented her laughing. She just couldn't see that what had happened to her was a laughing matter. She could never see that. And she never would. And she would never forgive the terrible land that had brought her so close to death.

36

Anne slept most of the next day and improved enough by the middle of the week to return to the hospital with Red. But she had been out in the hottest day of 127.4 degrees and it was two weeks before she was fully physically recovered. Even then her mind kept going back *there*. It would continue to until the day she died. And she would never get to tell her secret: well, never the full part of it to Red, anyway. Her secret was that she had loved him from their first meeting and she had hoped against hope that he would ask her to marry him. But now she could not tell him this.

Instead, in the days that followed their return from the Back of Beyond, she debunked the great Australian myth of the wonderful life on the land, or life on the land at all. Each time Red seemed about to have the discussion which, a few short days ago she had so hoped for, she pointed out with statistics, statistics for each sunset Red tried to paint for her, that there was no one on the land, absolutely no one, except a few dumb cockies leading hopeless lives alone because nine out of ten Australian women—more—would not, could not, leave the cities and towns, because life on the land, with their men away so many hours and days and weeks, left them lonely and unloved and dried out into early old age by the withering sun. She would doctor and help these people—but only by plane from a town base. She would not live on the land.

She told him as much. He believed he could change her mind but did not mention it at this time.

Kiwai came in to visit him at the hospital after his return to Darwin. His curly graying hair looked particularly distinguished. He wore a suit and looked a successful, suntanned business executive, which of course he was. Red told him this and they joked. He told Kiwai, who had a wonderful large family, that he hoped to marry Anne but that she'd had a terrible baptism of fire along the track.

Kiwai nodded. "First experiences stay long," he said.

"Isn't that the truth of it? Well, perhaps the beauty of the country will one day persuade her, even if I can't. She's seen it at its worst. She'll one day see its good side."

"Hard on women," was all the wise Kiwai said.

Red nodded and they turned to talk about business once more.

In January of '42, in the Wet, the evacuation of Darwin began. It was already an important Allied base, a supply point for the Allied forces and becoming more so and therefore more of a target for the Japanese as the Pacific War accelerated. So women and children were being evacuated. Kat and the children, Bluey's family, had been in to see Red in the hospital and he now sent word to them with Cathy that they could go to the Back of Beyond if they did not wish to go South. Kat said she would prefer to be this much closer to home and thought that that would be what Bluey would want. Red agreed and it was organized. He wanted Cathy to go, too, but she was a nurse now and needed, so he did not argue when she said she would stay in Darwin. She thought it was a huge joke when Red insisted that his .303 and pistol be brought from his kit, and put one under his bed and the other under his pillow. But he knew it wasn't such a joke and he had his batman looking for a Bren gun for him and plenty of ammo, if one happened to fall off a passing truck. Anne thought he was being overly dramatic but said nothing. She, of course, was staying. By early February all but a few of the women and children had been evacuated.

Yet despite these apparent precautions there were some amazing parallels with Pearl Harbor when on the morning of February 19 a coastwatcher radioed a warning. This was followed by a message to the Amalgamated Wireless Station in Darwin from Father McGrath of the Bathurst Island Mission:

"I have an urgent message. An unusually large air formation bearing down on us from the North-West. Identity suspect. Visibility not clear."

In the Timor Sea four Japanese carriers had launched two hundred fighters and dive bombers and they were within minutes of Darwin as the clock hands on the post office turned to 10:00 A.M.

The twenty-odd coastal defense guns were of little use. The handful of American Kittyhawks were wiped out, wharf and air force installations and bases destroyed and, in the confusion, personnel who were not killed became scattered, some believing they had been told to escape in the bush. Much of the city was smoke and flames and hundreds were killed and injured. Six bombs fell on the hospital, but miraculously no patients or staff members were injured in any way, although the hospital was blitzed half open, so that Anne and the other doctors, assisted by Red and anyone who could be made ambulatory, were soon tending to the casualties being brought in from the town. There were some terrible burns, great gashed wounds from which it was almost impossible to stop the blood flow, let alone patch up in time even if the main supplies of blood and saline had not been destroyed. The power failed and the doctors continued to work on into the night by flashlights held by Red and other volunteers, with water boiled on kerosene pressure stoves used for camping in the Outback.

By the next day most patients had been moved to a military hospital on the outskirts of the town, a staging hospital only for a hospital ship which was being brought in to take the wounded out.

Red was told to go but refused, and because no one could be found immediately with field rank to order him, although a doctor who was a major said he would put him on report, Red stayed, telling the doctor that in military matters he would decide, and what the doctor could do with his orders. For Red already knew Anne was staying and although there was now a mass evacuation in panic because an invasion was thought imminent, Red knew there would be more casualties and that as many soldiers as could must stay. And soon he found an American colonel who said anyone who could shoot should stay and told the doctor major to stick to his job and told Red to find himself a car or a horse, if he could ride, to steal one if he had to, and get down to Adelaide River, which was the main exit point for the town refugees, and enlist and turn back every man of military age. They were the orders from the Australian authorities he was liaising with, the colonel said.

Red smiled yes sir and said something about the only damned decent war being one you could ride to on a bloody horse, which the colonel apparently did not understand. But Red went off and commissioned a car from Bluey's garage because it really would be faster and better. And after finding Anne and telling her to be sure and be in one piece when he got back because there was something he wanted to tell the bottom half of her but he wanted the top half to hear it, too, so that she went red, he kissed her and was away with his driver on the road out of town to Adelaide River.

The bombing continued through 1942 until the end of '43, but none of the raids was as severe as the first. Darwin was again a makeshift town, as in Red's very early boyhood, yet makeshift with modern amenities. Of course there had been electric light there since the 1920s, and refrigeration. Yet the American occupation of the town, like any American occupation of any base, brought all those giant mechanical and modern things, those giants of American pragmatic inventiveness, crawling over the land like primeval monsters, building airstrips, bringing in jeeps and trucks and every little modern amenity of that country's utilitarian mind, as if the last frontier had been blitzkreiged by twentieth-century America. So suddenly, although it was 1942 and '43, suddenly the nineteenth century was gone for Australia in the North as it had in the South so much earlier. And although it was still the last frontier, the last encroachment on it—not the first, but the last, which would turn it eventually into something else—had been made.

But these were only passing thoughts in Red's head as he watched it happening, knowing it was necessary for winning the war, yet also regretting it in other ways and grateful that, when the war ended, he could head back to his beloved Back of Beyond and the peace that only the Outback gave. He hoped that Anne would go with him.

He had proposed, of course, but the discussions of marriage always ran dangerously close to arguments. So they settled for love. And, in any case, while the war lasted neither felt they could make a final decision, for that decision seemed, to both of them, to involve the land or not the land. So they found a house in the town and lived openly in it, in one of those de facto relationships of the time, lived there (not without some whispered criticism) as much as their duties would allow. They had some of their happiest times. They grew closer. Red hoped to change Annie's mind about marrying him. In a sense, she hoped to change it, too. The war ended. Then suddenly Red was busy again. The pearling industry was changing. With the war gone there was little demand for shell and it had gone out of fashion as an ornament. Cultured pearls were now the thing and they must switch as quickly as possible. He had to see Kiwai about selling the luggers off promptly as tourist hire craft, before the demand for them dropped as others realized the changing pattern. He must go to Sydney to see Douglas and discuss all their interests. But he knew his business was a cover for his feelings and his real priority.

A few months after the war ended he and Anne returned to the Back of Beyond together.

37

She had come to stay. It would be a serious attempt, they had both agreed to that. It would be as if they were married and she had settled down on the property for good. That was the only way it would get a proper trial. No time limit had been set. They would just try it as hard as they could. Red would go about his normal duties. Annie would do the paperwork parts of her research, and what little study she could of the limited number of black children nearby, and would supervise what interested her on the property. She loved him dearly, and his people, and knew they all intended such good and honorable things. It was just that they didn't fully translate that way for her, by the time the feeling reached her insides, and the only possible way she could explain it, the only completely untenable, unscientific way she could explain it was that somehow the land, the devil-god of the country, could turn good intentions into bad for those it knew could not live full-time on it and come to terms with it. The world war was over and soon the twentieth century would be half gone. Could such primitive bloody animism survive? Could the land have a spirit of sorts? It annoyed her even to think the thought, but she did think it, although only to herself, and went ahead with her quiet grace and warmth, with the soft sensitivity Red believed in so much, she went ahead, and compounded the problem, trying and smiling twice as hard, just like everybody else, and burying—dangerously, she knew—the other thoughts for another time.

The thing was, of course, that the land contained her. Its very immensity, challenging her to go wherever she would, contained her. And what could she really do here of her own work? She needed fresh children all the time, hundreds to study and work with, if she was to do anything meaningful at all on that damning infant mortality rate. But, more than this even, more than this and despite the inhospitable threat of the land, there was that question every woman has faced, one way or another, silently or not so silently, every day of her life: What, when the partner to whom she is seen as owing loyalty and responsibility is absent, does she do with her time? What, apart from husband, lover, children, cats and chores, what, in God's name or anyone else's, is her personal fulfillment? What does she do for herself to make herself happy, once the shock and frightened freedom of having a separate entity and existence from one's mate is recognized? This true individualism she had recognized in herself, despite her relatively young years, a long time ago. It was this same thing in Red, her tender and strong Outback cavalier, that she loved as much or more than in herself. But could the fulfillment of the freedom of each contain the love of both in a full-time living-together situation? There, there was the question. And it was heavily on her heart as she stood, like some Gothic heroine, waving good-bye from the veranda as Red rode off on the first of his series of six-week mustering camps of the Dry. She would not see him for six weeks. Then he would return for a few days to reprovision, and be off with his men again. Of course they had asked her to come along. Of course she had refused.

She watched them disappear finally off the skyline and went inside. It would be an interesting fight, this thing between her and the land. And perhaps of all the women who had faced it she was as well equipped as any to fight. Or had the land already won back *there?*

Red felt that day, as he rode out of sight so slowly that he

seemed to be slumped forward over the front of his horse as if
he and the poor animal were the classic cast-in-bronze statue
of dying rider and horse, Red felt that day more dejected than
he had ever felt in his life. He hoped Annie had not noticed,
except at the first. After that he had put a brave front on it.
But it was stupid for him to go on this drive. After all, they
had managed without him during the war; Jacky and the
team had done very well. Certainly things needed whipping
up a bit; there was the slight lack of what the books he read
called "entrepreneurial ability." In other words, the owner
had been away: it was very important to have a captain, the
real captain, however good Jacky was. But this first drive
Red did not need and did not want and in the end had only
taken because Anne had insisted in her quiet way by saying
nothing. Her silence had said that it was part of the deal for
him to go about his *normal duties* and that she must test
herself against life on the land as it really was, not as she
would like it to be, not even as he would like it to be.

Normal duties. There was a laugh. What were a cattleman's normal duties? What were a station owner's normal
duties?

The acid of desert despair was in his brain as he rode away
from the softest and most loving lady he had ever known,
rode away because it was part of his deal with her, yet he had
a terrible feeling that this one ride, which he could legit-
imately have forgone for cool swims and good talks and walks
and evenings with her, might be the *bête noire* of his life,
might be the nutcracker of separation for them. God, his leg
still gave him enough trouble for him to have begged off this
muster drive. Oh, he knew the owner had to see for himself,
of course. Even during the war he had got out as many
weekends as he could and that had helped keep the station
healthy. It was the planning that mattered. This had always
been Red's forte. It was how he was different from his father
and mother and Jacky, too. He had discussed it once with
Jacky, who used to say, "I do plurry hard yakka, Boss, but
need you plan." Red had remonstrated with him and pointed
out many ways in which Jacky himself had planned. He

planned ahead for water and feed for the stock for a start, Red pointed out, and there was no more important planning than that.

"You right, Boss," Jacky had said; "I plan pretty good, even better than most white station managers. But I plan what regular and we do all time, plan maybe one, two years ahead. But you plan new things that haven't happened yet, Boss, you plan what things will be good maybe five, ten years from now and then you do 'em now. You jump in, Boss, when no one ought be swimming but always work. Gambling run in family, I reckon, and in the end you bigger gambler than young Billy, I reckon."

Well, Red was that, and no mistake. He'd not deny that. He'd gambled all his life with the land—the Russian roulette of the land was all there in these extremes—he'd gambled and won, but he worried that he'd won too many times and the second half of his life might be the time when the reaper started taking it back in bits. Thinking of Billy, Red knew he'd already had *some* bits taken out of him, that was for sure. Would Annie be the next? God, he detested this drive and it wasn't half a day old and he had left so late it was nearly noon before they got away and the men had been annoyed, so annoyed he'd almost heard them grumbling that the bloody Boss was back and so what, why the hell didn't he take a day or two off and stay with his Missus? He couldn't explain the complicated tricky way in which he'd have loved to, but couldn't because of the Missus, he couldn't explain that to his Outback colleagues, because he was both one of them and a slightly different thinker as well. He was not sure they'd really understand a relationship of equality. In fact Red was not sure he really did, and on this particular heat-hazed day, wasn't sure he wanted to.

Stick to your normal duties, Annie had said in Darwin, that had been part of the deal. He hoped to hell she didn't quiz Fan-tan and all the others too much about what were his normal duties, because if she did she might be gone by the time he got back. Normal duties! Why didn't the boss take a day off? Hell, had he ever had a day off? He'd had more days off in the army—both wars—than ever on the land. He thought and he thought and he couldn't remember, apart from the odd weekends in Darwin, when he'd ever had a day off from the time he accepted full residential responsibility for the running of his property. He put it that way to allow for those early years of debt collecting and pearling until he got the capital together to make his run. But once he started, once he put his shoulder to the plow, days off didn't exist, not for him. For every farmer it was the same, he knew, and yet he wished to God he'd had a farm and that was all he'd had to worry about.

There were no farms in that part of the world, and that was what Annie was still adjusting to. He could see it in her face. There were runs and stations and spreads: no farms. A cow and a calf to an acre? No one ever heard of that here. A cow and calf to sixty, seventy, one hundred acres of the spread stretching for hundreds of miles and lucky ever to find them, even at mustering time. You never truly knew how many you had. But what you did know was that at any given time, somewhere, some place on that long stretch of land, one of your animals was doubtless in trouble: hurt, ill, thirsty, struck out by bad water, hungry. And even if all were alive and fit and well, or apparently so, though you never covered the whole place, you just did the best you could with the eternal muster camps, as the cattle helped by working their way in as the surface water dried up.

But even if all looked well, you might detect sooner or later too many scrub bulls, the bad quality resulting from times of overbreeding, weakening the strain, the bulls no good for anything but to be shot so they did not breed down the strain further. Even as he looked now, such a short ride out, he saw some of these. Well, it was to be expected after the war; Jacky was not a miracle worker. A day off? There was a laugh. What was that? Five in the morning, sometimes earlier, to midnight or later, seven days a week. That had been his existence these several years, these several lifetimes. Working and learning all the while.

He knew about the scrub bulls now and not to waste his

time on them. At least he now had a generously strong breed except for the few, a breed of seven-eighths Afro-Asian Brahman and one-eighth English Shorthorn. That would have been a good way to breed human prototypes to people the North if you could have arranged it in advance. But it had taken him years. Years of reading into the night before they had electricity from the diesel generator, reading about breeds and grasses—God, grasses, that was another problem and still not fully solved, although locally grafted stylos would be the thing—and one day if he had a kid, he'd need a degree in agriculture to run the place at a profit. What did they call it, what was the word? He'd need a permanent agronomist on the property. That's what station management would become. The boss eventually would sit in an office, as Red often did now, when not mustering. The men would gather at the veranda each morning for their instructions when they'd come over from the quarters after their six-thirty breakfast and Red would come out of his small front office and give the Boss's instructions.

He would give his right arm and left testicle to be a fully-chaired station owner right now. But he was not. He was in the saddle and even if he hated it this day, it was in his blood like his father the Overlander before him, and Red would not leave working the land until he dropped. He needed it, and perhaps that was how he understood when someone needed to do something the way Annie needed to do her doctoring. He owed his leg to her. He loved her. He'd not want her unable to do the work she needed as much as he needed his. But perhaps if he got her her own plane, and she learned to fly as she wanted to and must soon anyway, perhaps they could work it out so that she operated from the property and were both away roughly the same time. Of course; that should be possible. His spirits lifted. Then he must cull the mobs, cull the herds with a vengeance. He needed the money to buy a plane. Everything salable would be sold, sold immediately.

When they camped that night he went to bed almost happy.

Jacky had watched all this unspeaking, reading Red's thoughts like watching a silent movie. So Jacky's spirits lifted, too, when Red was up at the very first light the next morning, the time they called piccaninny daylight after Aboriginal babies—up at first light, whipping the camp into order and shouting that they were all to work their backsides off and make this six-week camp a five-weeker, and a record-breaking five-weeker at that, with each holding paddock full of stock to be sold, a record number to be sold and a bonus for everyone. He did it so well that everyone was soon up and jumping, for they all did truly admire him so and were really glad to see him back and now knew that the Missus would make no difference and the Boss's leg would make no difference and they had their old Boss back, Big Red, the best in the land, and for him, for the legendary Murranji Red, old but by no means dead, no sir, fought in two wars, but not dead by a long shot, for him they would break their backs without pay.

It was like a battle really, once Red had declared it so. Every day they were up and rousting about early, washing if there was a creek nearby or not if there was not, which was more often the case; eating breakfast quickly, sometimes just the old bush standby of cold beef and damper bread, eating a sandwich with one hand and swilling tea with another as they cleaned weapons and saddled horses and were off culling and shooting and burying the scrub bulls. In November would come the weaning, setting up the temporary cattle yards with a few posts and sugar bag burlap in rolls, as they mustered them in and drafted off the young cattle, leaving them in the yards as they drove the cows out again and the weaning thus over. But the work at this time of the year in May was different. It was calf-marking and castrating and branding time.

So each day they mustered in a mob of cattle to mark the calves and brand them. They mustered them into temporary yards, where they fire-branded all unmarked cattle and castrated the young bulls. Then they earmarked the calves— two nicks at the top and one at the bottom in Red's case. The two at the top meant they were "off Red's place," the one at the bottom was an age mark: the calf's first year. In addition to this process the salable cattle were drafted off: steers and barren heifers. These they took to holding paddocks—the paddocks Red wanted full, and quickly, so he could buy Annie that plane.

The five weeks went by like lightning, and by nightfall of the last day of the fifth week they were nearing home paddock with the holding paddocks all full of good cattle and Red and the men knowing that somehow, for whatever reason, it just all worked better when Big Red was around.

They broke out the beer at dusk at the men's quarters and Red sent one of the lubras from the women's quarters over to the station house to get Annie and presently she came and was so pleased to see him home early that she was soon Skoaling her way into the finals of the beer-drinking championship, explaining amid the laughter and the shouts of "Blimey, can the Missus drink," that she had learned at drinking boat races in the medical students' quarters. A gnarled old ringer with gray curly hair and a beard, whom everyone called Curly, was the undisputed yard-of-beer champion. It was a close thing, but Annie beat him down on the last glass by a whisker. Red wondered if Curly had let her win, but if he had, Annie had certainly not realized, and either way Red would be eternally grateful, for it gave her the acceptance she had felt lacking at the start. He saw this in her eyes as they stood her small frame on the table of planked wood and cheered and stamped and clapped as she swirled and shouted "Olé," her thin cotton dress swirling out and showing off her brown legs up to her panties so that the men shouted "More," and she did it one more time and then feigned a collapse into Red's arms and then waved good-bye as Red carried her out of the quarters back to the homestead.

"He didn't let me win?" she said, seeking reassurance rather than anything else, for Red knew she felt she had won fairly and indeed he was not sure she hadn't, for she was certainly deadly with a glass of ale and no mistake.

"Not Curly," he said. "Not him. He wouldn't let a woman win if his fucking life depended on it, begging your pardon, Missus."

"You beg anything you like of me," she said in her moist, sensitive voice into his ear as, still carrying her, he reached the veranda, kicked the flywire door open and took her straight to their room.

One could have been forgiven for thinking that the five days of bliss, in which they were the closest they had ever been, would have cemented this as a full-time relationship, as a marriage and the strongest of marriages for all time. Certainly both Red and Annie thought so during those days of sweet inebriation with the other's company. They lived turned inside out each other; everything hummed with sweet charity.

But they were only using parts of them, however much they told each other that the full person was committed to the other. And even then it did not show until the very last minute.

Red had talked about working hard to get the plane, of course, but made an excuse that he needed these five days at the station to organize the men to go out to the holding paddocks in easy stages and get all the steers and heifers to home paddock for a contract drover who would come in to take them to market. Annie had believed that five days were necessary and Red was thankful, knowing he could make up the time on the next muster camp. He and the men would do it in four and a half weeks if necessary. The men had even connived a bit in taking their time to bring the cattle all together during the week, for the truth was that they'd have normally reprovisioned and done the turnaround in a couple of days, leaving a few of the older stockmen who worked full time at the station to bring the cattle in from the holding paddocks. But it had worked wondrously well and Annie, perhaps because of her blithe happiness, had not noticed.

But the evening before the day of Red's departure little strains started to develop. They were just the smallest of things, like little awkward silences which they really never had. And then Annie at bedtime asking Red was there anything she could pack for him, did he have a spare pair of socks? It was out of character for her, and such a strange, unnecessary thing to ask a bushman, that he did not know what to say, so he just nodded and she said, "Good, you'll be all right, then," but in a faraway voice.

He felt the need to say something else. He came and sat quietly beside her on the bed where she was absentmindedly undressing. But the awkward silences were taking their toll. It was the simplest of things to say. It was an automatic, everyday Outback phrase. "The men will expect you to come, you know," he said. But even as he said it, he heard Annie involuntarily catch her breath.

The words were a trigger, an unintended trigger but a trigger nonetheless, a trigger causing her now to say something she did not mean, or rather perhaps did mean but had never intended to say, at least not that way. A very real part of her knew he had not intended what he had said to sound the way it had sounded; a very real part of her knew he had said it in the gentlest of voices, with his arm still around her. But he had said it, made the accidental conjunction of words which everyone at some time has done but which are the exact wrong words at the exact wrong time and in the exact wrong place however well meaning their intentions. She knew they were part of the context of a larger discussion and had been said in such a way as to be kind, gentle and understanding, but she flew at him, giving the words their face value and divorcing them from the person who had uttered them. She pulled herself away from his embrace on the bed and stood up as she pivoted away from the bed and turned to him, like any housewife, like any shrew, like any person who has hidden a resentment too long and taken the flash point of an unintended hurt to hurl it back:

"I can't come because I'm still scared out of my wits and I hate this place. I need a more civilized world and more civilized bloody people and I need my work. Can you understand that? Can you really bloody understand that in this bloody tall man's land the poor women you're all so anxious to protect need something as well? I need my work as much as you need yours. *I'm a doctor*. I need people to tend the way you need cattle. I need people to water the way you need land. I like to see bloody things grow, too, can you understand that? Can you? . . .!"

She had been shouting at him and he had sat looking at her the whole time, his eyes getting sadder and sadder, and now she noticed them and saw they were close to tears and she wanted to run away as she felt the first of her own tears she had been trying so hard to hold start down upon her cheek and she tried even harder not to break into heavy sobs. But when he said quietly and simply, in the hoarsest of voices she'd ever heard him use, "Yes," and stood and walked over and took her in his arms and held her just gently and stroked her hair, she broke into heavy, heaving sobs so that the whole of her frame was shuddering in his arms. And she felt him heaving, too, and knew he really did understand and knew that of all men in the world that her words might have been thrown at, he was the last she should have done it to. But they were closer now than ever, holding each other gently still, and his hand still stroking down over her hair to her back. She knew he did understand, understood she had not meant what she had said—or at least not meant it with the anger she had said it. He understood.

They both understood. They both now understood too much too damn well. That was the whole damn bloody trouble and after he had put her into bed and asked would she like a quiet ale and she had nodded appreciatively like a child, he had said he'd be back in a minute and walked out and down the hall and she'd heard him, but only just, talking on the two-way radio before he brought the beer back and sat on the edge of the bed, stroking her hair as she sat up to drink it. But she knew she had not been supposed to hear so she said nothing, although perhaps he sensed her silent thanks, and she hoped he did, and they were tender to each other all night. And it was only after Red got up while it was still dark and dressed to go on the drive, kissing her on the temple and saying, "See you," as he walked out the door, that she eventually fell asleep, in the unexpected way the body knows the mind needs a rest from the anguish of that particular sort of sense of loss which one has created for oneself, by being oneself, and which one will never know the full answer to.

She was still asleep when she felt the hand on her shoulder awaking her and saw the chubby face of Bluey, smiling gently at her so that she reached up and hugged him, and sobbed again a little until he said softly, "It's two in the afternoon. Let's get some breakfast into you and get you into town. Red thinks you'll be happier there for a while."

"I know," she said softly. "He called you on the radio last night, didn't he?"

"Yeah. I flew down this morning. There's a letter on the bedside table."

She nodded.

"I'll let you be for a while, then, and see you in the kitchen."

She nodded again and he walked out.

He had known better than to ask if she were OK.

Red's letter had said,

"Take your time. Whatever you decide, I'll learn to live with."

Kiwai was concerned when he heard the news. He kept encouraging Red to come over and see him. In the end they'd not sold the boats but had gone into boat rental themselves. Douglas was furious. He said it would never be profitable.

Red and Annie did not see each other for nearly a year. It took a lot of sorting out. But then it started to grow again, and they dined together again, and became friends again. Both knew marriage was out of the question. It took Anne a long time to come back to the property for a weekend visit. She was very committed to her career. But eventually she did come and little by little came to enjoy the weekends there.

There was a solution of sorts which they now began to discuss. Their friendship and love deepened and after a time it seemed the natural thing to do. And that was how, four years after the war ended, Alison was born, the last generation and the start of tomorrow on the last frontier at the Back of Beyond.

38

Red took Alison down to meet Kismet. He knew some people might have thought it funny. But not Jacky, not Crocodile Tommy. And sometimes he felt as much a part of these people as his own. His mother Beth would not have approved, although Red himself had been born close to this spot where he stood now with his daughter, just back by the rock pool there, the night Jacky had sworn he saw the Big Red kangaroo roaming a thousand miles out of his territory. But his mother would not approve now, any more than she ever had, of the crocodile. She thought the story of the Big Red kangaroo was a lovely legend, but that croc was something else. "Well, look at it, daughter," Red said, half aloud, "look at it sitting in the sun on the rock there smiling at you, and know that it's a part of the family and like we humans it's fine if you don't get too close."

He looked down at the baby in his arms and smiled. He must take her to see his mother in Sydney soon. She was seventy-six now, and whoever would have thought she'd have lived to see that, the way her early life had been? Perhaps there was something in the bush breeding them tough, even the women forced into it. She was old and crotchety now, but in a way warmer toward him and he knew for all her tut-tutting about him and Annie not being married, it was only a front and she was dying to see her first grandchild. He must take Alison down to Sydney soon, before his mother, with her stoop and her shuffle and that bush-creviced face that the city creams had never fixed, got much older.

Douglas would be a problem as usual, though. He'd gone from bookkeeper to accountant to gold-rimmed-glasses respectability and had refused even to acknowledge Alison's existence. There'd been some heated words when Red had phoned to tell of the impending birth and then the birth itself. So there'd be no question of Douglas seeing Ali, old Kismet, old son—you can bet on that, Red said to himself as he turned and smiled down at his baby daughter once more. Annie understood when he said he'd wanted to take Ali out to Five Mile Camp to meet the old fellar. Anne understood, as Lisa would have, that he had to come out and talk to the croc sometimes, that it was his way of thinking back and thinking forward and thinking things out. Sometimes Red thought life was largely good and bad memories: and if, during the interwar years, he had his share of bad to live with, in the postwar years he had his share of good to live on. Life was in a sense memories because so often the actual present was a happening so intense, or even so unintense, that one sat or rode there as a spectator, the events running the life of the liver, rather than the other way around, so that a spectator part almost looked at a participant part of you to see it happening, it was happening so fast, and you were not conscious of it happening until the memory occurred and of course that was always afterward, when all you could say was that it felt good or bad.

From the time Alison was born, Big Red had his share of years which, when they became memories, he called good. This was the overall feeling he ascribed to so many of the postwar years, a warm and good overriding sense, yet a sense tinged always with a sense of loss, that sense of loss, that separation anxiety, which starts as a child and continues throughout life for all but a special few who manage some sort of steady and creative relationship with a mate who accommodates their heart's desire. Such fulfillment was not

Red's, nor Anne's. The ache was all the worse because each sensed in the other that capacity for the full and deep fulfillment, the echo of one's own inside another that so few have.

Yet they were good years, and Anne was a good mother, however much in absentia. With the cheeky Cathy and the quiet, phlegmatic Roo, Alison had two wonderful companions. Black Roo was closest to her, although some years older. Cathy was older than Roo. Red watched silently as Cathy adopted Anne and gradually became her protector, confusing even the knowledgeable good doctor, as Red called her, with her Aboriginal logic and complicated kinship systems. Cathy convinced Anne that by the birth of Alison, marriage or no marriage, Anne was part of the extended family, and Cathy's responsibility, so that when Anne finally said all right, that Cathy could work for her although the pay was little enough for both of them, Cathy winked at Red and as she went out said, "Father and child see plenty of mother now, Boss, what you think?"

For the first two years of Alison's life Anne stayed a lot on the property, feeling it important for her to be there as mother in the formative years. So except for the odd forays into Darwin for books or talks with her colleagues, she stayed, happily, on the Back of Beyond.

The property expanded and Red, with one final big acquisition, having bought several smaller holdings around him cheaply during the war years, reached his magical target of one million acres. A big American firm had bought a large property to his east, where the boundary of that neighbor was nearly a hundred miles distant, but Red was the biggest for miles around, and certainly the best known and most respected. He had wanted the American property, however, and he saw it as an irritation so close to his consolidated holdings. The Americans had tied the previous owner to some commitment just after the war, and although he had always promised Red first option, the man had sold it direct to the Americans without consulting him. Red supposed they had paid an exaggerated price to get a foothold in the North. They were a big company, but he did not see them as a danger. Besides, the Americans often had different farming methods which did not always work in the North and Red believed that sooner or later he would pick that property up cheaply, too.

When he heard they'd sent a man out to run it who was more accountant and business manager than farmer, he smiled. When word filtered through from the black ringers, who always talked to each other when they met on the Track or on cattle drives, that the Americans were going to fence their property, Red smiled even more. Now there was a nice, capital-intensive, labor-intensive, maintenance-intensive pastime that was completely unnecessary. Territory cattle, however upgraded some of the large mobs were, such as Red's, were still in many ways scrub cattle: rather like wild horses that have been tamed and crossed and recrossed to improve the quality and yet, deep down, are still bush horses. Such were the cattle of the North. Their meat was often sold overseas for hamburger and processed meat—even pet food with the tougher and more muscled of the animals, for with a free range system the animals did not develop so much fat as muscle and therefore were not seen in the same category as the luscious, steak-producing, grass-fed animals of other regions. Still, there was a big market, and Red was pushing into the pet food and hamburger market with good quality buffalo meat, too—his "free" meat as he called it.

But the cattle were free range, or open range like the buffalo. They ranged over hundreds of miles until the real onset of the main Dry each year, and then they worked their way in, as if by instinct, from water hole to water hole, heading, always, toward the river and permanent waters of the home paddock area where the main muster was taking place, although outriders went out all the time, except in the Wet, to help herd the cattle in toward the permanent water. This was particularly necessary during bad Dries. The cattle could only travel a day without water. If an animal got weak, or a mother with calves slowed down, it could be disastrous.

So they needed some help to keep them moving in. In bad times, the animals who had stopped to rest or sleep might be so weak they had to be lifted to their feet. This was not at all uncommon: lifted and then driven mercilessly to the next water. It seemed cruel, but it saved their lives. If they were not lifted up, they would stay there until they were only bleached bones in the sun. So the ringers, the stockmen, the jackeroos, the property workers, were needed for this work, not fencing. When properties were so large, fencing did not help cattle stay alive. It just took men from such duties, or required the hiring of extra men so that your labor force became uneconomical.

So Red was happy when the Americans started fencing and did not see them as a threat.

The property ran itself, in many ways, with Jacky the head stockman and Douglas now in charge of financial matters in Sydney, although Red, by habit through the years, still checked everything himself and then subjected it to Bluey's always withering, but happy scrutiny. Bluey's son was in Sydney now, the eldest boy, doing law. Bluey was fatter and balder and more opulently prosperous every day. He and Red and Kat and Anne had some wonderful buying sprees, in Darwin and Brisbane and Sydney, buying extravagances for the Back of Beyond and for the Byrne cliff-top mansion although, as Bluey himself admitted, with the coming of the aircraft, with two-way radios, with the Royal Flying Doctor Service and the School of the Air for Outback kids each day, the Outback was changing. In fact, with generators and refrigeration and electric light and all the luxuries of the homestead, and the beaming, brimming lagoons of barra-mundi, or the thousands of magpie geese which took off at first light from the lagoons, which made beautiful shooting and beautiful stew, Blue had to admit that when Red had the good French champagne in stock, as he always did nowadays, that parties on the Back of Beyond were better than at his own place.

And so it was, after Anne moved back into the town, that the Back of Beyond became the party place for the weekend, for all who could fly and many who drove or rode in from neighboring properties. Anne came every weekend she possibly could: always by air. The parties grew, so that people were often coming from interstate now, cattle buyers, businessmen, even politicians.

Alison was four, Fan-tan was fat and happy, although going into Darwin more and more to gamble lately; Jacky was getting gray, and his lad, young Black Roo, now full grown. Nothing further had ever been heard of the crocodile hunters; the police had never come; Red and Jacky had never mentioned it again. Five Mile Camp was only visited by Red, Jacky and a few other highly trusted blacks.

One day just after Alison's fourth birthday, Fan-tan having been gone in town for several days, the old Ford truck, which he drove in a totally uncontrolled and hilarious manner on his journeys into town, pulled up outside the long, low bungalow line of the ever-freshly-painted white station house. Fan-tan got out and hurried up the straight steep steps which led to the wide veranda all around the house, set on thick timber stumps for coolness but hidden from outside view by clean white latticework. Red was in fact rummaging around underneath the house as he heard and looked and saw Fan-tan's arrival and desperate dash up the steps, with a bundle under his arm which Red supposed to be some food Fan-tan had bought in the town, for whenever he went to town, in whatever straggling state he came back, he always, always, brought the ingredients for making them wonderful Chinese meals for the next several days; meals of shark fin's soup, and octopus and lobster, and wonderful sweet and sour sauces with ginger and lychees, always tinned lychees with his special homemade ice cream. So Red thought this is what Fan-tan had, and kept on rummaging until he thought he heard a cry and so decided to investigate. He could bend his leg some now, and it was definitely improving so that soon he believed he would be able to walk completely again, although with a slight limp. But in such confined spaces as under the house, having to bend between the stumps which were not quite his full height, he had to be careful with his leg. So it took him some time, and he heard two more cries, before he reached the outside steps and mounted them and walked into the kitchen to see Fan-tan sheepishly holding a baby and saying, "Baby belong town, Boss, and need good home."

The baby in fact turned out to be aged two and that was all Fan-tan ever said about her, that she "belong town," and that her name was Jitangeli; although under Red's withering questioning Fan-tan implied, but did not say, that the baby was illegitimate by his sister, which certainly set Red to wondering because Fan-tan had never mentioned a sister before and he was certainly muddying up the questioning with his skillful and cunning use of his Chinee English. Red wondered if the child may have been Fan-tan's own from one of his earlier visits to town. Red also wondered, for Fan-tan was an anachronism in the twentieth century, still very traditionally Chinese in dress and manner, Red also wondered if Fan-tan had bought the baby on the Chinese black market. It seemed inconceivable that such a thing could happen, yet Red knew well enough that some of the old Chinese habits died very hard and it was certainly not above Fan-tan to have bought such a girl as company for Alison or, worse still, have won her in a fan-tan game. In the end, after all the questioning, Red suspected the latter.

There was no doubt Fan-tan had decided his four-year-old blond charge needed a female playmate of roughly her own age. And there was no doubt either, in Red's mind, that he had charitably to accept his old friend's good deed, for it was certainly that, and whatever anyone else might think, Fan-tan was in his own special way fulfilling some secret canon of Asian righteousness which he was entirely satisfied with. So of course Jitangeli stayed, a beautiful child of mixed Malay and Chinese blood, stayed and grew up as the younger sister of Alison, both watched over by their elder brother, Big Roo; they grew up and very close together, Black Roo the tall Aboriginal boy, and Alison the stately blond tomboy, always swimming naked and spearing fish with Roo, and Jitangeli, water-lily soft and precious and quietly smiling.

39

It was typical of the bush and its huge distances and accompanying attitudes that it took until Alison was nearly five before the trip to Sydney to see her grandmother was finally organized.

At first, despite the increasing use of light aircraft, Annie was not anxious her daughter should travel until she was at least one year old because of the heat. Then Bluey went to Sydney—he was going more and more and would continue to as the years went by and his empire's base changed to the city. From Sydney, Bluey reported that Beth's health had improved a little. So this, in the casual bush manner, caused another year's delay. Perhaps, too, there was hope that Douglas, the childless and unbending but hyperefficient Douglas, might change his mind. Even his wife, Joan, whom Beth had picked out for him and was a grammar-school-educated daughter of a social family, wrote nice letters saying they must come and stay, all of them, Red and Annie and the baby, for she would dearly love to see them all and she was sure things would be all right. Joan missed not being able to have children and Douglas had not been willing to adopt.

Nevertheless they planned to go for Alison's third birthday. But by then the negotiations had started for Red's final big acquisition.

So in the end it was Beth's eightieth birthday they went for, with the tiny blond Alison not so tiny anymore and skipping and jumping and laughing happily, taking to her grandmother with the wonderful openness of her nature so that Beth cried and hugged her so much, hugged her and Annie as well, hugged all three of them, so that it was too much emotionally for her and she had to sit down and Annie gave her something to take. Beth didn't want to take it, but Annie said it was only an aspirin, which it wasn't, and presently she had fallen asleep on the wooden veranda in her old wooden armchair in the timber frame house overlooking the harbor that she and Douglas had moved into when they had first come to Sydney.

Of course now Douglas and his wife lived in a mansion of a house overlooking the expensive part of the harbor. But Beth had never moved, and even her view was worth a lot of money now. Somehow, despite the fact that Beth herself was very rich, for Red had always kept a financial interest for her in everything he'd done, Beth's house looked remarkably like an Outback house: dry, bone-dry timber, needing paint, dried and bleached in her case by the salt winds off the harbor. And inside, the house was almost Spartan, as much like the early house on the Back of Beyond as you'd find anywhere. Beth had not gone out and bought all those creature comforts she had so craved for all the years she'd been in the bush. Annie, whom Red had told about the hardship of the early years, remarked on this and Red nodded.

"It's always the same with bush folk who move to the city," he said, as if that was end to it.

"Guilt," said Anne simply, without a hint of rancor. "Punishing herself for leaving you all."

"Perhaps. Anyway, she got what she wanted. She'd probably say she couldn't afford it. Needed the money for Douglas's schooling. It's only the last few years the real money has come, you know."

"I know," Annie said, taking his hand and walking to the veranda rail to search with her eyes for Alison who had run down into the garden to play.

Red put his arm around her waist and they stood still and silent and very happy for a time. Then they went and got some food. It was still only noon and they had planned to take Beth to lunch but felt now they should eat in.

But by the time they arrived back she was dressed and waiting, her eyes as alive and alert as they had ever been, flicking out from under her bonnet, so totally out of fashion she looked like an aged, frail and cloth-worn-smooth ancient female Salvation Army warrior.

"Must have dropped off—not like me at all," she said purposefully, to deter any suggestion that it had to do with age or had any frequency on her calendar at all. "Haven't done that in years, have I, son?" she said, turning to Red as if he'd been with her all the time.

"No, Mum, not like you at all. Never do that. Must have been the excitement."

"Yes, that's it."

"And the aspirin," said Annie kindly; "that could have made you a bit drowsy."

"Of course. Well, where are we off to then?"

"That nice restaurant overlooking the harbor that we went to the first time I came to Sydney to see how you and Douggie were doing."

"Can't go there, son. Too expensive. Douglas says so. Haven't been there in years."

She paused. Then she looked lovingly at Red, at Annie, at Alison, who had come up, skipping and talking to herself, from the garden.

Red inhaled deeply and said, "But Alison might like it, that's what you were thinking, weren't you, Mum—Ali might like it and although it's your birthday it could be like a birthday present from you to her—is that what you were thinking?"

The old lady nodded, choked up, but her eyes alive with happiness.

"I could pay cash, you know, Mum. Douglas wouldn't have to see an account or anything," Red said gently.

"Oh, bugger Douglas," the old lady said suddenly, the

tremor gone from her voice. "It's my money, too. We'll go and have a big spread and then take my granddaughter out on the harbor and we'll hire a private launch and you tell that Douglas to charge it all to me. I'll not have her growing up without knowing there's an alternative to that dry Outback."

Red smiled and they got their things together and ordered a taxi and drove to the restaurant overlooking the harbor, sitting there on the terrace in the easy sun, and looking across a whole world of blue ocean ringed around them.

Alison was at the questioning, inquisitive age and Beth's love was communicating itself, so that presently they fell to nattering, as the very young and very old sometimes will, as if they have more in common than any of us realize, so that soon Beth was reminiscing and Alison was joining in as if she'd been there. Then they went out on the harbor, Beth insisting on standing outside, hanging onto the rail with Alison beside her, the two inseparable now, standing like captain and chief officer on the bridge of *Defiant,* standing against the wind and the spray, the first and last of the breed.

They stayed until the sun was almost down over the harbor and then they went home and had a cup of tea and a snack and put Alison to bed. Beth had her second cup of tea and kissed Annie and Red on the forehead as she passed by on her way to bed, saying, "I've had a wonderful day, son, a truly wonderful day."

She died in her sleep that night.

Back at the Back of Beyond, Red sought solace again at Five Mile Camp.

Was it the camp or the crocodile which guarded its back entrance that attracted him so? No one on the property really worried anymore. It was his Shangri-La and he had a right to it, that was the view. And as Annie had to be away more and more, she was glad he had this strange but quiet comfort.

He sat on his rock in the early morning sun, his friend on his rock a short distance off in the water, and thought about his mother's life, about all their lives.

He thought about Billy's running away to war and his

subsequent death; of his father's death at the hand of the land he loved so much before that wet and dry mistress had enabled him to realize his dream. He thought of Jacky's Nora, whom his mother had missed so, of her death and how it had diminished their lives, only to be replaced by the bubbling Lily to be wiped out in her prime but succeeded by the quietly confident Cathy, who gave him so much love.

It was ebb and flow all right, old boy, ebb and flow here on the land like ebb and flow there in the billabong.

He thought of Lisa, dear Lisa, wonderful Lisa, who had come up for his mother's funeral and he'd realized how like Anne she was; or how like Lisa Anne was; or how like Anne, who was perhaps a little quieter to begin with, Lisa had become. He should have married Lisa. He'd known that for years and it didn't detract from his love for Anne. He loved Anne as much, maybe more. But he and Lisa had met at the wrong time; they'd been too young; both too hotheaded; neither willing to yield. If they'd known how they'd change, they might have had a good continuity of love. If life allows for such a thing. You tell me, you there on the rock. You've got all the answers. You've been around longer. You're supposed to know. I'm still a learner.

He thought of Douglas and how, at the funeral, there was a common bond of sorts still. But they were so different. And Douglas still blamed Red for Billy's death. He'd been so small then, he'd idolized Billy so, and, he'd been such a victim of Beth's propaganda, of her last attempt to cope with the exigencies of the land. But the thing with Douglas might heal. There was time. And Bluey was a help. Red missed Bluey fearfully, but Bluey's son, John, was in Sydney, his business interests were growing more and more there, and he was a bridge to Douglas.

Book IV

THE BACK
OF BEYOND

40

Ten years had passed and the parties, the legendary Outback parties of Big Red, became sporadic now, yet more formal, with engraved invitations sent out three or four times a year and always now including some overseas invitations, eagerly sought and always accepted by cattle buyers, knowing Red's breed of English- and Asian-African–type cattle to be one of the best, as good as the American Longhorn some said. And Red was always glad to see such men, and old friends who were also in cattle, and any with other interests from overseas, for Red was not above doing a little business at his parties.

Annie could fly herself now, and they had given her her own plane to work among the Aboriginal children. In 1963 Red was sixty-five. When Red was born Jacky had been seventeen. He was now eighty-two. Red knew Jacky was dying. Anne had seen him on her previous visit and said softly and with understanding eyes to Red,

"He's got a little time yet."

Now on this visit Red said to her,

"Is it anything in particular?"

"Just old age."

"Is he in pain?"

"Who ever knows with these people? All their thresholds

and receptors are different. I suspect just a little—just a little rheumatism."

"Can you give him anything?"

"Sure. Can you get him to take it?"

Red shrugged.

"Is he sleeping all right at night?" Anne asked softly again.

"Yes. Yes, I think he is."

"He's all right, then."

"Yes, for the time."

"Will you go down to Five Mile Camp with him when the time comes?"

"Of course. But I didn't think you believed in that sort of thing."

"Despite my hobby of anthropology?"

"Book learning. This other is like saying you believe a man knows when he is going to die, almost to the day. I thought you'd think that unscientific."

"Not in an Aboriginal."

"What about a near-Aboriginal?"

"*You* might know. But that would test my system—as I said, they've got different receptors and thresholds. We probably had them once and lost them, although I doubt we ever had some of their rich tribal mythology. Anyway, I don't think it's something you yourself will have to worry about for a while."

She was suddenly serious and leaned across from where they always sat on the veranda and touched his cheek with the back of her hand.

"You're a strange woman."

She gave a little smile.

"Why—? Because I didn't marry you?"

"Right words—sort of—but wrong feelings."

"Tell me."

"Because you make me feel so incredibly good with such simple words and movements like that."

"Is that strange?"

"Only because one thinks of those feelings going with people being together all the time."

"Perhaps we wouldn't have them if we were together all the time."

"You have been the nicest thing in my life and I seem to have seen so little of you."

She smiled her faraway smile and put her right hand on his thigh.

"I'll stay a few days if you're worried about Jacky," she said.

"Can you do that?"

"Yes."

"You've always been around when I needed you—you know that. From the time I met you, you have always come when needed. You're the most reliable, steadfast thing I know."

"More reliable and steadfast than Kismet or Jacky?" She said it kindly.

"Than both."

"That's quite a statement. I can live on that for a month. I think you're probably the most loving, supportive person I know. I wonder if those who have been married have come to know each other as well and to be nice to each other as we?"

"I doubt it. Took me years to understand, though."

"Me too. I had plenty of new, young ideas—took me awhile to work out that I actually believed in some of them."

"You don't hate the land anymore, though."

"No. I don't hate it anymore. It really came down to my career in the end. Otherwise I would have tried the full-time thing for you."

"We had some great weekends and always the Wet to look forward to."

"And we've got a teenage daughter who doesn't hate us. In fact she seems to like us both."

"We could sell the formula if we knew what it was."

"I think the formula is dying out there." She had become suddenly serious.

"Jacky—?"

"Well, him and his kind. Jacky and Nora and Lily and their whole system—which, incidentally, includes you."

"You, me and the matter-of-fact black extended family—that what you're saying?"

"Sure. Lots of easy love from all around and not an exaggerated childhood dependency. Want to go and see how the hyacinths are doing?"

"Not particularly. I was enjoying being a good father."

"You'll still be that when we get back. I just had a sudden fantasy of taking my clothes off in that lush green hyacinth patch."

He got up and they walked hand in hand toward the home billabong.

"I always feel like I'm stealing my first when you proposition me like this—"

"Sure beats taking it for granted, doesn't it?"

"—that I'm about to make love for the first time and have all the time in the world—"

"Yes."

"—that there's no age difference between us and that we're incredible first-time lovers—"

"We're always good. It's not a function of age."

"Yes, we are. Our bodies have always known each other well. If only we could have known then what we each would become."

"And told each other what was really in ourselves?"

"Something like that."

"And married and lived happily ever after?"

"Yeah—would we have got to understand each other as much that way?"

"Probably not."

"Well, it was better the way it was, then?"

"Not along the way."

"No. That's the strange part. It was as if we knew what we were missing. That mean we might have been OK together?"

"Maybe. Who knows? Will the sun rise tomorrow or do we buy a flashlight just to be sure?"

"Yeah. Great to be wise after the event—and even then you don't know. Guessing from the front is even trickier. Wouldn't it have been great, though, if we were right?"

"Don't think I haven't thought about it." Her voice had gone very low.

They had reached the paddock now and then they were in the special spot among the hyacinths and they lay together a long time in love before talking again.

"Jacky'll be all right, really," she said eventually, with a deep sigh.

"I know. It's just that he's always been there."

"I know. But you have Alison and me and Jitangeli and Roo and Cathy."

"That's quite a family, isn't it?"

"It is when they're all on your side. Your land and love on all four sides."

She always knew the right thing to say and, as if sensing one further thing were necessary, knowing how he worried about the Aboriginal's attitude to pain, she added,

"I'll leave you something to slip in his tea when he's not looking if you're worried about him being in pain but I think you'll find he won't need it."

His heart was very full, as it was more and more these days. There were still parts of love, parts of understandings between people that he kept discovering and wondered how he could have gone so long without knowing and wondered if others knew them sooner or even at all.

Among the hyacinths and the smell of the flowers and their bodies and the rich black earth, among the whites and blacks and deep greens, they were closer than ever before, as Anne had intended, so that the pain of Jacky's going was forgotten.

A month later Jacky took himself to Five Mile Camp. Red followed and they spent the night talking over old times by the fire. Just before dawn, Jacky, in kangaroo-skin cloak against the cold, lay down to rest and a few moments later he was dead. They wrapped his body in paperbark and, with full tribal reverence, took it to Coffin Swamp and placed it in the branches of the sacred banyan tree.

41

When Lisa heard of Jacky's death she came to see Red as
soon as she could. She brought her grandson who wanted to
be a jackeroo. Bill was three years older than Alison. Red had
kept in touch with Lisa in a strange way over the years—
strange because he kept thinking his whole life that it had
been over with Lisa the day she left to marry the doctor, but
it never really had, for both had kept seeing each other one
way and another over the years, or writing, or telephoning.
They told themselves it was one of those truly platonic
things. Annie didn't seem to mind, and Lisa's husband had
long since stopped trying to prevent the friendship and
eventually became friendly with Red in a mild way himself,
so that Red felt free to call in if he could find an excuse to get
to Adelaide. But the fact was, it wasn't platonic; they only
said it was. It had become a joke with them that one more
whiskey would do it and they never had that one extra drink.
But the desire, the same desire as on the beach of long ago,
the ambivalent desire was always there just below the
surface.

"You're the sort of person one can never really stop loving,"
Red said to Lisa, taking her a little aback when she came to
console him and talk to him about her grandson whom Roo
had taken for a look around. "You're the 'what if' person."

She was going to say something frivolous—deliberately, for she had got over her stupid frivolity many years ago now and sometimes cursed herself for ever having had it because she believed that that had lost Red to her, her frivolous impulsiveness. She stopped even the deliberate lighthearted remark now. Both knew each other too well.

"Well of course we should have married, if that's what you're saying, and perhaps it's better to have it out now. But you're happy with Annie? She's lovely."

"Of course. But you would have lived on the property. I could never forget that. Despite everything, you actually offered, wanted, to come and live here. You're the only one who has. You like it still, don't you?"

"I sometimes think leaving up here was the stupidest thing I ever did."

They had been walking and she was suddenly close to tears.

"It's a long time ago now," he said, taking her hand. She had the wonderful ripe beauty of a woman in her fifties, though she was really in her early sixties.

"Well, at least young Bill will have the opportunity to get back here on behalf of the family."

"You sure he wants to? It's not all just to please you?"

"You've met him. What do you think?"

"I think that in a year he'll make up his own mind."

"He's a lot like you were."

"He could do worse," Red said with a smile.

"You'll take him, then?"

"If that's what he wants—of course. Even if he didn't, I'd probably try to talk him into it to please you."

Bill had lost his father in the Second World War and Lisa had helped his mother to bring the boy up. He was now seventeen. But he hated school and wanted to get onto a cattle property. Finally Lisa and his mother had agreed that if he finished school he could go jackerooing straightaway if Red would have him and teach him the business.

"Why *did* we keep seeing each other?" Lisa said as they reached the station house again now. She had recovered from that terrible sense of loss she'd felt in the conversation earlier, which they'd both felt often over the years.

"Torture," smiled Red, "pleasant torture," covering his feelings with a joke as usual, and then a little more seriously, "because we've had that rare thing, a deep, abiding genuine friendship, and so we put up with wanting each other sexually and knowing we'd made a bad mistake but that too many people would get hurt if we tried to right it and, in any case, if we'd been going to, it would have had to have been done years ago and I was too proud then and you were still an unpredictable bitch. It's only in old age we've got nice, you know."

They both laughed, then hugged tightly just for a moment as they stood on the porch and then went inside to have some tea and wait for Roo and Bill and the fourteen-year-old Alison, the tomboy, who was tagging along, to come back.

Black Roo was now twenty-eight, and Big Red immediately appointed him head stockman in his father's place. This caused a little discontentment among the forty-odd ringers, jackeroos and rouseabouts they had on the place, a little discontentment among the stockmen, because of his youth and, with one or two, because he was black. But they knew Big Red and they knew that was an end to it, even if Big Red had not been careful to pass along the grapevine through one of his trusted white ringers that anyone who gave Roo any trouble could expect a knuckle sandwich and to be off the property by nightfall, if not earlier. They all respected Big Red too much to know that this was likely to be an idle threat. And, indeed, however much they bucked about it for a day or two, they knew Black Roo was the best of them all, as good or better than his father, and perhaps that was part of it. There was in Black Roo the happy geniality of his father, the almost lackadaisical good-naturedness, yet there was a slightly sharper cutting edge, too, as if the twentieth century he was a child of had added a slightly tougher dimension, not meaner but tougher, more like Big Red. They knew they would get away with less with Black Roo.

But there was a try-on, as there always is in the bush: a trial of strength. It was done well, Red would give them that. His men were not stupid. They used the American stockman with the Southern accent and tooled boots from the neighboring property.

From time to time Red and Roo went in for a drink either to the Adelaide River pub or to the town of Katherine and a pub there. Both watering holes were a fair distance, but Red either flew or drove, and he gave his men reasonable freedom with the Land Rovers and Nissans, for he well realized the necessity for them to get off the property and let off steam occasionally.

On a hot day Red and Black Roo had driven into Katherine for a drink. It was a long day and they had arrived thirsty. A few of the men were there, not many, and to be honest Big Red did not at first read it as a setup.

He ordered two glasses and he and Roo began to drink. Both were dressed similarly in their moleskins, more white like white jeans these days than the old gray ones, with half-calf, scuffed brown riding boots, faded khaki shirts and hats. Red, when he wore a hat, still wore his old Light Horse hat, which was beautifully stained with sweat. Roo wore a white and stained more traditional stockman's hat, with a low, tucked-in crown and broad brim curled at the sides coming almost to a point at the front over the forehead, where the two curls met.

The man with calf-high, tooled leather boots worn outside his neatly pressed trousers, in checked shirt with a newer, higher-crown American hat, a man perhaps six feet four inches tall, a strong man, a Coke machine with a head on it of a man, stood near them, and as Roo went to sip his beer, said in a low voice,

"Can't stand dirty hats . . . yah alwuz see niggers in dirty hats."

Roo said nothing. Big Red said nothing. Both kept sipping at their beers. Then the American said,

"I'm talkin' to yah there, boy, yah coon, yah hat's dirty."

Black Roo paused momentarily, put his glass down, half

turned so the American could see him, made a quick sign as if to tighten an imaginary tie around his neck, around his open-neck shirt, and then slouched back into his original position of leaning on the bar, as if nothing had happened.

But something had. The bar had gone suddenly silent. There was not so much as the sound of a beer going down.

It began to dawn on the American that something very strange was happening here.

"Well—?" Big Red said at last.

"Well, what?" the American said.

"Well, he's given you the high tie sign, that's what."

The man looked at him incredulously. "What the hell's that mean?"

"It means he wants to fight the bar."

"What—everyone?"

"If necessary."

"He'll get murdered."

"I doubt that—no one else is moving."

"But they're all whites."

"Sure. And some probably feel the same as you do. But they know one or two things you don't."

"What's that?"

"First, he's with me and no one fights me—not for a long, long time, anyway. Second, even if he wasn't with me, this son of mine would take out a good ten white men in any fair fight. But of course that's not the point, is it? He's not going to have to fight ten. He's only going to have to fight one."

"He only looks about half my weight. I don't fight out of my weight."

"Well, you're going to have to start, mister, because he's sure as hell going to fight you any moment."

"He hasn't even moved."

"Smart, isn't he? He's been using all the time you've spent getting wild and talking, sizing you up, watching how much energy you're expending, guessing your weight within a few ounces, assessing your age, any old injuries—and he'll know where they are, even if they're under your clothes, such as that weak right knee of yours—"

The white man looked askance.

"How could you—"

"Abo logic they call it. Really just glorified common sense. You can tell by your stance at the bar that you're favoring it ever so slightly, once you know to look carefully for such things. I'll bet that's where he was going to go for you first— *right* for that knee. . . ."

He turned to Black Roo, whose teeth spread in a delicious grin.

"Yes. One hit in the knee. That's all he was going to give you on the way past to the next man—if there was a next man."

"Why are you telling me all this?"

"For the joy of seeing the beads of perspiration on your brow and to make sure Black Roo doesn't let you off with a light chop in the knee. I've been a bit worried about him lately. . . . He's been getting very kind to strangers."

The man was perspiring very freely now, despite the air-conditioned bar.

"Black Roo," he said tremulously, "what sort of a name is that?"

"A rare and beautiful name for someone who moves very fast and hard. I'd watch his feet if I were you, mate."

The American could not believe this was happening. The others had said it would be simple. Just a scrawny Aboriginal kid . . .

But that was his last thought, because as his mind wandered disbelievingly and his eyes went to Roo's feet he did not even see the heel of the black man's hand come up at his nose. All he saw was the black blur of his arm and then he was on the ground, unconscious, his nose bridge badly broken as his head lay sideways in the blood running from it.

Roo was standing as if he had not moved. Only his right arm had moved as it had stiffened as his right hand had moved backward, simply, viciously, effectively, with the bone-hard heel of the hand going unerringly to one of the most vulnerable parts of the face.

He downed his beer and they left. It was a strange thing,

this Outback Code. The men from the Back of Beyond who had organized this trial of strength had used it to get back at the opposition American property, too, and were even now collecting their bets from the ringers from that station. They had given Roo his trial of leadership, yet they had, in a strange way because he was theirs, wanted him to win. Woe betide him had he not. He would have had trouble keeping his men in line then. Now, like his father before him, his leadership was undisputed.

The time passed so swiftly. They saw more and more of Anne, which was lovely, and if she couldn't make it to the property, but was within a couple of hundred miles, she radioed in, and they all flew out for the weekend, Red and the two girls anyway, Alison and Jitangeli, with all sorts of goodies packed by Fan-tan, and camped out and had barbecues and swims and wonderful walks and talks and campfires. The propensity of the countryside to please with its opal-hearted hills and purple escarpments and waterfalls and all manner of earth and rock and green and brown timber and plant texture seemed endless.

The property prospered, they found some bauxite to the north near the world's largest deposit of the mineral rock used to produce aluminum, they shifted from seabed pearls to cultured pearls, implanted pearls really, but still profitable, and converted the luggers they did not need for hire boats to prawning off Cape York where the king prawns were cooked and snap-frozen on board, for air shipment to America. Kiwai now had several assistant managers. Whatever happened, Red kept moving, moving on into new things, making his money work for him the whole time, knowing it was the only way, yet knowing, also, never confiding, but knowing that there was always a risk. But was that not what the textbooks called his kind: entrepreneurs, risk takers? This was how capital was accumulated. But however much he tried to pay it off, he always had to keep his mortgage going on the property to finance each new venture.

The one venture he did not approve, as the years passed,

was uranium. His discovery so long ago had been one of the earliest. But despite discoveries by others, and even a uranium treatment plant set up for U.K. production not far from his property, he stubbornly refused to mine his uranium.

Douglas pleaded with him; Bluey pleaded with him. It was worth millions, they said. Offer after offer to buy came rolling in. Douglas—and Bluey, too, in the end—were convinced that Red also knew of uranium at Five Mile Camp and that was why so long ago he had banned the place. For his opposition to uranium was well known. In a time when few questioned it, he stood against it. When asked, he turned into his truculent, seemingly semi-illiterate yet completely deliberate bushman mood. The stuff fuckin' burned people, he said, it was as simple as that, fuckin' burned people and kept on burning, like that bloody mustard gas in the first war. When they remonstrated with him he retorted that there was no argument: however much he hated the bloody Nips, the atom bomb burned them and he wasn't going to mine or allow to be mined anything that bloody burned people. Billy wouldn't like that. The Carlyons weren't in that business. The others could do what they bloody well liked, but they would not mine his uranium except over his dead body because as far as he was concerned the bloody stuff could stay in the bloody ground for bloody ever.

It was this trenchant attitude that led another newspaper article to imply that perhaps Big Red, the Northern Territory magnate, was the slightest bit eccentric. Red only laughed when Cathy sent him the newspaper clipping, saying, over-protectingly as always, that, whatever happened, even in fun he must never say he talked to crocodiles.

Red laughed and wrote her a lovely thank-you note for her concern, and then went out to Five Mile Camp to talk to Kismet about the arrangements for Alison's twenty-first. It helped him to think aloud, talking to the old boy, who was nearly three hundred years old now, with the history of the country on his back, with those cunning croc eyes old enough to have seen Captain Cook find the continent, it helped to talk to him and why shouldn't he have a say in his daughter's twenty-first, why shouldn't he and Red plan their daughter's twenty-first together, for it was going to be the best and biggest party the Territory had ever seen, and in some ways perhaps the last, or the last of its kind, for Red watched and noticed the start and middle and end of all things, like he noticed signs in the bush.

After the twenty-first he would go back to live in Darwin and be with Annie for a time, for she was mostly there now and he needed to be on the property less and less and perhaps they could finally have some time together.

42

Alison's twenty-first lasted a week and at the height there
were a thousand guests. Huge blue-and-white-striped marquees, with frilled canopies, were put up in the home paddock
for the celebrations. There were three bands which played in
rotation in the biggest marquee which was the dance floor.
The waiters wore white tie and tails, and white gloves,
despite the heat, although this was somewhat alleviated by
the air conditioning Big Red had put in the marquees and the
guests' tents, for the whole area resembled a gay military
camp, but with every modern convenience, including striped
canvas showers, for every tent. It was the party to end all
parties. Lisa and her husband and sons and grandsons came
up from several states; Douglas and his wife from Sydney,
along with so many business contacts that they had had to
charter a jet; then all Alison's friends from several states, and
Jitangeli's, and Roo's, plus the station hands and overseas
guests. In that week, five thousand bottles of Veuve Cliquot
were drunk—straight, with stout as black velvets, with beer
chasers, with orange juice for breakfast as the festivities
started once more.

Big Red said afterward that, given the young and old
people, some of whom seemed to be doing more swimming
naked in the swimming hole than the young, and some of

whose tents seemed to be moving more at night, too, he feared for a birth boom after the party. It went rollicking on, with Fan-tan and his broad apron in charge of chefs, and waiters and maids, all hired from a Sydney agency and flown in. Two thousand crayfish were consumed, five thousand king prawns, three thousand prime Darwin mud crabs. There was bullock on spit and pig on spit and prime young Australian lamb, there was turkey and stuffing, beef Wellington. There was freshly caught fish always for the entrée, with butter or asparagus, or capers and lemon, so fresh it fell away from the fork, or barramundi and banana. There were rock oysters being flown in all the time from Sydney, and strawberries fresh in every day, too, along with the flowers, festoon upon festoon of red roses, and yellow roses, and anything the florists cared to send to add to the banks of native water lilies.

There were farm fresh eggs, and bacon steaks, and home-made bread each morning, hot or toasted at the big outdoors fire, the campfire which was going all the time, the idea being that you could eat what you wanted, when you wanted it, at table or at log, so that there was always a mixture of people straying by that fire, men half in dinner jackets and half out of them, girls with towels around them after their early-morning shower, although no one quite going fully to bed for the whole time—well, never to sleep other than with someone for a time—so that the whole party mood caught on, and no one worried any more if a senator strolled down to get his breakfast clad only in his BVDs or noticed his daughter wandering around in her damp underwear after a swim.

Of course Big Red said afterward that the press got hold of it and greatly exaggerated it as the wildest party ever held in the country, adding in the hundreds of bottles of spirits which were also drunk, which was true enough, but it was not the biggest party ever, for that had not been held yet, he said, but he was enjoying getting back in the party mood so much that perhaps he would hold the biggest ever next year.

And so it went on, in relays, in captivating, capricious relays of people coming and going, arriving and unwinding and falling into the spell of the place and always, Alison, the blond and golden wonder girl, so soft and feminine and just slightly tall, brown and soft as milk chocolate, yet strong inside her body and head like her father, kind but smart like her mother, always Alison, in wonder and charm and fun, dominating the whole scene and warming Red and Annie inside.

Of course Bluey remarked—as only Bluey would, Red retorted, as only Bluey would to break his warm feeling of fatherly security—Bluey remarked that he had noticed his son seemed to be spending each night in Ali's room, and he hoped Red didn't mind him mentioning it.

"Well, they're bloody friends, aren't they?" Red said. "I mean, he's a special guest, got to be in the house, can't have him out in a bloody tent. I guess Ali must have told him to share her room. How the hell should I know? I just pay the bills around here."

"They like each other, Red, they like each other a lot."

"I know."

"Well, he's city and she's country."

"I know. I've thought about it. That's why I'm not paying it too much attention."

"Ali would die in the city and he'll not move back here to run the business. Says he can do it from Sydney."

"Yeah, they all want a home by the harbor and the city. You're right about Ali, though, but she's got to make up her own mind and I don't want her deciding for me because I won't be here forever. Anyway, she can fly. What the hell? We're worrying too much. Let's go back to Kat and Annie and get another drink."

The two tough old Territorians rose from the veranda and walked down to the party, like the last of the plainsmen coming in from the bush for the last time.

"What do you think about them using helicopters to herd cattle and computers to run a property?" asked Bluey as they walked.

"You know what I think. But I know the Yanks are doing it and maybe soon so will I."

"Seems a pity not doing things personally by hand anymore."

"Seems a pity? Christ, Blue, they hardly need the bloody

cows anymore. You just get yourself a pure breed Simmental, fertilize a lot of eggs, implant them by Caesarean section into any old scrub cow and bingo, you've got a row of purebreeds. That's what's coming. That's what's here. Ali was telling me the other day. We're entering a world, Blue, where the phrase lovesick cow won't even have any meaning anymore."

"Not sure I want to live that long."

"Me neither. But ill health seems to have passed us by."

"Must be all the tea we drink."

"Got to be. Reckon they'll find a way around that—so you don't have to make it and drink it anymore, just piss it out?"

"Sure to."

Red was knighted soon after the party, in the Queen's Birthday Honors list, leading him to remark that someone had obviously enjoyed the party and if people must call him Sir, would they please make it Sir Red.

He asked Annie if she wanted to marry him now she could be a lady, or would she prefer to stay a mistress, and they had a good laugh as they walked down to the home billabong together. She said she'd think about it, but she didn't mind the title doctor, to be honest, and indeed had given up quite a lot to keep it a working title, so perhaps, she said, squeezing his hand and thanking him for the offer, perhaps she'd stay plain doctor if he didn't mind.

Red said that was all right with him because he wasn't going to use the title at all, except when that younger brother of his, Douglas, got a bit upperty.

But although they did not marry, and they discussed it seriously once again, Red moved for a time into Darwin, visiting the property only occasionally, moved into Darwin where Anne was collating all her years of fieldwork, which would take a year or two to do, moved in so that they slept with each other every night, easy and old, old and easy, and such very good friends and lovers that it all seemed so very worthwhile after all.

During this period of about two years, Douglas made them all financially secure in terms of regular return on invested capital, by getting Red to agree to certain joint ventures to develop some of their big noncattle interests, including the minerals, pearling and prawning. He tried once more, but could not succeed to get Red to agree to develop the uranium.

After Red had lived two years in Darwin, beef prices started suddenly to drop and Red once more returned to the property. These fluctuations were not new, and they had been very subject over the years to American quotas on the import of beef, quite apart from seasonal conditions.

But the falling prices went on, and then there was a bad drought, and then something else happened. And that was when Red sent for Alison, who had been overseas. He had now entered his seventy-seventh year. Alison was twenty-five.

Book V

KISMET

43

On that Saturday morning when she arrived back in Darwin after receiving a cable in London from her father which said simply, "Need you, come home," Alison Carlyon was worried. A telegram like that would worry anyone. It was very early and the night was still in her eyes as she crossed the tarmac to the terminal, shaking out her long brown-blond hair and unconsciously running the flat of her left hand down her shirt and jeans front as if to iron them. She hunched her Adidas bag up her back so it sat jauntily short-armed, like a sailor's duffel bag, askew across her back and shoulder. She was tired, having come through in less than twenty-four hours since she got the telegram, changing at Bombay for Singapore and Darwin. Yet the tiredness could not contain the lively personality that showed in each frown or eye squint or self-smile or turn of the head and hair or nod to an airport attendant or body movement as she passed through immigration and customs. She knew the men, of course. Yet whether it was this, or her natural good looks, whether it was her bright-eyed vitality of anticipation of life which always seemed to show, whether it was one or all of these things, there was a certain breathlessness of character which gave the idea of exuberance, even from a distance.

She went straight from customs to the domestic section of

the airport. She had cabled ahead and the Cessna 310 was fueled. The mechanic smiled and made her tea from the urn to drink while he pushed the plane out away from the hangar. She drank hard into the heat and scalded her tongue, noticing the old tea stains on the inside of the white china cup.

She shook her hair out again and wondered about telephoning her mother in town. It was still very early and not quite light. But the plane was ready now so she decided to keep going.

Ali smiled her thanks to the mechanic, who was an old and easy friend, got clearance from the tower and took off into the pink rim of dawn already warming into orange as it lit the tropical sky. The broad country below looked fresh and washed in the morning.

The tower let her climb a little higher and then a voice it seemed she had known all the years she had lived came on the line, a warm Outback voice of nasal mock-rudeness which suggests that even to open one's mouth is an effort, to do a favor is monumental and that no help will ever be forthcoming again.

"So now I guess you want me to sign this nonexistent flight plan you've filed, now we've got you airborne?" the voice said.

"I guess I do, Barn," she said, her voice conveying tender thanks as the man's warmth reached into her.

"That's all right, luv," he said, "good trip home."

She blew him a kiss on the two-way.

"Oh, and let me know how your old man is when you've spoken to him, will you?" he added, as she banked to turn.

"Sure," she said, out of the immediate vicinity of the airport now but still searching the sky carefully for other aircraft coming in to land or taking off, and frowning deeply at Barney's words. "Sure," she said, and pondered the weight of what that meant as she flew on.

Yet the beauty below held her. The ten years from 1960 to 1970 had been bad drought years and it was still dry as she looked down and saw the tin windmill of an artesian bore as she began to fly over the start of the property. It was dry, dry at this time of the year, with rivers dried up and mudholes cracked like stale chocolate. But the mists were not gone. However dry it got it never quite dried up the mists which were always hanging just at the edge of every landscape as if to remind the returning traveler that beyond the mists were the unseen things and it was the unseen things that moved up here and tied people to the last frontier with a soft primeval intensity so that the land was sacred, as the Aboriginals said, and timeless back to the Dreamtime when things did not die but lived forever.

She flew on, her mind transfixed by the changing surrealist patterns of the Max Ernst painting below. She was home.

She landed easily and taxied in but there was no sign of her father.

"All right, where is the old bastard?" Alison asked of the black stockman sent to get her, as she slung her bag into the back of the Range Rover and they drove off toward the homestead.

"Fan-tan says he'll do all the talking."

"Oh, he does, does he? So the bloody place is being run by a Chinese cook now, is it? Where's that little Jitangeli? I could wring her neck."

The stockman, his bent cowboy's hat pulled low over his forehead, stared ahead and drove.

"I'm new," was all he said.

"Not too new. You've learned enough to know when to shut up. Who hired you—my surrogate mother, the Chinese cook?"

The black man might not have understood the word but he got the meaning and turned and looked hard at her, the way an Aboriginal will when tribal instincts a thousand years old warn not to underestimate someone.

"Roo. Black Roo hired me."

"I bet he did. You're smart enough for him to have hired you. But where the hell is he, that adopted half brother of mine?"

The look on the Aboriginal's face told the story of surprise and broke his silence:

"He's . . . out . . . out . . . mustering."

"He didn't tell you he had an unofficial sister?"

"No, miss."

"And you don't know anything else?"

"No, miss."

Something about him irritated her.

"Come off it, don't play that dumb Abo act with me—it's too late for that and I grew up on it. Probably know more bloody dialects and more about tribal totems than you'll ever know. Born in the Alice, right? Came bush to establish your heritage, right? Clever, little, city-smart Outback Abo with a sharp mission school education, right? My name's Ali but I suppose you've got some gifted name like Johnny Lightning?"

"Johnny . . . just Johnny," the black man said, softening a little.

"That makes six Johnnies on current staffing," Alison said. "But don't worry, Johnny, I'll get your tribal name out of you eventually, or help you to trace back and find it out yourself, and then we'll really be friends in your sense. But we're friends in my sense already, OK?"

The black stockman nodded, noting the combination of gruff orders and ready warmth, the same combination as her father, whose authority she obviously felt was hers at all times. Well, he hadn't been born in the Alice, or the other things, and he wondered if she knew, if these were just things thrown at him to get a reaction. Perhaps he should have reacted a little more. But, in any case, one thing was certain, all they said about her was true. She was smart and quick as a stockwhip, as well as being pretty. And there was no doubt she had come home to find out what was wrong with her father and was going to bang as many heads together as was necessary to find out.

"You wait in case I need you, Johnny," she said as she hurried out of the Rover at the entrance to the station house.

"Right, miss," he said and saw her glare back at him. If there was one thing she hated to be called, she was telling herself, as she ignored it and ran inside the big square house with the big veranda all around . . . and then there was Fan-tan, fat and smiling and with the skin of his face even smoother with Chinese old age, with his black pillbox hat and pigtail, and his white apron, an anachronism in the twentieth century, but the emotional sheet anchor of her life and next in love only to her parents.

She ran and hugged him and soon both were half crying.

"Where is he?" she said at last. "Where the hell is my old man?"

"Tea first, Missy, tea first, then I tell all."

"God, everyone's got the turn-of-the-century jitters today. Doesn't anyone speak English here anymore?"

"It not velly easy for simple Chinee." It was a game they had played since her childhood. It was his way of teasing her and exacting his full share of love in old age, wishing things could have stayed as they were when both were younger. Alison went along with it, in friendly banter. The old man was seventy and aging fast and the pigtail was white.

"It is velly simple for Chinee who live longer in Australia than China," she said, "particularly smartest gambler in Darwin and best cook this side of the equator."

"Ah, Missy most kind to honorable servant."

"None of the Charlie Chan stuff today, Fan-tan, please, I couldn't stand it. If you keep it up so help me . . ."

"All light . . . all light"—he really did have trouble sometimes with his r's—"I'll talk properly."

She had hurt him slightly and she had not meant to. She realized, although she claimed never to suffer jet lag, that she was tired, tired and anxious.

"Big Red down at Five Mile Camp and mostly OK but we talk," Fan-tan said, as if reading her thoughts, pulling out a wooden kitchen chair, one of the originals, with the wood scrubbed almost white over the years.

She sat and he made the tea. He made it from a huge metal kettle and he took it off the roaring stove which was half the room long, recessed under a giant brick alcove and chimney, and went by the name of a one-fire stove which she had never understood, and couldn't be bothered now, but knew it was what other people called an iron range fire. It was cast iron

and black, except for a couple of silver oven hinges Fan-tan
kept meticulously polished, and one of the fondest memories
of her childhood. Yet her not minding the heat did not stop
her some years later, asked what she would like for her
fifteenth birthday, replying, "Air conditioning."

"Been talking to your mother, have you?" had been all Big
Red had said, knowing only too well that she had recently
been to see her during the school long vacation during the
Wet. But the next day he had left for Darwin and soon was
back with the air-conditioning units and the extra generator
necessary to run them. Fan-tan sometimes switched it off,
claiming it dried him out, which with the stove going and the
temperature outside anything over 120, Alison was not
inclined to blame on the air conditioning. But there was, in
Fan-tan, that overlanding, pioneering, droving, goldfields
element—call it what you would, the same as there was in
her father—which seemed to resent any modern amenity as
almost a symbol of the defeat of manhood. To suffer, even
sometimes to suffer stupidly and unnecessarily, was noble.
This was particularly so with the heat. A man never admitted it was *too* hot. It might be bloody hot, or every graduation
of swearing up and down the scales not meant for childrens'
or females' ears, but it was never *too* hot. Alison was glad
Fan-tan had the air conditioning on today, for she worried
about both the old men in the heat. But then, as if reading
her thoughts once more, he said, although with a wicked
smile,

"I put air conditioning on when Barney talk two-way that
you left Darwin so it be cool by time you arrive."

"Thanks," she said, sipping the good, strong Outback tea as
he poured it now from a big blue enamel pot pitted with black
chips and smiling to herself that the timber house could not
possibly have got that cool in the two hours since she had left
Darwin.

"Now about father," she said quietly, smiling out at the old
man over her teacup as he sat with her at the long, scrubbed
kitchen table.

The old man was alternately very serious (sometimes

reaching across and touching Alison's hand as if to reassure her) and smiling, but in the forced manner that Asians have of laughing shrilly with a great show of teeth, and then swallowing the smile almost immediately, as if they have forgotten themselves in a country not their own and offended against the Mandarin-type virtues of quiet interiorness and inscrutability. She listened intently and patiently, not hurrying the old man. Her scientific objectivity had returned to her now, after the emotions of arriving home again.

She felt now she should never have gone. But it was her best school friend's wedding and because she was marrying an Englishman and staying, Ali had felt she should go. Her father had urged her to. She'd been away over three months and having a wonderful time when his cable arrived.

Almost as soon as Alison had left, Fan-tan told her, Big Red became very quiet and uncommunicative, although no one thought a great deal about it at first. They put it down to him missing Alison and the depressed beef prices—and of course his own bushcraft code of privacy prevented them asking too many questions.

Alison was hearing all Fan-tan was saying, and thinking about her father at the same time. The problem, according to Fan-tan, did not stop at "the Boss's" quietness. Soon he began to camp out more and more at Five Mile Camp. Now Five Mile Camp had been called everything from Big Red's Folly to Big Red's Alamo, the clear inference being that it was a last-ditch arsenal, dating from Red's middle years when, infuriated by Federal Government apathy toward the Territory—a continuing problem most of his life—he had seriously suggested secession. Big Red said that Five Mile Camp—exactly five miles from the main station house—was simply the nicest bit of his property, if not the Territory, if not the country, if not the whole damn world.

Fan-tan kept talking in his repetitious, circuitous way, but he was adding nothing that gave Alison a clue other than Big Red had got "worse and worse," spending more and more time at Five Mile Camp, camped out with the few old tribal elders of Jacky's day who remained, and their families, who

"guarded" Five Mile Camp. For although the family respected Big Red's wishes to keep the place to himself and, in
effect, really believed him when he said he wanted the place
kept unspoiled, and it was that simple, others did not. There
were men who refused to believe a man as astute as Big Red
Carlyon would be sitting on something for simple conservation reasons. Most, including the Japanese and the
Americans who helped comprise the uranium lobby in Sydney, believed it was a massive deposit of uranium.

This was the consensus. Some, of course, remembering the
gold rush in the early days of the Territory, said it was gold
and Red had kept it as a nest egg all these years and it was
his hedge against fluctuating beef prices. There were 101
theories, but one thing was certain—no white person other
than Red had ever been inside since he had been born there
more than three-quarters of a century ago.

Fan-tan said that about a week ago Big Red had sent a
message with a black that he would be staying at Five Mile
Camp "forever." Jitangeli had immediately gone down to try
to reason with him, but had come back saying she could not
get past the entrance and that although she had talked to
him there, he seemed very "unusual." Two days after that the
same black, Crocodile Tommy, had come in with a written
message from Big Red to send the telegram to Ali. Of course
by this time gossip was starting in the town, Fan-tan said.
Alison smiled at this reference to Darwin, as if it were just
across the river. In the Territory distance meant nothing.

"Well, he's acted funnily before and it hasn't meant
anything," Ali said at last.

"In town they say Big Red lose malbles," the Chinese said
hurriedly, bowing his head somewhat shamefully. He was
excited and anxious again and she gently calmed him with
her voice as she said, "You mean marbles. You think so?"

He nodded. "I no say, Missy. They say."

"I know. I just want to get a clear picture of everything,
that's all," she said kindly. "Now tell me what was so
'unusual' about a week ago?"

"He started to say someone was trying to get him, so
Jitangeli says."

"And you believed him? You know that's part of his Great White Hunter routine—how he tamed the Territory single-handed and has many friends but a few enemies, who have always tried to get him but he has outwitted them by his bushcraft stealth. He never means people are trying to kill him." God, she knew it by heart. It was like a bush ballad. It was a campfire tale.

"But different this time, Missy," said Fan-tan, again unconsciously breaking back into his bastardized English-Chinese way of talking, in the same way Big Red often broke into early Outback English when he got excited.

"Different in what way?"

"This time Jitangeli say him serious." Fan-tan said it without a hint of doubt in his mind and with the full weight of his concern for Red in his voice.

"I see," said Alison, rising. "I see," she said quietly. "Well, I'd better go and find out for myself, hadn't I?"

"Oh, not to Five Mile Camp, Missy, please. You know how angry that make him."

But Ali had smiled at the old man, almost a little patronizingly, as she turned and walked down the passage to the front veranda. She had not forgotten about the stockman. She had kept him waiting until she knew if she needed him. She now called, "You met Ghost Gum yet?"

He nodded a smile.

"Saddle him up and bring him over for me, will you? I think I'll go for a ride."

"I could drive you."

"I know. I'd have told you if I'd wanted that. But no, thanks."

"You're not going to Five Mile Camp?"

"You're not going to collect your wages, either, if you don't have my gray here in about two minutes flat."

"Yes, miss, certainly," he said, smiling so broadly that it was almost a laugh and emphasizing the word *miss* in such a way it left Alison in no doubt that he had picked up her dislike for its usage. She did not linger, though. She knew about not fighting little battles and keeping your strength for the main one. That was bushcraft, too. She would turn to

Johnny whatever-his-name-was soon enough. But she'd ask Roo about him first. She'd see her father and then she'd go and find Roo—which could take several days. But there was one other detail to be attended to, now that a logical order of things was settling in her mind. She walked back inside.

"Now Fan-tan," she said kindly, "I must know where Jitangeli is and why she is not here when my father needs her."

Fan-tan looked embarrassed. He did not want to speak.

Ali looked strongly at him. He knew he must tell her.

"I no know, Missy. I no know. One day she just go. I guess go Sydney, but I no know and even Chinese daughters don't tell honorable adopted fathers everything these days."

Ali would have smiled if growing concern had not been her dominant emotion. Fan-tan was on the edge of tears and she walked over and hugged him which of course made it worse so that he walked away and busied himself at the range. It was still only midmorning Saturday. If Jitangeli had gone to Sydney she would be at the Wentworth where they kept a permanent suite. But the only way Ali could contact her was by a relay call via Darwin from their two-way radio transmitter. She decided against it. This was family business and family business was private. To put the family call sign on the air—Sierra Zulu Victor—was to invite a listening audience.

44

When she was young she had wanted a white horse at first, but after a succession of ponies and station horses her father had bought her the gray, unusual for those parts, but he said he had got her the gray because he was a Goondiwindi gray from Queensland, and there were none better, and he wouldn't have a horse trucked all that way if it didn't have a large heart and lots of speed which he reckoned would about suit his daughter now she was getting close to her sixteenth birthday. Ghost Gum was named for the eucalypt tree of the same name and it said more about the North than most other things, and so they named the horse for the tree and anyone coming upon the pair from a distance, standing by a water hole, would have thought them planted there, both seemed to belong so with each other and with the land.

The horse snorted at the smell of her and whinnied around and she mounted, thanking the stockman and wheeling off in the opposite direction from Five Mile Camp yet conscious as she rode that she did not think she had fooled him. But she skirted around, nonetheless, until, out of sight of the station house, she turned for the plains and Five Mile Camp, giving the horse his head now and, alone on the open land, feeling again the indescribable thrill of gathering speed and open space.

There were places in the Territory that would never lose their sense of having been part of the first millennium on earth. Often it was in the nature of the rock sculpture—worn, shaped and creviced so that the mind knew it had to be that old—or in a simple but lyrical Aboriginal name such as Malapananbanjo, which seemed to belong to such early times. But often it was the sense of mist that supplied that mood of a past infinity. Alison saw it now, for it always seemed to hang over the humped-rock area of Five Mile Camp as she came upon it from a distance. Yet she knew much of the mist was in her mind's eye, the smoke of a thousand Aboriginal night fires and the legends told around them as a child. Oh, sometimes there was heat haze hanging, as today, and often there was a mist of sorts. But so often the mist she saw was at a distance, and not there when she got close.

But then of course she had never really been inside that rocked-out perimeter of Five Mile Camp, with the narrow gorge opening on the nearest side, and the Crocodile River on the other, and she did not expect today to be any exception, although she wondered that she had not seen any movement so far. Usually there was some sort of tattered Aboriginal camp at the small gorge, looking indifferent and deserted, until someone tried to enter.

But today, as she galloped on, there was nothing—or so it appeared. It was not until she was nearly on the rock outcrop itself that she saw the solitary figure, dark and foreboding, so it seemed, sitting high but against the rock, so that he was almost impossible to detect and it was not until she had wheeled her horse around, so that the figure and accompanying rifle could be seen against the skyline she had ridden in from, that she realized it was her father. He was sunburned nearly black and wore only an old pair of army khaki shorts and from that distance could have been an Aboriginal. She unmounted, and he stood up, erect and stiff before he moved, shining like an old bronze war statue against the sky. He wore no hat against the sun and his face was compact and tight and metallic like the round end of a bullet, with a grizzly gray haircut giving the impression of flint. His bare feet moved over the big boulders with ease, knowing each step with a sure intuition, and his tall, sinewed body moved toward her with ease and purpose despite his slight limp, as he slung the rifle from its strap onto his shoulder.

He came without a smile and they held each other tightly for some time until she felt the steel arms go from around her and he beckoned with his head to squat on a rock beside him as he put his firearm down and took the makings from his shorts pocket and said,

"Smoke?"

Though she had it given up she nodded, for it was a ritual between them, and she took the tobacco and papers and rolled and licked for him, then lit the cigarette with his proffered matches and took the first pull herself. It had been ever thus since her early teens.

Her father was not a man you ever said, "what's up, what's wrong," to. It must have been very hard for him to telegraph her to come home and now that they were face-to-face the telling of it would take some time.

"How come no camp?" she said.

"Gave 'em the day off. They're inside, way inside, but handy enough if needed. Thought I'd wait out here for you myself."

"Heard the aircraft?"

He nodded. "Knew you'd be along shortly. Had any breakfast? Want a swim and some tucker?"

"You mean you're actually going to let me in—?"

"Only the front part. Only as far as the waterfall and rock pond. Goes for a couple of miles back beyond that. Front part can't do any harm," he said, smiling now.

They walked in together through the narrow rock cleft, along a narrow path between the tall boulders, until it suddenly opened out and there, before them, was the most beautiful little waterfall running over a slated cliff into a big pond formed where the rocks ran down and into each other.

Over to the left there was a ledge and beyond it a cave, where Alison could see some of her father's things. They walked over, picking up dry twigs to start a fire, as they walked and talked.

"No towels," he said, smiling again, as she started to unbutton her shirt. This, too, was a thing from the past. When you were out droving cattle, as she had often done with her father and the stockmen, from her youngest years on, changing sheds and towels were not exactly considered necessities when you came upon a swimming hole in the heat of the day. She had only asked for a towel once, when quite small, and the men had debated whether it might spoil her if she were given one. The consensus was that it would be letting the side down, and by the time they'd finished joking with her, all sitting together laughing in the sun, and one man offering his khaki handkerchief with great dignity, of course everyone was dry and no towels were needed. In the heat of the Dry, towels could be very superfluous things.

"No towels," she said, laughing, undressing completely unselfconsciously, and wondering, as she sometimes did, whether her open attitude toward sex, whether the uncomplicated pleasure she seemed to derive from it, grew out of these free and happy times with the stockmen, from her times with her Aboriginal playmates before and after that, and their sweet, matter-of-fact acceptance of all things sexual. No one had ever told her not to go outside without her clothes, or to cover anything up, and, as she dived in, she suspected from what she'd read that if Sigmund Freud and Margaret Mead could have got together and developed a prototype for the healthy new generation, she would have been it.

She swam her fill, and then hunched on the rock to dry in the sun beside where her father had the fire going now, the eggs and bacon nearly cooked in the burned-black frypan, and the half-gallon, cylindrical billy, black and rusted over its original bright tin, boiling along on the fire, ready to make the tea.

"Ready?" her father asked.

"Yes, please."

So Big Red stood, and took the billy full of boiling water, and a handful of tea from his tucker bag, throwing the tea into the boiling water with a eucalypt leaf and clasping the tin lid on immediately, taking the billy by its arched, bucket-type handle, swinging it quickly in a couple of full, straight-arm arcs with his right hand and then putting it down to rest and "draw," or stand, until the brew reached its full strength, while he busied himself with a couple of chipped-enamel mugs and sugar.

"The milk's gone off. I've been out here for days. . . ."

"I know. It's fine. Black is fine."

"There's powdered . . ."

"I like it black."

"Milk is better."

"Yes, milk is better. But black is fine. I should have thought to bring some."

"I didn't mean that. . . . I'm just sorry I haven't got milk for you."

Soon now he would tell her what was troubling him.

In the meantime they ate their breakfast off the tin plates and wiped them with some bush bread he had made the night before, and drank the thick billy tea, which was hot and good and strong and which she knew her father preferred black and had only said that about milk for her benefit.

After breakfast she dressed and they shared another smoke and the quiet stillness of the bush was all around them and finally her father said,

"I'm really all right, you know. I just got a bit down."

"I know. But you were right to contact me."

"That Great White Hunter stuff I sometimes go on with is all campfire joke stuff, you know that."

"I know."

"Although plenty have tried to pull me down one way or another over the years."

"I know that, too."

"Well, they're trying again. They're going for the big lick this time. I'm not in any doubt about that."

"What's that mean? What are they really trying to do?"

"Take us over."

"You mean take over the property—take our land and our home and our cattle?"

"Exactly."

"But why?"

"Why not? They've tried before. It's the most valuable property around."

"Sure. But they've never got within a bull's roar of us before. Why is this time so different?"

"Well . . . it's different because there's more of them . . . big American consortium this time. . . . They're more determined and are obviously going to play very dirty . . . and . . . and I also think that bastard Douglas has finally thrown his hand in with them and he knows everything about the books and about me so that he could give them information that could really hurt us."

"This time it *is* serious, then? You're really worried?"

He nodded. "This time it's serious, all right. It's not a question of the family ever going broke. It's never been a question of that for a long time. But capital, as they say, has to be serviced like cows, and if the bastards do what I think they're going to do, I don't know if we've got the capacity to withstand selling off the property, which is, of course, exactly what they are after."

"I'm sorry. I would never have gone away if I'd known you were in this sort of trouble."

"Wasn't. Well, wasn't that bad then. Knew we weren't going well, but so did you. Ten years of drought and then the bottom falling out of the Japanese and American markets on the heels of lost European markets: it hasn't exactly been a picnic having a big cattle property. But we both knew all that. It wasn't—or hadn't come to—a case of facing the loss of the property. No, the crunch came on after you left."

"And when will you know what's going to happen?"

"When one of us is left standing, I suppose. You never knew the Great White Hunter to give up without a fight, did you?" He looked at her and smiled. "I mean all those campfire stories have got to be worth something. We'll figure something out. You and me and Jitangeli and Black Roo and the others will give them a run for their money."

"So Jitangeli's in Sydney on business?"

He nodded. "Got that worked out now, have you?"

Ali smiled at her father, half-wistfully, half-exasperatedly. "Yes, I've got that worked out now, thanks. I don't know how anyone would survive in your family if they hadn't learnt to do jigsaw puzzles at an early age."

"Wouldn't. That's why I gave them to you." He stood up then and put his arm around her and they walked a little distance together. "Hell, Al," he said, "it's not just the money. It's the land, the land and the country. The station house, the homestead. This is our home—every rock and croc and damn lizard, and I can't let them take it away now. It's the best damn place a man ever could live and they won't move me off it alive."

Alison was thinking clearer now and wondered if she should broach something that she had reminded her father of several times. It had first come up when she had boarded at Uncle Douglas's place in Sydney for the first part of her first university year. He had been very friendly and nice and she believed he had intended it as a constructive criticism, although she had flown at him when he'd said it.

"You know, Alison," he had said, "people are starting to talk about your father even as far down here as Sydney. I mean we've all known and understood about Five Mile Camp for years, we in the family, although none of us knows what is really there apart from that damn giant croc at the back entrance which he's always talking about and says is the oldest living inhabitant. But you know some people, particularly city people, might think it strange, a man having a place like Five Mile Camp that he's almost paranoid about . . . some people might even find it stranger that at that camp there's an old crocodile whom that same man talks to, says has more sense than most humans he's met and claims answers to the name of Kismet. Some people might say that there is a word that could be used to describe such a condition."

It was typical of Uncle Doug, the accountant who had graduated to the smooth world of the Sydney establishment, to avoid the use of the word he most intended—senility. That would have been impolite, improper, lacking in decorum, to attach such an epithet to his own brother, even if it might be true. By his studious avoidance of it, of course, he scored an even harsher, if subtler, point.

So Alison now raised tenderly what she had raised before with her father after her uncle had made his original comment. But she used the word honestly and without adornment.

"If you keep on about people being after you, about them trying to get you, there's always the outside chance they could try to get you declared senile. Then you *would* lose the property—or have someone else put in to run it."

"True. But I'll be damned if I'll tell people about Five Mile Camp or stop doing whatever I want to do just to prove I'm sane. I don't regard blue pinstripe suits and five-hour business lunches as any test of sanity, I can tell you. Besides, we wouldn't want a sudden change in my behavior just yet, would we? . . . I mean it would be better to keep people thinking whatever they've been used to thinking about me, even a bit more so perhaps, to get them off their guard. Then we might have time to find out a bit more about what they're really on about . . . about the main thing that's worrying me—the thing that really could lose us the property in a very short space of time."

"So it's not really the senility thing you're worried about?"

"Yes, yes I am. I believe they'll use that if they get half the chance—they'll use anything—but I don't believe it's the main threat."

"So what's our main problem, then?" asked Ali.

"Money," Big Red replied, "just money. Liquidity. Cash. Happens to millionaires, too—particularly when they have irrational loves about things such as land and wanting to hold on to huge tracts of it. It's just a question of whether we'll have enough cash at the right time after all these bad seasons and the market fall-off. You know we can expect to get a little help from our so-called friends to make it much harder to meet our commitments. Tell you all the details tomorrow—OK—? I'm a bit tired now and I've got some thinking to do. You know I'll do everything I can to save the place for you."

"Of course." They had stopped walking now and she leaned up and kissed him on the cheek.

They started to walk back toward the entrance then and they talked small talk for a while until eventually Ali asked, "You coming back with me?"

He shook his head. She would not ask again. They were too close for that. Asking again was to show lack of trust in the other's judgment and they did not have that sort of relationship. But she would try a future positive, for that was part of their Bush Code, that was allowed.

"Don't hang about too much if you can help it, though," she said, thus accepting his right to stay at his private Shangri-La, but also continuing, "If you hang around here too long they'll say you're going funny. If Uncle Douglas really is involved then that's the angle he'll try first with the banks and lawyers—something smart and sophisticated and plausible. He'll let the Americans make the obvious up-front moves and he'll try to twist the knife legally."

"Maybe. But he was also born in the bush and he's got enough of that cunning to know that's what we'll think he'll do. Whatever he does, if he is involved, he'll know how to squeeze so it hurts." He paused for a time as if almost testing for her reaction in advance. Then he added,

"But perhaps it's not Douglas."

"Perhaps not."

"It's hard to believe that one's own brother—"

"Of course."

"I've often been too hard on him, I know. I suspect him when I shouldn't."

"But you'd never get rid of him. I suppose there were many times you could have in the early days, before he became so involved in the running of the financial side, for you never really needed him, did you? I mean for a start he was really just the bookkeeper, wasn't he? One can hire bookkeepers."

"But one can't sack brothers."

"People like you can't."

He smiled again and then said, as if it were part of some previous unspoken sentence,

"Besides, Billy loved him. He loved us both. Douglas was

the kid brother, you see—the youngest—and Billy was more father to him than I was, and Doug was still young when Billy died, and he didn't understand and I think he's always blamed me, as if my going off to the war and Billy following had something to do with Billy's death, even though Billy came home from the war, as you know." He paused, and then went on: "But maybe it began even earlier than that when he was just a kid. I sometimes think he hated me then. I was pretty tough with him sometimes—because I loved him, I suppose, and wanted him to grow up a man."

"I know," she said quietly, touching his face lightly with her hand and then kissing his burnt leather cheek as she mounted while he held the horse. She would go now. He was starting his recollections again and he would be on his own for some time now, thinking and figuring back over the past.

"You don't think there's anything wrong with a man who talks to a crocodile, do you?" her father said, saying it half aloud only, as if he was not sure if anyone was there or not.

"I talk to my horse," she said, in soft, warm reassurance.

"Of course you do, of course you do," he said, animated for a moment as if by the joy of a fresh discovery.

"Of course you do," he said again. "How is the gray beast?" He leaned over and patted the horse on the neck beside the mane.

"Never better. I love him almost as much as you."

"You know Ghost Gum and the crocodile get on? I took him down to meet him once while you were gone. Gave him a run while you were away. They get on fine."

"You mean you've taken my horse right into Five Mile Camp and I'm not allowed?"

He was nodding in a wicked smile now and she almost cried to see the half-light back in his eyes.

"You're full of secrets, aren't you?" Ali said to him.

He nodded knowingly again. "Full of."

"Well, I'll have to ask Ghost Gum to tell me all about it."

"Don't let Uncle Doug hear you talking like that."

She laughed out loud, feeling better. "I'll try not to," she said. "Give my regards to Kismet, won't you?"

"Surely."

"Good-bye," she whispered. "Come home soon."

But he shook his head when she said that, and was smiling his faraway smile again so that she wondered if he ever intended to come back to the station house.

As she turned her horse to go she looked for and saw Crocodile Tommy, far up on the rocks above the gorge. Her look was enough, and the old man's nod, even from that distance, was full of the rich, unspoken knowledge of the tribal Aboriginal: his friend was in his sight and would not leave it and his daughter need not worry. Ali nodded back and headed her horse for the home paddock.

45

Kismet was, in a sense, since the passing of Jacky and despite the closeness of Crocodile Tommy, Big Red's best bush friend. He said bush friend to himself, because he was well aware that the animal was not human, although he had all those qualities of a sweet, capricious disposition mixed with innate treachery which might have qualified him for inclusion under that heading. He was just short of thirty feet, as close as they could get to measure him from overhanging branches, and that was pretty much a record. Age and length were strength for a croc and one shot wouldn't kill him and he was too cunning to take a poison bait and lazing in the sun meant nothing if aroused, although Red rather felt the croc would watch over his own, if it came to it. This was a sort of silent pact they had.

Red was on his rock, a few feet from the water's edge, and Kismet was on his rock, his favorite spot in the shallows for this time of day. He appeared asleep, and he might well have been, which would mean Red was talking to himself. On the other hand, he might simply be appearing to be asleep, which was why Red never went any closer than the rock he was on, sitting up just high enough with his feet on a small ledge so that Kismet's first lunge, if there ever was one, would miss him. He believed it to be a sort of Mexican standoff situation, with each showing sufficient respect for the other's territory.

When he came here to think like this, Red told Kismet everything.

Kismet knew plenty.

He certainly knew that in some ways, despite the bad seasons and markets, Big Red blamed himself.

He should never have let up a little. He'd settled back to enjoy the kids and the property and even, after all those years, reach out again for the gentleness of Ali's mother in Darwin, for the gentleness of Annie, blooming in her fifties, wondering as he touched it, knowing more than wondering, about the tenderness he had gone without because he would not move from the land and she would not become a permanent part of it. They were always easy together, despite the arguments over the land, and for two years he had spent all that time in Darwin with her, going back to the property perhaps only two days a week, when she was on extended flights doctoring the Outback. So he had, in a real sense, almost relinquished his hold on the land which he had loved so much (yet he thought never as much as her softness) but in a way that allowed him to possess it still, despite that part of his brain which knew that Darwin and Annie and a small pocket of country would have been contentment for him and his children.

Yet he had still sought and needed the power of the land, the power of acreage ownership, whatever the cost, apart from the mystic mistress love of the earth, for there was that, too, though he never fooled himself, for one could irresistibly hate the land when the sun was high and dry and your cattle dying. But during that one time, that watershed of getting old and seeking softness, he had not needed the power, or perhaps it was truer that he thought he had it and it would last forever, like some magical crop that would grow without tending.

But that was the time Douglas had been waiting for. He had waited with the parasitic, Pharisaic bloody patience of Job, waited his time until his brother eased his jackeroo's hand ever so lightly off the rein—paused for a lengthy drink at a water hole, no more. But it was enough. Douglas the younger, in his sixty-seventh year and with a cunning Red should have admired, had organized all those developmental partnerships. And they were good deals, too, for Red was not that asleep and Douglas wanted his own future secured and had large share-holdings in them as well. But it meant that by the end of that year, Red had partners in the pearling and prawning and minerals. It was good business: their families would live handsomely for more than the normal three generations from riches back to rags on those mineral royalties, but it was bad common sense. It was so because the thing Red loved the most—his cattle run with Five Mile Camp—the one thing he had never given Douglas a share in, became vulnerable. He was geared three to one with borrowing on it already, holding off selling in the hope the American Government would lift its quotas and put the price of beef up again. But if the tick fever was really there and he would know soon enough, then the banks would come at him, no doubt with some help from the American consortium offering to place all their business with his bank—no doubt advised by Douglas, no doubt with stock options making Douglas as close to owner as he was ever likely to be, and no doubt with everyone writing out uranium share certificates for themselves as a big fat bonus.

Well, he'd know soon enough, he told Kismet on that evening in 1974, sitting on the rock above the crocodile where he had been reviewing the whole Carlyon history. He should have the results tomorrow. Jitangeli had taken the swab to Annie to have analyzed on her way to Sydney to get Bluey Junior, whose name was John Patrick Byrne, after his grandfather. Hopefully Jitangeli would be back tomorrow with Bluey himself, and Bluey Junior, the smart lawyer accountant, and the results of the swab. Then with Alison and Black Roo they'd all sit down and have a family council of war. If it really was tick fever, and it was widely spread, Red was gone. He knew that. He needed what beef sales he could manage, however low the price, to keep the property. But he couldn't believe it was tick fever. It was easy enough to get it, in the Territory, but he'd been so careful all these years with his cattle, he couldn't believe it had happened now. And it had only been on the couple straying near home paddock that he'd thought he noticed the telltale larvae. But they could be like pinheads for a start and perhaps he had not seen them. He'd taken the swab secretly and secretly shot and buried the two cattle himself, buried after burning the poor beasts, down by the billabong, while the men were out mustering.

But soon he'd know. And then he'd tell Alison and the others the whole story and plan his battle—his last battle?

The next morning, when Red heard the Piper Twin Co-manche, and then saw it fly low over Five Mile Camp, and knew it to be Bluey's plane, he saddled up and rode into the homestead.

They were all in the kitchen drinking tea and eating one of Fan-tan's legendary breakfasts when Red surprised them. They were overjoyed to see him.

"The kids got in from Sydney last night," said Blue. "Too late to come out, so came first thing this morning. You OK?"

He nodded slowly. "Thanks for coming."

He sat down and Fan-tan poured him some tea and put more eggs on.

"Where's Roo?" asked Alison who, despite all her happy equanimity, got the anxiety of a little girl in her voice if she could not find, or did not know where to find, her elder brother.

"He'll be here presently," Red said kindly. "He'll have heard the plane, too. He's been out checking the stock for me for days, but he'll have been working his way in by now and be here soon."

He looked around the table. Beside Bluey was his son, John. He was Bluey's youngest, for, as Bluey always said, it had taken three girls to get John. But John was now in his mid-thirties. Despite his diminutive mother, the boy was tall, perhaps taking some height from Bluey and his thinner frame from his mother. He was quietly spoken in an almost whimsical way. He was not a typical hardened Outback case nor a typical hardened business cynic. There was almost a touch of Irish poet about him, with his softly curling and unruly ginger hair and boyish smile and thin, long fingers. He seemed more artist, more painter, more thinker, philosopher, academic or poet, than . . . well, than Bluey's son. Of course he *was* an academic in one sense. He'd done law, then a master's in business administration, which included computer technology. Bluey used to complain that he had a perpetual student on his hands. But by his mid-twenties his son had finished his courses and, with his father's help, immediately opened his own business consultancy firm. Of course as a boy he'd learned an awful lot about his father's operations, the mainstay of which was minerals, particularly iron ore, and soon Bluey Junior, or Bluey Mark II as he referred to himself, for the boy certainly had his father's quick sense of humor, had some of the metal industry giants such as Broken Hill for clients. He was now among the top of Sydney's younger group of business consultants, those who were into that whole new world of technology which neither Bluey nor Red confessed to understand. But Red knew that this time that was just what he was up against in the opposition and he was placing high hopes in Bluey Mark II coming up with a lifesaver.

Alison sat next to John, for she refused to call him Bluey, except when she wanted to annoy him. She was as golden of hair and sunny of nature as ever and was holding John's hand under the table—or tickling the inside of his thigh, more likely, thought Red—and although she'd had to cut short her London stay, with one of her girlfriends who'd married an Englishman, she was obviously glad to be home and see John. Red hoped he could save the station for her. Had his talk of the previous night really made clear to her, though he had withheld some details, that the property was truly in jeopardy? She had seemed to believe him, yet there was still an element of childish trust in Alison toward her father, and her brother Black Roo, who had now come in, as if they were infallible and could put anything to right. They'd need some powerful white man's and black man's magic to do it this time, thought Red. The cards were really stacked.

And what of Jitangeli, the Asian flower, still sitting in her city dress? Although on the property near the house she wore jeans—or sweet nothing, or half of it, half the time, like Alison—she dressed in formal Asian attire when she left the property, like Singapore Airline hostesses, Red thought, in those soft, unshiny silks, with delicate tropical flowers on them like the lagoon lilies and lotuses, the skirt cutting in ever so lightly around her beautiful Asian hips, almost in a Chinese fashion, and, indeed, she was half Chinese. She had these dresses made for her specially, in Darwin. Her black hair was shiny, yet soft, her face was indeed moonfaced, the ultimate Chinese compliment, round and pretty with big brown eyes in the most delicate yellow-brown face and the most perfect set of teeth, though she giggled rather than laughed, giggled gracefully, not like a teenager but with a deep sense of Asian grace. Yet she was the quiet one of the family, speaking ever so softly, her whole nature a fragile porcelain thing.

She was the one Red feared for most when he was gone. But Roo loved her like the brother he was, and sometimes Red wondered if he loved Jitangeli at that other level, too, and would not say, for you'd never know with Roo. He had the real old-fashioned Aboriginal interior thing, that one. Yet in this Red took comfort. Whether Jitangeli was the reason Roo had never married, never taken a lubra, or not, he would watch over her. Jitangeli caught Red looking at her, as she often did, for she had a level of quiet perception, Red believed, closer to Annie's than anyone's, and it was as if she had read his thoughts, for she reached her tiny, finely fingered, delicately thin-fingered yet incredibly tiny little brown hand across the table like a child reaching out, and took his hand and squeezed it for a moment, smiling thanks. Whether she had read his thoughts or not, she sensed he had been thinking protectively about her. Red marveled again at the ignorance of white men over the centuries who had failed to learn from the higher levels of perception and culture and quietly orchestrated interior levels of intelligence of the black and brown and yellow peoples.

He thought this as Jitangeli smiled again and let go and as he turned his gaze and thoughts for a moment to Black Roo. He seemed only a boy, he still looked so black and happy and ungray and youthful, like his father as Red first remembered him as a child. For although Roo had that extra touch of toughness his father had not had, Roo lacked none of Happy Jack's smiling, incorrigibly cheeky and happy ways. And, indeed, from Lily's cheekiness, and it seemed only yesterday she had been flashing her bare bum around the kitchen, from that cheekiness Roo drew another dimension of personality, for Lily's cheekiness, like his sister Cathy's, was a quick-wittedness, a quick-fire sense of humor. Yet he was thirty-nine and would turn forty next year. He was as strong a man as Red had ever met, or would ever wish his son to be, and as he looked quickly across at him, and then away, the old man fought back a tear, for he was his son in a real sense, as well as his friend and mate, and he loved him for the son he might have had, and the son he was, and the way he loved the land like no one else living in these parts now except Big Red himself.

Bluey had been watching Red's eyes wandering around the table, as they drank their big enamel mugs of tea, the mugs they still used in the kitchen, and his heart feared for his old friend, for he had heard the story now, from Jitangeli and his son and Anne.

"Well, I guess I'd better call this meeting to order," Red said at last. He thanked young Bluey, John, first, for giving up his valuable time to come and help, and then thanked Bluey himself, and then nodded to Fan-tan so that the cook and old friend would keep nit and see that no one came near their kitchen conference room. He smiled to himself as he thought this, thinking how many times Fan-tan must have kept nit, kept the watch at that rather less than salubrious gambling den and brothel he had brought him from over half a century ago. It seemed like yesterday, and then he realized his mind was wandering again a little, and there was silence and they were all waiting for him to talk.

"This is difficult for me to say," he began, "but you might as well know the truth from the start, although I suspect most of you know more of it than either Black Roo or myself, although we've been working on slightly more than a hunch. So let's get it over with. . . . We've either got some sort of outbreak of tick fever or we haven't. . . . Jitangeli . . . how was the swab—?"

"Positive," she said quietly, in her most unemotional voice, which she was good at the way Asian peoples sometimes talk without emphasizing one syllable more than another, yet with a lyrical sound.

Red kept himself well in control. He knew anger would not do. He needed his head now as much as on any Murranji Track he'd ever been on.

"Roo's been out checking the herd on his own, sampling as many as possible in the time we had. Roo—?"

"Nothing. No cases out on the range. Seems the only two are the ones you found down by the river near home paddock. You burnt off the grass, too, you said, didn't you?"

Red nodded. He thought for a moment, then he said,

"Look . . . I've got a couple of ideas and I want to get a full report from John here, who's been doing a bit of homework for me in Sydney. But before I do that, and tell you what I've got in mind, I feel I owe you a bit of an explanation as to what's happened and why and what it means because . . . I'm afraid what it very much does mean is that we might lose the property . . . even our home . . . because I don't think anyone's going to settle for just part of the property, although I'll certainly try that if it comes to it. But first, let me explain, and feel free to ask questions as I go along. I know some of you will know a lot of what I'm going to tell you, but I want to be sure everyone understands as best as I'm able to tell it. OK?"

They all nodded and some poured extra cups of fresh tea from the big, blue, chipped-enamel pot Fan-tan had placed on the table before resuming his place at the door.

"About three months ago," Big Red began, "just after Alison had left, McWilliams from the Yankee property came over to talk. Now I've never had anything against the man himself. I mean he can't help it if he's an accountant with thick-lens glasses who wears brand-new army hats all the time to try to look Australian. But you have to admit we all knew he was wrong when he started to fence that property. Anyway, he came over all perspiring this time and in his pressed whites with patch pockets as usual but with a brand-new Texas ten-galloner on his head, as if he had to make sure I knew he was American this time, which as you know I'd always been a bit confused about seeing the way he wore that slouch hat around—" Alison smiled to herself here, noting the way her father was getting into top gear as she had seen him so many times in the past, building up his aggression with his heavy bush sarcasm, feeding his indomitable spirit always with the harsh, tongue-in-cheek bush humor. "Anyway this Yank joker who you could have picked a mile off by his horn-rimmed glasses with those flap-over sunshades, without the bloody ice-cream-cone hat, comes over and says, without pausing hardly long enough to say g'day, that he was authorized by his principals to make me a firm offer to buy at one million dollars. Now one million, I ask you . . . a dollar an acre . . . what sort of an offer would you call that—?"

"Reasonable," broke in Bluey Junior; "I'd call it reasonable in this market."

There was a silence in which you could have heard a blade of grass drop. Big Red looked him up and down. Then he smiled.

"Well, I'll tell you, kids," he said, looking around the table but mostly at Alison and Jitangeli, "I'll tell you something. We are going to get honest answers from Mark Two here like we have always got from his old man and we should be grateful. I asked him here to help us and he's going to shoot straight down the line however much it hurts and for which I thank him. He is, of course, quite right. On current market prices that's not a bad offer. The European Common Market has hit us Northern producers bad over the past few years and the American quotas, preventing us sending as much beef into the States as we used to, has made it worse. So I'd say that's right, that a dollar an acre isn't such a bad price, although I reckon they'll go higher. So at this stage I need a family vote on something. I've decided that I won't vote. I'm not going to be around that much longer and you're all secure for life with the other investments, curse them, so the decision must be yours. So far as I'm concerned, it's a four-way split: Cathy, Roo, Alison and Jitangeli."

"What about Uncle Doug?" asked Alison.

"He's never been a partner in the property, you know that. In everything else, but never in the property. Never wanted it in the early years, wanted the money to invest in other things. He's worth a lot in his own right, you know. He invested on his own in a lot of other things."

"With income he was getting out of the property," Alison interrupted again.

"Sure, darling. He was my kid brother. Whatever I was making money out of in the early days went to him and Mum and then just to him until he got established, but he was never an owner in this part of the business. He said he didn't want it, and perhaps he didn't, because he hated the land like your grandmother did, or perhaps he knew I didn't want anyone in who didn't like the land and I was happy to pay him a big fat fee to look after our business. Anyway, I was part of it, too. I wanted one name on that deed for one million acres—mine. And that's how it stands. But it belongs to you four. I've phoned Cathy and I'll tell you how she stands in a minute. But first what about you three . . . want a moment or a day to think it over?"

They all shook their heads. He turned to them in order of age.

"Keep the land," said Roo, with that quiet ferocity only someone with a deep tribal background has.

"The land," said Alison, firmly and determinedly.

"Oh, the land," said Jitangeli, with her wonderful soft soprano sound.

"That's unanimous, then," said Big Red. "Cathy votes for the Land Party, too. But it's not going to be that easy, kids. Apart from the market demand, even leaving aside the tick fever thing for the moment, we had a bad Dry last year and this could be worse. And your old man is here to tell you that he is stretched as thin as he could possibly be. I know people always think of millionaires as having unlimited stacks of millions of dollars somewhere, but the fact is that rich men are often short of cash, too—liquidity, they call it. Rich men are short of capital because it's the one thing they never have enough of because they keep reinvesting it to expand and get more. Now this property cost me three million dollars, not counting the blood, toil, sweat and tears. Okay, property values are low at the moment because of generally depressed conditions around the world, because of low beef prices, and, because, I reckon the American offer means more American quotas are going on and I suspect the American consortium wanting to buy us out—and it's a bigger group than we've ever had to face before—have got an inside draw on supplying their home American market.

"So they want my cattle; they also desperately need my water because last year's Dry nearly wiped them out and of course all the sixties were dry years. That part of their company responsible for the Australian operation has got to be in desperate trouble, too, because of uneconomic running of the property. I'd say the vice president or presidents responsible for the Australian end, not to mention the manager McWilliams, are all in deep, deep trouble with head office or may even have been cooking the books so head office doesn't yet know. But those in charge of this end must know that the day of reckoning is at hand and they need my property to make their Australian operation justifiable. They can then make up one set of books and turn a quick profit on my cattle through their inside running in the American market. They are also, I believe, convinced there is uranium at Five Mile Camp."

"They're not the only ones," Bluey chipped in sarcastically.

"I've told you, Blue, there's none there. The only uranium is the stuff I found years ago and I'm coming to that."

Bluey shook his head a little disbelievingly and his son looked across at him.

"I have to tell you, kids, that I've thought of this every way

I can, and I've made a decision which is very painful for me and one I think you would agree with but which could lose us the property." He paused and licked his lips and Fan-tan waddled over, not as a servant given a signal, for it had not been that, but Fan-tan had noticed and came over and took the pot and put his hand on Red's shoulder as he leaned over and said, "I make fresh tea. Water still on boil."

"There are two ways," Red went on, "in which I could raise enough capital to bail us out at least for the time being. The first way, which would bail us out for all time, is to mine or sell my uranium deposit. This I cannot do. I am against it. I feel it would be a betrayal of Billy. If you want to sell that, you must do it after I'm gone—"

They were all shaking their heads and, in any case, he knew how they felt, for either because of his brainwashing or their independent decisions, and after all Alison did have a university degree, they felt as he did. But he had to ask.

"Well, given my—our—attitude on that, there's only one other way and I won't accept that either. You know how short crocodiles are these days and that they're starting to talk of making them protected. Well, that's fine and that's how I've always felt. But until they do, while shooting is still legal, seeing we're the one property so far as I know where they've never been touched, we have got a bloody fortune in hand-bags and shoes in every decent billabong and lagoon and river for miles around. If we shot them ourselves, or sub-contracted, we might make enough to get out of it, but I doubt it. I must admit I never knew the word conservation the way they use it now, when I first came here. I knew about the word in terms of conserving water in the desert and things like that. But I guess it's as good a word as any. But either way, whatever you call it, I just say that they've never touched me or mine, and they're part of the land, part of the bloody land like any other creature, and I'll not be a party to their killing."

"You know we all feel the same way," Alison said quietly, with full reassurance in her voice.

"OK, then," Red said, taking the fresh cup of tea which

Fan-tan had poured and sugaring it, "OK, then, we've got to play a very straight bat and bluff it out and play for time. Bluey Marks One and Two can check me out on this but roughly, as I said, we're capitalized here to at least three million dollars. We've got nearly fifteen thousand cattle and I can hold that number only two or three months longer at best, assuming we can do something about the tick situation. I held heavily from last season, hoping for better prices. There won't be feed or water enough this year to carry more, and in any case I've got to sell off as many as I can this year to generate as much capital as I can—because in three months at best, all my mortgage payments are due. You understand that; I'm capitalized at three, so I still technically owe money on the property. This might seem damn stupid to you, and it does to me now, but for years the banks and agricultural companies have carried us happily; most big property owners are the same. The banks and agricultural companies get their interest and I get the use of the money for other ventures.

"Pearling first helped finance the property; later the property helped it as we extended into prawning and later bauxite. But in the pearling we've got men, plant, equipment, machinery and every bloody capital-intensive device known to man and a few more our Japanese partners have just invented and I never thought I'd be partners with them; the boats that get us and the Americans their giant banana prawns are the same, and the bauxite, and the airline shares. I have, in effect, got partners in every one. So I get dividends, huge dividends, we can all live off very well all our lives—but not enough in one lump sum to get me out of trouble. Now, of course, my partners in the nonfarming ventures would be only too happy to buy me out. But they'd know I was in trouble if I asked, or they'd check and find out quickly enough, and offer me some ridiculous price so that if I sold, all I'd be doing would be destroying your financial security and I'll not do that. To sell the airline shares would be the same. With the share dividends and the dividends from the other ventures, you're all financially secure for life and that's not so

bad—you'll always be able to have a small property somewhere if you want to stay on the land—it's just keeping this
particular piece of land that is going to be the problem."

He drank another mouthful and then went on:

"I owe the bank three-quarters of a million. I owe Trans
Australian Stock and Station another quarter of a million. As
you know, this is like the farmers' trading post. Everything
from nails to posts for the stockyards to tractor parts, we put
on our current account with them. They also sell our stock,
repay themselves as it were, and send us the balance. If there
is a balance. But on current prices, whatever I manage to sell,
revenue from sales will be less than costs of operation—just
the wages bill can be pretty heavy here and I'm not about to
start laying off. But we are in a rural recession and the banks
and agricultural companies are going to start applying the
pressure in weeks if not days. I reckon they'll carry me for
three months at the most. But there's no guarantee—"

"Not after all these years—?" broke in Alison.

"No, darling. They might have dozens, even hundreds of
farmers in bad straits around the country. If they didn't start
calling in, they'd go out of business, too, and wouldn't be able
to help any of us with any credit at all."

Alison nodded.

"Well, that's about it," Red said. "I guess they'll carry me
for a little, but one way or another, I reckon I need at least
half a million I don't have and I haven't really got any good
ideas for getting it. All I've got is one or two ideas for slowing
things down. But before we go any further, I think there's
something we've all got to know, and that is exactly who
we're up against: who this big American consortium represents. Bluey Mark Two's been doing some homework for us
since I sent Jitangeli down to Sydney with a lot of my
papers."

He looked across at the young man, who started to talk. He
talked a lot softer than his father or Red.

"Yes, well, it wasn't all that difficult. I've traced most of it
through the Registrar of Companies office where all, or most
of it, has to be on file. The North American Pastoral Alliance,

Incorporated, made the offer, which is the company which has always owned your neighboring property since the war. Now, although they've made offers before, this time, according to Uncle Red, they made it on behalf of a bigger group, a group which McWilliams, the manager, called Territory Pastures, Incorporated. This is an Australian-American group, or rather a paper company, quite legal, tying together three other companies in partnership for the purpose of this exercise. First, the North American Pastoral Alliance is part of it—your traditional agricultural opposition; second, there is a company called Northern Minerals, a name which no doubt has an old and familiar ring to it, for it keeps cropping up in the offers Red gave me, the firm offers he's had in writing, for his uranium over the years: a mineral company comprising Japanese, Australian and American interests; and third, the last leg of the consortium is a company registered in Sydney and called Harborside Nominees. You may not all know but one of the things about nominee companies is that their shareholders are not listed on public record, at least not for inspection, at the Companies Office. Usually they turn out to be family trusts, a quite legal form of tax . . . I hate the term avoidance . . . of tax saving by making all members of the family members of the trust so that a man's income is spread over his wife and children, the latter, particularly, being taxed at a much lesser rate than if one man was taxed on the lot. There are some other advantages, but that's basically it. So I don't know officially who Harborside Nominees are, although my business associates have come up with one or two informed guesses. I was hoping perhaps that Uncle Red might be able to help me out on that one—?"

Red looked across at the young man and admired him. He knew only too well, Red supposed, who comprised Harborside Nominees. He would have done a thorough job of investigation and hired people to find out, if necessary, even although it was not a matter of public record. It was not easy to find out, mind, Red knew that. But this would be part of John's daily round of work as a business consultant. No, he knew.

But he had made a conscious decision to let Red decide if the others should be told. Red, for his part, wanted it all out in the open.

"When last I heard, that company belonged to Douglas," he said quietly, without emotion.

Fan-tan had been baking some fresh scones in between his bouts of watching and he now brought these out of the oven and put freshly patted rolls of homemade butter and cheese and jam and honey on the table and some fresh tea.

Red got up and buttered a hot scone. Alison got up and followed him. "Are you serious?" she said, and then, knowing that he was, went on before he could answer, "The hypocrite, the bastard, the deceitful bastard."

Red cut a thick welt of cheese and put it on the scone, and munched into it as he went to the refrigerator to get some beer, shrugging, "What can you do?" back at Alison. He and both Blueys and Roo and Alison drank the beer. Jitangeli had tea as always, black tea without milk or sugar. As usual she was keeping her anger in. But Red could see she understood the full weight of what he had said.

Red knew that the company had been Douglas's family trust company for years. He had suspected but not known who the members of the new consortium were. The Americans and Japanese would have been brought in by Douglas to get the capital necessary for such a venture. In turn, they would be happy to have a local partner, for the government was getting touchy about selling off the farm, as it was called, selling off the country to foreign interests. But with a local partner such as Douglas, they would have no difficulty. They would play dirty, too, there was no doubt about that. Red was sure now that the tick fever was a scare tactic. A very risky scare tactic which could affect everyone but, nevertheless, a scare tactic. He confided this to the group at the kitchen table as he began talking again. Having explained that he thought it was simply a tactic, he went on:

"So, much and all as I hate it, I'm *not* going to report the two incidents of tick fever. Now you all know I should—and the penalty if the Agriculture Department finds out. But Roo has samples checked fairly thoroughly and what we're sure about is that there is no major outbreak. Any more cases and I'll report them, that's a promise. But our only hope is to buy time. I guess you're all sitting there asking how did I let things get in such a state? Well, I've asked myself that plenty over the time I've been down at Five Mile Camp. I was wrong to leave myself so short of capital in one sense, by agreeing to all those joint ventures; yet in another sense I did not think I could ignore the very real way in which they would make you all financially secure for life. I mean, the land, which we all love, is a very contrary mistress at the best of times and the farmers in the South aren't driving Rolls or Mercedes anymore either. People are going bust on the land all around the country.

"So you might say, well, how come I didn't foresee it last year? How did I intend to meet my payments quite apart from the American threat? Well, the answer to that is that the man on the land often sees what is coming, but he's so used to the good and bad seasons, he hopes something will turn up and keeps going. I thought that perhaps we would have a moderate Dry. It was terrible. Perhaps the Americans would ease their quotas. They made them worse. But still I thought I might get out by selling off as much stock as I could as quickly as I could to the pet food companies here, along with the good price I'd get for my quota to the American market. Now that that has been cut even further it seems hopeless. There's no way revenue from sales will cover costs. It's the end of August now. We've got until the end of November— roughly the start of the Wet. If I can't pay by the end of November, that will be it. I'm afraid, kids, that I gambled with your home and lost. You'll all be rich—and dispossessed of your home. I've named you officially as heirs to avoid contesting, by the way."

"We'll think of something," Bluey's son John said.

"I hope so, son. I hope so. But you'll be a bloody genius if you can pull us out of this one. I think, maybe, I got a bit old and started to lose my touch. Thought my golden luck would run forever."

He poured another glass of beer for the others and himself and then said, "Anyway, we're not going down without a fight. John, I must buy some time and to do that we've got to hit back, or appear to, hit back hard enough to make the opposition think we're stronger than they realize. So I want you to make them an offer of three-quarters of a million for their place next door. Can you do that on my say so, knowing I haven't got the cash but not letting on, without getting yourself into any trouble with any authorities anywhere?"

"I think so. It's only a verbal offer, after all. And Big Red is still Big Red to the public and the business community at large. They'd always expect you to pull a rabbit out of the hat somewhere along the line, to have a pile of gold stashed away for a rainy day . . . you don't, by the way, do you, Uncle Red . . . at Five Mile Camp or anywhere else? . . . I mean forgive me saying this, for we all admire your cunning tremendously . . . but now would be a good time to tell us if you do."

Red looked at him and loved the man and the way they were all looking at him and he looked back at them and said with his faraway look that took him back down the years to him and Kiwai diving for pearls, risking their lives to get started, Kiwai who was back on Thursday Island now with his great-grandchildren, he saw all this in his mind's eye as he answered,

"No, son, I don't."

Yet as he answered he knew that Bluey did not believe him, and Bluey's son doubted, too, and they all still expected a miracle from him, which he did not believe he could deliver. But he was certainly going to try.

"Well, make the offer, son, and make it sound good, and release it to all the papers and feed them stories to keep it running as long as you can."

"Any way I can?"

"Any way."

"You sure?"

"Well, I'm not against uranium for publicity, son, if that's what you're asking—only against taking it out of the ground."

John nodded. "I'll make it sound good."

"I bet you will. You young sharp businessmen and your methods frighten hell out of me. Just as well we're not listed on the stock exchange."

"Wish you were," chipped in John quickly, and with such a devious smile that Red and Bluey exchanged glances which said they would prefer to stay out of jail if at all possible.

They were all accustomed to Red and Bluey exchanging looks, and read the old men's faces much better than either realized, both still thinking that this part of their bushcraft was still sacred. But it was not, and there was a general titter around the table.

"Oh, well, at least we can all still laugh," Red said, and then added seriously, "Oh, and, Roo, see what that new black stockman is all about while I'm away, will you? I'm going into Sydney for a few days. He was near the home paddock when I found the two tick cows and someone has got to have put them there, I reckon."

Roo nodded quietly and intently. Alison looked at her father and then her brother.

"I might give a hand there. He seemed just a little more than met the eye when I arrived yesterday."

"Always trust your sixth sense, daughter," Red smiled. "Now Fan-tan, my best blue suit. I'm off to do battle with the pinstripe brigade."

They all knew what he meant. It was the way he talked when he was going to Sydney to see Douglas. This would be a different sort of meeting from the others.

46

Despite everything, John and Alison were desperate to be alone. So the moment Red had flown off with Bluey, they headed down home paddock. There they made love hurriedly in the grass by the river, hurriedly and perspiringly, with the deep intensity of wanting that Alison always had, and John loved so in her, as if all the beauty of the countryside, all the rich sense of the ever regreening of nature, she held between her thighs.

"God, I've missed you," she said, in many ways the more volatile of the two and the protagonist in the relationship, yet loving John's steadiness as he said to her,

"You know the offer is always open."

"I know. But I must sort myself out first."

"What's there to sort out? Come and live in Sydney."

"Well, we certainly can't go on like this forever. I can't live on four or five trips to Sydney a year, plus your yearly visit at Christmas."

"Is it your father?" he said at last.

"You know it's not. I wouldn't leave the station now, not for anything. But even without him you know I love it here. Why can't we live in the country?"

"Because my work is in the city," he said quietly.

"But there's your father's whole empire. Who'll run that?"

"I will, when he goes, from Sydney. But my work is different. I want to build my own work."

"Well, it looks as if I mightn't have any choice," said Alison glumly, turning over on her tummy so her own dampness was against the thick, richly greened grass, also damp it was so close to the river.

John stroked ever so softly down the back of her gold-brown long hair, down the blond fuzz that ran between her shoulder blades down to her bottom, and with the flat of his hand over her bottom and down as far as he could reach to the backs of her knees.

"It'll be all right," he said, doing it again and again and speaking to soothe her, for he knew how upset she really was. "It'll be all right, really. We'll put up the money. My father and I have talked about it."

"But don't all the same things apply to you? About borrowing and lending and all that and using your capital?"

"Yes, with one exception . . . we're not on the land—and our property has never been mortgaged."

"Oh, John," she sighed, and then began to cry, "not the house on the hill, the beautiful place on the cliff with the square white tower we used to sit in as children. . . . I couldn't bear to lose that, too."

"We're not going to lose it—only mortgage it."

"He'll never let you."

"He's got no choice."

"Oh, yes he has. He won't do it without paying you interest and he won't be able to afford to pay you interest any more than he could the banks without selling something."

"But just for three months, three or six months, wouldn't he let us help with the interest that long?"

"No. Would what he'd get for the plane pay the interest?"

"No."

"Then he wouldn't do it. Not unless he could physically pay, or see his way clear to pay virtually right from the start of your commitment."

"I know. That's what my old man said. But he'll try an offer that he sell part of it to us as partners, though Dad says he'll refuse that too because he knows our business interests have never been in the land, although we've often thought of it, and we'd only be doing it as charity. Is that correct?"

"That's correct. Your father knows my father as well, if not better, than I do. That's exactly what he'll say and do."

"Well, I can't see any way, then."

"Neither can he, otherwise he wouldn't be going cap in hand to Uncle Doug, the bastard. Have you any idea how hard that is for Daddy?"

"If he's anything like my old man, which of course he is, yes, I know how hard it is. They don't make them like those two anymore. There's a sort of stubborn pride in oneself that they've both got and which we tend to denigrate almost as a stupidity these days yet which in a funny way we still worship and wish we had, too. Know what I mean?"

"Sure. Except that I've still got it."

He smiled, though she could not see him, for she was still lying facedown in the grass she loved so and feeling her body warmth against it with every soft downward movement of his hand over her back and buttocks. He smiled where she could not see him and said,

"Yes, you have, haven't you? That's part of our whole problem."

She rolled over onto her side then, and moistened a finger and put it to his mouth as if to say "Sssshh" and then moved her hand so that her open palm was lightly and tenderly against his cheek, and she said softly to him, "We'll work something out so that we both keep the property and you and I are together. Perhaps I could live in Sydney and just come and visit here. . . . I'm just frightened of having the same sort of relationship my parents have. . . . It's sort of the same thing in reverse—I want the land and you want your work which is elsewhere. They've had a wonderful time in some ways, but there was always the hurt of missing and I couldn't bear that myself, I don't think, after seeing them go through it. . . . But," she added, something inside her as strong as a giant steel clock spring reverting her to type, to the Bush Code she had grown up with and could not now let go of, "something will happen. Red will find a way. We mustn't trouble trouble until trouble troubles us."

"Of course," he said gently, not adding what he was thinking, for he did love her so, particularly in her almost childlike, innocent mood of bushcraft and Aboriginal logic, "of course," he repeated, not adding that trouble was indeed troubling the Carlyon family and it was not trouble of a kind that would easily disappear with the sunrise of a new day.

The meeting between Douglas and Red was very subdued. Only the texture of Red's face and hands—that telltale ruddy, worn and beautiful thing that the Outback gives—would have singled him out from the crowd as other than a businessman as he made his way, with his slight limp, through the Martin Place city people to his and Douglas's office. It was technically *theirs,* he thought, for he was still paying the rent. He wore a finely worsted blue pinstripe, with cream silk shirt and pocket handkerchief and navy spotted tie and black imported English shoes. He went in through the marble foyer and up to the top floor into Douglas's office, the biggest office he'd ever seen, with a sweeping view of the city's skyline. He had been there plenty of times before on his biannual visits to Sydney and he smiled as he was ushered in by Douglas's secretary after she had announced that Sir James was here to see him and Douglas had gruffly asked back, "Sir James who?" to which she had replied, "Your brother, sir."

"How many of us do you know, Douggie?" Red asked as he was shown in.

"Two others with the same Christian name of James," he said lightly, almost too lightly. Christ he's in a cocky mood, thought Red, bloody cocky. Douglas motioned him to a seat, and offered whiskey and cigarettes. Red shook his head: it was too early in the day for him for a drink. Douglas lit up a cigarette. He wore a blue pinstripe, too, and a gold watch chain across his waistcoat, and half-frame, gold-rimmed glasses like the best of surgeons, or eye specialists, or whatever those pukka blokes who wore them were, that's what they were all wearing in Sydney that year, waistcoats and watch chains and half-lens glasses, as well as their pinstripes. Next year it would be something else. It had to do with the club you were in. Not a real club with buildings, though they had those, too, but the club in the sense of being in the club, such as being pregnant, for it all had to do with who was up who, as far as Red could see, in this business world. It didn't have to do with loyalties or Old World honor or friendship as it used to and as they pretended it still did when they went to their clubs which actually had buildings and dining rooms and cardrooms and billiard rooms and whiskeys and sodas and men to brush off your dandruff and hand you a towel in the washroom, it had nothing to do with any of these Old World charm things as they pretended, but it had to do with who was fucking who for a dollar—not even pounds anymore, but for a dollar.

So Red sat there and eyed off Douglas in the way he knew Douglas hated and called him Douggie which he knew he hated, too, and which he'd been doing for years and now regretted in a way because he knew he'd never loved Doug as he should have but they were such different people, so unalike, one city and one country, wherever each was born, both with the same mother and father and on the same earth and under the same Outback sky, although Douglas had been born indoors, perhaps that was it, perhaps it was that simple, perhaps that was why so many preferred the cities and their deadly, devious smoke-filled rooms of plot hatchery.

"Harborside Nominees still yours?" Red said at last when he saw Douglas was playing what he considered his smart city game of waiting for the other man to talk to find out what was on his mind first.

"Sure," said Douglas, leaving a deliberate silence again. What was it Alison called it? She'd lived with Douglas and his wife for her first term doing agricultural science at the university before she cabled to say, ATMOSPHERE STIFLING. MOVING INTO SPARE ROOM IN BLUEY JUNIOR'S FLAT. Hadn't fooled Red for one minute. What was it she'd said about Douglas when he visited the flat? That's right: "He always gives monosyllabic answers in a smirky, confident tone," she had said. Smart girl that Alison. She'd be all right. He wasn't really paying much attention to Douglas. He knew what his answers would be. He'd got over the betrayal bit. Although he'd only known for sure yesterday, he'd had three months of being fairly sure. The more he thought about it, the more he thought that he really should have expected it sooner or later and that if it hadn't been Douglas it would have been someone else, which of course he would have preferred, but there you were. You had good luck and you had bad. His had been good for quite a while. He hadn't ridden a Murranji Track in a long time. Sweet Jesus, it was a lifetime ago and yesterday ago. What was it Douglas was saying? Had he actually outlasted Douglas in silence? Yes, he had. He was saying, "I'm serious, Jim."

"Oh, I know that, Doug. I just wondered if you realize how much the property means to us all. I mean, if I can get a lot of my cattle to market quickly on the road trains and your people don't push the banks too hard, then maybe I can ride it out. If not for me, for Mum, for Dad, for Ali's sake, by Christ: the property means everything to her. Leave us just the homestead and Five Mile Camp and I'll do a deal. The rest for the one million, how's that? You can have the river, and all the water except for the little bit at Five Mile Camp and the property between there and the homestead."

"We want Five Mile Camp."

"You'll be disappointed. There's nothing there."

"I don't believe you. But we want it anyway. My friends need the property to rationalize their Australian operations."

So that *was* it, thought Red. They needed to spread their books over a wider field to get out of it. They still hoped for uranium but it was a considered risk and would be a bonus.

"It's just my private Shangri-La, that's all—nothing else. No riches there. Just nature. The last bit of unspoilt bush around. You can understand how I wanted to leave my kids that, can't you? To leave them some bush the way I knew it, the bush that I was born in. That bush goes back seventy-six years just with me alone, apart from our father the Overlander, and you know it's got a resident three hundred years old."

"We intend to farm him and all his friends," Douglas said. He did not raise his voice, nor did Red, but both knew it was the cruelest thing he could say. Red knew they would have their eyes on the income from the crocodiles before any bans were placed on. But Douglas was saying something else which he was only just hearing, "Oh, and, Jim, I wouldn't talk too much about crocodiles like that in the city, people might think you were . . . well . . . incompetent, which would have certain legal consequences."

Red did not even raise his voice. "Who taught you to hit so well below the belt, Douglas? Is that what all those accountancy classes taught you? Is that what the city teaches?"

"I'm a businessman."

"Well, something like that. You're my own flesh and blood but I think perhaps I enjoy talking to Kismet more than you. Do you have a recorder hidden? Would you like me to say that again, that I am the man who talks to crocodiles and don't find that so damn funny?"

"He'll turn on you one day."

"Of course. Don't you bloody well see—that's why I like him. Everyone's got one but none as good as mine. . . . I can always see where he is and what he is doing and we've got respect for each other."

"You really mustn't talk like this. People will misunderstand."

"What was it, Doug?" Red said quietly. "Was it Billy? You loved him so. Did you blame me for him, for him following me to war and getting the bad lungs or because I represented the land that took him away?"

There was a long silence.

"Perhaps, Jim, perhaps that was it," Douglas said in a moment of dropped pretenses, for a second the Douglas of old, of so many years ago whom Red could still talk to, though he'd been Jim then, and Doug really Douggie and not minding it. "Perhaps it was," he went on, "perhaps it was partly that and partly wanting to do something for myself.

Perhaps I just got sick of being Big Red's brother. Have you any idea what that has been like all these years? It's as if everyone knew and treated me as if I owed my success to someone else. Which, of course, I did. However successful my investments were, I was just your business manager, not anything in my own right. I'm sixty-six, Jim, sixty-six, and I want something for myself. Can you understand that?"

It was a terrible moment for Red. He had that terrible longing, that sense of wronging someone, the feeling one gets like butterflies before a race, only worse, that terrible sense of wronging someone, of just by being himself having caused someone else deep, deep hurt. "Oh, Douglas," he said, holding in his tears, "you were always part of the family, always loved. I didn't mean anything by not making you a partner in the property. You could have had something to yourself, the prawning when we first started it, anything; you had only to ask."

"Yes," said Douglas. "I had only to *ask*."

"Is it really too late?"

"Yes."

"All right, take the property. Take it all. Just leave us the house and airstrip."

Douglas shook his head. He was a tall, fattish, balding man, with a touch of reddish curling hair, the color of Beth's.

"Then take the lot, Douglas, and good luck to you. I'm sorry I never properly understood."

For a moment, despite everything, despite all the years of misunderstandings, or perhaps because of them, a moment of genuine emotion passed between the brothers and for a moment Red thought Douglas might break down and cry and he was sure he himself would.

But it passed. Douglas spoke kindly now as he said,

"I'm sorry, too, but it's been too long and the principle would still be the same—you'd be giving it to me. I'm afraid I'm going to take it from you, Jim."

Red got up out of his seat and walked over and shook his brother's hand. "You are certainly welcome to try and I wish you every success but I want to tell you now that you won't succeed and the secret of Five Mile Camp, whatever it might be, will certainly die with me. But you're a Carlyon and you should try. . . . Friends—?"

Douglas smiled ever so slightly over his half glasses as he took his brother's hand. "Friends," he said as Big Red turned and walked out of the office and wondered if he would ever see his brother again. He knew now what he must do.

He went to the Qantas Wentworth Hotel, where he'd kept a suite for years, after the developers pulled down the beautiful old Hotel Australia where you could get thickly buttered toasted chicken sandwiches with proper thick chicken at 3:00 A.M. in the morning. He told the manager at the hotel to cancel his permanent suite, that things were getting tough on the land and he couldn't afford it anymore. Of course the manager laughed and Red laughed and said that he really did want it canceled and then the man got serious and said he hoped Sir James hadn't found anywhere more satisfactory. "Not unless you're rebuilding the old Australia," Red said over his shoulder as he moved off, leaving the manager somewhat perplexed.

He went straight to the airport and there boarded an aircraft for a destination other than Darwin. He had to go and he had no way of knowing what would transpire on the property while he was away.

47

When Alison had not heard from her father after the Sydney meeting she became anxious and spoke to her mother in Darwin on the two-way radio.

Her mother said she'd phone Sydney and call back. When she did, it was to inform Alison that her father had left Sydney, no one knew for where. She had spoken to Douglas's secretary and to the hotel. He had even canceled the suite for good, she said, which was certainly a straight economy measure he would have had to take anyway so Alison should not worry. It was difficult over the two-way, for they knew others listened in, including the American neighboring property. "Probably just part of the plan, do you think, darling?" her mother said and Alison replied, "Yes, probably," but would she keep trying and she hated to ask but because they had no phone at the property would she mind terribly calling Lisa and seeing if he'd gone there? Perhaps there was something from the old days he'd remembered. Alison worried it would hurt her mother for her to say this, but there seemed no hurt in Anne's voice as she said of course she wouldn't mind, she'd be happy to, and Alison realized how really secure her mother's relationship was with her father. Her mother called back shortly to say she couldn't contact Lisa but she'd keep trying to reach her and let Alison know the moment she heard anything.

But suddenly things started happening on the property which took all Alison's attention, and Black Roo's, and John's.

The first day after Red had left, John and Alison drove over to the American property and delivered the counter bid to the agricultural company's Mr. McWilliams. He was taken aback, particularly when he saw John's business card. John was very offhanded, telling the man to make sure his principals received the offer and took it seriously, because Sir James Carlyon had always promised himself he would buy their property one day to round out his own holdings and as land prices were likely to go down even further it was a very generous offer and they'd be foolish not to accept it right away. He said the man could send word to the property for the next few days or after that he or his principals could contact John at his Sydney office.

When they got back to the Carlyon property John got Alison to fly him into Darwin where he briefed his office manager by phone and then spoke personally to the head of the public relations firm he retained to ensure that a constant barrage of publicity would be kept up and he told them to leak the uranium stuff in a few days if the publicity started to lag.

They saw Alison's mother on the third day, after overnighting together at a Darwin motel. Still no word. They flew back to the property.

Black Roo had been out of sight for three days. Alison knew what this meant and determined to speak to the new black ringer herself. She questioned him in more detail now about his background and he became very defensive, so she dropped off for the time being.

That night, not long after midnight, she and John, who was sleeping in Ali's room despite Fan-tan's muttering, were awakened by a shot. They all went tumbling out of bed, Alison grabbing for her father's gun and a large flashlight and John running after her, calling to come back.

"Get the Land Rover started," Alison shouted behind her as she struggled into a housecoat.

"Roo—" she shouted as she came running out onto the veranda. She knew the shot had been close by . . . probably in home paddock. "Roo, oh, dear God—Roo—?"

She was running through the grass of home paddock now in the direction she believed the shot had come. Behind her, Jitangeli was out ahead of John and starting the Land Rover as John came running. Jitangeli got it started and headed for home paddock, throwing the lights onto high beam and ahead of Alison.

First they saw the cow. Then someone lying beside it. Alison ran to the slumped body. It was facedown and had been shot through the shoulder and passed out.

But it was not Roo and presently he emerged from behind a nearby stand of trees.

"Oh, thank God—I thought it was you who'd been shot," Ali said.

"You should know better than that," Roo said quietly.

"How the hell should I—I didn't know how many of them there were? Why the hell didn't you answer?"

"For just that reason. To see if there were others around. Haven't I told you never to run to the sound of a single shot like that without someone backing you up?"

"What about the kid sister?" she said as Jitangeli skidded the Land Rover to a stop. "I thought she backed me up pretty well."

"Sure did," said Roo, "made you a perfect target in those lights."

"He doesn't care that we care for him," Alison said over her shoulder to Jitangeli.

"Ungrateful bloody black man," said Jit with unusual relish in her soft soprano voice, "they're all the bloody same."

"Speaking of ungrateful black bastards, what are we going to do with this lump of carcass?" Alison said.

"I'm for a barbecue," said the innocent, wide-eyed Jitangeli.

"Me too, Jit," said Ali fervently.

John had never been with the three of them all together in such a mood before and his mind kept swinging from thinking how close a family they were to whether or not they might actually mean it.

"Crocodiles are less messy," said Roo.

"He might die while you're talking about it," John said nervously. Alison looked at him as if he were some kind of nut.

"If Roo had meant to kill him, either quickly or slowly, he'd have shot differently, lover," she said testily. "We mightn't have computers but we're pretty precise in our own way."

They all laughed and John felt a little out of it.

"I guess we'd better take him to the house for questioning," Roo said at last. "You three handle him until I get there—?"

"Sure," said Ali nodding, "the cow—?"

Roo nodded. "Lend us your flashlight for a minute, will you, Al—?"

She handed it over and they all watched while Roo took a stick and prized open the cow's mouth and looked into it from a distance. He threw the stick onto the dead cow's body and came back to the group. "We're going to have a barbecue of one kind or another," he said. "Not a word to anyone. I'll fix it and see you back at the house. Leave your spare petrol can off the Rover, Al."

"Righto, brother," she said, picking up the jerry can from the back ledge of the rusty, dirt-streaked khaki vehicle, dumping it on the ground, getting in the driver's seat and starting the engine with a call to Jitangeli and John, "Come on, you two, the quicker this is all over the better. Help Roo with the shot bastard, John."

But John was not needed, for as she had been instinctively doing her part, Roo had been doing his. They each had bush instincts which John and even Jitangeli, though she had a few of her own, marveled at, at times. Roo already had the wounded black stockman over his shoulder, and now dumped him in the back as Alison prepared to drive off.

At the station house they patched him up and got some spirits down his throat, sent Fan-tan back to bed and told him not to worry, and presently Roo came back as the black ringer was waking up.

"Morning, brother," Roo said as the black man came to, "morning brother," Roo said, placing the nozzle of his .303 beside the man's head and loading it so he could hear the click. "I could have killed you earlier but thought everyone deserves a second chance. You've got five seconds to tell me who and why before I pull the trigger."

"The American property . . ." he stammered out . . . "they hired me . . . they want you quarantined for tick fever . . . thought it would happen last time but you were too quick."

"Are there any more infected cattle around?" Roo said, pressing the gun barrel harder into the ringer's temple.

The black man shook his head as best he was able. "Don't be silly," he said, "no one wants an outbreak, just a scare on your property. We were just infecting them one at a time and feeding them in."

"No one wants an *outbreak!*" said Roo indignantly. "You took an awful bloody risk. If Red—and I—hadn't got to them so quickly and burnt off all around, we'd be having ticks for breakfast. Don't you know anything over there? We still mightn't have got them in time. Your cattle could all go, too."

The black man was nodding.

"Oh, I see," said Roo. "You don't want an outbreak but if everyone happened to get it, it would sure solve the manager's problems with the books. Some outfit. You're supposed to look after your animals, you know—tend to their every need, keep them healthy at all costs . . . that's a cattleman's job, a drover's job, an Overlander's job . . . Oh, what's the use? We'll send for the air ambulance and have you taken out in the morning to hospital. Don't go back there or come around here ever again, understand?"

The black ringer nodded his head. Then they moved him into another room, locked him in, called the Royal Flying Doctor base in Darwin, had some tea and waited for the plane to arrive at first light.

No sooner had they got rid of the air ambulance, and showered and dressed, but they heard another aircraft coming in.

"Department of Agriculture?" Alison asked, grimacing at Roo over tea at the kitchen table.

"Could be, Al. Sounds like their big old plane."

"It does indeed. Fan-tan, put on the scones and bring out the cream. We are going to have to do some awfully fast talking here."

The men were kindly enough souls, but said, quite frankly, an outbreak of tick fever on the Carlyon property had been reported to their office late last night. They had no alternative but to investigate. They appreciated Miss Carlyon's statement that, to her knowledge, no case of tick fever existed on the property, and that the head stockman agreed. Alison had had a mild argument with Black Roo before the men reached the homestead that she'd do the talking and take the consequences because whatever else happened, he'd be needed to help Big Red more than she would.

However the officials said that although they accepted her statement it was not that simple. Tick fever had been reported. They had flown over the property and there were two burned-out pieces of land in the home paddock. Alison breathed a sigh of relief at Roo's thoroughness. He had obviously removed the burned carcass and bones. Alison said they should talk to her father about the burned land. She kept trying skillfully to avoid a direct lie which might implicate her or the property. Well, the men said, they would wait to talk to her father but, in the meantime, the report having been made, they must start the laborious stock check, which could take weeks, and in the meantime the cattle would be quarantined. There was a procedure, as she no doubt knew, for her father to apply for an injunction against this, but for the moment the quarantine must stand for the statutory period and they were sorry because her father had such a spotless record. They would try to be as little trouble as they could, but would appreciate a couple of stock ponies.

"Of course," Alison smiled. "And whatever provisions you need. Will you stay here overnight or at the bunkhouse?"

"At the bunkhouse thanks, Missus, just for the night. We'll check around here today and then get started tomorrow. Sorry for the inconvenience. We realize it's probably only a scare. But you know how these things are."

"Yes, indeed. Don't give it another thought. We want to

find out, too. We've got the cattle and the other properties to think of."

"Thanks, Missus. We'll be taking our leave now." She nodded.

"Couple of old-timers," Alison said wistfully as they walked out.

"Yes, I saw you warming to them," John said. "I suppose with your father away you are the Missus?"

"Well, to those who can remember, that is certainly the way it goes. It was rather nice. It's the first time I've been called that."

48

There were several versions told afterward, in Darwin and indeed around the Territory, of what happened next, and whether it could have been avoided; whether it was just one of those things; whether it was accidental; whether it was planned; whether it grew out of a drunken conversation. The truth was, no one knew, or if they did they weren't saying, which may have meant that someone had deliberately planted an idea.

In any case, it appeared to start in the bar of a Darwin pub, the place where so many Outback stories started and so many of which never happened anywhere else, however strong they grew in the telling of them. But this one happened all right, happened on the night of the day the wounded black man was brought back to the hospital in Darwin, happened for a start with a conversation in the bar, over those quart-sized bottles of beer called Darwin stubbies, happened around the fifth or sixth stubbie, as the two Americans got talking to the two professional crocodile hunters. The Americans were expensively dressed, though in country-style clothes. Each was very wealthy and they said they had been on many hunting and fishing safaris together around the world. Whether this was the truth, no one ever knew or asked. For the Americans started talking to the professional crocodile hunters because the hunters were bemoaning the difficulty of finding good croc hunting sites anymore: of finding one decent, old-fashioned, strong and worthy croc opponent for sport, let alone for monetary gain.

The croc hunters were neither old nor young, mean or kind. They had that inevitable Australian Outback look about them, yet you could tell immediately they were neither bushies nor townies in the traditional sense. Perhaps they did have that slight look of men of prey about them, perhaps that was there in the hard-etched lines down their lean faces which seemed to pull their whole face masks down to their tight and thin-lipped mouths. Each had unruly brown hair, and a touch of stubble, and worn sunburn rather than a fresh-faced suntan. They were dressed in torn and tattered denims, with the sleeves torn out deliberately. They were in their mid-thirties, or their mid-forties; it was hard to tell. One had a heart and scroll tattooed on his left bicep; the word on the scroll said Mother. They had deep eyes, yet there was something lean about the eyes and nose of each, too. They looked very alike and indeed should have, for they were brothers, whose surname was Digger, and no one ever heard either of them called anything else, either as Christian name or surname, and no one ever seemed to mind which one answered, for each seemed to answer the same way, say the same things and with the same nasality. They had been hunting crocodiles for years. Between them, it was said, they had shot more estuarine crocodiles, more crocodiles of all kinds if it came to that, but more estuarine, too, more of the big ones, the giant, man-eating ones, more of them than any other two hunters alive; more kangaroos, too, if it came to that, and more wild dogs.

Whether by design or accident, the two Americans got talking to the two professional hunters. Whether by design or accident they asked them why no more big crocs could be found, for the Americans would pay highly, very highly indeed, they said, just to see and take a photograph of a big one. They had heard there was one nearly thirty feet long: about three hundred years old and thirty feet long. Could that be true? Could that possibly be true?

The two hunters exchanged glances, and then a smile (ever so slight, for smiling was not their forte), and they said it could be true; yes, possibly, it could be true. But it would be very risky and costly to find such a crocodile and they could not guarantee a photograph. If they got close enough to see him, they would have to shoot him, it was the only safe way. Well, said the Americans, if it couldn't be helped, it couldn't be helped: shoot him, then, by all means. As to the cost, that was nothing to them. Five thousand dollars—one thousand dollars a day for a five-day safari? Nothing. Happy to pay it. Where would they be going? To Crocodile River? Oh, good. But they must not mention it? Of course not. To the Carlyon property? Yes, the famous one, but they must not mention that either. To a place called Five Mile Camp, to the back of it where the old croc lived, so it was rumored. To Five Mile Camp? Wasn't that where the uranium was supposed to be? Hadn't they read about that in the morning paper? Sure, said the hunters. Had everything on that property, old Big Red did. But he was out of town, they said, so there'd never be a better time to try for his pet. His pet? Oh, yes, they reckoned he treated the croc like a pet. Impossible? No. True. They'd take some other croc skins out at the same time, if that was all right with their clients, said the hunters. Of course, said the American clients, whatever the hunters got out of it was their business. It was the big croc they wanted to see. Lived near Five Mile Camp, did it? What a fascinating sounding name—what interesting names so many places had. Yes sir, they'd look forward to this trip. Start the next day? Right. They were ready. Oh, better to start while Big Red was still away? Yes, they got the picture. They'd be ready at first light.

Those who overheard pieces of the conversation afterward said this was how it started—what they could remember anyway. Did the Americans deliberately start it? Of course not. It just grew out of a conversation over a few beers. Anyway, no one could foresee then what was going to happen, could they? How did they know it would turn out to be the biggest hunt in the Northern Territory's history? And over nothing, really. One simple complaint. It all got out of hand

and then every hunter wanted to get in on it. Poor Red, and him away.

It is said that of all creatures, big and small, domesticated and undomesticated, who have a sense of territory, the crocodile's is the strongest. A guard dog who snaps at the fingers even of little children who try to poke their hands at it through wrought-iron fences in the city?—nothing compared with an animal in the wild and no animal anything compared with a crocodile whose sense of territory is intruded on and old crocodiles nothing compared with the biggest and oldest who had reigned in the territory for three hundred years undisturbed, used to some human beings and their smell but not to the sudden movement and noise that came upon him that night at Five Mile Camp.

It was the night after the talk in the Darwin hotel, and however quiet and careful the hunters, the group of four, thought they might have been, they were sensed, or heard or smelled some miles off. A sense of noise—hearing—is very important to crocodiles.

The men had driven out from first light and made the part of the property they wanted by dusk. They were careful, for over the years the reputation of the Carlyon strictness and where the guards were placed, even the Aboriginal guards at Five Mile Camp, were known, although Big Red used a rotation system. But forty men over one million acres was hardly an army and now the agriculture inspectors were there looking for tick cattle; the ringers were out helping, too. It was a convenient time, almost a time that couldn't have been better if planned, you might say. Yet still the hunting men were wary. They knew, not by design or error, to tread anywhere near the front of Five Mile Camp, not to drive near or around it, for there were Aboriginal lookout points on the rocks no man could see from the outside. Of course everyone said it was just a stupid, bloody Abo game which Big Red joined in and it didn't mean anything at all; and then some old hand in the bar would say if the young buck saying that was so smart and wanted to come up against Big Red, why

didn't he bloody try to front the place, then? Hadn't they
heard of the Murranji Track, the old men would say. And the
young men would say, indeed, not only heard of it but driven
along it. And it was true; you could drive it in less than a day
now. And yet, some still didn't get through.

But these hunters this night were not foolish men. They
were cunning hunters, in torn jean suits, yes, but with special
cartridge holders stitched onto their sleeveless jackets, and
cartridge belts around their waists, and hunting knives
which they looked as if they could use, and beautiful modern
rifles, yet sweat-stained enough on the stock to see they knew
how to use them. These were men with portable spotlights
and a metal-bottomed boat upturned on the roof of their
Nissan four-wheel drive, with the thick treads and the crash
bars for wild boar charges and crash bars overhead, too, so
the cabin wouldn't crush if they rolled. They had spare petrol
and spare water and shovels to dig themselves out. They had
a small outboard for the boat; they had groundsheets and
tarpaulins and proper small tents. They had maps and
studied them, though they knew the terrain well enough
from landmarks over the years. They drank whiskey but not
too much. These men would bite the bullet. They knew their
business and now it was as much that as anything to them.
They were professional hunters.

They skirted well around Five Mile Camp and they
traveled in the last of the light to reach the back of it near the
river but far away enough not to be seen.

Then they quietly unloaded their boat, the metal boat, and
put the outboard motor on, and took their rifles and their
spotlights, and got into the boat and started the motor.

So much of the Outback is open, yet so much, too, is covered
with all sorts of unusual foliage and trees and undergrowth
and dead and regrowing bark that there are always natural
barriers to sound or sight of one sort or another.

But on this night—after a twilight like any other which
had been watched so often before by the old Aboriginal
guardian Crocodile Tommy, lean and stringy and muscly old
Crocodile Tommy, long and lean and grizzled around the eyes

by the sun, like all old black bushmen, and with a full head of pure white hair, thick and curling—a foreign sound was heard.

It might seem strange that for almost three-quarters of a century after the invention of the internal combustion engine, no such engine had been heard in that billabong by the river at Five Mile Camp; that a place could still exist on earth that had not heard the sound at least of an outboard motor, or smelled even the tiniest puff of petrol smoke. Yet it had not. There had never been any need. This was the place they had kept. Red had never seen the need to put a boat in there. Even their fishing for their beloved barramundi they had done downstream. This was, to all intents and purposes in the twentieth century, untouched land. And the animals knew it, and reacted accordingly.

Despite the natural barriers of tree and thick green growth at the water's edge, Tommy, high up in Five Mile Camp, in his waist string and pubic cover, and with his lubras near him by the campfire, heard the sound. There was no Aboriginal army guarding Five Mile Camp, as legend had it. With Jacky gone there was only Tommy now and his few lubras. But at the sound, the old man stirred from his place by the fire, where he warmed his old bones beside his women as they prepared supper, he stirred from the bark, lean-to wurley shelter near the rock ledge, he stirred and took up his woomera spear-throwing stick and his spear and his heavy pole club and nodded for his women to hurry to the main and narrow entrance near the rock pool, and to build a fire to warn Black Roo, while he went to find the outboard motor. For he was not an ignorant man, although he knew, as he walked gracefully but swiftly in his full tribal nakedness except for his cover, as he walked in the full pride and wisdom and fighting cunning of his eighty years, he knew that many thought tribal men stupid these days. But he had known and seen airplanes and cars and trucks and boats with outboard motors which Big Red used farther down the river. Tommy's acutely trained and inherited bush ear recorded and remembered such sounds, and as he went toward the Five

Mile Camp billabong, at the back entrance, he knew he went to trouble, for none of the people on the property came with boats and engines to this sacred land.

Of course, to the old man, not only was the land sacred, but the crocodile as well.

With bush instinct he hid where he could not be seen but could see and watch. And when he saw them with their lights upon the water he knew they had come to kill the precious and sacred thing. Yet he waited, waited hoping Black Roo would come with his rifle before he had to move. For if they caught Kismet, the three-hundred-year-old one which they all loved, if they caught him in their lights, then the old man would throw his spear—not to kill but to frighten.

He waited and watched. For a long time he stayed in the dark, watching yet thinking back over the years and missing Happy Jack, his friend, though he was from another tribe, for Crocodile Tommy was a local black. He remembered when Jacky had come and he remembered watching the night Big Red was born, watching from the rocks, for Tommy was one of the original inhabitants of what became known as Five Mile Camp. Soon he, too, would go to the Dreamtime. He would already have gone had it not been for Jacky's going and Red missing him so, and then his trouble, so that Tommy had stayed on, and, as he thought about this, it did not strike him as anything strange, for he knew, as Jacky had known, that a time comes.

But he did not expect it to come this night, suddenly, out of the dark; he did not expect to be wrenched from life, pulled like a tooth by the roots after such a gentle, leisured time on the wild, warm land of the North. But that night he was. For a moment later, he saw the boat slow, and the light drop down low, and, in the water, just a few feet from the boat, the light stopped on a giant croc's head. It was what Tommy had feared. Kismet was not an animal to let a strange noise disturb his territory. It was the noise that had brought him to the boat, a noise he would not distinguish from some other primeval animal that had come into his territory. Tommy saw a man in the boat rise to his feet and draw his rifle to him. Tommy's spear was already loaded in his spear thrower and he held and threw, threw to hit the man's rifle, which he did unerringly, taking him off-balance so he fell and went over the side. But as he threw he saw the flash of a light from the boat a split second before he heard the sound of the bullet fired toward him, and the old man in his eighty-first year threw himself to one side and the last thing he remembered, as another man in the boat turned his light to see the black man fall into the water, the last thing he remembered was the sound of a great thud against something and in his dying moments, as the water took him away, not as peacefully as he would have liked, but at least with the soft flow of water, he knew that the crocodile, his beloved crocodile, had struck the boat. At least he had given him that much time.

What ensued for the men in the boat was a nightmare in full force—a confused and strangled and frightened pattern imposed on the air of the night. As the denim-clad hunter had been knocked off balance and gone overboard, the croc had struck. But not for the hunter. The crocodile did not distinguish between man and boat and rifle and light. All was one. Here was a big animal with a strange sound and in all his three hundred years of strength Kismet struck first at the boat, biting right through the tin, and then at the source of the sound, crunching hard at the forged metal of the outboard motor. At the same time as trying to pull his brother back into the boat, for the men did not know the crocodile wanted to eat their boat and engine more than they, the hunter shouted at the American who had shot at the direction the spear had come from.

"Did you hit him?"

"How the hell should I know?" shouted the American who had acted on reflex and should never have been allowed a rifle anyway, though he was there to get close to Five Mile Camp or create an incident and he had, however unwittingly, done that.

"It doesn't matter if he hit him or not," said his friend who had turned the light on Tommy. "It doesn't matter if he hit him or not. The old man went down and into the water and he hasn't come up."

"How the hell do you know?" the hunter said. He was hauling his brother in and somehow, miraculously, the croc had gone. He did not know this was because the sudden shudder and biting at the motor had stalled the idling engine, thus stopping the foreign sound.

"I kept my light on him, that's how I know," said the American. "Jesus, do you think I don't wish I could say he was all right?"

"I don't know," said the Digger brother as the other lay gasping on the boat. It was holed where the teeth had bitten and filling with water rapidly. "I don't know," the man said, "but I do know that anyone who shoots nervously like your partner is a fool and that whether he hit him or not we have killed one of Big Red's blacks instead of his bloody crocodile and there is going to be all hell to pay."

He kept pulling at the cord on the outboard and finally got the engine started again and turned the boat back along the bank hurriedly to where they were parked, hoping he could reach the spot before the boat filled too much or before the croc struck again.

They barely made the riverbank and the two brothers dragged the boat in and drained and inverted it and left it where it stood and hurried the Americans into the four-wheel vehicle and drove off in great urgency.

"It can't be that serious," the American who had shot and who was the coolest of the two said, "it can't be that serious, it was an accident."

"Try telling that to Big Red when you see him—or any of his kids for that matter. Listen, mister, you'd better hope and pray we get off his property tonight without being caught."

"But you've left the boat."

"Sure. That's our insurance. We've only got one hope now. We've got to blame the crocodile. We've got to report to the Wildlife Department that the croc attacked us and the old Aboriginal tried to come to our help. We'll show them the boat to prove it. We were close in to shore and he tried to spear the croc away when my brother slipped overboard but the croc got him and nearly us. That's the story. It's our only hope."

"But that's admitting we were here. Wouldn't it be better to take the boat and say nothing?"

"No. They heard us in the pub, talking about it. Besides, if you want to risk taking the time to put the boat on and getting speared or shot in the back, go ahead."

"Are they really like that?"

"Do you really want to find out? Our only hope is to leave the boat as evidence, I tell you, and get official permission to go after the croc as a threat to human life. It'll help if you blokes post a bounty. Then we'll get some help and the attention won't all be on us. I know a lot who'd like nothing better than to come here for a shoot."

"That means there'll be hunters climbing all over the property, then?" the American said.

"That's the general idea."

"All right, if you say so," he said hesitatingly enough to sound as if he were being forced into it. "If you say so I'll post a bounty."

"Good," said the hunter. "Now let's make sure we get off of here before daylight and let's make sure everyone understands that the croc got the old man and has to be found and destroyed. It's the only way."

Black Roo had already arrived at Five Mile Camp in answer to the signal. He was freely allowed in as his father before him. When the lubras who were crying told him as much as they knew, he went to the river and searched all night. Later Ali came out to the river, and Jitangeli and John, and all the ringers who were on the homestead at the time. But it was no good. Crocodile Tommy was gone. When they found the boat, Roo immediately returned to the station house and radioed a complaint by two-way radio, reporting the boat registration number. But he feared what might come. The boat was evidence of a dangerous croc. And Crocodile Tommy was missing.

Alison felt physically sick to her stomach. John spoke to his father on the two-way radio—the only means of communication with Darwin from the property—early the next morning. Bluey said unfortunately it was already in the paper. An American tourist had offered a five-thousand-dollar bounty for the giant crocodile the paper described in its heading as a "rogue crocodile." He had said the crocodile was responsible for the death of an Aboriginal who had tried to help the tourists, who were simply on a bush safari to take photographs. The American said the crocodile had nearly killed one of his hunter-guides; it was a danger to human life and should be destroyed. But there was no word from the Wildlife Department yet. Alison had been thinking half the night and she now asked Bluey to send some documents out as soon as possible.

Ali and Roo then went down to the back of Five Mile Camp to search again in the daylight.

"Are we really sure he's gone?" Ali said hopefully as Roo picked his way along the riverbank, looking at footprints and signs, examining trees. Secretly Alison hoped it might be some cunning Aboriginal trick, that Crocodile Tommy might be in league with her father, who was not missing but hiding on the property after all. But Roo said,

"I'm afraid so, Al. All the signs suggest he stood here for some time and then slipped or fell. There's a chip on that mangrove tree which I suspect means they shot at him. It looks like a bullet grazed the tree, but I can't be sure: could have been a wild buffalo or a boar or anything. But probably was a bullet and I suspect he jumped aside. There's no sign of any blood. He was very old. I think he slipped as he jumped aside and probably hit his head as he went down on that rock there."

He pointed. Ali looked and felt sick to her stomach again. It was, ironically, the rock just below the water in the sun which Kismet loved so: the place where he had lain on his belly in the sun for so many hours, for so many years.

Despite all their fears, no open season was declared. The men in Sydney who had so carefully orchestrated this thing did not want mass slaughter of crocodiles by men not in their

employ. That would come later. It was true that they had
wanted a closer look at Five Mile Camp. They had not
foreseen that the crocodile himself would be such an immediate protagonist for his own domain, striking almost as soon
as they entered his home waters. Nor had they foreseen that
an old black man would accidentally die. They had known
Big Red's thought patterns well enough, these men in
Sydney, for they had expert family advice, and knew that,
within reason, he would not murder to keep men off his land.
The threat was in the man himself, and his presence, and his
ability to frighten, persuade, outwit, all who would come. But
with him off the property, perhaps with the captain away, the
soldiers would be sleeping. But they had not reckoned on the
black man's determination, nor had they reckoned on the
absolute fearlessness of the animal itself. Of course, these
were city men, and they did not realize the full extent of the
saying that, among all beasts, and species of beasts, there are
leaders, too, and kings, and that, on that particular night,
their hastily contrived expedition had met the sleeping giant
of the land with three hundred years of history etched in
every ring of his shining white and armor-plated belly. He
was, by all accounts, a giant. The biggest croc even the
professional hunters had seen. The two Americans from the
agricultural company were terrified as they spoke to Douglas
on the phone. They had indeed been on millionaires' safaris
around the world. They had even seen crocodiles before. But
this was a giant. This was thirty feet long. It was like a
primeval leftover, a prehistoric echo, a dark, Freudian,
atavistic image, a phylogenetic shadow of the past.

Douglas let the hyperactive American, with his college
ring on his finger and his college education, talk himself out.
Then he said with a business coolness, almost a bush cool-
headedness that his elder brother might have approved,

"I told you not to go near Five Mile Camp—just to get the
crocodile. We'll find out about Five Mile Camp in good time.
But we need the property to incorporate in our books before
the next financial year. All of us concerned with your
operation in Australia do. The books have to be right for the
auditor before the next board meeting or you won't be safe

either. So just do as you're told. I know what will hurt him most. We've got his cattle pinned down so he can't sell; we've got his lines of credit blocked beyond three months. Now I want to hit him where it hurts. To him that crocodile represents everything he stands for. Get it and you get him. By your ill management it now looks as if we're going to get others to do the job for us. But you make sure our man in Darwin does his job, and does it properly. I don't want any open season. I just want that one croc. We'll cash in on the others when we get the property. And stay away from Five Mile Camp, I tell you. I want to know what's there as much as the next man. But knowing what's there won't fix the books for this year. And I'll tell you one thing. Try to invade Five Mile Camp and you *will* start a war. Remember old Red is just missing. He could be cooking up anything. But even without him, those kids of his will defend that place to the last ditch. So no more shooting at people and no more trying to do anything other than get the crocodile. Anything else and we'll have the police in and inquiries and God knows what else and we'll never get the property in time. Now you people get down there and identify the boat and keep up your tourist story and then get on with the business of getting that croc. That's the body blow we want. Unless I miss my guess, that will send him reeling. Then he'll sell. Make it look good. Make it look like righteous indignation against this terrible rogue crocodile: this man-eater. Get the TV people in on it. Make it a media crusade. But you handle it from up there. You're just an indignant American tourist."

"All right, all right," the man at the other end of the telephone said angrily, lighting a large cigar. He was a millionaire in his own right and hated being talked down to like a schoolboy, particularly by this uppity Australian. But he and his American friend had backed the Australian project, and then covered it up, with the help of this sharp Sydney accountant. They were in it together now and must rationalize the books before the parent company which had recently taken them over found out. But the American wanted the uranium. Then he could tell the parent company to go jump; then his company would be the top one in the operation once more. But the Australian was right. They must get the cattle property first. "All right, all right, I'll fix it," he said, and hung up heavily.

He puffed on his cigar and then dialed a local Darwin number from his hotel. "No open season," the American said as an Australian voice answered. "Absolutely no open season. Just the big crocodile. Just the one."

Alison had let Roo ride back alone and now sat on the rock her father always sat on, looking at the large, flat stone ledge which was Kismet's invariable resting spot, except for today.

It was now the fourth day since her father had left. Although she put a brave face on it (for little Jitangeli looked as if she might cry any minute—well, not so little, she was twenty-three now), she was worried. She could only assume he was doing something he would not trust to be communicated over the open line of the two-way radio. She worried, but also, like a little girl, had childish faith that he was again hatching some wonderful plot to get them out of their difficulty. Yet with that strange dichotomy of the human race, which she had studied thoughtfully enough at the university, but found so hard to put into practice, there were her feelings, and the objective truth. Whatever her feelings, her fantasies, the state of innocence she would like to regress to where these things did not happen, they were indeed happening, unfolding before her eyes: the last of tomorrow, as Red used cynically to call it, was unfolding before her. The Territory way of life they had known was changing. They had, indeed, despite all the vicissitudes, lived in a sort of protected innocence for over a century. But now it was changing and disappearing. Big Red's dilemma, the loss he faced, the loss they all faced, was part of a larger pattern. She knew that. She knew there was this strange old and new in her, too. When on the property, she reverted to her truculent tomboy role, the outdoors golden girl. Yet there was the quieter side of her, too: the side that appealed to the sensitive, businessman-poet John, she supposed. He seemed to hold old and new in a much better balance than she. He loved the new technology, he loved his work, yet he did not harshly use people. Perhaps the latter was an inheritance from his father. Perhaps the next generation, perhaps their children, if she had John and they had children, would have lost this . . .? common touch. Was it that? Was that what this part of the world gave? Was that what was passing? If it was, it was a sad day. For to the best of her knowledge none of it was left anywhere else in the world.

She rose and walked over to her horse, walked to the beloved Ghost Gum, the Goondiwindi gray, the best of the breed, who was old himself now, and she patted his flank, and nuzzled him, and gave him a sugar lump from her pocket which she took with her always when she rode, always something for her horse, for in this country she sometimes thought he was the best and truest part of it and when so many now did everything from the seat of a four-wheel-drive vehicle, a vehicle padded all around with cruel metal crash bars for herding and charging the wild buffalo and the wild scrub bulls and even kangaroos they all said were such a threat to the land, eating out the feed for the prime stock. She indeed wondered where the world was going when they were not even happy with this and were bringing in helicopters to herd and computers to record and air boats so that even the Wet, the blessed, locked-in Wet when everything and everyone took their rest, and chatted idly and let things replenish as nature watered, so that even the Wet would be gone: they would even take a season away.

She knew she was foolish to think this way, for she was an educated woman. Yet education could educate feelings out of you, make you so smart that you had a label to knock everything, so that everyone was thinking up sayings to outsmart everyone else. You could study psychology and not come into contact with yourself. She wondered which might be better: an honors degree in a fashionable modern subject, or a pass degree on the land? But *there* was the trouble. You wouldn't be able to get the latter anymore. The next generation of jackeroos was going to be helicopter pilots.

Yet as she thought this last thought, something had slipped into her field of vision so that she looked, and there, on the rock, in the sun, on the rock ledge he loved so much, was Kismet the Brave.

"Oh, darling," she said to herself but half aloud also, hardly aware she was talking, "oh, darling," she said, "please don't let them get you. Be smarter and more cunning, please. Find an underwater cave. Go back along the river to the ocean. It'll kill Red if they get you and I'll never forgive myself if anything happens to you. But everything's changing and it's not safe here anymore. The hunters have finally found their way in and they're at the gates of Shangri-La."

A tall shadow fell over the water between her and the crocodile and she gave a sudden start, thinking first it was a stranger and then that it was her father. But it was just Roo back again.

"The men from the Wildlife Department are here," he said softly. "They're along the river inspecting the boat and the outboard. The men who came last night are with them. Will you come?"

She sat for an instant longer, coming back from a long way, coming back to the present, almost it seemed, from a part in which she had recollected more than she had known.

"Yes, I'll come," she said quietly, as she got her grip back on reality. "Yes, I'll come. I've got something to say to them."

As she walked quietly with her horse, Roo walked beside her but did not talk. With his unerring Aboriginal instinct he knew when she needed personal space, knew when she had been to the Dreamtime of his ancestors and back. She loved him so for understanding, and for his protection, and for the way he loved Jitangeli but would not let himself know. Soon she must find a way to tell him, or Jitangeli must. Alison had this terrible feeling that so many things had to be done in a hurry now. As she walked she looked at the sky and even thought it might rain, although she knew full well that the season of monsoons and cyclones, the season they called the Wet, was a full three months off. Well, it could be a little unpredictable. Three months: give or take.

She steeled herself for the conversation with the men she must talk to. She was really feeling quite down, depressed.

But she must be in full control; she must be her father's daughter. She wondered how well the others understood the conflict that was always in her: her tomboy exterior and her yearning feminine interior. Her mother understood. Alison was half-and-half, all right. Is that what parents want? Well, let's call up the father part.

She sighed with relief when she saw Bill was there. He was one of the two wildlife officers who had accompanied the men, the four men who had started this and at whom she stared in disgust, completely ignoring the introduction from Bill but greeting him warmly with a kiss just under the chin. He was a little older than she, although he always looked so freshly washed and laundered in his uniform, and too young to be anything, he was so boyish. But he was good at his job and smiled and gave Ali a hug as she kissed him. He was not intimidated by the look of the Americans. The two professional hunters were staying right out of it. They didn't want any more trouble than there was already.

"Bring the warrants?" Ali now asked Bill.

"Sure. Old Bluey phoned me early—just after you radioed in. Want them now?"

Ali nodded. "First things first. Got a pen?" He handed her some documents and a pen from a slot in his neatly pressed khaki shirt. Ali bent down and signed all four on her knee.

"There now, gentlemen," she said, turning to the two Americans and two hunters, "there's a civil charge of trespassing, and a criminal charge of attempted murder. We'll see you in court."

The Americans looked at each other, then at the wildlife officer.

"How can you do this," the stronger of the two said, "you're just a wildlife officer?"

"Yes, that's right. I was just delivering some mail to a friend. A friend in town asked me to bring some papers out to the lady here. We all deliver mail for each other in the Outback—it's an old custom."

"But *we* came to swear out a complaint."

"Well, we've got that and I've seen your boat and now we can be going."

"I'll keep the boat, Bill, in case Big Red wants to do something more about it."

"Can she do that?"

"I suspect so. It's her property and the boat was left here by trespassers. The old man's home, then, is he Al?" Bill said, giving her a wink away from the others.

"Got back just before you. Just having a shower and a change."

"Oh, good, give him my regards. I'll pass these forms on to Bluey."

"If you'd be so kind. Sorry there's not time for tea but I want the vermin off the place and locked up by tonight."

"I think that would be the normal course of events. I suppose someone will radio ahead so Bluey can have the appropriate authorities meet the plane?"

"I guess," Alison said.

"What about the hunt?" said the American, still disbelieving.

"I'm afraid others will be doing that for you, mister," the wildlife officer Bill said. "Other vermin . . . because there's not one decent hunter in the Territory will come on this place knowing how Big Red feels. Even if they disagree with his stand they'll respect his wishes. In any case, only hunters with permits will be allowed and I doubt you four would get them."

"Are you threatening us, officer?"

"Don't be a stupid smart arse with me, mister. You walked out on a limb on the Carlyon property. If you don't expect them and their friends around here to help saw that limb off legally, you've got rocks for brains. If you weren't with me today I'd fear for your safety if you went near the river, despite the good nature of these people. That poor old croc will probably finish up dead, if that's what you wanted, but you won't get to do the shooting. This lady here has tied you up with enough papers to keep you in Darwin for about a year, I reckon. Things get awfully slow here, with all the red tape."

He turned to Alison slowly. "I'm terribly sorry, Al. The department had no alternative. Looked for a while as if we might have to declare open season."

"Yes, we were worried about that. What happened?"

"Some joker rang and put up a good argument. Don't know who it was. Course we didn't need too much convincing."

"Thanks."

"You know we're on your side within the limits but we'll have to issue about a hundred permits. None of the true bushies will come, but there'll still be some good shots among the bounty hunters. Of course some of our own people will have to supervise, although most of us have been shooting terribly lately."

The Americans looked at each other as if they could not believe what they were hearing. The two professional hunters remained quiet. They knew they were in enough trouble as it was.

"When, then, Bill?" she asked as she walked him to the Land Rover which Roo had driven them in from the plane.

"We've said starting at first light tomorrow, Al. For ten days from tomorrow. Then, if they haven't caught him, we'll review the situation. If there haven't been any more alleged attacks by then you might be away free because I can't see them tying up too many field officers beyond that."

"Thanks for everything, Bill." She kissed him again as he got in the vehicle.

"Anytime. You're riding back?"

She nodded.

"Is that still Ghost Gum?"

"Yes."

"He's getting on."

"Yes, yes, he is. Come out and stay for a weekend when all this is over, huh?"

"Sure. Take care."

"And you."

She nodded to Roo as he drove off and as she nuzzled her horse again she thought about Bill who had come up to the Territory as a jackeroo when he had turned eighteen and worked first on their property. He had been her first boyfriend, and the tenderness was still there, and he loved the bush and her family so. He was Lisa's grandson.

49

Red was in the air, on his way back from America. He was certainly impressed with the service of this airline he had helped to found, although he'd had the dickens of a job keeping his trip quiet. He'd rung one of the board members and said please could he slip him on one of the aircraft quietly, for he had to make a quick trip incognito to the States? The man had said yes, that would be fine, assumed name and everything. But somewhere along the line someone had got carried away, for Red had not previously flown in one of the big double-decker jets as he called them; hadn't seen the need. So when he'd arrived at the airport, it was like the most open well-kept secret he'd ever seen. It was wink, wink everywhere and such hushed, red-carpet treatment that everyone wondered who he was. Well he hoped no one would recognize him, for it was important to get to America and back without being recognized. He was worried about the kids and not telling them, but, what the hell, they'd been trained to be independent, and now was as good a time as any to be thrown in at the deep end. They'd have a few heart stoppers without him, but that was life.

He'd read about the crocodile thing in America, and that had been a heart stopper for *him*. The American newspapers loved those last-frontier stories about tourists being chased by crocodiles in Australia. When he'd first gone to America many years ago someone had asked him whether he had learned to speak English before he arrived in America. Red had replied that he didn't speak English, it just sounded a bit like it, well, not even that really: ask an Englishman. The same man had then been subjected—much to the amusement of Red's host, who had spent a little time in Australia—to Red's string of bush campfire stories: most, if not all, were apocryphal. Red explained how he told the difference between a crocodile and alligator by opening the mouth of each and looking in with a flashlight to count the number of teeth. Yes, the flashlight was very important: it got very dark very quickly in there. Red neglected to tell the man there were no alligators—only crocodiles. Of course the man didn't quite understand all of Red's jokes, especially some of the kangaroo ones, and certainly not the one about what a man did in the Outback if a kangaroo jumped in beside him on the front seat of his four-wheel drive. Although Red suspected the man's wife understood when Red had said what you did depended on whether the kangaroo was male or female, and he reckoned that American women were good on the whole, and he'd had a wonderful time, but that was all those years ago and he had only seen his American friend once in the intervening years until this trip, but he'd loved his earlier trip to America, loved the whole damned big country and loved to tell them that Australia was bigger than America, which some didn't swallow, so Red brought the maps and statistics out of his pocket to show them. That had been a great party stopper for a while. That had stopped some of the asinine questions about kangaroos.

But that was the previous trip, not this one. He was recollecting again. That was a nice word. Wandering was more like it. Hell, everyone did that on a plane, didn't they? Wasn't that what planes were for—so you could daydream in the clouds? Not in the war, no sir, not in the war over the Somme: not when he first flew, not yesterday, not over half a century ago. Was Douglas right—was he really a bit off? He'd seen men go very funny after even one day without water in the desert: go right off their scone they would. Scone? Head. Why was he using so many words from the old days? *God, that Douglas knew how to hit below the belt*. Poor old Kismet. Red wasn't as worried as the kids would be, though. He knew Kismet better than they did. He and Kismet were like that, just like that. They knew each other backward. It'd take more than a couple of dumb American businessmen trying to be cattle farmers in the Outback to outsmart his old croc; more than a couple of good hunters, too; more than a hundred good hunters on a ten-day shoot, though that would be a problem; but he would be there to help. He and Kismet, he and Kismet and Captain Bluey: Kismet and Major Red and Captain Bluey, they'd take 'em on.

"Another drink, Sir James?" (Sir Red, son: red like your chief steward's jacket, red like the kangaroo on the plane's tail, red like the country, red like blood. Understand all that? No? Not sure I do, but don't worry, I'm not going to confuse two of us by telling you.)

"You're very kind. A little more of the Dom, and easy on the name."

"Of course, sir, you're right. I was told. It's just there's no one around up here in the lounge—just you and me."

"Don't take any notice, it's just that I'm tired."

"Of course, sir. It's been a pleasure to meet you."

"They're nice aircraft and you're nice people."

"You must fly with us again one day, sir, one day when we can take you up into the cockpit."

"I'd like that but I don't think so."

"Oh, well, you never know, sir."

"That's right, you never know—that's the one thing you always know."

The flight steward smiled and moved off quietly. He was young to be so senior. He shouldn't have called him son, even to himself, but he didn't seem to mind. He did seem genuinely pleased to meet Red. Was Red a living legend? There was a thought—a legend in his own lifetime. What the hell did that mean? Old and well known? That a newspaper had written about you? Kismet had that now. Old and written about. Did that make him a living legend? Hell no: Kismet had been a living legend before Red was born. Three hundred years old, the old bastard, and they reckoned they'd finally get him, did they?

Getting back into Darwin was the hard part. In the end he flew to Brisbane and phoned Bluey and asked him to fly over and pick him up.

"Christ, you sound happier than anyone around here," Bluey said on the phone, almost sounding disappointed, as if Red had deserted him in his hour of need, cheated him out of his one chance to comfort Red for a change.

"Well, is anyone playing taps over there yet, Blue? I sure to hell haven't heard them playing the last post for me yet, though I do admit to having some qualms about hearing angels' feathers on the way home if you're going to do the flying."

"Hire a plane and fly yourself, then."

"I'm broke—you know that. Millions of dollars and no liquidity. It's so bad I'll even trust myself to *your* flying, there you are."

"Where the hell you been, anyway? The kids have been frantic."

"They'll be all right. Don't tell them, though. Need secrecy. They'll wake up I'm back soon enough, but don't want the opposition hearing anything over that bloody open, homestead, air-ambulance, school-of-the-air, two-way radio invention."

"You didn't say where you've been."

"Correct. Not saying. Kismet comes first. See you in a few hours. I'll wait at the domestic hangars for you. Know a bloke there I can trust."

After he hung up, Red had a few hours to kill so he went to a pub and propped and had a few beers and thought how long it had been since he'd had just a couple of quiet hours to himself to have a few quiet glasses of ale, and what a luxury it was to lean against the bar, and not be known, for the public didn't really recognize him in a crowd, he knew that, he wasn't that well known. And he thought this was a good part of Australia, this easy camaraderie, these suburban blokes just having a few jars before going home, a few jugs, just one or two or ten. And what the hell, for he knew that in not being one of these city jokers he'd missed something, too, and wondered whether he had really been cut out to be a living legend, or whether it was something he'd had to be, whatever you called it, had to be like a disease; and if the cruelest part of all wasn't to get to this time of your life and face losing what was most important to you, and wonder if you wouldn't have been just as happy with a few drinks after work, and a timber house and the wife and kids and flowers in the garden and the beach to go to on the weekend. Perhaps, if he'd married Lisa, and moved to town, which was what he'd always feared she'd somehow manage to get him to do, or later, moved early into town with Annie—for she'd have married him for a steady proper home, he knew that— perhaps he'd have been happier.

Oh, well, he'd had a good time, one hell of a good time when you considered it, and no regrets—well, no more than most, no more than anyone, no more than an ordinary human's life cycle of luck. He'd had his good luck and his bad, and he'd taken the latter on the chin and the former with a happy bursting heart, and he'd take what was coming his way now as he always had, with his face in the wind, his body bent to it, driving hard into it, telling it come what may, this tree would not snap easily against it and there'd be a bit of old-fashioned, good-humored acceptance along the way, however hard and dry the track, and he'd been along one or two of those, yes sir.

They went about their preparations, these two, secretly, at the stables at the back of the gracious old home where so long ago Red had tethered his horse when he'd first come to stay; they went about them secretly as if preparing for the first and second wars they had fought in, combined; though their ammunition was little enough: a host of spotlights and car batteries and jerry cans of kerosene. The plan, which Red had thought about on the plane coming back, and now explained to Bluey as they loaded up the Land Rover, was simple enough. They would hide along the banks of the billabongs at the spots which Red knew over the years Kismet liked most to frequent. They could not hope to cover the whole hundred hunters or so who would be there, but they could cover those who came near Kismet's favorite spots—all of which were in a reasonably small area close to Five Mile Camp. "Got lazier and lazier, the old bastard, as he got older"—Red explained to Bluey.

At nighttime, if any of the hunters appeared to sight Kismet, then Red and Bluey, from the banks, would shine the powerful spotlights in their eyes, or at least on their heads. "Funny thing, you know, Blue. For years hunters have been trapping all sorts of animals by hitting them with a spotlight, so that they freeze and then the hunter shoots them, doing this and acting as if the animals were particularly dumb to freeze in the light, as if they were afraid of the light. Well, we're going to do some experiments which old Pavlov and the rats-and-stats scientists would be proud of. We're going to prove that a human hit suddenly with a heavy, fierce light coming out of nowhere in the middle of the night gets just as surprised as the so-called dumb animals he's hunting."

"And the kero?" asked Bluey.

"We'll pour it on the water and light it, if too many hunters get too close to old Kismet. One bullet won't kill him, that's for sure. And he hates fires that old boy. If we light the surface of the water, he'll swim under it way out of the region and it'll be interesting to see the intrepid hunters scurry out of the way."

"Will the rangers allow all this?"

"I don't know, Blue. But first, they've got to catch us—if, indeed, they decide to try, for most of those guys will be on my side, I know. Then, even if they do catch us, which might take them a day or two, if we're any good at all still, what's to stop me using spots on my own land? They'll all be doing it. I could even claim I was just giving them a bit of extra light. As for the kero, well, it's coming up to the Wet and tick fever has allegedly been reported on my property; a man would be a fool not to be burning his billabongs off, wouldn't he, getting rid of all those mosquito larvae and making sure there were no tick eggs around? Now in the daytime, all we're going to do if they get close, or someone fires at old leatherhead, is just bang loudly with sticks on the kero cans: just bang loudly in Aboriginal fashion. You see, noise is both our big danger and big weapon. Crocs hate any foreign noise in their territory. I bet that's how those guys even got to see the old fellar last time. It'd be the sound of the outboard for sure. That'd be a new and strange sound to old Kismet. Well, if the outboards attract him again—which they won't necessarily as much the second time, but they might—we'll just bang very loudly to turn his attention to another foreign sound elsewhere."

"And if all else fails—?"

"If all else fails and someone appears to have a good quick bead on him, we shoot over the bastard's head. The noise of the shot—probably use duck cartridges—should disturb both the hunter and the croc. No danger, no real danger in any of this for human life, and I don't see how anyone can prosecute me—even if they do come looking and find me—for shooting at wild geese in the air, burning off the water, banging cans or using spotlights on my own property. The only thing you've got to worry about is that you might get classed with me as being a bit crazy if we're found walking around banging kero cans. But don't worry, you get used to it. After a while you don't even notice their sideways looks."

"You're almost enjoying this, aren't you?"

"Operative word being *almost*. I wish to Christ it had never happened—none of it. But no one wrote me a mortgage on good luck to the end of my days, and I'm sure to hell not going to stop looking danger in the eye at my age, or stop trying to do something about it, when it threatens me or mine, or stop trying to live life with a smile. That'd be mean and miserable. Life's too good for that, whatever happens."

Bluey went to find some of his gardener's clothes, which would be closer to Red's size. They had two slugs of whiskey each while Red changed. Then they loaded the rest of the stuff, in silence, and headed out of town toward the bush. They had missed one full day already.

That morning, just after dawn, just after the geese had lifted off at first light, one hundred hunters, exactly one hundred, licensed by the Wildlife Department, had invaded the cattle station, the cattle run they called the Back of Beyond: the lands that had been closed so long. The species, regarded as predatory by so many of the hunters, yet which had been protected so long, unreasonably they felt, by this idiosyncratic old bastard, Big Red Carlyon, was now open to them—or at least the oldest living representative of the species. In Darwin, and in the Territory, there was no doubt that this was the hunt of the century. At dawn that day, in convoy, in their four-wheel-drive vehicles, from where they had camped in the bush outside the boundaries during the night, the hunters finally came to the last of the last frontier.

50

What makes a hunt so special? It could hardly be the life at stake, Alison thought, as she sat and shivered a little beside the fire Roo had built for her at the back of Five Mile Camp. He'd still not let her enter the camp, although he himself was back there now, while she watched from the fire, with her rifle beside her and Bill sitting next to her, Bill whom they'd put in charge of the hunt and who'd agreed that Five Mile Camp was out of bounds and an unlikely area to find the croc anyway.

John had finally gone back to Sydney. He'd hated to leave, but he had his business to attend to and there was still the matter of keeping the publicity and business rumors going to support Red's counteroffer for the American property. No answer had been received yet, so John had assumed they'd not deliver it personally to the property but to his office in Sydney—if they delivered it at all. So he had flown out that morning and Alison was glad of the company of Bill and glad he was in charge, for things would be done properly. But for the moment she was hardly aware of his presence as she sat on a rock by the fire in her jodhpurs and riding boots, and her knees hunched up to the white cotton man's shirt she wore, an old shirt of her father's which was a little too big for her, except at the front, for she had a country girl's front, no mistake about that, she said to herself, as she hugged her legs to it and felt the warm and pleasant sensation of this self-comfort. Her blond and brown long hair hung loose over the shirt collar and the yellow firelight was unkind to the tiredness under her eyes.

What did make a hunt so special? Life was at stake every day for everyone, in one sense, on the land or in the city. One could be hit by a car, electrocuted, charged by a wild boar or bitten by a snake. But these were accidents. She knew that was really the difference. It was the intent, the cold-blooded, deliberate intent, that made a hunt so chilling, Alison decided. It was quite different from any other form of killing. It was planned, deliberated killing: killing by agreement, by design, by contract: assassination decided upon in advance. She could better understand, though she did not like it, the killing of the introduced water buffalo, whose proliferating members were trampling out the scarce and vital feed for so many natural species; or the wild boar pests; or the feral cats who ate baby wallabies, baby kangaroos. She understood about survival of the species and the natural versus introduced species. But that was just the point. The crocodiles were indigenous: part of the whole ecosystem. Whatever his reasons, her father had kept that part of the property as it had been since the world began. But no longer. The billabong, the lagoon out beyond her eyes, was now full of metal boats loaded with men and spotlights. Though there'd been no sign of Kismet. Two other crocs had nearly been shot, however, and Ali began to see that the accidental shooting, or claimed accidental shooting, of other crocs could be a danger. Bill and his men had been very strict about this and the ones nearly shot at had not been big at all. But it was difficult to tell from a quick look at a croc's head going by, or coming out of the water quickly, what the size really was.

"Well, how will we know if it's really him?" one of the hunters had asked Bill, for these men, though professional hunters, had made their living by shooting blindly at any croc for years, not always seeing the full size, or lack of it (for many shot the baby twelve-footers), until the croc was dead and out of the water.

"I reckon you'll know it's him when he bites a hole in your boat and attacks your outboard motor," Bill said.

The man looked at him as if he were crazy, although all had seen the marks Kismet had made on the boat the other night and stood in awe of him. The teeth marks looked as if a heavy metal pick had been driven right through the metal hull of the boat four times. And the metal casting of the outboard motor revealed not only three places where the black paint had been chipped right off with the teeth marks, but two places in which not only was the paint gone but the metal indented slightly, too. It was incredible the strength of the jaws, and every hunter had seen the boat and the motor where it still lay on the bank, and however brave and tough these Territorian hunters appeared, and one or two from the South, and the television crews, everyone was scared as hell. It might be five thousand dollars to the winner, but that had to be placed against the Russian roulette which the land and its waterways always managed to put up against anyone who would intrude upon them. Every man in every boat, every man jack of them, knew that at any moment, without warning, this biggest of all crocodiles could sweep up from beneath them and without warning the teeth strong enough to bite into a large metal outboard motor would be around them. Against the metal on that motor, bones were minor matchsticks.

Yet although this was a comfort to Alison in a sense, that Kismet could indeed defend himself, it was also her greatest worry. There had never been any guarantee that he would not attack a human. There was no agreement, however much Red joked about him and the croc having an understanding to leave him and his alone. Red had always been careful to sit on the same rock in the same place and never tempt Kismet with an idly dangled foot. Now Alison knew the croc had not killed Tommy. There would have been some sign of it. But if, in addition to the suspicion of killing Tommy, he actually killed one of these hunters during the next nine days, then he would be labeled a man-eater for sure, and any chance of a remission after the hunt ended would be gone forever. But if they cornered Kismet, if they harried him or hurt him, if someone landed a shot but did not kill, oh, would he come at them, and then there would be all hell to pay. Some did not believe that crocs could live that old and be that big. But they could; and, to a croc like that, every extra year, up to a certain point, was a year of strength. She believed him to be at the height of his powers now. Soon they would wane. But if he was going to strike out at those who came for him, he certainly still had the strength to do it.

Bill put his arm around her, like the old friend he was, and she wondered what it was she felt for him. It was something quieter than what she felt for John, something less intense in a way. She and Bill had been such amateur lovers, and each made so many fumbling mistakes, for each had been the first for the other, that it seemed to give them an easiness with each other whenever they met afterward, as if each had known the other's innocence and ignorance, and been kind to it, so that it was carried as in a pocket by each of them, so that forever afterward the words would be soft and the feelings kind and one could put one's hand in the other's pocket and find there still the absolute freshness and inno- cence—sensitive touch of the first hand holding hand, and then all the other wonderful things that make up one's first love. It was an interesting feeling to articulate after all these years, Alison thought, for she'd seen Bill a few times off and on since then, but somehow the feeling had come up from her unconscious stronger this night, strong enough to point itself out, perhaps stronger because she was, in a real sense, weaker herself this night, and needed to regress, needed to run away to that state of innocence where nasty things didn't happen. And she wondered, wondered and then knew that if Bill were to ask her, she would sleep with him that night for old times' sake. At least, that's what she'd tell herself.

As the hunters roused themselves at first light on that next day, as the mist lifted and a hot wind sprang up with the sun, it was like a ghostly dawn on a battlefield, like some pre- Napoleonic day of reckoning, the men strangely quiet and disoriented as they awoke in singlets and trousers with braces hanging down and shaved absentmindedly with lather and old-fashioned cutthroat razors some of them, shaving by feel, rubbing the flats of their callused hands over the stubble of their chins to see if it was close enough, then stoking up the campfires, and making tea, and finding khaki or checked or denim shirts in their tents.

Then the mood changed, and as the camp became finally awake and knew what it was about, that they had a common purpose this day, a common yet competitive purpose to find and kill for money, the mood changed all right, and rifles were checked and oiled, and cartridge belts filled, and hats pulled on tight and determinedly as the anxious ones set off without breakfast, just with a cup of tea and some cold beef and bush bread from the previous night as a sandwich, set off to stalk the banks for signs, for signs in the sand or the light undergrowth at the edge that would tell them the creature they sought had passed that way during the night. These were the true professionals, these men who were out early for the battle, before anyone could trample down the signs of the night, these were the good bushmen and the ones Red feared, however much he hated them, as he watched from the trees back from the bank on the opposite side of the billabong of Five Mile Camp.

He and Bluey had arrived just after midnight and driven down and hidden the Land Rover in the brush and rolled out their swag and gone immediately to sleep, for only a handful of the hunters were out on the water after midnight, and nowhere near any spot Kismet liked to be.

But these others were the men who concerned Red, these men who were out early this morning. They wore old army battle fatigues, purchased from disposal stores, no doubt, yet they looked the right age to have fought in the war and they all wore slouch hats, army slouch hats all of them, with the pinup side down against the sun, and the hats looked old and worn, and the men looked like old and good diggers to Red, who did not agree with what they were doing, but he knew by looking at them they knew their job and they were the enemy and he wished he didn't feel a slight sympathy for their professionalism. He'd bet they were the ones who were out late last night. They were systematically searching for signs, these men. They were in no hurry. They did not mind if they wasted five or six days putting the crocodile's geography into their heads. They would not shoot the wrong crocodile. They'd watch the mistakes the other hunters made, watch where any sighted crocs made for, looking all the time, with their bare eyes, through their field glasses, looking all the time for a pattern.

Red took his field glasses from his eyes for a moment and turned to Bluey, who let his fall down onto the strap around his neck.

"What do you think?" Red said.

"Yeah, those boys know their business, all right. They're the enemy. In a few days they're going to have as good an idea as you have where to find the old boy—maybe better because they can move around and see his latest patterns. He might have changed his routine, you know."

"I know. I'm going to have to deal Roo in on our little operation. There's no alternative. I didn't think anyone as good as these guys would come. Most as good as them know me and wouldn't set foot here at this time because of our friendship."

"Could be down from New Guinea."

"Yeah, probably. Anyway, we've got opposition we didn't expect. I'll need Roo's blacktracking ability. Have to leave Five Mile Camp to Ali."

"We'd better keep moving if we're going to keep up on this side with those four on the other side of the bank. I guess that is the idea, is it?"

"You're right. Got your kerosene tin?"

He looked at Red down his nose. "Some last battle," he said with feigned disgust, "two old jokers with a stick and a kerosene tin apiece."

The men on the far bank moved purposefully. "I don't like this," the leader said, "I don't like it at all. We shouldn't have taken this job from those Americans. They didn't tell us the full facts. They didn't tell us this was a bounty hunter's job. Half the blokes in that camp are vermin I wouldn't let near the worst man-eater I've ever shot."

"The money was too good *not* to come. What they're paying us makes the bounty incidental. What are you going to do now, anyway, go back home so we make a loss on the job? Half now and the balance at the end of the ten-day period, that was the deal."

"I still don't like it. I was talking to the head ranger last night and he reckons the joker whose place we're on is a good bloke."

"Well, he can be a good bloke and still have a mean croc, can't he? Half the blokes we've shot crocs for around the world have been good blokes. Half the crocs we've shot in New Guinea have probably been good crocs. But you can't stop and ask them, 'excuse me, you three-hundred-year-old leatherhead with all those lovely teeth, excuse me, sir, but are you good, bad or indifferent? We'd so much like to know before we pump six shells into your lovely old hide.'"

The second man who had spoken was the key man of the four-man team, they all knew that. The leader was the businessman. They were all ex-army who'd stayed on after the liberation of New Guinea. They lived like kings in that tropical paradise to the north of Australia, lived like the British in Colonial days, lived still with gin and tonics and servants in long-verandaed bungalows. But when they worked they worked and they were the best at their job there was. These were the best crocodile hunters in the world and the mention of New Guinea by Bluey had sent a chill down Red's spine, for he knew of these men. But the gun among them was the second man who had spoken, he was the gun hunter, the best shot and the best tracker and at fifty at the height of his powers in cunning. He'd grown up in the Territory, fought in a war and had thirty years experience in New Guinea. He was a man capable of tracking and killing Kismet. That was why Douglas, through the Americans, had hired him.

So the group of four kept on looking for croc tracks and Red and Bluey kept following them. The four men stopped briefly for lunch. The shortness of this stop made Red think that they were on to something.

After lunch they moved quickly on, and when Red saw one of the group start to make notes in a small notebook he was both relieved and more worried. He was relieved because it meant they didn't have anything yet. But he was more worried because the notes meant that they had found some old tracks. Not last night's, but perhaps the night before: still recent enough to be there and recent enough to note down. These men were making notes to draw a map. They were systematically narrowing down the area of their search before they went in for the kill. Red was not sure that spotlights or banging on tins or even firing over their heads would deter these men. They would have a boat twice as strong with an engine twice as powerful as the others and once they sighted Kismet, as Red began to be surer and surer that sooner or later they would, they would stay with him, whichever way he went, they would have four pairs of eyes trained enough, trained to watch every direction away from the boat and trained enough not to be drawn off by distractions, so that they would follow and go in for the kill. In that moment Red decided what he must do if this happened.

Nightfall came and still the men did not stop. They had sandwiches and tea quickly again—no alcohol, none of them, all day, Red noted—and then moved off to use all of the last light, to watch where even crocs might come out at the traditional animal watering time of twilight, and then moved off again, into the night, on the water this time, with their boat, which one man had been sent to bring up on their Range Rover, one man detached as in the army so that the others could keep on with their job until the boat arrived. Then they went out on the water, and the boat was big and thick-hulled with an eighty-horsepower Johnson, and even Bluey, who being on the coast was more used to these things, said, "Jesus Christ," and Red said, "Yes," and knew that his spots would hardly be seen from the bank against the huge spotlights these men mounted on their boat, and the hand-held ones, all of which they used so professionally.

It was after midnight before they quit and Red could slip across to Five Mile Camp to see Roo.

Red came in the front way through the canyon entrance and spoke to Roo quietly, who was not surprised to see him. He told Roo where they were camped and told him to send Ali over quietly later if she wanted to see him, but without Bill knowing. Then, from first light the next day, Roo must start blacktracking, Red said, blacktracking as never before, blacktracking with all the wisdom of his father, Happy Jack, and his father, and all their fathers, for these men were good and Roo was not to underestimate them.

Roo nodded. He'd been watching them with glasses from the rock cornice high up in Five Mile Camp. He'd intended to come down in a day or two himself. They hadn't seen enough signs for them to be getting close yet. Red thought to himself how foolish it was for him not to have realized that Black Roo would have things more in hand than he himself could in the tracking department; that this man was a boy no longer, but even as a boy he had been, with his father's training, the prince of trackers. He could see a leaf out of place when the best of their opposition, even the men Red feared so much, might have looked at an area of ground and seen nothing. Roo also had heightened senses of smell and hearing, and a sort of sixth sense that alerted him, just as animals' ears will prick up as something foreign is about to invade their environment. Roo seemed able to sense when animals were worried or frightened or even just noticed something new, something different around them. Red realized that this almost intuitive thing would be their best protection. If Roo kept close to the hunters, and if they got close to Kismet, Roo would read the signs, almost hear the bush telegraph of the other animals sensing that a crocodile had come into their area.

Red explained all this to Bluey and Bluey nodded but Red knew that very few except the absolutely convinced bushcraft practitioner believed men could become so attuned to animal thought patterns. Yet Red had seen it in Roo's father, and there was no reason it should not be in the son, too. He should have realized earlier. Roo would lead them to Kismet to protect him when the time was right.

Late at night Ali came over with Jitangeli and there was a tearful reunion while Red apologized and said he had had some business to conduct in secret and did not wish to have anything said over the two-way radio or in a telegram. In any case, they should get more used to being on their own, and doing things themselves, as they'd always been brought up to do, for he wouldn't be around forever. Then they made a fuss over him and said what nonsense and explained everything they could explain about poor Crocodile Tommy and what had happened at the billabong, though Red had heard it all from Roo earlier. Then the girls asked him if there was any news from the secret business he'd been doing and he smiled kindly and said nothing definite and for them to tell Fan-tan he was all right when they saw him, but to keep it quiet, and they must all keep on their toes, for it wasn't over yet, not by a long shot, and no one was going to take Kismet away before his time, no sir, not if he could help it. He saw their eyes light up when he began to talk that way again, in his old determined bush way, and he wondered, after they'd gone off happy again, or reasonably so, he wondered how much of this bush optimism was to keep their spirits up, and how much was to keep his own up, and how much was real.

Bluey had long since gone to sleep while Red was still pondering that one.

By the middle of the next day, the third of the hunt, the four men whom Red was worried most about had worked their way around to the back of Five Mile Camp. He wondered if they might try to enter it, indeed what might happen if anyone did, for the arrangement was that two shots in quick succession would be fired so that a ranger could come running if anyone tried to enter. But there was no guarantee a ranger would be close enough to get there in time before the men got in, although Bill was mostly manning his end of the operation from there, for which Red was grateful. While Bill stayed there it was no problem and he had a walkie-talkie to reach extra men if needed.

But the men did not try to enter Five Mile Camp. Red cursed under his breath and would have almost been happier in one sense if they'd have tried. But these were men with enough confidence in themselves and pride in their work to know what they were after, to know it was not croc country in there, and more, to be able to look at the back entrance quickly and tell that the quarry they wanted had not passed by there to hide. But they spent a long time looking around the rock where Kismet so often lay. Then they spent a time talking, making notes and nodding among themselves.

From what Roo and Alison had told Red it was now more than three days, nearly four, since Kismet had been there. This meant these men could read signs three days old. They had worked out that this was a spot the croc favored, and, as if Red needed any further warning of their professionalism, they immediately dumped some baited blood meat right on Kismet's rock. It made Red almost sick to see it, and it was another thing he had feared, but he still had a grudging admiration for the men. They knew their business. But Red had no way of knowing whether the bait would attract the old croc or not, if he would sense or smell the poison. These hunters did not care how they caught him. There was no sense of justice compelling them to stalk and shoot. They would get him by poisoned meat bait or any way they could, although it had appeared to Red from a distance that one of the men had argued with another about whether this method should be used. But now it had been. Now the die had been cast. They had found a spot they were sure the croc frequented. So they had baited a trap like hunters, a trap to catch their quarry, and, if any further evidence were needed of their determination, they left one of their number behind, hidden on the bank, so that if the croc came, but did not take the bait, as Red hoped he would be smart enough to do, yet the hunter would have a clear shot at him while the croc was deciding.

Now was the most crucial time of all. Red did not know why

Kismet had avoided his favorite spot so long; he did not know why he had not attacked any of the boats. Perhaps his hunter's sense, his animal cunning, told him the difference between one foreign sound, like the boat he had attacked on that first night, and many. Perhaps he knew that he faced a herd of invaders this time, not a single one. Perhaps he knew instinctively not to go to any of his favorite haunts. Yet, as he thought this, Red feared that sooner or later he would. What if early one morning, before the rest of the camp was up, but when these four determined men were already out and about, what if, without the noise of the motors, and in the first gentle rays of the dawn, Kismet slipped quietly onto his favorite rock? Quite apart from the blood bait, at that distance, with the rock so close to the surface, he would be a sitting duck. One good shot from the man left behind—and Red had no doubts they would leave one man there in shifts all the time now—one good shot through the eye, or into the side of the head, would certainly disable Kismet long enough for the hunter to get the remaining fatal shots home. Damn it, why had men as good as this had to come? With the others it would have been easy. But Red really knew the answer. To get men as good as this someone would have had to hire them separately, pay them more. So now he had no alternative, and, as the other three moved off, and one man stayed, Red turned to Bluey and said, "This is a bad business now, Blue, and I'll have to stay."

Bluey nodded. He had learned over the years to read as much from his friend's expressions as from his words. He knew when Red was biting the bullet.

"I'll get your .303 and some ammo, then," Bluey said.

"If you would, as soon as possible."

Bluey hurried off. The time for kerosene tins and sticks was over. He returned presently with Red's .303, ammunition, their largest spotlight and battery and some food and water.

"I'll follow the other three until they stop for the night." Blue said.

Red nodded without speaking. When it got dark he picked his position carefully, so that, although on another bank of the billabong, he had a triangulated line of fire equivalent to that of the hunter. Red would have to shoot roughly the same distance, at roughly the same angle as the other man: as if both had a line of fire along either side of a triangle with the point of the triangle joining their lines of fire where Kismet's rock stood.

About 2:00 A.M. Roo found Red. Roo said he had seen a sign late in the afternoon: a paw print on the sand along the bank in the direction away from Five Mile Camp on the west side. It was bad. There was a spot there where the bank was hard mud and then fell away, although you had to have swum underwater in the billabong to be able to tell. The water was not the clearest at the best of times, looking down from the surface; and with water lilies and lotuses and varieties of mosslike growths there was no way to tell from the top. But Red and Jacky had come on the mud ledge while swimming when Red was a child, and they had swum away the moment they saw the underwater mud cave, for inside was the biggest crocodile they had ever seen. It was Kismet, of course, but that had been the first and only time, to their knowledge, anyone had got a good look at him in entirety. They had looked down on parts of him from different angles before; once they had looked down on the top of him from an overhanging branch. But that had been the first time he had been seen in full length and girth from the side.

And now it appeared he was there again, in his old hiding spot, and late that afternoon, perhaps because the main body of hunters had been farther downstream and it had been quieter, he had come out. Did the others know this, too? They'd be fools not to have seen the obvious foot mark. They wouldn't know about the hiding place. But they'd know now he was about. Kismet could even have smelled the bait from that distance: it would be getting pretty high by now. In the morning, in a couple of hours' time almost, Red feared his old friend-enemy would come out.

In those next two hours, from 2:00 A.M. to 4:00 A.M., before the hour which the dawn broke in, before the early, often unpredictable dry-Tropic dawn, mist-filled dawn, clear dawn, chill dawn, Red reflected again on the nature of luck. It was an awfully simplistic philosophy, he knew that. He wasn't even sure it deserved the label of philosophy. But he was sure of his theories: well, up to a point, anyway. But he didn't talk them out loud too often. He talked the bushcraft out loud; that was different. These were things you did to limit the bad luck, to encourage the good. But in the end you had no say in it, no say in it at all. Why was he born so beautiful, why was he born at all? Because he had no say in it, no say in it at all. Everyone had been singing that at birthday parties all their lives. And why did they sing it? Dr. Freud would say that they sang it so frequently, that it was part of the lingua franca, because they believed it. Red believed it. He'd believed it before he met Dr. Freud in his books which Alison had shown him.

Of course Red had read all his life, because of his mother at first, he supposed, and his father, and because somehow he got to know that learning was above everything. Not just books—though you got plenty from books and they were important. People often sneered at bushmen as if they had no book learning. The fact was books were very important in the development of the Outback. Most portable thing there was and very close to—what did Ali call it?—ah, yes, the oral tradition, the campfire stories. He was wandering again, he knew that. Wandering a lot lately. Hell, who wouldn't wander when an era was coming to an end? If old Kismet came out, as somehow Red believed he would, would come to face his enemies finally, then an era could be ending this day, three hundred years since the settlement of the country. Kismet had been there since the Europeans came and if they got him today that would be the end of the last frontier and it would mean the twentieth century had finally intruded on the Back of Beyond. Now anyone who heard Red say this out loud would certainly think he was screwy. But Red knew Kismet would not think so and that was the very reason why Red was almost certain Kismet would come out. It was as if he knew the game was up, or at least had to be decided: that now the others knew that the unspoiled things that Kismet represented were there, they would not stop until they spoiled them.

Hell, he was getting morbid. Kismet mightn't come out at all. It was nearly 4:00 A.M. Fan-tan had sent tea and sandwiches out by Ali earlier, and Red, from his hiding spot, looked out at the lagoon, at the billabong, at the stretch of water, whatever, and thought what might happen there this day, as he munched an egg and lettuce sandwich and drank the hot, white, sugared tea from the thermos. It was billy tea. He smiled at how nice it was to be loved. Despite the range fire going in the kitchen all the time and the tea from the water there which Red loved, old Fan-tan had put on a blackened billycan, and made the brew, and tossed in a eucalypt leaf to stir the flavor and put the century-old ritual of bush tea into a modern vacuum flask and sent it out to the man he had served so loyally so long. Red thought about Ali then, and Jitangeli, Jitangeli's devotion and the loyal love of Fan-tan, of Roo, and the beloved Annie, and long ago the brief and transitory but very special thing Lisa had given him, and the friendship of Bluey and his family, and Happy Jack and the Territorians who had known the Back of Beyond as the best place to pass through on their drives, the place you'd be treated with decent bush hospitality still, and how grateful they were. Red thought of all these things as the light began to lift, and thought how loved he'd been, and how happy, despite everything, despite the bad luck there had been the good, and he would not complain—no, not even now.

Roo was standing far down the bank, just within Red's range of vision, so that Red could see if Roo nodded his head. This would mean that Kismet was coming out from his hiding place.

Just before full light, just as the last of the dark was lifting, Red saw Roo nod. So it would be today. The fate of the Territory would be decided today. And it would not be decided in some dark corner in some unmanly way. For no sooner had Roo nodded than Red saw Kismet himself, on dry land, coming fast along the bank, his five hundred pounds of muscle and head and jaw and tail—watch out for the tail, son, if he gets within range—five hundred pounds and three hundred years of the heart of the old Territory was coming out to do battle with the new. And it was coming, God bless it, not in the dark as the hunter had first come, but in the full, fresh light of day, coming at full speed so that even the waiting hunter was shaken, pulling his rifle up quickly now that he had seen the croc and realizing that, after all this, it would be no picnic shoot. Red knew now that Kismet would not take the bait, and indeed as Kismet entered the water momentarily, the large croc cut through the cool, quiet, green billabong waters swiftly, sniffed once, and then with the skewered turn of an animal used to his domain, flicked the tainted carcass from his rock, from his territory, like the foreign thing it was. As he did this, the hunter, who had aimed too hurriedly fired. Red did not see where the bullet hit, although he knew it was not a vital hit, for Kismet came out of the water in the direction of the shot as if untouched, snarling and angry and teeth bared, yes, but slowed down?— never. He knew how and where to strike now, the shot had directed him, and he was moving with more force and speed than even Red had imagined him capable of toward the hunter who was out from behind his tree now and aiming again, trying to take his time, but he had a croc on land coming at him now, a croc on land at full speed, like a train coming at him unexpectedly through a tunnel, and as he aimed, Red knew that he could never be sure that one more shot would do it, and the hunter would only get one more, that was for certain. Red had been taking quiet, cool aim all this time. He had thought about every possibility in advance, planned out all the likely and unlikely moves with all the cunning of his years and his bushcraft and despite every contrary emotion he felt. In that split second, with a clear line of fire, he did the only thing he could now do, and pulled the trigger: once, twice, three times; four; and then five, until his magazine was empty and the croc, his beloved croc, lay dead a few short feet from the hunter.

Red came out of hiding then, and people were coming from

everywhere, the hunters and the rangers, so that the crowd was gathering as he took his time and limped slowly around the billabong to the other side and they watched him walk up quietly to where the croc lay and bend down beside him, with his rifle still in his hand, and pat the head of the dead and bleeding animal, and talk quite openly to him now, not caring what they thought and hardly conscious of them being there and saying, "We both knew that time was running out and it's better this way. I'd not have them say that you killed a man, even if you had every right to try. They don't understand that the place is really yours."

His eyes were full as he stood up, and his look at those around him, as he walked off, and limped up into Five Mile Camp alone, needed no words.

Just before nightfall, when all the hunters had gone, Alison rode out to Five Mile Camp. Her father was sitting by the rock pool where they had gone swimming what seemed like half a lifetime ago.

"Come to get your old man, have you?" Red said as he saw her come through the narrow canyon entrance, walking Ghost Gum and his own horse, the last of the Firecracker progeny, as old as the Goondiwindi gray himself.

"Yeah, thought I'd come and see if you were still in the land of the living."

"That was nice. Yeah, still here. Knew you'd be out before dark. Reckoned I'd wait until you came."

"Not too bad?" She had let the horses go, for they needed no tethering, and sat down beside him now.

"Not too bad," he said. "One more wound on an old soldier at this stage?—hell, you get used to it."

"Still hurts, though. Hurts me."

"And me. But he'd had a good innings. It was the way it all happened that got me. But then, if you could predict bad luck, know where lightning would strike, it'd be one hell of a world, wouldn't it?"

"That's too deep for me."

"And me. Anyway, that's as far as it goes. Not much of a theory."

"No one's ever explained beyond it in anything I've ever come across."

"Nor me. He'd have felt no pain, except for a moment. I couldn't have him getting off into the bush wounded and hurt, or killing the hunter."

"I know. You don't need to explain. We all understand. He'd have understood and preferred it that way."

"I reckon."

"Let's go home and eat."

"Yeah, good idea. Want to see the camp first?"

"You mean all of it?"

"Sure, it's the best time of day. What it's all about, really."

She took his hand and they began to walk.

The river itself wound around at Five Mile Camp but underground, so that inside the back perimeter of tall rock, the river surfaced again in a beautiful lagoon.

It was a spot such as exists in a few places anywhere anymore. It was untouched. The water was green, but a clean, translucent green which at times, for all the dark green and lighter green things around it, could, at the right time of day, with the sky coming through in the right spots, appear almost a deep blue washing into the green. At other times, depending on the lights of the sky coming off the rocks of sandstone and ocher, the water could appear tinged with rays of light yellow. But at this time of day it was the clearest of clean, pure green, still, quiet. There were the most exquisite mangrove trees all around: those trees that truly do stand on their roots, like soft, gray pelicans, although each with a dozen or more spindled feet that have taken root, just barely, but taken root in the earth very tenuously at the edge of the water, a delicate thing on legs, drawing its life from those thinly planted water roots, giving the scene a thin gray-green beauty and an entwining lacework around the edge of the lagoon.

They had walked down past the rock pool, by the escarpment high above them that threw up those purple mists Ali had always thought she saw, past the twilight-hushed rush of the waterfall over each tiered and staggered slate-rock ledge, past the lush greens and the lilies and lotuses, so that now they gazed at the beautiful and quiet and still lagoon and Red whispered as he sat her down on a rock beside him at the edge,

"It's just about time. Any moment now. Just sit and wait."

Their quiet presence seemed not to disturb the normal nature timetable. The thing about Five Mile Camp, whatever else it might or might not possess, was that here nature still felt at home, undisturbed. Here was the most popular spot. So at dusk, which was the really and truly best time, every night throughout the Dry, on the soft summer evenings, the inhabitants of the region came down to water. There were magpie geese and pygmy geese in pecking order. There were bigger birds like pelicans, of incredible vermilions and grays. But of all the things that came, the roos were the best. They came in their hundreds, bounding through the camp, for it was five miles long by two miles wide inside its rock perimeters and it had many open spots. You would have thought there was no water anywhere else. But there you are, you see, Red used to say, they're just like us in the end—all those other places, but they like to come together at one favorite spot. Perhaps the water tastes better to them here, who knows? And so, in their hundreds, on this night in the last light of twilight, bounding in that soft, vaunting grace over the salmon dust which is the form the red-brown earth of Australia so often takes in the Territory, the kangaroos came. They came and stopped, and dipped forward, almost pecking at the water like birds and twitching their furred and cat-whiskered rabbit faces as the water went down. For beauty, for dusk and last-light beauty, here was the heart of things.

How disappointed so many people would be, he thought. All Five Mile Camp had to offer was beauty.

She took his hand and they got up and walked, arms around each other, back to the horses. So he was all right. And yet there was something: perhaps a resignation, but almost a contentment she'd not seen in him before. She had always felt her father to be a man at peace with himself, despite his vigorous ways. Yet despite the fact that this thing had hurt him deeply, and a trace of the anguish was still in his eyes, there was something deeper, too, some other reality that he had come to terms with, as if he had finally accepted something and it had given him a tranquillity in which to rest his anguish.

"I've sold the property, by the way," he said, as she held Firecracker for him to mount, "but the deal is that you all get to keep the station house and Five Mile Camp and the land in between. Not exactly a million acres, daughter, but that was *my* dream and it's gone now, but you'll have the heart of it, the good and true heart, and enough land for you and Roo to work and your home. Is that OK?"

She took his hand as he sat in the saddle.

"Of course, that's a good deal. That's all I'll want. Who'd you sell it to?"

"Some Yanks—the main opposition to the lot Douglas has thrown in with. Always a good theory, daughter, if one group wants something pretty damn bad you can bet your bottom dollar you'll get a better price from their competitors who'll do it just to spite them if for no other reason. Sold it to the opposition who will have just as much pull with the meat lobby as the others and sold it on condition that Roo stays as manager for as long as he lives. I mean they'll bring in helicopters to herd and airboats for the Wet and the whole damn lot but they don't hate blacks and they're good people: I've met one or two of their top bananas over the years, so I reckon it's a good deal."

"Sure," she said softly.

"Well, no, who am I kidding? It's not a good deal. A good deal would have been if I could have kept it. But seeing I couldn't—and I did know that there was no way out of that squeeze play—seeing I couldn't, the next best thing I could do was use the one thing no one can ever take away from you. Know what that is, daughter?"

"Your right to choose—?"

"Half right. Perhaps your individuality would be better; your right to do it your way. I mean they can take away rights to choose from people. When they kill people they do that. Sometimes there's no choice whether you live or die. But the manner in which you face it, that is something else. Old Kismet, he had no choice, or very little, after a certain point of time, and he knew it. But he sure to hell exercised his individuality in the way he went out, did he not?—and I certainly helped him with it."

He'd been sitting in his saddle all this time, with Alison standing beside him, squeezing his hand now and then. As he finished this sentence she looked up, wondering for one terrible moment if he might be just a little manic. But he looked down at her and smiled. He said nothing, but his smile indicated that if he were a little manic, it was something he was conscious of, and that what he was saying he had thought through. He patted her on the head then, as if to reassure her, and said, "Come on, mount up now or we'll be late for dinner. I could sure use a beer. What do you say?"

She nodded her head heavily, and was glad that her face was half away from him and easily capable of being turned a little farther, for God she loved this dear old man of hers and suddenly she wanted to cry awfully badly and knew she must hold it in whatever happened.

So she mounted up and rode off quickly, so he would not know. But he knew, for he did not try to catch her. Both horses were old, but Firecracker still had that little extra, plus the greatest rider in the Territory on his back, still the greatest Outback rider, and the things that made him this, the things inside his head that made him the man he was, told him to let his daughter ride ahead this day. So as the light fell out into night, he galloped lightly along behind her on the plain that led to home.

And in the kitchen, with Fan-tan chuckling merrily to see Big Red back and in good spirits, with the tops coming quickly off frosted bottles from the fridge as Red declared to Bluey and Roo and Jitangeli, to the whole assembled household, that Kismet deserved a decent wake just like anyone else, and so did the property for that matter, and the whole bloody Territory, too, if not the whole damn country, if not the whole damn world, as he declared this, and explained about the property but they could keep their home, he saw their eyes light up again, and knew that they were good kids and good people all of them, and that nothing abides forever, whatever a certain book says, and that the one thing that must come to pass, sooner or later, they would have the ability to cope with.

So they all got bloody drunk, everyone as drunk as a skunk, excepting Fan-tan, said Red, for he was drunker than that and how anyone could cook such a fine roast that drunk was beyond him, said Red, and just as he was saying it Anne came in the door, having flown in and taxied up to home paddock without them hearing, they were making so much noise, and with her arriving they broke out the champagne and stout and had black velvets, and then Bill came in after getting the last of the hunters off the property, so Red poured him a few beers and told him and Ali it was about time they woke up to themselves, and then got drunker and told Roo and Jitangeli the same thing, so that Anne said she understood he believed in complete freedom but would he mind not organizing people's lives, to which Red replied that Anne was, of course, quite right, and that he and Anne were going to bed anyway and all he'd been trying to do in his simple bush way, because life got so bloody complicated these days, was make sure the right people went to bed with the right people, because that was surely part of what was wrong with the world, that they didn't always, which meant they didn't have the right sort of children, which explained why there were so many bastards around.

He was very drunk, and very funny, and very sad, and presently Anne blew a good-night kiss to the room and took him to bed.

The property was declared free from tick fever and the last of the strangers on their land left.

Before they knew it, Christmas was almost upon them. Anne had stayed a few days and they'd all gone out to Five Mile Camp together for a grand tour.

After that Anne had gone back for a time to Darwin, and

Red had spent his time visiting old friends, and chatting, and even flying out to Thursday Island to see Kiwai and talk about the old days and pearling. Kiwai had told him the Wet would be late that year, and a bad one, and Red had said he was inclined to agree. But he said nothing to the others.

So they prepared with great happiness and glee, all of them, noticing Big Red's great tranquillity and being glad for him, they prepared for their last Christmas on the Back of Beyond with the property fully intact. They invited everyone they could think of, who were family or close friends, and it was going to be the best Christmas of all. Red said he would fly in to get Annie as usual. On Christmas Day he always flew in to pick her up, as a courtesy and loving thing, and to bring her out himself.

On Christmas Day he got up early before the house was awake and looked at the sky and the wind sock on the home paddock strip. He showered quietly and shaved and parted his hair and dressed slowly in his best khakis which Fan-tan always kept so meticulously clean and creased for him, creased even down the large, button-down shirt pockets, so that although they were Outback and not army clothes, he always had a military precision and cleanness look to him. He took his old Light Horse infantry hat with him in his hand for company, though he knew he would not need it.

He walked outside and thought how good and white the homestead looked and how green the home paddock looked. He unchocked the plane, and checked that the tank was half full, as he'd left it, and climbed in and started up and took off, noticing the wind rising as he banked and turned to the sea, and thought of all the beautiful land he could look down at before he reached the coast, all the beautiful brown and green land he loved so, and if he had judged it right, he'd meet the real wind, the true wind, just as the land ended.

THE DREAMTIME

On Christmas Day, 1974, Cyclone Tracy blew in from the Arafura Sea. It blew for six hours, and when it was gone so was Darwin. There was nothing really left, and those who survived it would never be the same again. With the cyclone went the heart of the Territory. Now it was gone and with it a way of life which would never return. If it seemed that those who lived there had some foreknowledge of what was to come, then it must be pleaded that perhaps they did, perhaps they knew intuitively, with the mysticism of the first dark inhabitants which has always haunted the brown lands and purple hills of the Top End, perhaps they knew the time they were living in on this true and last frontier, living in the last of tomorrow.